A novel by
J. C. Dreger

Arizona USA

GRAVE.

First Edition.

Published by Cactus Rain Publishing, LLC
San Tan Valley, Arizona, USA
www.CactusRainPublishing.com

ISBN 978-0-9962812-0-1

Cover Design by Junior's Digital Design
Typeface: Bleeding Cowboys licensed from Segments Design

Published August 1, 2015
Published in the United States of America

Grave.

A novel by

J. C. Dreger

J'ai vecu

Verite' sans peur (truth without fear):
Anonymous French proverb

Chapter One

The Stranger

The dusky orange light spilled over the high, jagged rim of the plateau, bathing the desert in an effulgence; eldritch and boiling. The dust and sand spewed up from the ground in great swirling cylinders and wild spastic howling squalls that sent it scattering; ashes from a ceaseless fire.

Upon an especially lonely and forlorn stretch of that barren and acrid wilderness was the form of a man, sunbathed yet strangely pale. He walked quite erect and with an odd sort of resolve, as if he had some dire task to perform, some magnificent purpose beyond all reckoning. So tiny and insignificant in the vastness of that flat expanse, and yet wholly pivotal, for without a granter to grant significance, who was there to say that there was any at all?

None, but he.

The traveler wore a broad-brimmed hat of black felt which shaded his keen green eyes and a pair of purple-tinted, thick-lense spectacles that rested upon a sharp, slightly downward curving nose which he used to sniff the wind.

The smell of sulfur.

The brewing of a storm.

Dry lightning roaring in the distance; those fickle forms of frozen lightning like afterimage plants from a blue world of dreams.

His parched mouth moved soundlessly to the cadence of the squall, red lips flexing like two worms glued together upon an aberrant scarecrow. He raised a large, dexterous hand to his sharp, small chin and ran it along his ten-day-old stubble wonderingly.

With him he carried only what he wore; everything he had possessed had been taken upon the road save his clothes and his life.

The man passed a row of rummy white plants. He walked closer and peered at them, discovering that they were not plants at all, but rather the milky ribcage of a wild steer, long lost to the hungry land. The ground heaved and breathed with ants where the dead creature's guts used to be, a red writhing pool of animated innards and shimmering carapaces. He walked on and found the skull of the dead beast looking up at him, eyeless and cracked with the heat like a helmet sundered by some incorporeal mace.

A little blue skink darted suddenly from under it and ran up and over the traveler's boot and then darted under a pile of rocks and vanished from sight; a gaudy wayfarer decked out in a regal suit of mail. The man watched the little creature with amusement and then passed on. He kept on across that forsaken plain of sand and rock until he fell to his knees with the strain of it. Nearly passing out, the traveler slumped to his side and lay like a puppet long cleaved of its stings, clinging to consciousness by sheer force of will alone.

A few minutes passed by and a shadow drifted across his brow, then another; he looked up. Two enormous blackened things wheeled eagerly above him, turning low and predatory over the wide, windswept wastes.

Vultures.

One of them landed and hopped toward him, stopping merely a stone's throw away and cocking its long, ugly head at him inquisitively.

"I don't take kindly to being looked at like a sausage."

The huge avian remained unfazed by his remark and hopped a bit closer, the stench of carrion hovering about it, thick and reeking, maligning the air.

GRAVE.

"Oh no you don't, you over-grown varmint! Shoo! Go on! Git!"

He rose, with considerable effort, to his moderate height and removed his hat, flapping it madly at the vulture which recoiled with a squawk, took flight and was gone.

He muttered a curse under his breath as he watched the avian rise up into the thermals in a cloud of falling feathers.

"Damn rats with wings."

Getting to his knees nearly winded him and standing upright made his head dizzy; his vision blurred, nearly going black outright. He was about to damn the sun as well as all the birds neath it, but couldn't find the point in it nor the heart in himself. He sighed and dragged one leg after the other until the sun had dropped from the sky and the landscape was a cool glistening sea of jewels, sparkling in a ghostly opal pall.

A bone-thin coyote trotted before his path, stopping and staring up at him, curious and cunning, and him staring just as curiously back.

"Hi."

It barked a little bark, as if in reply, and then padded away into the night and was swallowed up in the blackness. Only a pair of yellow eyes remained, and they looked back once at the tatterdemalion form and then were gone like elfin lanterns shuttered in some other plane of existence.

The man stumbled on.

☼

In the enkindling light of the newborn sun, rising lofty and arrogant upon the clouds like a fiery heathen god of yore, a city appeared upon the horizon, through an obfuscation of heat. The man wondered to himself if it was a mirage. He thought about that for an hour as he walked, then the town he had been headed toward was found in the foothills of the mountains, and that was just where it was.

No mere mirage, but a sprawling multitude of rickety wooden shacks and busily moving bodies, as real as the earth beneath the traveler's boots. There were tin roofs baking in the sun like giant tea kettles flattened by a scornful and capricious force, and the high towering edifice of an oil derrick digging into the bowels of the earth; a mindless miser on an endless quest.

He smiled like a fool, threw his arms up in the air and danced a merry jig round and round until he fell over and lay there, exhausted and gasping like a drowning man. Then he rose and started toward the buildings at as much of a jog as he could muster, the ground becoming firmer and the sand becoming scarcer as he progressed.

He reached the outskirts of the town by midday and collapsed under the shade of the first tree, lying there panting and half delirious. So affected was his mind by the haze and fog of the great and burning sphere that he was quite certain that the grass was singing to him, a lovely falsetto, as he rose and grabbed hold of the first man he saw.

The man looked to be an oil worker, so slick was this fellow with a patina of blackened grime that he looked to have been marked by a diabolical sentience for transgressions unspeakable beyond all computation.

"Steady on, man!" the oiled figure shouted with concern and surprise. With an effort he kept the traveler from falling to his knees, bracing him with a massive forearm.

The traveler, in his quasi-madness, kissed the big bearded man like a long-lost lover and then fell to the ground like a sack of rags with a wolfish grin, half conscious and nearly dead.

Confounded and perplexed to the outer reaches of absurdity, the oil worker stood in confusion for a moment with a blank look upon his grease-covered face. Then he bent to the traveler and dragged the poor fellow into the nearest house.

☼

"Ms. Whitum! Ms. Whitum! We've a man near dead here!"

"They lawd above! What did you do, Henry?"

Henry shook his mighty head and shut his eyes tightly, as if doing so would produce a different woman whence they opened up again. Unfortunately for him it wasn't to be, for the old lady still stared out of her little shack at him with that scornful, disapproving expression he had come to disdain.

"Damn it woman, I ain't a done nothing! This here fella came from the desert, crossed the badlands, I reckon."

"The desert? They lawd above! Bring him here whilst I fetch the preacher."

"The preacher? This fella needs water and food, not no blasted sermon!"

"That's the devil speaking in you! He flapping ya tongue like that yon flag, they lawd knows it. He sholly does."

"Oh, shut your trap, ya crazy old bat!"

She shook her long white mane and went out with her hands thrown up in the air like a defeated soldier of a surrendering army terribly humiliated and at a loss for words.

Henry pulled the fellow's limp, ragged body to the large fur carpet that lay in the middle of the room. The big man stooped and removed the fellow's hat and set it aside upon the creaking wooden dining table and then ran out back to the well and returned with a bucket of water.

The traveler had regained his senses and had propped himself up by his elbow into a semi-sitting position, looking about frantically as if someone had just set fire to his mustaches. When Henry reentered, the first thing that the stranger said was, "Where is my hat?"

"I put it on the table when you fainted away. Here, drink."

The big man gingerly handed the bucket to the drained and pallid figure who tipped the container up and completely over his head, his maw agape. When he had satisfied himself and drunken his fill, the stranger rose and cast an eye about and then set his hat back upon his crown with loving care, bending the brim just so and no further.

"Looks like I owe you some gratitude," said the traveler.

The big man held up his hands, "No need. I done had enough of your gratitude!"

"Whatever do you mean?"

"Y'all don't remember none?"

"Not at all. Should I?"

"Oh. Well, no. Never you mind it."

The big man laughed heartily, his voice fairly booming from his throat, and then he walked forward with one massive forearm outstretched, a great animate tree, yielding, amiable and welcoming.

"Name's Henry Collins."

The pale man took the worker's hand and shook it in a surprisingly firm fashion.

"Glad to meet you. I'm Eisen. Eisen de Torquiam."

"What now?"

"Torquiam."

"Tor-kee-am? That's a funny sort of name, ain't it?"

"It always is to the party not concerned."

The big man laughed again and Eisen rubbed his chin and smiled.

"Ya'll should eat something; reckon there wasn't much in the desert in the way of victuals."

"Yes. Oh and yes, that would be nice."

Collins headed for the stove and got the burner going, putting on a pan, greasing it and breaking a pair of eggs with peculiar skill.

"What do ya do, Eisen?"

"I make coffins."

"What?"

"I'm a coffin maker, not a carpenter. I can make most anything from wood, but I specialize in coffins, as they are the only things I can seem to make particularly well."

"I ain't never met no coffin maker before."

"Well I wouldn't get too excited. Thank you."

He took the eggs and ate them straight from the pan with the fork he was handed. They went down, slimy and searing, but tasty all the same. Starvation had a way of reinvigorating the taste buds to turn even the most base and mundane of meals into a gourmet fit for the ficklest of regents.

"Now tell me stranger, how you come to luck blacker than I don't know?"

"By way of men. Road agents."

"Led by an Irish fella?"

"Yes. You know him?"

"I wouldn't say I know him, but to be sure I know of him. Everbody round here does. His name's-"

"Kavaria Kallista. Wouldn't shut up about it, wanted everybody to know his name. Curious fellow if ever I met one. What kind of name is Kallista for an Irishman? Probably a pseudonym."

"And your companions and the driver?"

Eisen shook his head, his face expressing more words than his mouth could ever hope to conjure upon its own.

"That's a damn outrage! Y'all talk ta the sheriff and we get a posse together, you'll see, or I'm a Spanish fly!"

At that moment Ms. Whitum came darting through the door looking considerably happier than she had been previously, though her visage soured some upon seeing that Collins lingered still.

"Oh! He awake!"

"Yes, ma'am. And I thank you for your hospitality. I'm not sure how to repay you, but I'll surely try my best."

"Well, they is something."

Whitum walked to the stranger and handed him a little piece of paper, a small white square.

"Ya'll kin read, kantcha?"

"Yes, ma'am." He took the paper and held it up to the light. There was no maker's monogram, and the words on the other side shone dimly through the momentarily translucent square. Collins eyed it and said, "That from the preacher?"

"Never you mind who it's from, foo!"

"Crazy old bat!"

"Shoo!"

Eisen turned the square of paper over and then righted it and read it aloud, his rich, velvety voice filling the rustic confines of the humble little abode:

> Have heard of your unfortunate circumstances. I regret that I am unable to meet and pray with you in person, but there

is, at present, a pressing issue that detains me. I would be very much obliged if you would join me and the wholesome people of this striving little community for church tomorrow morning at seven sharp.

Faithfully,
Reverend Luce Montferiat

Eisen reread it once more, this time silently and to himself, an eyebrow raised, and then he rose to his feet and set the paper on the table. He turned to Collins with an inquiring gaze and a thin artistic hand raised, beckoning.

"Tell me, Henry-"

"Yes?"

"Is there an inn in this town?"

"Just the one. Swanson's."

"Can you show me there?"

"Certainly. It's on the other side of town, so it may take some time gettin, perhaps you should rest some still."

"No. I am well as ever I was."

"All right then."

He turned next to Ms. Whitum with a kindly smile and made a flourish, bowing elegantly like some exiled functionary from times long gone or still to come. There was something like the flavor of the vaudevillian about him and his stately gesture.

"Oh, shoo!" she replied with a smile.

"Good day, ma'am."

Collins and Eisen headed out for the hotel at an easy pace.

"They lawd above."

☼

It was the dead of night when they arrived at the inn like footpads stealing off from a crime, and a thick and freezing fog had fallen about the town, rolling down from the lofty, jagged peaks of the mountain that pierced the earth and sky like a titan's smoldering brand.

"This is it, sir."

"Sir?"

"Yes, sir, uh, sir."

"Tell me, Collins– "

"Yes sir?"

"What have I done to earn a sir?"

"Well, don't rightly know. Is it important?"

"Once you realize that nothing is important, everything takes on a dimension of importance that can scarcely be reconciled."

Collins squinted and pursed his lips like he was tasting some kind of exotic viand, measuring, weighing, confused.

"I'm not sure I follow all that wise-an-were-force."

"Very likely not, as it is a long and obfuscated path. Thank you, Collins, for everything."

"Ain't no need to make nothing of it."

"Well, if you say so, then I shan't. I hope to see you at breakfast tomorrow, as I should very much like to get to know a man of such artistic mustaches, what say you to six?"

"I'd be right proud to, sir... er, Ibsen."

"It's Eisen."

"Uh, sorry."

"Well, it was close enough. Good night, Mr. Collins."

Henry Collins waved one massive hand as he departed into the shifting blackness and was gone.

The reddish crescent moon drifted rouge-like through the sky, a glistening, grinning, wayward satellite; a toothless bloody mouth.

Eisen looked at the moon and stood there for some time staring, then he spoke aloud, the voice of a fearless challenger.

"You may have the last laugh, but I shall laugh best."

Then he nodded as if to confirm his words and turned on his sore heels, walked up the low wooden porch and passed into the hotel like a man passing from a dream into the waking world.

☼

Collins came in a few minutes late and took a seat next to Eisen who had donned a brand new suit of spotless dark cloth and a matching hat with a sharp flat brim that he tilted low over his eyes.

The inn was quite large, considering the small size of the town, and could well fit upward of one hundred people quite comfortably. The lobby level was sparsely furnished with five small circular tables, though more were available upon request, just like the gin and sarsaparilla.

The short, roguish Englishman behind the counter was not only the innkeeper, but also the barman, the janitor, the chief and the most renowned and colorful liar in the town (or so Eisen had been told the night before by a man of equally dubious credulity whom had upon his arm a live mongoose). This multi-talented man's name was Arrgilius Mersan, and he had instantly taken a liking to the young, taciturn coffin maker.

Due this amiable turn, both Collins and Eisen were treated to a large, cream-filled sponge cake that Mr. Mersan's girl had made for him. He told them he couldn't stand the stuff and was going to throw it out, so they were welcome to it. Welcomed they certainly were at that, they ate and ate until they could barely stand. They leaned back in their spindly, creaking wooden chairs and smiled both and all.

"It's the little things in life, eh, Collins?"

"It certainly is. What did ya'll say ta the keep ta git em to fancy ya so?"

"Why do you ask?"

"Cause he'd typically spit in one's eye as quick or quicker as look at ya."

"Why is that?"

"Cause no one listens to him anymore, his stories that iz."

"Because they think he's lying?"

Collins nodded and took a sip of tea. It was a strange, somewhat surreal sight, him, an oil-stained, hulking brute of a man gingerly holding a tiny white tea cup in a hand that could have held four with ease.

"I see. So tell me about this preacher. Your Ms. Whitum seemed quite ready enough to talk of him and highly so."

Collins grunted.

"Well, she ain't mine, thank God, but she likes the preacher well enough, most do."

"You don't seem like most, Henry Collins."

"Neither do you at that, Eisen Torquiam."

Eisen grinned his sly little grin and leaned slightly forward to showcase his interest in Collins' words, and at length the latter continued.

"Well, I can't says I ever been treated foul by the man, the preacher that is; been treated quite well I suppose, and far be it from me ta speak foul bout folk hind their backs, but I'm not easy in my mind bout him."

Eisen had lifted up a sugar cube from the bowl on the table before. He was about to drop it into his steaming cup of tea when he stopped and gestured with it theatrically between his thumb and forefinger at the big man. As if it somehow illustrated his question more vividly.

"Why is that?"

"Well, I cain't rightly say. There's just something what's off bout him. Had the same feeling bout that there Irish."

"Which Irish?"

"Your Irish, I reckon."

"Kallista?"

"That's the one. It's sort of a gut type thing, I ain't never been one much given ta superstition, y'understand, but there's something in it, intuition that is, and I'll wager well enough."

"I suppose that I shall see him for myself soon enough."

"The Irish?"

"No. The preacher, he did invite me to your church... or are you not a religious man?"

"Course I am."

"Why do you say it like it's so obvious?"

"Ya'll a stranger here so's you wouldn't know none, but this here town, or rather the people in it, are very fervent in their faith."

"That's very edifying. Who is that man over at the door eying you up with such displeasure? Morose specimen."

Collins cast a quiet look over his shoulder and smiled. "My boss, Old Elroy. Gotta run."

Collins rose, shaking his great, shaggy head and tromped across the floor like any behemoth that had ever walked the land. When he reached the door he had some words with the man named Elroy, and then they left, enveloped in the searing sunlight to such a degree that a man of less faculty might have thought them disintegrated with the heat of it.

He watched them go and then Eisen, too, rose and headed out for the church, then realized that he had no idea where it was. Returning, he asked the barkeep where to find the church.

The barkeep replied, "In the town."

Eisen gave him a stern glare. Arrgilius held up his hands in entreaty, "Go out and follow the people, as there would be plenty enough to lead you better than a beacon."

So he did, them streaming peaceably up to the north, and arrived outside the stately looking construct very nearly the time that the letter-sending preacher had specified. It looked, at a passing glance, very much like an ancient Gothic cathedral, only gussied up in bright and fanciful colors. Fulgent ribbons hung from the archway of the heavy, ornate wooden double doors.

The plot of land upon which it sat was verdant with greenery and gaudy flowers of every color that caught the eye. Strange leering grotesques sat upon their stony haunches and grinned their perpetual disturbing grins as if some queer humor was upon the air.

Looking up and up and up, Eisen nearly toppled backward, too far did he have to crane his neck to gaze upon the five razor-like spires of that grand baroque monolith. The tallest jutting up from the very middle and being the bell tower, ringed round by four, one in each corner. One of the towers, the southern-most left one, had partially collapsed some time ago, for there was a great quantity of moss and birds and vines in the exposed innards of the conical and stony ream, like the guts of some great primordial beast of olden times, fossilized by sheer inaction, coated in stone.

GRAVE.

There was something unsettling about those remaining towers, like an extraordinary decaying mouth baring its mortared fangs and threatening to swallow up the sky, and, unsatisfied, feast on and on until it had devoured the whole universe in its black and terrible maw.

As he watched the people file in through that gigantic yawning portal and disappear into the misty twilight within, some chatting to each other, others solemn as the dead, and about as animate, he reckoned that all the building needed was a portcullis to complete the narrative of the place that he had constructed in his head.

He waited until they, one and every man, woman and child had vanished inside before commencing onward.

Walking inside was like diving into a frigid pool of water when one didn't know the temperature. A gust of icy air passed over the coffin maker like an eel through a slipstream; he shivered and braced himself for the cold by hunching his shoulders and stuffing his hands into his pockets.

He took a seat in the very back so as not to bring undue attention to himself and looked out across that great cavernous space. A stranger in a land stranger still.

The pews were as old as the church itself and they looked it, wood-battered, chipped and worn as the stone floor upon which they set. The seat cushions were red and appeared deceptively plush, though they were rather thin and about as good as sitting upon a strand of painted bark. In the back of each of the pews was a hymnal and a piece of paper with a selective quantity of Bible verses printed upon it in a long discontinued font.

Each pew could fit twenty people, and there were two rows of ten each, one upon either side of the podium. Upon the oratory platform not a soul was to be seen, but the tense and expectant staring of the patrons foretold of an impending appearance.

A man walked from one of the two side doors that led directly to the stage, but were concealed by low-hanging curtains suspended from the rafters much like they would be in a theater. There was decidedly something of the performer about the man as he strutted forth as if ready for a fight, and threw his short arms wide and smiled at his welcoming congregation. He was of medium height, neither fat nor thin, but peculiarly bloated, like a drowned man long adrift and swollen, but with excellent skin, very tan.

Despite all this, there was something undeniably charismatic to his fiercely energetic eyes, deep blue and probing, his long, flat, supple hands, like beautiful white spiders, or his debonair hazel hair, elegantly combed upon his head, to one side and well down.

"Blessings be upon you, my brothers and sisters!"

"Blessings be upon you, Reverend!"

This exchange took more the form of a ritual call-and-response than any kind of commonplace and congenial greeting. The churchgoers were taunt with their fervor; Eisen could see it glistening in their eyes, burning like brain fever. They seemed unable to relax, and some had moved forward to the edge of their seats, clambering for a better view.

Eisen wondered what kind of man could exert such an influence by his mere presence alone. He reckoned he was about to discover just that.

"It has been a hard six months. A hard six months, has it not, brothers and sisters?"

Most of them shouted yes indeed or something similar, but a large black woman directly in front of Eisen threw her hands to the air like chickens scattering from a danger and said, "Six months of misery, lawd know it true!"

He wondered what misery she was talking about.

"Six months of shooting and killing, and travelers and merchants being waylaid by the road agents who besiege us like a plague! Cutting off our supplies and forcing us to fend for ourselves in matters we don't know much bout fending! Six months without a new oil well and our town all but worn to a shadow, and that saying nothing of the people what's in it! Six months of that bigoted oilman sucking the blood from our marrow like a wild beast and running this town into the ground with every fiber of his being! Six months of those so-called intellectuals and liberals who are trying to get their hands in matters that don't concern them! Governmental meddlers, telling us that we can't teach the Lord's honest truth in our own schools! Our own schools, brother and sisters! Six months of cattle rustling and theft! Six months, my brothers and sisters! Six months of misery!"

The woman in front of Eisen repeated her mantra, throwing her hands up in her exuberant, chicken scattering fashion once more and then shook her head violently as if the very culprits that the preacher had been ranting about were standing there upon the stage for all to reprimand.

Eisen raised a brow and turned back to the preacher who seemed to be growing more and more filled with indignation with every uttered syllable, the veins upon his neck standing out like blood stains in a frozen field or green worms beneath drifts of melting snow.

"I say it again, brothers and sisters, six months of misery! But the Lord giveth and the Lord taketh away and everything He does, He does for a reason, of that you can be sure. For no other animal has reason, save man and man alone. Thus it stands to such that something had to give man that reason, that reason that led him to that brilliant spark in the darkness of the universe, the lantern in one's time of need, that eternal beacon to tranquil shores, and that spark was God!"

At this point in the speech Eisen's eyes misted over, and he looked much like a man shipwrecked upon an island with natives who spoke nothing but their own tongue, and not a lick of his own, and him likewise so. And it was a tongue of mad howls and insane piercing screams to shatter and stir the placid air.

"Ledru would have us buried like the dead! Buried like those unfortunate souls in China toiling neath the Great Wall, constructed for their own demise by their very hands! Buried neath his corruption and greed, his insatiable appetite! His enduring sin! Yes! And Kallista, a devil's hand in his own right, predatory fiend of the plains, hiding deep within the badlands like the serpent himself coiled in his right own cave! And what's the cause, you might ask, my good people, of all this meddling and interfering?

"Well, I'll tell you. I'll tell you straight. It's infidelity to the Lord. It's your own fault each and every one! Yes! You, and you, and YOU! Worshiping the false idol of wealth! Of oil! Myself included, I no less guilty than thee! I take no pains to spare you the truth, oh my brothers! For truth is pain! And those who strive through adversity are tempered by their pain and emerged steeled of mind and body!

"So what's the remedy, you ask? It is war! War, brothers and sisters, not waged upon the flesh, but upon the mind! And all earthly slag what besets you, oh yes, my brothers and sisters dear, it is war! For if your faith is strong you will find comfort in the Lord, and he will ask of you in return to take up His word like a blade and cleave with it all the black and sneering villainy in your sight! What I ask of each and every one of you is nothing less than a call to arms, to battle in His own name. For we are all Warriors. Warriors of God! Amen, brothers and sisters, amen!"

The frenetic din that then followed, surging forth from the crowd like fire from the rim of some primordial volcano, was such that Eisen's ears rang painfully with the brunt of it. The preacher's words fumbled about in the coffin maker's head briefly, but when the pain of the applause and adoration had passed, he didn't feel any stronger at all, and he certainly didn't feel like a warrior, of God or anyone else. His ears just hurt slightly less.

The preacher then called forth a young, studious-looking man to walk the rows with the offering plate, which he did with great solemnity. Collecting here and there. Not saying a word, never smiling.

Then the preacher asked all his "brothers and sisters" to take up their hymnals and sing with him in praise. In total they sang four songs, everyone save Eisen intoning like zombies these old and gaudy words. Eyes fixed upon their respective sheaves of paper, their deadpan voices drifting ghostly and colorless up high into the rafters and reverberating the cathedral throughout; a phantom dirge.

Only the preacher seemed to have a true passion for the words or any notion of their meaning, and he put the whole of his heart into each syllable and every noise. He alone had no book, the words coming to him from memory or some deep and secret place within. His huge spidery hands upraised and outstretched, with the words pouring violently forth, arcane and ominous, like a misplaced bocor or conjurer of eldritch days, long gone from living representation. A fey invoker raising some form to function from the imponderable places of man's mind, breathing life into the ancient scribbling of some devout delusional long since passed into the absolution of the dust and darkness.

When they had finished, the people rose and began to mingle with a kind of easy, yet formulaic companionship. Chilled drinks were served, and food was laid out upon two tables which were set near the doorway through which everyone had come, one on either side. The preacher was the life of that gathering. He moved with great animation, swift as a dancer, as if his sermon had never really stopped; perhaps he didn't think it had. Perhaps it never did. A swirl of black cloth and he would swoop in upon a group and ask them this and that and the other thing and end by telling them that they were blessed, and they would smile. How they smiled. This ritual never varied. When finally he came upon Eisen he stopped, looking exaggeratedly sympathetic, raising his hands up, beckoning, summoning.

"Why do you abstain the fellowship of your brothers and sisters, my friend?"

"None here are kin to me."

"All men are kin in the eyes of God."

Eisen nodded absently and picked a glass of tea up off the table and sipped it, looking out toward the crowd, then returned his attentions to the man before him and extended his hand warmly, cracking a faint smile.

"My name is Eisen. You sent me a letter of invitation."

"Ah, yes. I recall it. I am Luce Montferiat."

"Interesting name, French?"

"Indeed. On my father's side."

Eisen nodded again.

"You've been quite the subject of discussion, young man, are you aware of that?"

"I am now."

"Indeed. A man that's escaped Kallista's gang and survived the badlands, and on foot! Such feats are bound to bring about some curiosity, unseemly as it may be. I confess that I myself am curious to get to know you. Did you enjoy my little talk?"

"Well, it was certainly interesting."

"Have you had a chance to get acquainted with the any of the locals?"

"Not really, too busy setting up."

"I understand. What do you think of Ledru, I hear he is the one whom paid for your trip in the first place?"

"You are very well informed, preacher."

"I must keep abreast of all details that pertain to my flock, and in a town this small, it's fairly easy."

"Oh, I wouldn't exactly call myself a member of your flock just yet."

"Haven't won you over yet, eh? Well, can't have everything one's own way – but you will stop by again?"

"Certainly, when I have time."

"Good day, Mr. Torquiam."

"Good day, preacher."

Chapter Two

Ledru and Co.

Eisen took the dirt road from the church, headed toward the inn, then stopped dead in his tracks, realizing that he had nothing in the way of cash. He decided to speak to Ledru Monteblanc as quickly as possible and stopped the first person he met.

"Excuse me, where can a body find Ledru Monteblanc?"

The dapper old man turned round and Eisen drew back suddenly, for the old man had no eyes. None at all, as if they had been torn free of his face by some horrible bird of prey, nothing but dark, empty holes stared back at him.

"Monteblanc? Why do you ask?"

"My name is Eisen de Torquiam, and I was offered the position of coffin maker in this town by Mr. Monteblanc. It is only now that I have arrived, and I desire to speak with him."

The old man smiled, but it was not the smile of an old man, it was the gesture of a vibrant and devious youth.

He drew up his cane, black as ebony, tipped with the golden figure of a wolf, and pointed at the coffin maker.

"Then speak you shall. Come with me."

"You work for Mr. Monteblanc?"

"No. I work with him. My name is Percival Statletter. I keep Monteblanc's books."

"His books?"

The old man laughed as a youth might who has just dropped a wedding cake upon an unsuspecting passerby, merrily and with wild abandon.

"I shall explain everything in due course. Will you come with me? I have a carriage that can take us at the ready. "

Eisen nodded, realized his mistake and said yes. Statletter smiled again and placed his crisp top hat back upon his hoary head and struck out with tremendous speed, tapping here and there before him, spindly legs moving with remarkable precision.

"Have you ever thought about getting a dog?"

"To assist me, you mean?"

"Yes."

"Not in the slightest, I cannot abide a creature that would so easily give its alliance to one that has not paid for it with anything other than treats."

"I don't follow."

There Eisen turned a corner and came upon the first dense sprawl of houses since he had left the church. All about it in a large circle was an abundance of space, as if from reverence. A hot, dry wind was blowing in from the desert, and dust was whipping up in heavy sheets all around them. Some people walking beside them darted into the nearest shelter, while most others kept on about their business as if it were nothing, and to them it was not.

Snaking up and around the two wayfarers, the squall snatched the blind man's hat from his head and took it up and away. He flung out his left arm, the one in which he was not carrying the cane, and caught it, as if by some miraculous ninth sense.

"Accursed wind!"

"I fancy you can't abide that either, Mr. Statletter?"

"Not in the slightest. But it's not because of its allegiance, for the winds have none."

He put his hat on with a haughty thrust as if to rub his victory in the face of nature.

"Now dogs, on the other hand, will most oft give their loyalty to any fool what throws them a steak. But not so with cats. Cats are clever beasts, if they're a thing; there's a loyalty that must be earned, for it is never freely given."

"I suppose that's true. Is this some kind of analogy to people?"

"Not in the least. But there are certainly people what are cats and people what are dogs."

"And which one do you think I am, Mr. Statletter?"

"A cat, to be sure, a cat and nothing other."

"Why are you so sure?"

"One cat can always recognize another."

They shared smiles and turned into an alley that passed behind some stables. Behind the low, flat boarded building was indeed a horse and trap with a large, sullen-looking fellow sitting at the reins.

"Is it there, Mr. Torquiam?"

"Yes, and a man as well."

"Sievers?"

The man answered without turning, a glum look upon his drooping face.

"Yes, sir?"

"You'll be taking us to Mr. Monteblanc, Sievers."

"Yes, sir. Right away, sir."

Sievers' "Yes, sir," sounded more like a subtle curse; however, he said nothing further, only looking straight ahead, waiting for them to enter the cab.

Eisen helped the old blind man into the double-seated carriage and then joined him, closing the door and fastening it by an inner latch of shiny brass. Everything about the trap was lavish and expensive looking. Clearly this Monteblanc and his people were the upper crust in this town, the high hatters and suit men. He could understand the churchgoers' animosity to these people; it was an all too stark example of the haves and have nothings. He wondered absently whether or not that had anything to do with the rampant and frightening religious fervor he had witnessed in the cathedral. It seemed all but obvious that it was so, for no other outcome seemed reasonable.

Once comfortably situated, Statletter rapped hard upon the wooden carriage ceiling. Sievers gave a hearty, "Hup!" and they were off, winding up a long serpentine trail that became steadily greener the higher they rose into the hills.

"I'm glad you ran into me. Mr. Monteblanc has spoken of you a great deal and the correspondence that you had struck up."

"Yes. I saw his advertisement in a paper and I thought I'd give it a try. I had grown weary of my residence and I thought a bit of travel would do me good. Never thought it would lead to such an adventure."

"You must be referring to your little excursion with the Kallista gang?"

"Yes. The way I've heard people speak about them I gather that they have been around for a while."

"That would be correct. Six years, in fact, they've gorged themselves on the blood of our town."

"Why haven't they been apprehended?"

"Because no one can bloody find him. Kavaria Kallista hides out somewhere in the badlands, or so it's been rumored by members that have left his band and passed through town on their way to the border. They say that without a proper knowledge of the desert, it's nigh impossible to reach. Not that there have been many attempts."

"So, essentially, everyone has been too afraid to look for him?"

"Well, well! You've got some hard bark, don't you! What a cantankerous young man!"

"That was not my intention. I didn't mean to come across as such."

"Oh, it's quite fine, quite fine indeed! You breathe some color and life into this sordid little dung heap."

"If I hadn't been able to deduce from your accent that you weren't a local, your previous statement would have made the fact just as starkly evident."

"Quite so, I moved around a great deal before the," he gestured offhandedly to his eyes, or lack thereof, "accident. Then I met Ledru and we stuck up this prosperous little business. You know, it's rare meeting someone of such perception, I think you have a future as a detective, Mr. Torquiam. Torquiam, what is that? French? Italian?"

"Spanish."

"Is your family from Spain?"
"Some."
"Oh, how you open up, just a fountain, full of words."
"If I haven't got anything to say about something, I see no reason to fill the air with meaningless jabber."
"Oh, Ledru is going to love you, or utterly despise you. We shall see, but ever does he find a cagey man to be a source of interest."
"Cagey?"
"You're not very self-aware, are you, Mr. Torquiam?"
"I'm not sure. I mean, if I wasn't, then I wouldn't ever really know, would I?"
"No. I suppose you would not."
"Why are you smiling so?"
"You have just made my day, that's all, Mr. Torquiam, that is all. Nothing more. Nothing more."
Rather tersely, Sievers pulled back on the reins, and the carriage came to a clattering halt.
"Ah! Home at last! It is horribly stately, but I've missed it."
With exuberant energy to quite belie his age, Statletter unlatched the door, threw it open and leapt out. Without stopping or looking back he called to the coffin maker over his hardly existent shoulders, "Onwards and upwards young man, onwards and upwards!"
Eisen got out of the carriage and nodded to Sievers who glared back with such ferocity that a bystander would assume that the coffin maker had committed some horrible atrocity against the man.
Eisen arched a brow and then turned his sharp turn and walked his purposeful stride on and up the long, hard-packed dirt path to an enormous mansion that sat on a plateau in the foothills. Eisen paused and looked back over his shoulder. He could see the twisting path up which they had rode, and far beneath it was the town, clouded over in dust so thick one would think that the desert had over-flooded. Then he walked on up the path.

The trail suddenly pattered off and was replaced with a fine coating of white gravel that ran round the mansion in a near perfect circle. Parked there were several other carriages; one of them rustled to life and clattered past him.

The sound of a whip.

A shout.

Boots on gravel.

The satisfying crunch.

Somewhere in the distance the screech of a wild hawk.

The old man was already at the door to the extensive house and beckoned the coffin maker with his ornate cane. Eisen quicken his pace and ascended the steps. As he rose up and up and up he had the strangest feeling of walking without moving, as one might in a dream. The kind of dream in which one must run from some ominous and terrible thing that eludes all reckoning, and the legs move yet the ground does not. When finally he reached the top of the lofty concrete steps he was sweating, both from the heat of the day and his own selfsame exertion. Statletter handed him a rag, or rather, he produced a rag from his pocket and held it before him, saying, "You'll be sweating, I wager, take this so as to make yourself presentable."

Eisen turned to the old man with humor on his tongue, held there like a child might a sweet.

"And what is so reprehensible about sweat? Is the farmer or the steelworker any less deserving of aesthetic praise than the socialite or the model?"

The old man laughed aloud.

"I take back all skepticism, lad, Ledru is going to love you! Come on then!"

He then rousted up his cane and rapped upon the door, once, twice, three times, the last the hardest. Almost instantly the doors were opened by two elegantly liveried servants, one a Moor, the other an Asian.

Eisen found this choice of doormen telling but said nothing, his mind working too furiously to be bothered with voicing his opinions.

The two dark-skinned servants motioned with white-gloved hands for the men to enter and they did. Statletter bounded forward with the ease which with one acts in realms of familiarity. Eisen followed him down a long, white corridor, studded with ornate golden gas lamps every ten feet. They burned dimly like giant, dying fireflies resting on that milk-bone expanse of wall.

A clack of boots. The sharp sound of the old man's cane upon the marble floor, then carpeted with stately red velvet.

Door after high, silver-inlaid door went by as they walked along. Some were open and Eisen could see other servants busy with their toils. In the kitchen some were washing, some cooking, all dark skinned and dull eyed as automatons from some joyless dystopian future.

Eisen wondered at that.

"How many retainers does Mr. Monteblanc have?"

"Enough to make his stay as carefree and comfortable as possible."

"And what of their stay?"

"Whose?"

"The servants?"

"I'd call that a symptom of youthful naiveté."

"I am twenty-seven years of age."

"Like I said, youthfully naïve."

"Ha!"

"He's down that hall."

They had stopped in a large open space where the four main corridors of the house intersected underneath a large glass dome, from which Eisen could see the drifting red-orange clouds in the twilit sky.

They made a sharp turn right and came to a set of doors very much resembling the ones at the entrance to the vast mansion. The old man opened them for him and motioned for the coffin maker to enter.

The young man strode quietly through and beheld a most singular sight.

It was a library, as cavernous and vast as any Eisen had seen, yet there was something about it, despite its garland grandeur, that was singularly off-putting. The first thing to strike him was the color of the place, such a gaudy, vibrant shade of red, ruby-bright as the wardrobe of a gadabout. The floor was carpeted and of a rich purple hue, dignified and ornate with a repeating spiral pattern that would make one dizzy if looked at for too long.

The books themselves were shelved in grand cases that soared up to just below the stucco ceiling of the room, protected by thick sliding panes of glass, which betrayed not the slightest sign of dust or mildew. The books retained not the faintest hint of wear or tear, clearly they were intended to be seen, not read.

A great, jagged chandelier hung almost threateningly from the center of the ceiling, and was, of itself, enough to adequately light the entire room, yet numerous gas lights, six upon each side, left and right, provided additional illumination. Neath this chandelier was a circle of arm chairs and a small coffee table of polished mahogany, rimmed on the sides with hammered gold. There were six chairs in all and only one of them was empty, awaiting the newcomer.

Eisen recognized Ledru Monteblanc first; he was not a man that could easily have melded into any crowd, however motley. If one were to describe the character in but a word (a feat rendered impossible for any man, despite how banal) it would be flamboyant.

The whole of Ledru's personality and wardrobe was garish and colorful; his bright red hair hung down to his shoulders, and his bushy, similarly colored mustaches contrasted starkly with his deep blue suit and the yellow dress shirt he wore beneath it. His shoes were made of alligator skin, and with his silken pants of verdant green, a motif of eclectic fashion began to form. A fire-haired fop looking more like a noble giant from an ancient and fantastical court than any mere businessman of mortal strain.

Ledru was the first to greet Eisen, though the last to perceive him.

"Mr. Torquiam?"

"Yes. Mr. Monteblanc, I presume?"

"Indeed! At last, you have arrived! And what splendid timing you have, my good sir. Come, sit, do sit. Be merry. Will it be a glass of port or sherry?" With a snort (for he always snorted before he laughed, and he laughed often) he erupted into a cascade of booming humor, praising his witty rhyme.

Taking in the faces of the other men clockwise, Eisen discerned that he had come in the middle of a business meeting and, apparently, quite an important one at that. All the men wore rich suits and comported themselves with a bearing of grand self-importance (as it was in the nature of such men to do).

"Who is this, Mr. Monteblanc?"

"There's no need to get excited, Chester."

"Mr. Torquiam, meet Mr. Chesny."

Eisen walked forward, said, "Good day, sir," and offered his hand for a shaking, but Mr. Chesny simply thrust his nose in the air, his vexation clear as a purple moon. Eisen let his arms fall to his sides and turned back to Ledru.

"Shall I come back later?"

"No, Eisen, no we were just finishing. Isn't that right, boys?"

Some of them nodded, others said, "Yes," all answered, save for Mr. Chesny, who was still glaring at Eisen as if he had just called his wife something he rather shouldn't have.

After a brief moment of silence Ledru looked around and motioned to the door with his garishly bejeweled hands. "Well, be off then, lads! Be off wit ya! I must entertain my guest!"

They departed, all save for Mr. Chesny who stood a moment longer, staring at Eisen, and then he, too, left as well.

Ledru pointed with his sherry to the empty armchair directly before him, "Sit, please!"

Eisen pushed back his coattails and sat down soundlessly, a figure of solemn and poetic composure.

"So, you need a new undertaker?"

"Well, it's not so simple as that. I mean, it is, but it isn't."

"I'm not following, Mr. Monteblanc. It appears the common lot for me today."

"Oh, call me Ledru. Mister just makes be feel so damnably old."

"But you are old."

Ledru looked aghast for a moment and then caught the sly little smile playing up the corners of the coffin maker's mouth.

"I am but forty-seven, you little rascal."

"Oh, pardon me, then."

"We'll see. Anyhow, as I was saying, it isn't just that we need a coffin maker; we need a damn good one. The people around here, you might have noticed, are a God-fearing lot."

"I have."

"They don't want to stick their loved ones in any old box what kin be put in the ground. They need to find the presentation comforting, you understand?"

"I believe I do."

"Good. I've got a place already set up for you, and I'm prepared to give you a bonus."

"For what?"

"Nothing."

"When a body wants nothing, then that is precisely what they give; however, you and the people of this town most certainly want something from me."

"Aren't you suspicious!"

"No. Pragmatic."

"Eh, a realist, aye? Well, I was hoping that a cash advance would be able to compensate for any inconveniences you might have experienced."

"Like being robbed and shot at?"

"Yes, like that."

"Do you think you can buy yourself peace of mind?"

"No. No, it's not like that."

"Yes, I fancy it is, however, you needn't worry. I don't blame you for what befell me, and if I did I'd make little enough sense in the blaming."

Ledru visibly relaxed and leaned back in his chair with an exhale.

"Oh, good. I thought you'd be fuming about it," Ledru said.

"Do I look like I'm fuming?"

"No."

"Well then, what is there to talk about?"

"Nothing I suppose. It's just that I had ordered that carriage, planned the line, your trip, everything. I blame myself for what happened."

"You shouldn't. After all, you didn't force Kallista nor any of his men, I fancy, to do what they did or what they have been doing. But I am curious why there hasn't been more of an attempt to capture them. Your associate, Mr. Statletter, told me something of the matter, that it has to do with a hidden fortress? Is this so?"

"Yes, or that, at least, is the rumor. Seeing as it comes straight from the horse's mouth, Kallista's drop-outs, it seems quite reliable."

"Ah. But back to the matter at hand, you mentioned that residences had been prepared for me?"

"Yes."

"And they would be?"

"I'll fix that right as rain. Statletter! Come here my dear, come here!"

"My dear?"

Ledru laughed his booming laugh and downed his huge chalice of sherry in one final gulp and then jumped up from his chair in a swish of blue coattails.

"The measure of a man's masculinity is his ability to seem otherwise and remain unfazed."

Eisen arched a brow and rose to greet the blind old man as he returned with characteristic haste.

"Hello again."

Statletter inclined his head to an empty chair.

"No. I'm here."

His mouth formed a grim line.

"Well of course you are, I know well enough where you are and where you are not!"

"Ack, don't be such a crab, Stat. Show the boy his rooms, take him to his lodgings."

"Um, it is rather awkward, as I already have a room."

"A hotel?"

"Yes, Mr. Monteblanc."

"Well, well, I'll fix it. You don't worry none. I'll make sure Arrgilius knows you've left. I'll have him send your things to the workshop straight as an arrow."

"Thank you."

Monteblanc smiled warmly and held out his beefy arm, his thick red fingers, the hair matting upon the back of his hand. They shook firmly and then Statletter motioned for the coffin maker to follow him, and they left the rotund tycoon to his sherry.

"Boisterous fellow, isn't he?"

"Are you always in the habit of asking rhetorical questions?"

"Why?"

"I don't like them, Mr. Statletter, not at all."

And with that they said no more until they began to cross the gravel lot which encircled the haughty manse.

☼

The drive to the workshop on the extreme southern edge of town took far longer than Eisen was expecting. The land lay in a thickened darkness that smothered the light of the firmament. It was a small, low lodge constructed nearly a century ago, its continued existence a testament to its durability and the craftsmanship that had long since vanished from the region along with all the gold. Statletter rapped his cane on the carriage and Sievers pulled the bit tight, bringing the horses to a stop.

The lodge laid a ways off in the thick and tangled skein of the forest in that binding outer dark, and on foot it would take a man some good half hour to reach it from the road.

The blind man turned to the pale youth and smiled.

"If you need anything, you know where I'll be."

Eisen tipped his hat cordially to the man, wordlessly exited the carriage and trekked on through the deep oak and the ferns and moss. The air was sweet and thick with the fragrance of flowers which brought a humming multitude of tiny minstrels in off the southern winds. Crickets and grasshoppers, cicadas and other things nameless sang their shrill deluge up into the night and down into the grassy floor of that flower-covered expanse.

From the road the land tilted and fell off a ways, dipping down, so that one had to descend a small valley and then ascend a little rocky hill before reaching the auberge. It had once been an inn, so Statletter had related earlier and with great animation, and one of the very first buildings to be constructed by the hand of man in these parts.

It was set upon a flat stretch of ground beyond that second hill where the land leveled out and the trees and bushes grew less densely. The front porch was falling into utter disrepair, and two of the three wooden steps had rotted away completely or been eaten by the hungry denizens of the earth.

A single lamp, a strange shade of green, rendered even more so by the light reflected off the leaves of the forest, hung ominously from a rusted brass hook near the door. A peculiar harbinger of what was to come with the fall of the moon and the rise of the sun. The door itself was a mess entire, small, square, and the paint so peeled and chipped that it could barely be said to have any upon it at all. Additionally, it seemed that some rapscallion had pried off the one and only lock and stolen it away, probably to melt and sell the metal, thought Eisen.

He went in, the door being unlocked and unlockable, and trod upon an even more distressing sight. The first room, presumably the hearth room, if judged by the dilapidated fireplace, was almost indiscernible as such for so thick lay dead leaves upon the floor, blown in by the northern wind. A venerable carpet crafted by the sky and the trees below it in a grand and tricky scheme, but to what end Eisen knew not. There were two floors, but he bothered not about the upper heights of his new lodgings, as he had no need of it.

He cast his eyes about and discovered that Ledru had well kept to his word and had indeed had his personal effects delivered. They lay in the corner upon the one and only chair; the frame of the backrest all that remained to indicate it. He was delighted to discover that the big Scotsman had procured a brand new wood crafting kit, the caliber unmatched in the register of any he had ever seen. In addition to this, a new clean bedroll had been laid out, and someone or another had kicked or swept a clean, or rather at least, leafless, spot upon the ground. And it was the only spot in the entire room in which the coffin maker was able to make out the dark lines where the planks had been drawn together in the process of the building's construction.

He unrolled the mat and spread it out on the small patch of leafless floor, laid down and was soon ensconced in the languid depths of dream-bound slumber.

Chapter Three

Dreams and Little Hats

The man with the top hat stepped gingerly and vaudevillian from his shadow, taking a low and knightly bow. Eisen withdrew but so did his shadow, and so did the man standing within it. Eisen found this strange only because there didn't seem to be any light from which a shadow could be cast, but it remained nonetheless.

"Who are you? Where am I?"

"Need I be anyone and need we be anywhere? Nowhere is a fine place to be, since then you never have to worry about going somewhere. Worry, after all, makes worry."

"But wouldn't nowhere be somewhere?"

"Of course not, else ways you wouldn't be nowhere, you'd be somewhere, and if you were somewhere, then you couldn't very well be nowhere, now could you?"

"I don't know. Could I?"

"I haven't the slightest idea."

"Oh. Well at least give me your name."

"What makes you think I have one – oh look, there he goes."

Eisen followed the shadow man's gaze and came upon the preacher walking down out of the clouds with a merry smile. And behind him, upon the low-lying, trailing and billowing clouds, a great and terrible castle sat erect and formidable. A huge and ghastly sphere of radiance shining above it, all colors and all hues and all the lack thereof contained within that arcane orb.

"My son. Oh, my son."

"I'm not your son."

"Oh, you are all sheep and I the father of them, and so all sheep are my sons and all sheep are my daughters, and so you are my son and your selfsame enemy."

The shadow man cackled wildly, and with large and manic eyes he turned to Eisen with a flourish.

"Well, you'd better go on then and kill him, otherwise he's never going to shut up."

"You are both insane."

But when he turned to the preacher he lay in a bloodied heap upon the ground, and the shadow man stood above him, a savage pose of nihilistic victory; a grain scythe in his long, pale hands, a crescent moon grin on his dark-obscured face.

"You were never going to do it anyways. Mustn't waste any time, no, no, no, you mustn't."

He gestured feverishly toward the castle with the scythe and then again and again. Then he turned back to the preacher and knelt and flung back his arm, a tension of muscle and the glistening blade was driven into his face, once, twice, thrice, on and on until the coffin maker lost count and the dead preacher lost his visage to the red and the wet and sticky congealing pool. Eisen turned to flee, but tripped and fell on what he knew not and to where he took some time to discern. A moment later he lifted up his head and realized that he had somehow fallen into the castle in the clouds. How he knew this, he did not know, but he knew it nonetheless, and that was enough for him. After all, why shouldn't it be? He didn't know the answer to that question either.

The grand vaulted cavern of exquisite, inexplicable masonry was swallowed up in an all but impenetrable gloom so deep-chested that Eisen could barely see his hand held there before his veiled and black blotted eyes. The only light was a small dying torch far off and away down the corridor before the disorientated coffin maker. An expiring star in the vastness of space, a fickle ember in a distorted void without sufficient form to give shape to the malaise inherent there in that rangy blackness.

GRAVE.

He moved down the shadowed hallway with his hands to the cold, perspiring stone, drawing himself along like a blind man down an alley without his dog.

Hard soles of his leather boots going tok, tok, tok, whence they fell down upon that hard and unmoving floor of hidden marble cobbled from some mountain long since gone to the eternal molten flow of the world and all worlds therein. As he came closer to the end of the hallway, or at least what he perceived was the end of the hallway, he discerned a light. A strange green light, the luminance from the lantern of his new-found, forest-wrought residence. And as he drew closer he realized that it was, in fact, the lantern he had seen before, one and the same and hanging from the porch of that old and abandoned lodge.

The door was open and the green light seeped in like eldritch blood to some fey wound, illuminating a solitary figure within that seemed to be floating in midair, buoyant in the darkness, elevated by shadows or something else within them.

Closer he drew and gasped as he realized that this grim figure was suspended there in that gloom not by shadow or queer magic, but by a noose and the rope of it. When Eisen turned the man round, he faced only himself. He screamed, fell backward and disintegrated into a pile of leaves.

He awoke with eyes wide and feral as an antelope which sees the esurient lion give bawdy chase, a deadly machine, coveting the quarries' blood, devoured, into the strength within. Having rolled about in fits of restlessness during his dream, he had unintentionally covered himself in leaves, and after the contents of his mind had poured themselves into the glass of his well-known skull, he found them utterly repellent.

With a manic exclamation he swatted and swept the leaves from his clothes and hair and face as if they were poisonous reptiles intent upon his utter destruction. Then he rose and breathed deep the chilled night air, rolling in from underneath the door and the cracks in the broken windows as if from a world of ice and the cold, white expanse of snow.

Aside from the wind, the cold breath of the night and the world, all was still and soundless.

In the morning he was awoken by an urgent rapping upon his door which caused it to swing inwards and then completely off its ratty and rusted hinges.

Eisen arched his brows and smiled but said not a word; quiet, expectant, curious.

"Um... I didn't mean to. I'm really sorry about the, um--"

Eisen held up his left hand to the man in a manner of commanding entreaty.

"Push it like refuse from your taxed and harried mind, as I observe from your countenance that you are troubled by something."

The man who stood at the doorway was a short, stocky, sun-kissed fellow with rosy lips, a dark, neatly trimmed beard and a broad, very symmetrical and reddish nose. He was smiling at his own clumsy blunder, but there was a sadness to his large dewy eyes that belied it.

"Tell me your name and problem and I shall assist you with all my heart."

"It's Tavis. Tavis Wellington. Are you the coffin maker everyone is flapping about?"

"Yes. I observe that you are either not from around here or you have traveled extensively or for a great duration?"

"Yeah, but how could you possibly know that?"

"Your accent."

"What?"

"It's different from the locals, markedly so. I assume there has been a death?"

Tavis averted his gaze as if he had been struck by some invisible hand.

"Yes. My... father."

"Ah. I lost my father recently as well. I imagine most people tell you that they are sorry for your loss or something like that?"

"Yeah. I'm glad you didn't, doesn't make any sense of course, they had no hand in it. I always knew it'd be the cancer, smokin like he did, just like a bush fire. But anyway, I was wondering if you would build a coffin worthy of the old man. Always was his wish; and he very set on it. He was very keen on looks, you have to understand, and he was exceedingly adamant that he should be buried in his finest clothes in the finest coffin crafted by the finest hand, and I mean to see that his wish is fulfilled."

"You must have loved your father very much."

"I'd like to say that were true, but I never really knew him. Er, that's not really the right way to say it, it's more like, like we never really..."

"Connected?"

"Something like that and when– "

"When you went into the military you didn't see him for years. Yes, that kind of absence can put more than physical distance between two people, even a father and his son."

"How on earth did you guess I served?"

"I didn't guess, I induced it from your tattoo; it was hard to see at first, concealed as it is under your shirt-sleeve there. But please, come in and have a seat."

"The seat."

Tavis smiled and Eisen smiled with him, a unison of humor in that humorless dwelling so cold and lifeless without it; a balloon without a burner.

"Yes, the seat. I just moved in."

"Yeah, I could tell. Where did you blow in from anyway, heard you came in off the badlands, but I know that's nothing more than rumor. Folks round here gossip more'n a hawk kills mice."

"No. I crossed the desert, I had no choice; got stranded."

"You crossed the badlands on your own?"

"Yes."

"Without a horse?"

"Nary llama nor ass."

The whole while they had been talking Eisen had been moving his personals off of the lone wooden chair and stacking them in the far right corner against the wall. He then lifted the chair up and set it down before Tavis, who had walked hesitantly into the middle of the leaf-strewn room and stood with his hairy hands in his pockets. The ex-soldier took the seat after thanking his host and then watched as Eisen contemptuously kicked the leaves from of a small patch of ground six or so feet in front of the chair, as if they were something poisonous and foul. He sat like a native with his legs folded neath him and his arms crossed at his chest, his back erect and his bearing one of formidable concentration.

"Now then, what kind of coffin did your father want? You said it was his desire to be buried in a specific kind?"

"Yeah. Well, actually it's right here. The specifics, I mean. Here."

Tavis withdrew a large piece of fine-looking paper, neatly rolled, and handed it gingerly to the carpenter, holding it as one might a piece of expensive china.

Noting this, Eisen extracted it with equal care and looked it over with a solemn but curious expression. It didn't say much as it wasn't particularly long, but it was quite specific about the coffin. Black, all black, no exceptions, for he wasn't a woman or a homosexual and as such wouldn't even be caught dead six feet under in gay colors (these were the dead man's words). The box was to be gilt with brass, for of it he was particularly fond, and there was to be brass lettering of his initials over his head. It was to be made of the best wood to be found but he neglected to say just what that was, and was to be as narrow as possible so as to make him look sleeker in death (him being a man of quite notable girth). And that was all there was to the dead man's directions.

Eisen stifled a smile and then carefully set the paper on his lap and looked up warmly at the morose ex-soldier.

"I'd be happy to make it for you."

"In the matter of your fee--"

He held up his hand, "We shall come to that in good time. You needn't worry about it now. You've a family to console, have you not?"

He nodded sorrowfully. "Many thanks, Mr. Torquiam."

Then he rose and left with Eisen not watching him leave, staring intently at that clean, exquisite piece of paper. The shape and form of the coffin already congealing in his precise and methodical mind, turning like so many gears beyond all other reckoning, their orbits shaping things in the turning.

He rose early, before the entirety of the town had even culled themselves from that nighttime place where madness sharpens to a grave and serene tangibility, and set out into the forest for both his breakfast and the wood he needed. He found some mushrooms growing next to a strange face-like rock, festooned in a green mange of moss like some verdant, living mask. He didn't recognize them. He set down the ax he had been carrying and plucked one and sniffed the pale brown cap; it was moist and it hung heavy with the heady scent of earth and living things and spores. So pleasant did it strike him that he decided to nibble a small piece from the edge of the fungi's umbrella; he mulled it about and found it tasted quite good. He sat down and waited and waited for a minute entire, and when nothing happened, he ate the rest of the mushroom and six more.

He would later regret his haste.

When the woman came upon him, he lay upon his back laughing wild and loud with manic abandon into the high, vaulted ceiling of the sky, a microphone for this singular entity. His eyes wide and showing the whiteness of them and the green in almost equal parts, and both shining like a furnace flame. She knelt and felt his forehead, lolled her head to one side and chewed at her thumbnail and then rose and knelt once more at his feet, gathered his legs into her delicate hands and then dragged him off into the shadows.

He awoke to the smell of smoke and the sound of running water.

A pair of eyes watched him from the darkness of an overhang in a cliff face that ran up beyond his dazed and bleary eyes.

"You ate the little hats, didn't you?"

The woman who posed the question sounded strange, almost inhuman, certainly not like the locals. It was as if speaking was new to her, or something she seldom did, as arcane to her as deciphering the runes of stone. Indeed she looked wild and feral as any other animal ever he had seen or expected to see, but not fierce or dangerous, rather whimsical and half-mad.

"Little hats?"

"The umbrellas for the tiny workers. The busy ones."

"You mean the mushrooms?"

She paused a moment, lost in thought, then nodded. It was a peculiar movement, almost like a wet dog shaking its head, only up and down rather than side to side.

"Yeah. They must have been poisonous. I swore I was being chased by a giant snake. "

"You must not eat the little hats; they are only for the little workers, the busy ones."

"I'll try and remember that next time. Not that I'm hoping for a next time. Say, uh, miss, where are we anyhow?"

"My home."

"You live here?"

She smiled and it was a beautiful smile, though her teeth had yellowed some and her lips were chapped. It was as if all the happiness that Eisen had ever experienced were exceeded by that simple gesture.

"Yes. I live here, there, and there too!"

She was pointing all about her and she seemed absolutely enthralled with it; her movements, gestures, the wind and the trees swaying like dancers.

"It's nice here, no bad men or noisy tongues. Just the little workers and the tiny hats and the big armed silents and the blue snakes and me."

"What do I call you?"

She seemed confused.

"I mean, what is your name? You have one, right?"

"Oh yes! I do love names! I name most everything. My name is Kindle. But you don't have to call me that if you don't want."

She was at least twenty-five years of age, but she spoke with the innocence of a child in a quiet, energetic voice that spilled over with melody. She wore a tattered old skirt that had once been white but was now a patchwork of stains. Her face was smeared with mud, and leaves stuck from her hair as if they had sprouted there.

"I don't want to sound ungrateful, but... why did you drag me here?"

"It's not safe along the main way, lots of bad men come through there and the Keeper of the Mountain."

"Keeper?"

"Yellow Eyes."

"Who?"

"Old Yellow Eyes."

"Wolves?"

She shook her head and held up one index finger with her palm facing inward.

"A wolf?"

She nodded, "I've met him before, you know. Well, you didn't, but you do now. He's scary. It's like the place that stars go when they die -- his eyes."

Eisen cast a glance about; the ground beneath him was damp but comfortable, due the moss that grew like a great patch of carpet laid down by some lazy sprite in the deep times. All about golden beams shot through the high green canopy of the woods. Birds sang their riddles from their bough-borne thrones, like feathery kings mocking the earthbound with haughty but playful contempt; beaks yellow as trumpets and just as loud. Insects were chirping, and the heaving hum of water came from a great but lumbering river that sparkled with the sunlight that it caught and carried out like spinning crystals of fire. Fish jumped within it, and the light shined from their slippery backs, and their mouths opened and closed like the mouths of dying men uttering a curse to the deaf ears of their respective gods.

"Do you swim?"

He turned to his questioner, the young woman.

"Sometimes."

"Would you like to now?"

"Go swimming?"

"Yes. If you're feeling well enough."

He nodded and rose to his feet, "Yeah, I think I am."

She rose to and fairly danced down to the water, leaves spiraling from her body and hair and the latter spinning out and around like so many tiny brown snakes. She was barefoot, and her callused heels and toes made deep impressions in the soft green ground, like the mold for some verdant facsimile.

"The water here is soft and calm and warm. But up there, up there by Yellow Eyes, the water gets angry and cold and you can't swim in it at all."

He began to say that he would remember that when she reached up to the shoulder straps of her thin white dress and slid them over her shoulders and straight to the ground. The filthy dress billowed round her feet, and she stood thin and naked and pale in that fiery daylight, levin-brands of warmth falling through her terpsichore hair and glinting strangely off of her wide blue eyes. Eyes that were as blue as the water and as blue as the sky and deeper and more beautiful than both.

He found that he was suddenly unable to speak, and though Eisen had never been a particularly bashful young man, he found very much to his irritation that he was blushing a furious shade of red.

Quick did he avert his eyes to the ground and turn full around as if he had been grievously insulted. He slouched and thrust his hands deep into the pockets of his grass-stained corduroy pants. She didn't seem to notice the effect she was having upon the hapless coffin maker as she dipped a toe in and then smiled and slid her white body down into the cool and calming water.

He heard her splash about and then her voice floated out from the distance over the waves breaking slothfully upon the speckled and mossy rocks.

"Aren't you coming in?"

"I'd rather not, ma'am."

"Why? You said you like to swim – and the water is so warm!"

"I'd rather not, ma'am."

"You're scared."

"No, ma'am, I'm not."

"Yes, you are! Big scaredy is what you are!"

He turned with an arched brow and beheld her sticking her tongue out at him like a mischievous little child.

"You act like you're fourteen."

"And you act like a baby; scaredy cat!"

He rolled his eyes and began taking his shirt off; moments later he too stood naked in the sunlight on that soft, sandy shore. He didn't test the water, only calculated the depth and the length of his jump and then leapt full in and underwater.

When he emerged breathing the sweet, scented air, she was laughing merrily and made a peculiar wiggling gesture with her hands.

"Careful, there's fish down there."

"I'm not scared of fish."

"Bet you tell that to yourself every night."

"You're being a real pest, ma'am, if ever I did see one."

"Doubt that."

"Why do you doubt that?"

"Figured a scaredy cat like you'd run away before you got a good look."

He made a disapproving gesture and then leapt forwards and dunked her underwater; she emerged moments later, laughing and splashing and him likewise so. And both swimming and circling the other like merry-making siblings at play. They swam for hours until they were both exhausted and lay in the shallows of the river, each against a giant rock that surged up and out of the water like a great stony tooth. The stone was covered in moss and lichen and it was shaded by a tree.

"You're certainly unusual, ma'am."

She looked at him with those big, strange eyes, her expression searching and uncertain.

"I've never seen a woman what would get undressed in front of a man she never met without blushing."

"Why should that bother me? I'm not scared of anything."

"No?"

"No."

He shook his head slowly and pushed himself slightly up in the water and allowed his body to ease down the rock until all but his face was submerged.

"Everyone is afraid of something."

"I'm not."

"We'll see."

"Will we?"

He turned to her and discovered that her face had brightened considerably, as if he had just offered to build her a house or buy her candy.

"I suppose, I'd kindly like to get to know you, ma'am, what with you saving me and all, least I can do."

"You'll be my friend?"

He wasn't expecting such bluntness but found it charming nonetheless; he smiled and sucked in enough air to float at the surface, folding his arms beneath his head upon the rock and the rest of him bobbing and sparkling and white in the lazy river.

"I'll certainly try my best, ma'am."

The woman looked to him and smiled again, then became quite meditative, gazing out across that wide and glistening expanse of clear blue on blue, and here and there the occasional pink of a salmon flank or the brown of a piece of driftwood.

"It's been a long time since I've had a friend."

He turned to her, letting his body sink again, moving lethargically through the warm, flowing liquid, and propping himself up with his arms, half out of the water.

"How long have you been on your own?"

"Ever."

He didn't know what to say to that, so he didn't say anything; they sat there calm and cool and naked under a great old willow watching the mayflies dance in crazed pirouettes, like a ballet from another world where there was no concept of direction nor direction of concept. They sat sunning on the rock until they were both dry. Then they clambered over it and dressed and sat by the fire she made, watching one another and the forest and all the small wiggly things beneath it that watched them.

They shared smiles and stories and much laughter and very soon, much sooner than they would have liked, it was dark and cold, and somewhere a wolf howled into the blackness. Eisen wondered if it was the one that the woman had spoken off: Yellow Eyes. Something mythological in her mentioning of the beast, something that probed the inner mind, the reptilian brain. He asked her if it was the wolf of which she spoke that now screamed out through the void, and she said that it was, for never had she heard such a fearful sound, nor would she ever forget it. He heartily agreed, and they sat there in the darkness like sleeping dogs, peering into the fire as if it would divulge some grave and powerful secret long hidden from the world of men and known only to the nameless and terrible things that moved deep within the world and other worlds not yet known or long since gone and forgotten.

"Would you like to come back with me?"

"Where?"

"To my house."

"You have a house?"

"Wouldn't have invited you to something I don't have."

"A proper house with windows, tables, chairs, beds, and all that?"

"Most of it. I still need to sort the table and bed part out, but aside from that, yeah. Besides, it's much warmer there, up off the ground and away from the river. I'm surprised you haven't caught your death of cold."

"I told you I'm not scared of anything."

"Being scared and being dead are two very different things."

She screwed up her face and stuck her tongue out at him.

"Scaredy cat."

"Pest."

They laughed and sat in silence for a moment before Eisen put the question to her once more, more earnestly this time.

"So? Will you come back with me?"

She nodded and asked him when he was going back and where his house was.

He told her he didn't know the forest well enough to say, but told her that if in the morning she could guide him back to where he had passed out, he could lead them back to his lodgings. She agreed and then rose and vanished into the blackness like steam going off and up into the tall vastness of the sky. When she returned several minutes later she was carrying a tattered old blanket in her wiry, alabaster arms.

"I only have one."

"You use it then, it's getting cold."

"We should share, like you said, it's getting cold."

When he paused to decide she mocked him, saying, "Don't want to catch your death of cold, now do you?"

"Fine, pest, give me an end."

"You're not very gentlemanly."

"Well I guess that's your loss, not mine, isn't it."

"You're so mean!"

"Do you really think that?"

The sudden seriousness of his expression caused her to halt for a moment, then she sat and handed him half of the large, hole-ridden blanket. His look was such that she wagered it'd burn a hole in the blanket were she to veil herself with it.

"No, I think you're nice. Very. Are you from the town?"

"Not originally, I moved here for a job."

"What job?"

"Coffin maker."

"What's a copphin?"

He raised a brow and then realized that she wasn't joking; on further reflection, she did say that she had been alone her entire life, alone in the woods.

"A coffin, it's a box you put dead people in."

"That's disgusting! Why would you put dead people in a box?"

"I don't, I just make the boxes."

"Why would anyone want to put dead people in boxes, that's just sick!"

He couldn't help it any longer, and the laughter burst from him like a train through a wall of wattle and daub.

"What's so funny?"

"It's just that I've never met anyone who didn't know what a coffin was or what it was for."

"Well, now you have."

"Yes. Yes, I certainly have."

So he told her of his work and the ceremonial use of coffins and how they were for the living and not the person inside, and he told her of his early life. She said not a word the entire time but sat rapt in the words and weave of his narrative. The fire dancing a crackling jig and casting its warm orange light all about their faces and up and out feebly into the outer darkness beyond the scope of their myopic vision.

"Why don't you tell me about yourself?"

She didn't turn to him as she spoke, she just peered into the fire searchingly, like she had been doing before, "I already did."

"If you don't want to tell me, that's fine."

"Okay."

"Okay."

She stole a quick glance in his direction, once, twice, now three times, then four; he had first noticed the attention he was receiving the second time.

"What is it?"

"What?"

"You keep looking at me from the corner of your eye and thinking that I don't notice, something is on your mind, I can tell."

"Maybe I just think you look funny."

"I do look funny, nobody wears a mustache anymore, after all, thin as it might be, wouldn't take more than a few seconds to figure that out so it must be something else."

"I was just wondering, if I, uh..." She froze all of a sudden, blushing several shades of red and turning slightly from him and biting her lower lip.

"What?"

"Could I lay my head on your shoulder?"

"Sure. Was that all?"

"Yes."

"Why'd you make such a big deal out of something so silly?"

"It's not silly."

"It's silly to me."

"I haven't felt another person in many years."

"No one?"

"No. I just wanted to feel someone again."

Despite her declaration, she had hardly stirred, moving only to further avert her gaze, as if her loneliness were something of which she should be ashamed.

Eisen scooted across the ground and put his muscular hands over her cold, pale ones and found that she was trembling, in the vile throws of some terrible vexation. She whirled instantly, and they locked eyes for a moment as if through an unstoppable, immaterial force. Then she curled her fingers up through his and let herself fall lightly up against him, her head lolling on his sloping shoulder. He could feel the warmth of her skin through his clothes and smell her hair; leaves and flowers and fish and dirt and something he couldn't quite place.

The next time he looked at her she had fallen into a deep and peaceful sleep, and shortly thereafter he did as well.

☼

In the morning he woke to the sound of rustling leaves and found Kindle dancing in the sunlight; just whirling and twirling, unstoppable and unbearably elegant. She was smiling in her charming way, and the slanting luminance fell upon her like stage lights.

"Isn't it a beautiful day!"

"It certainly is. I've never seen anyone get so happy about it before."

She threw back her head and laughed with wild abandon as if his words were the funniest thing she had ever heard, and then she spirited herself away, on through the leaves which spiraled about her limber feet.

He rose and brushed himself off and looked around and then called to her and asked if she was ready to leave; she said yes. They rolled up the blanket and departed wordlessly, moving without sound, save for the rustle of dead foliage or the occasional snapping branchlet. He noticed that they had woken before the birds, and he said as much. She turned to him and made a disdainful fluttering motion at him, as if she were powdering a cake, saying, "The birds here are lazy."

"If birds don't know what lazy is, does that still make them so?"

She stopped and thought about that with the intensity of the sun; he waited next for her to answer, though when he had posed the question, he had not expected one.

"No. I suppose that it doesn't make them so. I take it back."

He shook his head.

"What?"

"You're just interesting, ma'am, that's all."

"Am I?"

It was only then that he realized he had never given his name; she had never asked.

"It's Eisen by the way."

"What's an Eisen?"

"My name."

"Oh! Nice to meet you, Eisen."

"Yes."

He chuckled as she stared at him as if for the first time.

"Nice to meet you to, Ms. Kindle."

They trekked on through the thick and unrelenting foliage with an amiable gait, not hurrying nor vexed by even the slightest malady. Everything was golden and green, and Eisen felt that his heart must be fairly likewise as well.

When they arrived at the spot of the coffin maker's mental bane, he could see the face-like rock in its little clearing only thirty-odd or so feet away; from then on he knew the way. It was only when he returned to his cabin with the feral woman in tow that the birds began to sing, and it was as if all the song-like sweetness that sound could muster was priming forth from their shrill little beaks.

When Kindle set her eyes upon that shabby house there in its small and unkempt clearing, she rushed toward it and round it like a babe playing in a sprinkler. She ran her delicate hands round the wood and felt the grain and she beheld it with wonder in her eyes.

"It's been months since I seen such as this!"

"Months? Why don't you ever come down from the forest? Go into town? Meet the people?"

"Town, oh no, I couldn't. No. I just couldn't."

"Why?"

She stopped at the doorway without its door and the square of wood that had once been hinged lying flat on the floor like a corpse.

"I just can't."

"All right, don't get all excited."

"But I am excited! Why shouldn't I be!"

He was standing directly behind her, and she had whirled upon him with a demanding expression; he held up his hands in entreaty. She grinned wolfishly at his gesture and then slunk into the dark gloom of the tattered old house.

She called from inside, "How old is this place?"

"As old as the town or older."

"How old is the town?"

"I don't know."

"Because you're not from around here, or there?"

"Yes."

This seemed to sate her rambunctious curiosity about him, but not at all about the dilapidated construct she had invaded. Up and down she went across the floor, from corner to corner, wall to wall. Bent low to the heavy mahogany planks like a detective at a crime scene. She sniffed the air wherever she went like a bloodhound, and after she had tramped up and down the length and breadth of the first floor, she ascended the creaking stairs and disappeared from Eisen's view entirely.

He went in and up and followed her quietly and with great concentration; a scientist studying a particularly anomalous specimen beneath his lens. And the lens were his eyes, and they curved upon her like bent light under and full with the strain of a black hole.

The upper landing was a wide hallway with a high, vaulted ceiling; flooring much the same as the lower level. There were four plain oak doors that ran the length of the corridor's left side and two small windows that occupied the right, one of which was missing the pane entirely and was decked with cobwebs so thick they obscured all vision without.

She walked up to the first door and poked the handle as if it were some overgrown and rummy button. Nothing happened, she tried again; this time he stepped forth and grasped the handle and turned it, allowing it to swing in upon the hinges. Creaking away the door revealed a small storeroom, so narrow that two full grown men would have been unable to stand shoulder to shoulder within. He and Kindle were barely able to fit, one and both, and he examined the shelves, of which there were two that ran nearly the length of both walls. In the middle of the room were a number of chests all stacked atop one another, from largest to smallest. All seemed extremely old and fairly expensive, or at least, very well fashioned. And in the very back left-hand corner, pushed up against the wall as if in punishment for some childish transgression, were several tall black iron coat racks, from which hung a number of hats and canes and other oddments.

She turned to him in her innocent and intensely inquiring way, "You look like you've never seen any of this."

"I haven't. I only just moved here, I hadn't even got the time as yet to search the upper landing until today."

"Oh. Eisen?"

"Yeah?"

"Do you think a house is a home without anyone to call it such?"

"I'm not sure. No. Probably not."

She nodded as if this confirmed all her suspicions and then set to examining the coats and hats, belts and canes like an affluent concierge of some ancient bazaar. Whilst she labored in childish delight and curiosity, he made his way to the chests and began rummaging through them, looking for something specific which eluded him; though he was sure he'd know what it was once he found it, he wasn't sure as to why.

The first chest, the smallest; old photos of a dour-looking family of Moorish descent and a young, mirthful priest, previous owners of the lodge and their friend, or enemy; nothing else. He set it aside and picked up the next one, second smallest. Inside there was only one item, a strange silver mask. It was plain, a simplified human face without expression, save for the slightest of twists in the left corner of its mouth, a subdued smirk, portents of some ominous and terrible calamity. There were two small incisions made in the middle of each side of the mask, and from these ran two thin lengths of silken thread, with which one was to secure the facade. He held it up to the light of the window and it glinted like an otherworldly jewel.

The next moment, almost without thinking, Eisen had lifted the mask even further and placed it upon his face, tied the string and risen to his full height.

When Kindle turned, wearing a gaudy Duchess of Devonshire-type hat, she gasped and stumbled backward, nearly tripping over her own feet in the process.

"You wicked, wicked man!"

"What?"

She scowled and shook her head; he only laughed and removed the mask. "Did I get you? I didn't mean to frighten you."

"Sure."

"I didn't."

"Right."

She tried to continue her begrudging, pout-lipped countenance but was unable to muster the zest and finally relented, saying, "Can I see it?"

He nodded and walked round the chests, his arm extended, the mask sparkling within and ghostly. She took it eagerly and tried it on; she looked to Eisen as if she might have just stumbled from the inner reaches of Faerie. Bone white, delicate and thin, garbed in a tattered gown and silver mask with wild hair tangled and strewn with leaves, she was the very image of some mischievous fey, a wood nymph or elfin queen.

He stepped back and watched her where she sat, legs crossed and her thin hands upon her sharp little knees.

"It suites you."

Chapter Four

Death and Caravan

When they finished exploring the storeroom, he remembered that he had work to do and told her as much, but added that she was free to look through the rooms as she liked.

He said a goodbye and left her to it, descending the steps, entering the woods and retrieving his ax from where he left it by the face-like rock and the treacherous "little hats."

He began cutting down a mid-sized tree deep in the forest. By the end of the day he had cut down two more, though both smaller than the first. He stacked the wood in neat little piles of ten and then walked back to the house in the dark.

When he arrived she was sleeping in a pile of coats on the floor, the hugely oversized hat of red felt still perching upon her crown and the fey silver mask held in the crook of her arm. She made a strange sound as she slept, like the purring of a kitten.

He tread the floorboards cautiously so as not to wake her, and he didn't.

In the morning he woke early, dressed in white cotton and plain brown corduroy and went to the stove to make some tea and fried eggs. He ate them with sweet blackberries he had found the previous day, and then he made another batch and set them on the lone chair near the stove for Kindle. Then he picked up the fallen door along with his tools and headed outside to see if he might be able to fix it. He laid it down on a clear, thin patch of dull green grass and went back into the house and upstairs. When he came back he had two sawhorses, and he set them down and laid the door full upon them. When he looked up from his work he could see a figure walking toward him. A man in black with a staunch white collar at his throat, as if he were the pet of some invisible and vindictive elephantine being.

"Mornin', preacher."

Luce seemed both pleased and confused that there was no mote of derision in the coffin maker's cheerful voice.

"I just came to see that you weren't ill at ease about us, as I haven't seen you round the past couple of days."

Eisen looked to the preacher and shook his head.

"No, I'm quite at ease. Just busy, country life is new to me."

The preacher smiled faintly at that, and Eisen bent to his work, fixedly examining the busted brass hinges with an eye as keen as any diamond carver.

"You see, Mister Torquiam, this community was built on faith, and kept going on it; we are poor in gold but rich in our love of God; you must forgive our exuberance."

"I've heard something similar from a man, name of Henry Collins."

"Ah, young Mister Collins. Yes. He used to be a frequent member of our congregation, but once Ledru's prospector, Statletter, came and began hiring up men and buying up land, he faded from us. I have seen little of him since but much of Statletter. One wonders with how much hesitance the Lord took his eyes."

Eisen furrowed his brows momentarily and filed that comment away wordlessly, still bent to his work.

"Is there something else you wanted? I'm kind of busy at the moment."

"I heard of your first job, now that Wellington is resting at the right hand of Providence. But to answer your question, yes, there is something else I wanted. Eisen, I want you to be a part of our church."

Eisen raised a brow; if nothing else, he could appreciate the tenacity with which the preacher purported himself.

"No, thank you."

"Aren't you in the slightest concerned about the prospect of death?"

"Right now I'm concerned with my work and the grain of this wood."

"I'm trying to be serious."

"So I realized, and I respect your principality. Of course, I'm concerned about the prospect of death, but I figure I'll cross that bridge when I come to it. No use in worrying over wheat before it sprouts."

The preacher turned his back and said, "Very well then, I'll take no more of your time. I will pray for you."

Then he walked away.

Eisen watched him go then turned back to his work and toiled the whole of the day. By the end of it he had fixed the door hinges, remounted it to his new house and moved half of the firewood (with Kindle's help) from the forest to the yard.

That night he began building the coffin with the firmament over his head burning with its dots of bright in that cold and endless void, he burning brightest of all.

In the pale light of the morning Kindle awoke before him and roused him from his slumber with a strange song he had never heard before. He asked her who had made it, and she pointed to herself; he told her she had good prospects as a singer and she laughed and danced away.

A couple of hours later he dressed and told her he was going into town for supplies, both for his work and for his wardrobe, and he wondered if she would like to go.

She replied that she would love to, and side-by-side they began the walk to their destination with the sun above them, as if devised just for them and burning thus.

When they arrived at the outskirts of town on its southern side, where the land was flat, dusty and sparsely grown over with dying grass, there was a great commotion. Several men lay on a cart and two rode before it on horseback. Both were bloody and it was their own blood that encrusted them.

Vultures turned wide, eager arches above them, and one of the great, feathery beasts dropped low and attempted to land on the dead men in the cart, but was promptly chased away by the smaller rider.

The townsfolk encircled the riders and their grim cargo. They were jabbering madly and asking so many questions that no lone voice was distinguishable from the rest, all moiled together in one great flowering blare of hissing and rasping.

Eisen cast a glance over his shoulder at his companion and found that she was shivering with fear and had withdrawn into the shadows of the nearest building, a little trading post.

"What is it?"

"Something bad has happened, something terrible."

"Yes, but nothing bad is going to happen to you, I promise."

"Can you keep it?"

"I wouldn't have made it if the wise was other."

She nodded and slowly emerged from the shade and walked hesitantly behind the purple-spectacled man as he made his way to the death cart and the riders who pulled it.

It was a grotesque circus where everything, no matter how depraved, was an instrument of spectacle, even the death of one of their own.

The bigger man told the nearest sprightly lad to run get the doctor.

The boy sped off with haste, an expression of solemn purpose showing on his round face, rare for his age but appropriate, given the situation.

Someone shouted, "DAMN THIS NOISE! SHUT YOUR BLEEDING MAWS AND LET THE MAN TALK!"

Everyone grew quiet and whirled; it was the sheriff, and he a great and burly man with a bright yellow mustache, hazel green eyes and a vest made of alligator skin.

"What happened?"

The bigger rider seemed too weak even to utter a syllable, and collapsed suddenly on the steps of the inn as his friend dashed to his side.

"Hell Ed, don't you quit me like this! Don't you dare!"

But it was too late, he had breathed his last and lay there silent and unmoving, as if he had been crafted of clay and dead things to begin with and not living matter at all. Nothing but an effigy of the man that once loved and had been loved in that small dust-clothed town.

"Ed..."

"You musn't despair, Daniels. All is as God wills it, his design is inscrutable, but just, in the end; Brother Braze is in a far better place than could ever have been afforded him by his lowly mortal coil."

Daniels whirled viciously upon the preacher who had appeared suddenly and quietly from the inn, a wide-brimmed hat shading his eyes from the midmorning sun.

"Damn your soul if that's what you think! Damn mine as well!"

"Why do you spit venom so, dear brother of mine?"

"I'm not ya brother and wouldn't want ta be. If God so intended this and you behind him as well!"

With that the doctor appeared with the little boy at his side. Both helped Daniels to the medico's house and were gone. The sheriff cussed loudly and then looked bashfully at the preacher, tipped his hat, made the sign of the cross with haste and left after Daniels.

Eisen walked forward from the dispersing crowd like a figure emerging from a pall of living smoke and stood full in the sunlight, peering through his glasses at the preacher.

"You should measure well that man's words."

Luce shook his head, "He was consumed with grief, driven from his right sense by it, driven even from his faith. His words went the way of his confusion."

"I'd wager that if what you said was true, it'd be his faith what drove his sense from him, not the other way round."

Before Montferiat could reply, Eisen motioned with stern command to Kindle and the pair departed silently, and left as the wind picked up and began to howl. A curse thrown at their backs like shattered glass, unheard as it was unheeded.

All the while the preacher watched the barefoot woman with a surging and avid intensity, gears turning in his mind, falling one by one into place.

There was an empty stall yet for another sheep, and a shepherd walked among them.

☼

Eisen went first to the general store and purchased a large quantity of glue and nails for the coffin, then some baked goods, cheese and a dozen pints of the local ale. When he turned from his purchase to ask her if she wanted anything, he discovered to his dismay that Kindle had disappeared.

He called her name in a low tone, but to no avail. He shrugged and wagered that if she had been living alone in the forest for most of her life, she'd make it alone half a day in town. A wood sprite indeed.

After she had gone he, too, left the general store and bought four pillows and twice as many blankets, half for himself, half for her. It was then, as he was shouldering his jean pack of supplies that he heard the church bells chime.

Two women passed before him, and one of them wore a large antediluvian hat of red felt; it was Kindle. She and the other woman were laughing and conversing quite jovially. The other woman looked to be about seventeen years of age, and a charming and spirited girl at that.

Eisen recognized her as one of the large group of teenagers who had laughed at the challenges he had made to the priest and the latter's inability to reply. But whether she had been laughing at the priest or him or both, Eisen knew not.

He walked to them, siding up to Kindle with a wave hello and a tip of his hat to the younger woman.

"Oh, Jen, this is my friend Eisen - he makes boxes for dead people!"

At this the girl named Jen stopped roughshod in her tracks and nearly doubled over in laughter as Eisen rolled his eyes and shook his stately and immaculate head.

"Coffins, Miss. I make coffins."

Quickly, her laughter subsided and she straightened up the better to view him.

She was an athletic, tomboyish young girl with long red hair and freckles all about her face.

"You're that stranger, the one everybody's been talkin bout?"

"Yes, ma'am, I suppose I am. Though I still can't get my head round why I'm so damned popular."

"Wish you wouldn't cuss."

"Why? Wouldn't want to take my change? You don't have a swear jar do you?"

She smiled and held out her hand. "Name's Jen Arlington, pleased ta met ya."

"Eisen de Torquiam."

He took her hand gingerly and shook, then tried to withdraw, but she held onto him, firm and warm and demanding.

There was something in her sparkling emerald eyes which he hadn't seen in a woman for a long time, and it made him uncomfortable. Worry gripped him suddenly and wholly; worry that if he kept gazing into those deep wells of green he'd fall in and never get back out. A worry that she wanted him to fall. He withdrew his hand forcefully and broke from her grasp. He told Kindle he'd some things to do on his own, tipped the brim of his hat and left off with dust at his heels rising like lazy wafts of pollen.

A silence fell same as sunlight, the two women watched him go, the younger speaking first, "He's a clever sorta feller, your man."

"My man?"

"He is your man, ain't he?"

"No, I reckon he's his own man and always has been."

"You ain't no couple?"

"You mean as in two people?"

Jen looked bashfully to the ground as she spoke next, "No, not just two people, I mean. Ya'll not lovers?"

"No. Why? Do we seem like we are?"

Jen smiled and shook her head.

"I just teasin ya, now you come with me to the church and I'll introduce you to the preacher; ya'll like him I'm sure enough, as he's sure to like you."

"Okay."

☼

Eisen watched them go with foreboding into the gaping maw of the cathedral, something pricking at his mind like whatever incorporeal ice picks there might be in the world or any other. When they had gone into the stony, twilit place, it was as if the whole of their collective being had been erased from the fabric of the land like so much chalk wiped from a blackboard.

It began to rain, cold, fat drops, and there was a crash of rolling thunder in the distance; the afterimage of dry lightning in the badlands. He wondered absently if Kavaria Kallista feared the storms and then uncrossed his arms, jammed his fists almost angrily into his pockets and went to find Henry Collins. He figured that if he were to be living here with any permanence, he'd need to get to know the people; Collins would be a good place to start, and maybe he'd even get another commission in the meanwhile.

He tried Ms. Whitum's house first, though it was little more than a shack, as he carried the memory of it so starkly in his brain. She was also the only other person, aside from the preacher, whom he was positive knew Collins on any kind of personal level, and he had no intention of making another pilgrimage to the church and the zealous, frenzied mob that waited within like so many hungry beasts in a cave.

Knocking, he heard only, "They lawd above! What is it now? I told you already, Mr. Aires, I don't want no strawberry jam!"

There was the sound of shoes on a dirt floor, the rattle of a chain being jostled, a lock turning, and then the door swung inwards on its hinges to reveal the old woman's scowling, prunish face.

"Oh! You that coffin man."

"Yes, ma'am, I was just wondering if you'd a notion about where Mr. Collins might be?"

"Henry Collins?"

"Yes, ma'am."

"They lawd!"

"Is something the matter?"

"With me? No. Save when that boy about, well... he's as like a man now as ever he'll be, but I've known him since he was a suckin his thumb, yes indeed."

"Do you know where he is?"

"Oh, oh right. Well, he went on up to work hours back, should be coming round, he lives but two houses over."

"Thank you for your candor, ma'am."

"Where all you from?"

"Not around here."

"Yeah, I kin tell by ya accent well enough - you smarten me?"

"Smarten? I don't understand."

"Nere mind, oh there he is now."

Collins was walkin amidst a small group of workers who had come back from a hard day's toil on the derrick. They were slick and shiny with oil, looking as if their very skin had turned to polished obsidian. Henry was easy to spot as he stood a good foot taller than any of the other men in his midst, or rather, they in his.

Eisen called out his name and waved him over. The other men held off as if wary of the stranger, some exchanged concerned glances, and they all whispered among themselves.

Curiously, Collins seemed hesitant to approach; when finally he did he was wringing his hat in his hands.

"Good morning, Collins."

"Morning, sir."

"Whatever is the matter?"

"Nothing."

"Nothing? You look as if someone has just killed your dog."

"I don't got no dog."

"Your hypothetical dog then."

"Some of the boys," he looked over his shoulder, "some of them been saying some things, been talking about ya. Some of them heard what you said to the preacher, and he himself been talkin about you as well."

"And what has the dear man been saying, Collins?"

"That you're the devil's harlot, that ya best be avoided."

"Really?"

Collins nodded grimly. "That's what I hear anyway."

"Thank you for your candor, Collins, now let's be the adults here. Invite all of your friends to the inn for a round, if you'll be so kind. They may listen to the preacher but they work for Ledru, and so do I. That and the brew should shift things a bit."

"I don't know, I don't want no trouble."

"Neither do I. What trouble do you expect? Do you think I'm looking for a brawl?"

"That ain't what I mean."

"I know what you mean, but I'll not let these Bronze Age superstitions muddle my affairs. And more is the pity for you, if you do."

Collins nodded vaguely; Eisen didn't know how to take the gesture.

"All right. I'll ask um."

He trotted back to his boys and they chattered amongst themselves. The big man seemed to be struggling with a few, but most, upon hearing the words "drink" and "free" in conjunction, brightened and began to make their way to greet the errant coffin maker. They shook his hand, introducing themselves and told him it was a pleasure and that hospitality from any man, no matter what one says about him, was always welcome.

Eisen wondered whether they would have been so friendly and obliging if he had not offered them liquor and decided in the negative. He led them into Arrgilius' tavern, and they all sat round the scratched and scathed bar stand, stooped shoulders and dangling beards and bits of grime and sweat.

Eisen seemed but a painted shape, so stark was his artistic form contrasted with the blackened, sullied oil workers that one or the other of them seemed to have come from another domain altogether; but who and what realm, none could say. One of them, a pudgy black man, remarked that Eisen was an ermine among piglets, and another of the workers told him to stop acting like a poet.

He turned to the smallest fellow, a cagey Brit named Stockholme Johnson who seemed to be the leader of the gang, or most of it, at least.

"So what can you tell me about what Mr. Ledru plans to do once the oil runs out here?"

The little man laughed and pushed his derby cap back on his head with the dirty back of his hand, less filthy than the front.

"What do ya think, that I've got me ears to hiz bleedin' mouth? I'm just a worker ere, he don't talk none to us, do e lads?"

They replied in surprising unison that he did not. There was more than simple indignation there, there was a positive will to bite the hand that fed them.

But Eisen remained undeterred in his curiosity, saying, "Well of course not," that it was not the nature of business, at least that kind of business, nor of the men that run it. "I'm only asking what you think, not what you know."

"You're a curious one, you know that?"

"It has been remarked."

"So it has indeed, sir; you know what they been saying bout you at the church?"

Everyone but Eisen turned as Arrgilius came tromping in from the storeroom in the back with his question and a bundle of packages under his burly black-haired arms.

"That I'm the devil's harlot or some such nonsense?"

"Yes. How did you know that?"

He jerked his thumb at Collins, "A little bird with a big mouth told me."

"What do you intend to do?"

"Nothing. Wouldn't be no point in it; just be stirring the hornet's nest."

The foreman Johnson turned on him sharply, "You calling the reverend a wasp?"

"No, I'm calling him a hornet."

"That's downright disrespectful!"

"Why? What's wrong with hornets?"

Johnson rose and motioned to his men. Only half stood, the others either not loyal or sober enough to stand.

"I'll take my drink elsewhere, with respectable like folk, if'n ya don't mind."

"Not at all."

Collins held up his massive hands and stood before the foreman with a sad, mendicant expression, as if some terrible calamity would befall them all if he was not stopped.

"He didn't mean nauhtin by it. Give him a second chance, will ya?"

"Out of my way, Collins, you've wasted enough of my time already, I kin see that what they say about him is true, no doubt in my mind. Now you git or by God, I'll make ye!"

With weary hesitation Henry Collins stepped slowly aside and allowed the foreman and his boys to pass, Johnson giving Collins and the coffin maker one last indignant scowl before exiting the building.

"What very amiable friends you have, Collins."

"He's excitable, that's all. He just needs time ta cool his head."

Suddenly one of the workers turned with a whiskey grin and leaned uncomfortably close to the coffin maker and began speaking in a lax, oft slurred manner, as if his tongue was glued to the side of his mouth.

"He could stick his bulbous dome in an iceberg till hell freezes over and he'd still ave steam ta puff! The bugger!"

Eisen smiled slightly and reached for the bottle. Sliding it over, he poured the man another drink, sensing a loose tongue and a gossip-gathering mind. Information was information after all, regardless of how it was obtained.

"Is that so?"

"Ey, tis at that! Always belligerent, telling ma dis and dat! Where e tinks e kin just give out de ourdas I know it not! Better ta ave Daniels, he a man of caliber iz true!"

Arrgilius looked at the grinning inebriate and shook his head as he took up a stained white rag and began to clean the glass mugs he kept under the counter next to his shotgun.

"Daniels? You mean the man whose friend was just killed?"

"The very same! And that's not the end a that, I kin tell ya straight!"

"Why? What's he planning?"

"A reckoning." Another of the workers piped in with a serious countenance and a solemn tone, as if to smile would be to spoil and scathe the entirety of his company. He was a large man and his head was shaved, and it shone white as polished stone.

Collins was lost and he made it well known, "A reckoning?"

"Vengeance. For his friend. He plans to kill Kallista," the drunkard scoffed.

"Ain't no man kin kill him. He ain't even human."

The bald man shrugged and turned to the rummy.

"I reckon that Daniels doesn't much care bout whether he iz or whether he ain't. But one thing I know, and that's he's planning on rounding up a team soon as he's all healed. I asked; Doc told me he'd be right as a rivet in no time flat."

At that moment the medico entered, as if the mere act of talking about the man, the mere evocation of his name, had pulled him inexorably to the spot.

The bald man nodded gravely to the medico and raised his glass, and several of the others tipped their filthy, grime-crusted hats, following suit.

"Morning, Doc."

"Good morning, Ramsey."

"How's old Dan?"

"He's fine, he's fine. Well, least most of him."

"What you mean?"

"I mean his body is well, but his mind ain't. He keeps going on and on about killing that there Irish."

"Kallista?"

He nodded, took a seat next to Eisen, and looked him over inquiringly.

"Ya'll new, aren't ya?"

"Yes, my name is Eisen de Torquiam; it's ironic to meet you just now, doctor."

"Why is that?"

"Ramsey here was just talkin about you, you and this man, Daniels."

"Good man, stout heart, but he's always had a bit of a sharp drive, if you know what I mean."

"I just make coffins, so I can't say as I do."

"Oh, when he sets his mind to something, he's seldom pulled from it and liable to blow it out of proportion."

"Out of proportion? Hell Doc, it was old Braze was kilt!"

The doctor turned to his challenger, a lanky, greasy-haired youth of maybe twenty or twenty-one years, but scant more.

"Well, whipping up a posse and spillin more blood isn't going to bring the dead back, boy."

"Something needs be done, it's what ever-body is thinkin, you know it."

"I know it, I think it meself sometimes, but thinking a thing don't make it right, no sir. More bloodshed ain't ever gonna stop this, maybe nobody can stop it."

"You saying there's nothing we can do, saying we should just give up an lay on down in our graves?"

"What's your name, son?"

"Rit. Gerald Fairson Rit."

"Well, Gerald, let me tell you something, and it's a truth if ever I knew a one, and I've known my share."

"All right."

"What we got here ain't nothing new, there have been killers and madmen for as long as there have been bodies for their twisted souls to inhabit, maybe even before. I've seen a lot of it in my day, killing and thieving, and violence and hate. Destruction and desolation. And all of it bred by the destruction and desolation that came before it. A cycle. A cage. It's been said that slaves make the worst masters, and I cain't think of no advice better. We all too often turn deaf ears to the past, to our history, to what we think of as nothing more an a bunch of something what has already happened, and it just a bunch a nothing. Costume posturing and maps and dead words. Dead languages. Fallen creeds. Nothing. But it ain't nothing, it's the lesson that no one ever learns, much less tries to improve upon. Damn it, that's the truth, and all of it."

The boy was struck a little silent, and he worked his jaw soundlessly as he mulled the medico's words over in his mind like a lamb turning slowly upon a spit above the fire that stripped flesh from bone.

"You're wrong, Doctor."

The medico turned to the speaker and addressed the coffin maker with something akin to betrayal in his voice.

"Bout what, sir?"

"About it being the entire truth."

"How's that?"

The youth, Fairson, turned now to Eisen, brows furrowed and a question in his eye, a small, spiny langouste obscured in a riptide pool.

"Ignorance is the great tormentor of humanity, the grand executioner of our tiny vengeful lives. Ignorance and bliss within it, my dear Doctor, not merely a failure of scholarly historical endeavor. For ignorant bliss is the laughing man on the gallows, manic and slipping from this world like so many grains of sand from an hourglass. That is the truth, and some of it."

The doctor considered this for some short length and then nodded gravely and said it must be so, and that he himself had been wrong for many years and that Eisen should be writing books rather than pounding nails.

"Paper is cheaper than planks and glue, if truth be told."

The medico laughed and slapped the table and Eisen felt, for the very first time since he had come to the town, comfortable. It was something in the old man's face, a certain strength of will, a will to kindness, a glittering bird borne up and aloft from the cesspool of experience and suffering therein. Eisen smiled faintly and held out his hand and the doctor shook it firmly.

He noticed that the indignant youth, Fairson, was staring at him fixedly and that strange questions still lurked there in his eyes, only Eisen lacked the perception to discern the integrality of their forms.

Shortly thereafter the doctor invited Eisen to his house for dinner and, feeling pleasantly elevated from the chilling psychic floor upon which he had been supine for so long, could do naught but agree and heartily so.

He bid Collins and all his friends farewell and they said it was a pleasure; he replied likewise. Arrgilius winked at him in his fashion, and Eisen tipped his hat ever so slightly in his direction, then departed for the door with the doctor leading the way.

However, just as he was about to pass over and through the threshold of the inn into the burning, golden, sun-laden land beyond, Fairson Rit strode forth and called his name very quietly. He turned with an enigmatic expression and faced the younger man, saying, "Need you something, Fairson?"

"I just wanted to say that I'm very glad I met you, I was so... just so damned angry that I couldn't think straight. But listening to you... I mean, to you and the doctor, it really made me feel... I don't know, but it helped. So I just wanted to thank you."

The coffin maker smiled his ghostly smile and held out one pale hand to the younger man, sun kissed and awkward and beautiful in his awkwardness.

Fairson took Eisen's hand and they shook, but not firmly, nor limply, but gingerly, delicately and precisely. Then Fairson worked his lips together very briefly, looking into the coffin maker's eyes before he nodded, almost imperceptibly, and then departed.

Shortly thereafter, Eisen did as well.

Chapter Five

Medico

The doctor lived in a thatch-roofed house near the foothills of the mountains far from the main sprawl of town, above which sat Ledru's magnificent, gaudy pleasure palace.

Eisen couldn't help but feel a strange prickling sensation every time he viewed it. A bother in the back corners of his mind.

The medico's house was a modest dwelling, old but sturdy, and designed in much the same fashion as the rustic lodge that Eisen himself had moved into.

There was a cultivated patch of earth to the immediate left of the building, and there lay a neat little garden of many plants made possible only by the slightly richer soil of the foothills; most a mystery to Eisen's eyes.

"I confess I didn't catch that you were a gardener."

The doctor seemed perplexed.

"Catch?"

"Deduce it."

"Are you a detective as well as a philosopher?"

He shook his head and chuckled.

"Not in the slightest, I'd make a terrible detective."

"Why is that?"

"Because I've too many problems with red tape and the bulbous waists they tend to stretch around."

The doctor burst out in a volley of boisterous laughter that only began to subside as they took each their respective seats, directly opposite one another, at his dining table.

"Maria? Maria!"

"Yes?"

"We have a guest. I'd like to introduce you to Mr. Eisen de Torquiam. Am I saying that right?"

Eisen nodded and rose to take the woman's hand, but she curtsied instead, so he smiled, drawing up a brow, then bowed in as stately a manner as he could manage.

She was markedly aged but graceful, and though no longer beautiful in the fashion of a woman, she was beautiful to Eisen in the manner of a sage. A beauty that one was not born with, but rather it was a beauty that was earned through trial and tribulation, through wit and wisdom, through stone and fire.

"Have you supper ready, my dear?"

"Yes, my love. I'll set the table presently."

"Shall I help you, madam?"

But surprisingly, the doctor assumed an irritated expression and motioned for Eisen to resume his seat.

"What is it?"

"That is not the way it is done."

"What?"

"Setting the table; it is a woman's job."

"Ah."

Hesitantly, he sat down and said nothing more about the matter; the doctor seemed pleased and had his mind turned to matters he viewed as infinitely more important.

It had scarcely been four seconds since Eisen had resumed his seat when there was a furious pounding at the door, the handle jigged about and then spun to one side. In strode the wounded man, the sole survivor of the previous bandit raid: James Daniels.

The doctor rose and a tension seized the totality of his being.

"What is that meaning of this, Daniels! You can't just come barging in here like this!"

"Apparently I can."

He pointed a bandaged left hand toward Eisen and said, "I need to speak to him. Now."

"What about?"

"I'd like to speak to you in private."

"Well, it must wait."

"If it must. Meet me tonight at ten, it is a grave matter and I speak of it gravely."

"Where?"

"My house, know it?"

"Yes. You have my word."

"Yes. I suppose I do."

He left tersely and as soon as he had gone, the medico turned direly to his guest with great urgency in his old black eyes.

"Don't go to him."

"Why? Because you think he's dangerous?"

"I know he is. There's no more dangerous kind of man than one that's just lost someone he loves. Braze was like a brother to him and now he's dead, killed by that Irish. Of course he's dangerous, he means to kill him. I don't blame him, but you can't get mixed up in it, you'll just die like the rest of um."

"Them?"

"Every man what's gone after Kallista has met with an early death as his only reward. Won't be any different with Daniels." The doctor shook his close-cropped head and sighed heavily.

"You shouldn't tarry upon your problems so much, Doctor, you of all people here should know the detriments that stress can cause."

The older man looked up finally at Eisen and peered into his face as might a child into a fog bank. An eager crowd searching the stage for the illusionist's apparatus, looking for the secret but never knowing whether they really want to find it or not, for the secret of the greatest tricks is that they are not tricks at all.

"You're not like anyone here."

The coffin maker tilted his head as if to better hear the medico. There was curiosity in his eyes and a question on his tongue, but he waited for the old man to finish, as he knew he was far from through.

"You talk to everyone as if they were your brother, even people you clearly don't much care for, like a few of Collins' friends. Not even the preacher is like you. He has a good heart, but he leads his flock more like a military commander than a sheepherder. That's one of the reasons why I wanted to talk with you. I have a patient. He's dying, and he knows it. It's the cancer, he's had it for a long time now and, well, you, me, we only ever have just so much of that. Time. His is almost gone and he's all broken up about it; he's just shattered. I've tried talking to him, tried bringing in distant relatives, I've tried everything I can think of, but nothing will make him any better, nothing. I just don't want him to die as he is; I couldn't bear the thought of anyone so worthy of a peaceful death passing from this world wreathed in nothing but terror."

"You want me to talk to him?"

"Comfort him, yes. Do you think you could do that for me?"

"I don't even know the man."

"First time for everything."

"I've never tried to get someone who was about to die to accept it."

"Like as I said."

"Doctor, do you understand what you are asking of me? Have you not even considered that I may make this man's fear and pain worse?"

"No, I need not consider that, ain't much possible. The preacher calls you the devil's harlot, but I know what you are."

"And what is that, Doctor?"

"You are a prophet."

"Excuse me?"

"Eisen, are you a spiritual man?"

"What do you mean by spiritual? This may well sound numbingly pedantic, but, as terms go, it's a bit of a blanket. A wide net."

"Yes. I mean, do you believe that we are here for a purpose not our own?"

"Some grand design? Karmic clockwork and all that?"

"Yes, in a fashion."

"Absolutely not. And even if we were, we'd have no way of knowing. At least I can't think of any."

"That is a pity; I thought you'd be less cynical."

"Cynical? You think disbelieving something when you have no reason to believe it is cynical? You misjudge me."

The doctor looked aghast. "No reason? What of us? Are we not proof of the soul?"

"I doubt it. At any rate, it is of little consequence to me."

"But why do you say this?"

"Doctor, you act as if I am personally attacking you."

"I apologize; I perhaps have grown complacent in my old age, too uncomfortable around different ideas and youthful bluntness. You understand?"

"Yes. I believe I do. But you needn't a cosmic purpose, to tell you what is and is not important, simply pick and choose that yourself. You needn't any immortal soul to enjoy life or for that enjoyment to matter. Why should our own plans and desires be considered lowly simply because they aren't divine? Desiring is in and of itself valuable. For there is no value without it."

"But if it is simply going to end, then what is the point?"

"Now you sound like the preacher."

"He has asked you this?"

The doctor laughed.

"Indeed I just might, I've known the man a long time. But I wish to talk of another man. This man, the one I want you to talk to, his name is Ennio, Ennio Farrara. And he thinks as you do. He lost his faith along with his youngest daughter, and she only twenty-two years on and agued something miserable. It was terrible. He believes that once he dies he will be swallowed up by unending blackness, a great and dismal void. Is that not a valid concern?"

"Of course it is, Doctor, of course, I never said it wasn't. But that void needn't be filled with talk of souls and karma and gods, at least not singularly. There is a far simpler alternative. I see no reason why having friends and family can't fill that space."

"He ain't got no family."

"Friends?"

The doctor slowly but surely shook his head.

"Ah. Now I understand. It would seem that he simply needs to be more selfish."

"What?"

"Why Doctor, you look as if I've slapped you with a salmon; there are no fish in my pockets, I assure you."

"Son, I plum don't get what ya saying."

"I'm saying he needs to value himself more. You and the priest and most of the people in this town think selflessness is some kind of absolute virtue, and selectively this is undeniably true and certainly a benefit to all mankind. But the completely selfless man is the completely joyless man; moreover, in what sense is he a man at all?"

The doctor considered this gravely but spoke not at all and merely looked to the kitchen where his wife was returning dutifully with plates of food and drink.

His wife sat and looked expectantly toward Eisen, smiling warmly.

"Would you like to say grace?"

"No. I feel strange talking out loud to myself."

She looked quickly to her husband as if expecting some kind of explanation for this eccentric and unsightly behavior; he remained passive and did little more than make a dismissive gesture with his hands.

"It was good talking to you, Doctor, but I should go now, things to do, people to see."

"Will you see him? Will you speak with him?"

"Yes. I will speak with him. I'd have spoken to him even if you hadn't explained his loss. The quickly dying, I find, are inexorably more interesting than the slowly living."

Then he got up and left without another word as his hosts thought of him wonderingly.

Chapter Six

Daniels

He found Kindle sitting with the young woman, Arlington, on the porch of one of the larger general goods stores, owned by a man named Ellis, though he was nowhere to be seen. They were chatting amiably, and the sunlight danced through their hair like gold, like fire, and they waved.

Eisen approached with the sun in his eyes and the dust rising about him like scales from some giant moth. Catching the light and spinning it, arcane sand whirling and alight liken to a thousand tiny lanterns.

"Hello Ms. Arlington, Kindle. I'm going to meet someone, would you like to come? I only ask since I'll be going back to my house directly afterward."

"Is he interesting?"

"Yes. He's certainly interesting."

She perked up and smiled her innocent, beautiful smile and rose, bidding her new friend farewell. Then she took his arm and they departed into the radiant effulgence of the tremendous burning sphere that hovered high and mighty, the prophetic orb of some invisible overlord; much to the redhead's derision and building gloom.

"What's his name?" she asked naively as they walked; he looking a little uncomfortable with her arm about his.

"Daniels."

"The man from earlier?"

"Yes."

"Is his friend all right?"

He hesitated a moment and stared ahead vacantly then steeled himself like the cliff diver before the plunge.

"No. He's dead. I'm assuming that's why he wants to see me."

"You mean he wants you to put his friend in one of your boxes?"

"Something like that."

"That's very queer."

"I suppose it is. So, tell me, how did you find your trip to the church?"

"Creepy."

He laughed and she looked to him with a curious expression.

"And tell me, Kindle, how did you find the preacher?"

"That's what they kept calling that odd-looking fella with the big spider looking hands."

"Yes, I know, but how did you find him?"

"Easily. In the creepy old building with all the big stone monsters, he wasn't hard to find."

"No. I mean, what did you think of him?"

"He was really nice, kept calling me his sister, can you believe it? It was wonderful, it was like he'd known me all my life. I did think it kinda strange that he wanted me to call him father, but after a few times I didn't really mind, and everyone there was really enthusiastic. Only, I didn't really understand what they were so happy about, he explained it to me but I fear I must be very stupid, for it didn't make much sense."

"Did he ask you to come again?"

"Yes, he said he wanted me to be a part of his church."

"His church?"

"Yeah."

"Interesting."

Eisen stopped briefly and crossed his arms and gazed off into the falling sun and the rising dark, then he kept on with the young woman in eager draw.

They got mixed up twice in direction, and finally Eisen had to stop in at the inn to get the proper avenue from Arrgilius before they finally found Daniels' house and rapped upon the battered wooden door.

Footsteps.

Coughing.

A child crying and the voices of solemn children, their heads at play, their hearts all but absent. A shout and silence descending like a foul and festering plague.

The door opened and a sickly woman of perhaps thirty years peered out warily at Eisen and his companion.

"What do ya want?"

Her eyes were bleary and red and puffy like the eyes of one emerging from some terrible sadness.

"Didn't he tell you I was coming?"

"James?"

"James Daniels, yes."

"He did but he ain't said nothing bout two people."

Kindle looked with innocent concern and stepped from behind the coffin maker, her eyes fixed sympathetically on the woman.

"Are you all right?"

"What?"

"Are you all right? I feel for you; something is terribly wrong."

"I'm fine."

"You don't look fine."

"It ain't none of your damn business!"

Daniels appeared from behind the sorrow-stricken woman, took her by one arm and led her forcefully away from the door, whispering something to her as he did so.

She gave Kindle one last look; no longer indignant, now concerned, curious, regretful.

Eisen watched all of this unfold wordlessly, with a detached expression, greeting Daniels similarly.

"James."

"Eisen, I'm glad you came, come in. It's warm."

"Yes, it's quite warm here," he replied as he stepped beyond the threshold and removed his hat, straightening the brim compulsively as he did so.

"Make yourselves comfortable. Sit anywhere, but sit, cause folk prancing round when I'm talkin makes me nervous."

"All right."

The interior of the little house, scant more than a very large shack, was rather respectably furnished for people of such low social standing. A mere oil worker, and yet he could afford a couch and a mahogany table with six elegant wicker chairs.

"You seem to be doing well for yourself, James."

Daniels turned to Eisen with a disdainful expression.

"My friend just died in front of my eyes; do you think I called ya here to chat bout my furniture?"

"No."

"Good, cuz I didn't."

"And what exactly did you want to talk to me about?"

"Does she have to be here?"

"Yes."

"This ain't got nothing to do with her."

"I don't even know if this has anything to do with me, but nevertheless she stays with me, she's new to the city, could get lost."

"She ain't no child."

"But if she were she wouldn't be yours, so stop prevaricating and tell me what is on your mind, elseways I'll be unable to assist you."

Kindle flicked her eyes from one man to the other, sitting directly across from each other at the table. Eisen leaning back with a calm, icy confidence, like a king upon a throne whilst James Daniels fidgeted uncomfortably and kept glancing over his shoulder at the wild girl sprawled upon his couch. She, to his eyes, seemed all but intangible in that distorted space, too narrow to confine her.

"All right. On with it then, I hear tell ya'll kin read Latin. That so?"

"It is, but I'm not following. What has that to do with Braze?"

"Everything. The only detailed map of the badlands was done awhile back by some prospector who was convinced the area was a gold mine. He wrote it in Latin so that no one from town could read it; most here cain't even read English. It was back near a forty years ago. Anyhow, what this fella thought was a gold mine was nothing more than a minuscule pocket of the shine, and afore he could even finish gettin it all out, he got bit by a rattler and died. Some luck."

He rose and went to a cabinet beside the small black iron stove and pulled down a book from the highest shelf and from it produced a carefully folded piece of paper which he spread out upon the table. He smoothed it down carefully and then resumed his seat with an expression of obscene pride.

"This here is the map. Take a good look."

Eisen had been studying it from the moment it had been unfolded by Daniels' careful, calloused hands.

"And this is the town? Here?"

"Yes. It was called by a different name back when but same place, yeah."

"Then this fort, here, this must be Kavaria's hideout?"

"Great minds think alike, eh?"

"Maybe."

Eisen looked over and found that his host was smirking deviously.

"What is it? Why are you smiling?"

"You just talk funny, is all. Like a storybook character. Where ya'll from, anyhow?"

"Let's concentrate on the matter at hand."

"All right."

"Now I assume you want me to help you in some way."

"Yeah."

"How?"

"I was just coming to it."

"Then speak your mind, I'm on a deadline."

"Yeah, I heard about that soldier boy coming ta see ya, real sad business, his ole man passin like e did. This map may show where the hideout is, but it's damn near useless without the measurements."

"Yes, otherwise you would only have a vague idea of where you were headed."

"Precisely. And I hear tell you kin read this Latin gibberish, yes?"

"Yes, quite well. But it's not gibberish, otherwise I'd not be able to read it, would I?"

He was silent a moment before he spoke.

"Well?"

"If I tell you, then what are you going to do? Find Kallista and kill him?"

"That's damn right. Braze was a... a brother to me, and I'll be more an damned if I fail him."

"You'll be shot dead as soon as they see you. Even if you do get Kallista, which seems unlikely, since Statletter told me he was the deadliest draw he'd ever heard of."

"Statletter, the blind man?"

"Yes."

"Shifty bastard; trust him bout as much as you kin trust his aim."

"This conversation doesn't concern Statletter; it concerns you and what you're planning on doing. Revenge might be the path you want to go down, but I assure you that it is not a place in which you will wish for long to stay."

"You haven't got the first clue about what it is I want."

"You may be right, but I've seen my fair share of misfortune. Most of it came about from grudges, compulsions for vengeance; the knife can still the beating heart, but it can't heal the wound. Not ever."

"I didn't bring you round for a sermon; I've had it up to my dick with sermons and preachers."

"I'm not preaching gospel, I'm preaching truth."

Daniels rose angrily and began pacing back and forth; two sets of eyes followed him as he moved, Kindle's and the coffin maker's, one curious, the other concerned.

"I won't do it. I won't give him a pass! Especially not no two-bit piece of shit like that damn Irish! He's the one who pulled the trigger; he's the one who put that bullet in poor Braze, in my shoulder! He's gonna burn. There's no two ways about it. No, he's gonna burn, and my hand is the one that's lighting the match."

Eisen cast his eyes to the floor and inhaled meditatively, then he crossed his arms and leaned back in the chair. A dire meditation draining his features and them all but inscrutable in the shadows of that gloom.

"I won't help you. Not with this, you'll have to find someone else to translate your map for you."

Daniels froze and turned slowly; his body was rigid and tense, and he had momentarily stopped breathing.

"What?"

"I said I won't help you."

"He's a killer, he attacked you, stole from you, killed your friends, killed innocents, raped women! He's nothing but a monster."

"No man is ever solely but one thing. And becoming a monster is an easy way to best another, but you clearly haven't considered the cost."

"I'll pay you whatever you want, within reason, I got money, I'm a hard worker, name your price. Go on, name it."

"I said cost, not price. I don't want money, nor was I speaking of it. But the cost will be yours to pay, of that I assure you."

Eisen held the older man's gaze for a brief moment longer, and then he rose, gathered his hat and motioned for Kindle to follow him out; she did so without a word, glancing back once at the dejected and morose form of James Daniels before she passed through the threshold and disappeared into the failing light.

"Is he going to be all right?" She whispered in the coffin maker's ear.

"No, probably not."

Chapter Seven

Cruor sub Luna

Outside they walked in the windless town neath the glittering blanket of blackness that shimmered above like a sea of jewels; strange fish, finite and finless therein. Their legs were heavy and their minds bound in a fog of fatigue and fast encroaching sleep.

No one moved about them; nothing stirred, save that which they primed for their own way through the dust and the sand and the dying grass. The tin roofs glowed strangely with the moonlight, as if they were themselves burning liken to an oven, heated with blue flame.

The baying of strange and aberrant organisms shattered the stillness like a stone to a mirror as their footfalls descended upon the outer dark of the city's limit.

Very soon they crested the hill road that lead into the forest and began the long and silent journey toward the lodge.

Footprints in the dark.

Silver in the sky.

Eyes in the trees and fangs neath the eyes.

The small shabby tin-roofed houses and wooden porches and sleeping beasts now far behind them. Between them nothing but the solitude of intimate companionship.

Everything now seemed far behind them, save for the rustle of the bushes upon the narrow path.

Eisen kept on, deep in thought. Kindle whirled instinctively, her ears molded to the detection of even the slightest disturbance.

Wise in her movements, as in her attention, she was able to throw herself in the path of the jagged blade as it arced up through the ghostly moonlight and down into her arm. She howled and lashed out with a furious kick as she fell, turning and twisting like a psychotic child in the throes of a ghastly seizure.

The man who assailed her was not alone, and the very next instant they made that fact known, emerging from the gloom of the forest on either side like unearthly predators.

Eisen backed up and let his pack fall from his shoulders as he shifted his feet ever so subtly and turned his head in such a fashion so as to take in all the faces. He stood next to Kindle defensively, but so complacent was his poise that, had one not known of their friendship, one might have thought he didn't spare her the slightest thought.

"I advise you all to reconsider."

The man who spoke next was the man that had stabbed Kindle, a huge broad-shouldered fellow with the look of a boxer said to him, "Shove your considerations and fess up the gold. Your money or your life."

"And what of your life?"

"What the hell of it?"

"Exactly."

The boxer's confederates seemed confused, but the big man obviously understood the carefully veiled threat and reacted precisely as the coffin maker desired: with blind, insurmountable rage. His muddled mind a boisterous zephyr stirring the waves of the world easily overcome by the calm shoal of precision upon which Eisen stood. As the boxer rushed him, the coffin maker leaned back, only half a step and the bend of a spine, a fencer's dodge. Head over heels the brute tumbled and fell, seething with ire, uncontrolled.

As soon as the boxer had fully hit the ground Eisen was upon him, looming over the brute with the moon glowing in his eyes; some fell demon or harbinger of unholy destruction.

Eisen inhaled deeply and then stomped down upon the man's face, fracturing the brute's skull. Then crushing it. Then again and again until there was scarcely anything left of the man's head that could be construed as such.

The boxer's men looked on in horrified silence, daggers held limply in their feeble, trembling hands, yet the wild girl remained strangely passive.

Eisen turned quickly upon the two remaining footpads, simultaneously wiping his bloodied boot upon the dewy grass as he did so. They gasped and withdrew, dashing off into the forest like nocturnal beasts fleeing the light.

Eisen walked to Kindle where she sat and helped her to stand, ripping off a large portion of his left shirt-sleeve and using it to bandage her wounded arm. It went red and from red to black.

"Are you fit to walk?"

She nodded and then began drawing round him, all the better to see the dead man that lay in a pool of moonlight like a soldier lying in grisly outflow; casualty of some monstrous battle. But the coffin maker intercepted her with a firm hand on her shoulder and a dire look in his eyes, mixing with the ghostly light, incandescent in its entirety.

"It would be better if we went a different way, else those footpads might return, perhaps with more men."

She nodded absently once more, whispering only, " All right." He tightened his grip on her shoulder until she winced with pain.

"That's no sight for one such as you."

"I want to see."

She looked to him pleadingly, and after a brief moment of deliberation he released his vice grip upon her shoulder and let her free. She began walking forward and stopped, once and briefly, to gaze back at her protector before she advanced upon her fallen foe. Then she stared down at that crushed and ruined form for a spell, how long, no one could say, perhaps a minute, perhaps a thousand years.

Finally Eisen walked up to her and motioned with his head toward the direction he knew his lodge to be. She didn't even seem to register him there in that well-traveled place, now nothing more than a mausoleum built upon a trail of sacrilege.

A place that would now seem all but alien to even the most familiar footfalls and those that made them.

"Let's go."

Then, to his mortification, she spat upon the corpse and shambled off down the road and disappeared into the darkness. He looked after her a ways and then once more at the man he had slain, then he too departed into the sullen void of shadows and ferns and all that stirred therein.

Chapter Eight

The Odd Principles of Eisen de Torquiam

By midmorning the next day Tavis' coffin had been finished and stood proudly against the side of the lodge, mere feet from the door; a beautiful, if somewhat macabre, decoration.

Kindle had gone out into the woods, where precisely Eisen knew not but he wasn't much worried. She could handle herself; he knew that well enough from last night.

The coffin maker stood upon his porch and surveyed his domain; it was a peculiar feeling, living within so much that was living and vibrant itself. His entire life he had lived within the sheltering confines of large cities and heavily guarded settlements. He thought, in his younger days, that such stifling security measures would render danger obsolete, but he quickly came to realize that it just replaced one threat with another yet more terrible. As threats from without are rarely as dangerous as those from within.

He thought of the man he had killed in the night and the look of terror upon his face, the look of a man who had foreseen his own demise and yet remained unable to escape it. Unable to accept it. He had seen that look before, and he knew it would never leave him; it had wormed down, deep inside, to a place that could not be touched by the corrosive light of forgetfulness.

He thought it was, perhaps, for the best. So many that live in bland contentment within those cities that were now but fragmentary vignettes within the microcosm of his mind had no notion of true despair.

The truth behind his wanderlust was borne upon the wings of disgust, a disgust of men, yet it was only the coffin maker's love that propelled him to such contempt. For without love, men would be almost wholly without bloodshed. A contempt of those pathetic cries and sobbing moans: I deserve so much more; I am under appreciated, no one understands me! Yet they had never had to face their own death, and yet they had the gall to complain of such trivialities?

Eisen had met many such men, women, even children, but always was he confused by their reasoning; if you deserve so much more, why aren't you getting it? If you are under appreciated, then you must teach appreciation. If no one understands you, make yourself understood. To the coffin maker's mind it was all so dreadfully obvious, but always he was met with the shrill cry of, It's not so easy!

Why not? Always he would ask: Why not? He never heard a good answer to that question and had no reason to expect one anytime in the foreseeable future.

Why not indeed?

He looked down at his plain brass pocket watch and then up at the road where stood a shabby-looking man with a hat wrung tightly in his hand. He stood beside a wagon pulled by two huge Appaloosa that stamped their feet as if in impatience.

Tavis Wellington looked on eagerly.

Eisen waved him over and stopped with his arm in an awkward limp over his head; there was a young woman with Wellington, Jen Arlington, Kindle's newfound friend. The redhead with the deep green eyes.

Those beckoning eyes.

He paused and then continued to wave, forcing a smile to his lips though he was uncertain if merriment was the emotion for the occasion, so obscure and fresh did it remain. Ebbing liken to a tide and he nothing but the flotsam upon it; carried away.

"Mr. Torquiam! It looks beautiful!"

"Yes, I'd hoped you would think so. It took far longer than usual."

Jen pranced up and took the coffin maker's arm with a wide, boisterous smile; a flash of perfect white teeth and sunlight shimmering on her screaming red hair.

"I understand Mr. Wellington's presence, but, if I may ask, why are you here, Ms. Arlington?"

"Well, to see you, silly."

Tavis averted his eyes to the ground and shuffled his feet as if to distract himself from the situation.

"Why do you want to see me? Has someone died?"

"Gosh, no. You're so weird."

"It's undeniably been said, Ms. Arlington."

She rolled her eyes."Please, call me Jen."

"All right, Ms. Arlington."

She glared.

"I mean, Jen. Is that short for Jennifer?"

"Nope, just Jen."

Eisen nodded absently and then turned to his customer and appraised him with a keen eye.

"I cannot fail to detect, Mr. Wellington, that unlike young Ms. Jen here, you appear quite exhausted from your journey. Been riding hard?"

Jen nodded exuberantly, "He was scouring the badlands with Daniels, rode furthern than I'd evera. If'n ya don't git carried way by the bandits, then ya'll git carried way by the buzzards. Once I seen one big as a man! It's the Lord's honest truth it is!"

Instantly the ex-soldier whirled upon the young woman with a baleful expression; she flinched and withdrew closer to the coffin maker.

"But it's the Lord's honest truth, why ya scowling at me?"

Eisen arched a brow and flexed his fingers up and down, curling his digits inwards and outwards.

"You said Daniels. Do you mean James Daniels?"

Tavis looked hesitantly to him and then nodded very slowly, as if it caused him a certain lingering, exponential pain.

"He told you not to let that slip, didn't he? Well, you needn't answer, it's painfully obvious that it is just as I have described.

Come in, come in, it's nothing to get excited about, you too, Ms. Ar – Uh, Ms. Jen. I'll put a kettle on and we shall have some tea."

"Blah!"

Eisen cast a glance to Jen over his shoulder with eyebrow preemptively raised, a bent black bridge on a pure white plain that folded round an unseen tumulus.

"Blah?"

"Tea, it's disgusting."

"Jen! That's no way to treat a host, especially one what's being so hospitable an all!"

"Oh, shut up!"

"Please, please, settle yourselves, there's no need for all the animosity, I assure you. If she doesn't want tea, sadly, it's her own loss, as it's become something of a secondary craft for me. And as for 'treatment,' I fail to see how it is mistreating me to speak the truth, rather it should be the other way round. If she were to have taken tea and drank it and pretended to like it, true, she would have spared a lesser man's feelings, not that I am one, but she would have lied to him all the same, or rather, me. Once a web of deceit is woven, however small, the spider, architect of its construction, all too often strangles itself there and lingers in its garrote like a broken marionette. So it would seem completely, patently obvious, provided that preceding insight, which the more noble act should be. Wouldn't you say?"

Whilst Tavis gazed on in utter confusion, Arlington smiled and said, "Ya'll got to be bout the smartest man I've ever met."

"Why is that?"

He posed his question offhandedly, without much interest, as he went to the cupboard near the stairs at the far end of the room and began ferrying dishes to the table. As he pirouetted about the wooden planks, his guests stood near the doorway in that fashion which people who are new to a place adopt in their uncertainty.

"Why? Because you're so clever. I'll bet ya a philosopher, ain't ye?"

Tavis, who had only just shaken himself from his stupor of befuddlement, seemed mightily troubled by this high-flung notion.

"What about the preacher? You used to do nothing but brag bout him. This coffin maker here your new idol or something? Hey Eisen, I think ya'll got a fan."

"Shut up, Tavis."

This time Eisen didn't even bother intervening betwix his two bickering guests, instead he focused solely on making the special blend of tea which his mother had departed to him, having acquired it on a long and whimsical journey to the Orient.

"A fan. Well I certainly hope not, please, make yourselves comfortable, take a seat."

"I'm sorry about her, Mr. Eisen; she's got me so flustered I haven't even thanked you for the coffin. Must have taken a lot of work, yes sir."

"And what did you think of it?"

"It's beautiful. My old man would be proud to be buried in it."

"He is proud."

"Don't mind her; she got a mouth twice as big as her brain."

"Bigger'n your pecker, leastways."

"You jus watch it now!"

Eisen broke in with a steaming kettle of tea and spoke dryly as he poured their respective drinks.

"Why don't you both shut up and praise my handiwork?"

They both looked abashed, concerned and then, finally realizing it was but a jest, hesitantly smiled and lifted their cups to their lips; one not realizing it was hot, the other not realizing it was tea.

With sheer serendipitous unanimity they spat out their respective drinks in great steaming spouts, cursing loudly.

Eisen stroked his short pointed beard as he resumed his seat and uttered a cautionary statement. "It's hot."

☼

They spoke for several minutes of the weather and of the bandits and the ex-soldier's journey into the wastes with Daniels.

And of Daniels himself much was said between Jen and Wellington, who seemed so in tune with each other's speech patterns that never did the other interrupt the speaker in the slightest. Despite the quarrelsome demeanor they projected toward each other, they seemed, to Eisen at least, to be the closest of friends. He had always considered himself something of a natural psychologist; to him people weren't open books, they were unrolled segments of greedily scrawled parchment, stark white and plastered upon the great black wall of the world. Often in the midst of the conversation Jen would cast those dangerous green pools toward the coffin maker who, though he desperately wanted to avert his gaze, held them there where they struck like white hot bolts of flame with a fresh and eager fearlessness that was alien to him. Alien, but exciting. Exciting like the first kiss or kill or the beginning of a long trip down a foreign road to places seldom sought and oft less arrived at.

Suddenly a large noisy wasp dived down toward the table and spiraled into free fall, striking the wood with a dull buzzing and striking about with its multiple crustacean legs.

Arlington shrieked like a man afire and Tavis cursed loudly.

"Goddamn, I hate these things! Scared the wits out a me!"

As Tavis spoke he raised his hand with every intention of smiting the poor defenseless insect neath his knotted fist, but with haste Eisen intervened.

"Hold."

"What?"

"That's just rude. To show such malice to he who's come down to make merry music with the sweet buzzing of his wings, and you not putting a thought to it at all. Not at all. Come here little fellow."

Having wiped the inside out with his rough coat sleeve as he spoke, he scooped up the injured, madly whirring creature within the milky white confines of the china cup and carried it safely outside of the building.

The duo waited with quizzical expressions adorning their respective faces until he returned a few moments later with a scornful air that was more evident in his movements than in anything his facade betrayed.

He resumed his seat and meticulously adjusted his dapper blue waistcoat before he decided to commence with his reprimand.

"Had that wasp harmed you, Mr. Wellington, in any way?"

"No, but what's that got to do with anything?"

"If it isn't starkly evident to you, then I fail to see how I could bring the matter into the light for your peculiar sense of mental digestion."

"You shole do talk funny."

"Allow me a reversal. What has that to do with anything?"

"Well, it's just that the boys..."

"The boys?"

"The folks I work with."

"Oil workers?"

"Yeah."

"Ah. Go on."

"Well, the boys I work with said that you had a run-in with the foreman, a rather unpleasant run-in at that, as well."

"If the run-in was unpleasant for him, it was doubly so for me, only because he was doubly as unpleasant as I. But presumably they were gossiping about me, and they've been lipping off about how strange I sound? Is that right?"

"Well, sort of, I mean, I wouldn't exactly call it gossip."

Jen sneered, "I would."

"Shut up you little runt, I ain't a talkin to ya!"

"Well I ain't talkin ta ya neither!"

"Xenophobia seems as endemic in these parts as bad manners. But, ah, what can one do?"

"Come now Eisen, ya don't think I have bad manners, now do ya?"

"Oh, no Ms. Arlington, not at all."

She smiled and rested her head upon her left hand, gazing up intently at her host with admiration of a subdued but respectable magnitude.

"I think you have terrible manners, not merely bad ones."

The smile quickly faded from her face as if struck from it by some ghostly cudgel.

"I came here to have a friendly conversation and get to know you, and you go off saying insults when all I'm trying ta do is defend you! If I had wanted to spend my day being insulted, I would have just as like stayed at home!"

Wordlessly she cycloned from the room, a swirling torrent of red hair and stiffly working limbs, pale and shimmering in the sunlight like a polished bone set alight.

Tavis looked to the host's confused aspect and shrugged with a wry smile.

"Women, ya know?"

"No, not really."

The ex-soldier rose first, swiftly followed by the coffin maker.

"Well, anyways thanks for everything."

"Sure. Though it does not pain me to say that I hope we never do business again."

Tavis laughed and patted Eisen on the back.

"You and me both."

They both laughed and then exited the lodge. On the porch Tavis examined the coffin once more; studiously did he apply his senses, striding intermittently back and forth, leaning in and out, closer then farther away. Squinting and working his lips, brows furrowed in his concentrations as if looking for some hidden panel or secret switch. With his tousled hair and hands stuffed by their thumbs into the pockets of his waistcoat, he looked, to Eisen's eyes, like some hard-boiled Victorian detective (if that wasn't a contradiction in terms). So amusing, in fact, was Tavis's unconscious performance that the coffin maker was loath to interrupt, but the urgency of the matter dancing upon his brain was such that he knew he couldn't leave it a single moment longer.

"Would you tell me something, Tavis?"

"Don't know, depends on what ya ask."

"If I ask you to tell me if you intend on accompanying Daniels on his suicide mission, would you answer me?"

"Yeah, but I'd rather not, he didn't want me to talk bout it."

"Did you make a promise to him not to?"

"Cain't say as I did, cuz I didn't."

"Ah, then it's all fair play, isn't it? He should have been more cautious."

"Eisen... you didn't see him, he's crazed with it, if he finds out I toldja something, anything, he'll kill me, stone dead."

Eisen paused momentarily and furrowed his brow with a great degree of consternation.

"Literally?"

"Ain't no other way ta be kilt. Ya'ver seen a man metaphorically kilt afore?"

"I didn't expect you to trust me with this, it's just that I've seen this kind of thing before, more than once, actually, a lot of people died, and I want to make sure that doesn't happen again."

"Why? Daniels ain't one of yourn."

"Need he be?"

"Well, no."

"Precisely. Else ways that wasp would have needed to be as well."

"So what happened?"

"When?"

"Whenever it happened."

"I'm confused. What are we talking about again?"

"You were talking about Daniels' obsession, said you'd seen it before, what did you see?"

"When I was eighteen I had two friends, woodworkers both, and all three of us worked for the same company. A little cabinetry shop run by a congenial old man with impressive chops, both literally and figuratively. And though we knew he was the wisest man in town, he was ironically considered something of a doddering, sentimental fool for taking so many apprentices on at the same time. He had a rather good deal of rooms for let and, as was in keeping with his generous spirit, allowed us to use them at our leisure and free of charge. This latter bit was what actuated the feelings of derision that beset the poor old man, my dearest mentor and friend, long since gone and cold and in the ground these past seventeen years." Eisen paused, bemused, and then continued.

"Anyways, it was like that with all of us, if you got to know him, really got to know him, bypassed all the oddities and eccentricities, then he was really the most lovely man there was, and you couldn't help but like him. We all did. Aside from me, the other apprentices were named Will and Daren, the former a cool hand but a bit of a rogue, and the other a hot-headed, self righteous do-gooder; essentially, polar opposites. Needless to say, they were always at each others' throats, in deed nearly as much as in thought, and I the partition betwixt them.

"Both were far more skilled than I and infinitely more dominion hungry. The reason for this is that our mentor had made it quite clear to us when he took us all in that over time one of us would be chosen to head the shop, to lead in case the old man was absent. So naturally neither of my fellow workers could help but compete from the position of privilege; what began as a friendly rivalry escalated and escalated until it was something so twisted and grotesque that there are few words for it.

"Not to make a labor of it, one day I came in and found him lying on the floor... my mentor, my friend, a second father really. His skull bashed in and Will lying beside him barely breathing but still alive. You can guess the culprit and his motives. Well, I managed to save Will, and he lives still to this day, but there was nothing I could do for the old man, nothing. And another thing I can tell you is that no matter how much you talk to the dead, they don't talk back, not ever."

Eisen sighed deeply before speaking again, his eyes downcast and glistening feverishly, full with the terror of his memories.

"Do you understand?"

Ever so slowly Tavis nodded, like a man moving under the barrel of a gun or on ice thin and delicate and cracking all around.

"Yeah, now I do. Can you tell me something?"

GRAVE.

"What?"

"The culprit, Daren, what became of him?"

"He escaped and fell into a life of crime, robbed a bank and set off from the city. I've no idea what happened to him, but he's most likely alive. Ruthless men tend to live longer than those without a spine, even if that life is a miserable one entire."

"It must be painful."

"What?"

"Thinking about all that, you might have forgotten, but I was a soldier, I've watched men die, hell, I've killed them. So, I understand."

"Yes, I reasoned, given your background, that you would understand even better than me. That is why I'm concerned with this affair, I don't want to see revenge wield its scythe upon those bold and deserving once again, and neither, I'd wager, do you."

"Well of course not, but... all right. Meet me tonight, I'll tell you everything. His whole plan. Maybe together we can... maybe we can stop him."

"I certainly hope so. Here, let me help you with that."

"Thanks."

With synchronous movements both men bent to the coffin and hoisted it up and off the wooden boards that suspended it from the ground.

As they made their way through the verdant expanse so pristine and unblemished to the wagon with the coffin at their waists, Eisen posed a question.

"Tell me just one last thing."

"What's that, Mr. Torquiam?"

"Do you think she'll still be angry with me?"

"She'd bear a grudge against herself till Judgment Day if the mood took her right."

"Thank you, Tavis, that's very reassuring."

Tavis laughed and then nearly put his right leg down a gopher hole that lay beneath him veiled in the tall and scarce-trodden grass as if waiting for him or some other prey to be swallowed up its black and toothless maw. The songs of the birds and the whistling of the wind were swiftly replaced by an unpleasant deluge of such irreverent perversity that would shrivel the ears of even the most hardened of sailors.

☼

Eisen stood silent, save for his subdued breathing and his calmly pacing heart; still as a statue, and what was he but such and such an effigy to any passerby, were there any. He watched them go, Tavis, bent and troubled at the helm, whip and reigns in hand, horses clopping to his beat along the hard, clay-packed road, and Arlington, lips pursed and arms crossed in steady resentment and dejection.

He'd make it up to her, he thought, and decided to do just that the following day. But there was much to attend to in the meantime.

He waited until Tavis' wagon had gone from the stage of his sight, the curve of his eye and then strode purposefully to his woodpile and began splitting the fibrous cylinders into long, thick planks which he then proceeded to ferry inside the lodge. Once he had made a suitable stack within, he set his ax in the corner and rummaged through his toolkit until he found his hammer and his nails.

Chapter Nine

Somnium nex Quod Atrum

When Kindle finally returned from her venture, she discovered that all the windows had been barred up with thick, flat crossbars of oak. When she entered Eisen addressed her immediately.

"You shouldn't wander off like that anymore."

She began to give him a disputatious look, but he sundered it with but a single word.

"Bandits."

"You handled them all right."

"You were no slouch yourself, but that's not the point. The point is the man I killed had friends, friends who are still out there, friends who just might have followed us or tracked us down. Friends who might, even now, be staking us out. The less you know about your enemies the more likely you are to underestimate them, thus the more likely we'll end up on the sharp end of the stick, perhaps all too literally. Until we know that those men are gone or dead, we need to stick together, no more going it alone. I know it's a lot to ask, but I don't want to see you come to harm, all right?"

"Of course it is, and it's nothing much to ask, I owe you everything."

"I don't see how."

"You saved me, you barely know me and yet still you chose to stay and fight them. For me."

"Did you expect I'd turn tail and run?"

She averted her gaze.

He rose from the table and walked calmly toward her, the dull thump-clack of his boot soles upon the floor boards and the dust rising from them like little sunbeam infernos.

"You can be honest with me; in fact I'd much prefer it that way. Friends who give false consolations are false friends as far as I am concerned. You are my friend, aren't you?"

"Of course I am."

"Then look at me and answer my question."

She bit her lip and clenched her thin callused fists but said nothing; her eyes still fixed on the floor. Anything to avoid his stare and the shame that would accompany it.

"Kindle, answer my question."

Slowly she pivoted her head toward him, craning it out elegantly, her eyes wide and moist, her lips trembling. She reached up and caressed his face gently; he began to move his arms as if to extricate himself from her grasp but hesitated and then stopped altogether.

"You are my friend, my only friend. No one has ever treated me like this before. Whatever you say, whatever you want from me... it's yours."

"All I want is for you to stay close to the house when I'm here. You needn't be so... melodramatic."

Slowly he reached up and gently but firmly entwined his left hand about hers and then slid it from his visage, looked long into her eyes and then turned round and went back to his work.

She looked on with a mixture of emotions that was so homogenous in its outgrowth that it was difficult to tell exactly what wormed therein. Then she departed upstairs to the treasure room, as she called it, where she spent the majority of her time not devoted to wandering in the woods.

His hand moved upon the solitary gas lamp, his thighs pressed firm against his chair, ears not listening to the woman's footfalls retreating upwards, upwards, up, then gone.

Graphite fairly flew as he dashed a line here, a circle there, chiaroscuro and the sublime but arrogant marks on the many pieces of cream paper spread before him; schematics for a new design.

But not the design of a coffin.

☼

The last thing Eisen remembered before he fell asleep was the gas lamp burning low, a silver moth circling his head, his papers before him with his project nearly finished, the grinning moon, pale blue tearing through that vast vaulting dark; then nothing.

Then light; faint orange light, like the dusky glow of burning amber only intensified a hundredfold; molten lead in the eyes of an immortal.

He stood amongst a barren, stony moor, totally bleak and cold and ruthless in its wide, joyless expanse.

He felt unease.

A noise in the distance.

No clouds in the sky.

The whole place permeated with queer vibrations and odors.

A nameless dread slithered through his gut like some aberrant fetus prematurely developed and rending its mother's womb. He stumbled as the ground shook with some impossible force that caused the stones around him to crack and then lift defiantly into the air, heedless of gravity's code; Gaia's will sorely broken.

The curious noise in the distance grew louder, and louder still.

Closer.

And, after a moment, a short spell in which he cocked his ear and rose above the shattered stones of that endless, infertile plain, he realized what it was.

Singing.

A seething, swelling multitude from above.

A hundred voices.

A thousand.

A hundred thousand, growing ever stronger, ever louder, ever more senseless and intractable.

Each seemed to be trying to out do the other for sheer visceral impact, and all trace of harmony was long since buried beneath this dire incentive.

He turned full round, following the direction of the mad cacophony and beheld a marvelous wonder; a great red tower stretching up clear into the fickle embrace of the clouds; a needle of blood that could pierce through the eye of the world. All about this fearsome, brick-dust monolith were the tongues of the vocalists and them working and moving, hither and yon upon and through the endless terraces, bridges, stairs and parapets. They ferried great slabs of stone between them, four men to a block, or twenty, depending on its size. Others hammered away, pounding in tune to their unintelligible warbling.

"What madness is this?"

To him those figures, so tiny and obscured in the low, whirling mists and the high, veiling clouds appeared as vestiges of a half forgotten memory. The taste of a delicious meal that could never be appropriately recalled save till it was partaken of anew. But this meal was poisoned and already in his belly and him full and sick with it through and through.

The higher they built the louder they sang, and the louder they sang the less sense they made, and the less sense they made the happier they seemed to grow. The happier they grew the sicker Eisen felt until he fell to his knees with the pain of it.

He whispered to himself through his pain, a mantra forming through his flicking tongue, "What madness is this?"

"Not madness but the sweetest of fruits plucked from the tender heart of the last man, succulent in its decay."

He gathered himself up and cast his senses round for the voice in his head and found that it was there contained solely no longer.

A man stood behind him and dressed in a business suit of steely gray, drab and flat and immaculate, a red satin tie at his neck like a thick stream of blood; his face all in shadow. He held a black umbrella in his left hand, and it seemed to suck the very light from the sky, for though the sun blazed as an inferno, not a speck of it shone upon that dark-webbed shroud.

Nothing of the man's face could Eisen see, save his unnaturally white teeth, white as bleached cotton, shiny as polished steel.

From the pall of shadow the man's crescent moon smile beamed and burned with obscene relish borne of feral intensity. Eisen gesticulated wildly toward the looming artifact, "What is this perversity? What is this sordid waste?"

"Waste? Is the delight of frictionless contentment any less profound than the delight of insatiable confrontation?"

"Your profundity to the dogs! Even they would choke on it, so sickly is your offering upon my tongue!"

"You'd discard insight in the same sling as discord? For you cannot have one without the other – it is the fisherman without his net – the fish without its gills."

"I'm no fisherman, my net captures nothing but air, and more is the privilege and the joy for it."

"A fish then?"

Eisen's visage darkened considerably and he scowled, crossing his arms pithily, his head tilted upwards in boosting challenge, "No. Schools offend me."

"Then why do you fret so at their illusion?"

"Because it is an illusion! They grasp but they cannot reach! They drool at fantasy without recognizing it as such!"

"There are some that say everything is."

"Not I."

"Nonetheless."

"Well, their existence certainly is nothing more than one big schadenfreude of obfuscation."

"So waspy is your tongue; might it yet sting even you?"

"Be gone from me, as I wish to be gone from this place!"

"There is no leave for those who are in the only place that is; and they the only ones that are. Come – I will guide you. And yet, might you learn of truth – if you can swallow such bitter poison."

Then, wordlessly the man with the black umbrella departed at a brisk pace, headed heedlessly toward the sanguine monolith, that fearsome red brand that beckoned insidiously, ceaselessly, irresistibly. He seemed not to walk at all, but rather to glide over the ground like some aberration of a nighttime delirium, a fever dream phantom, a fickle form kheft of shadow and fog. And yet when Eisen looked away from him, to the tower and back again, the man seemed not even to be gliding, it seemed as if the very ground beneath his beetle-black shoes were rushing to aid his momentum.

Eisen muttered to himself irritably, "I'm not going. I'm not... no... damn it."

With great self dejection he mournfully clambered down the rock-strewn decline before him, scampering nimbly over the jutting rocks that, contorted by time and its vile hosts, leered out at him from faces of bone. He could fairly hear them taunting him with reasonless malice, and at every step was his progress deterred by their jeers.

"Fool!"

"Centrist!"

"Traitor of emotion!"

"Turn back O' herald of destruction, for we are the keepers of Man, and he resides in the clouds alone! We are the foundation; the rock and the dome! The ladder to the gods! The ladder to ghosts!"

"The clouds belong to the birds and, of a certainty, your Man has their brains' equivalent."

They moaned with rage and agony, mingling to a singularity, and then they cracked and burst, fracturing like shale dropped from a great height.

Then there was only silence and the faint aroma of incense wafting on the indistinguishable cross currents; breath of the world and all that breathed within it.

The compulsion to follow the umbrella-shrouded man stood starkly out in Eisen's mind; so much so that he could think of nothing else. There was nothing in all the world, it was his only goal, his only desire; he would follow him, and that man would lead him to the tower, and then he would ascend to the gods, to the ghosts. He would take them all on shakes, were he able.

Strange purple lightning crackled and convulsed through the sky and then froze there, encapsulated as if in some quagmire of lofty, unseen tar, hanging, motionless; luminous as the absent moon.

He tramped blindly through the thick foliage, grasping and groping sightlessly in that impenetrable darkness, and the further in he drove the less he could see, and the less he could see the more he flailed and panicked. A blind man would have fared far better, he wagered with nothing to no one at all. For in the complete and total darkness, in utter oblivion and the wastes of the void, the keenest set of eyes availed less than the dullest set of ears.

But he had always been too busy, everyone had always been too busy to listen; always turning, stomping, killing, screaming and swearing; moving hither and yon, back and forth, up and down, east and west, north and south. Always moving, always looking, always tasting, never listening, not to anything important, not to anyone or anything at all.

Suddenly a strange slithering noise and then his legs were ripped from underneath his own control. He went head-over-heels and hung upside down from some massive column of substantial shade, what he could only assume was some mammoth tree. And all about him were withering, slithering, sliding vines, that seemed to materialize out of the air itself or something more sinister hidden covertly therein, from all discerning eyes, however worthy. What was worthiness to any vine but listening to any man? He tried to scream, but the tracheophytes drew round his lips and forced themselves, as if with some malign intent, down his throat and into his heart. He could feel them planting seeds there, breeding within him like any horrible parasite that ever there was. And the whole of his chest swelling and swelling and swelling with the monstrous tendrils until he was sure he would burst. Until his ears rang with pain and his veins grew bloated and blue and his eyes bulged nearly from their sockets entire.

Then he burst apart in a sanguine swell of pale gray rheum and gore.

☼

He awoke to a low light and something wet and warm upon his forehead; sure it must be some remnant of his intestines, he screamed and flailed wildly in grotesque contortions, striking Kindle fiercely upon her left cheek. He convulsed like a man set afire and wheeled back from her, delirious with dream-fever; a savage puppet to his fear.

She raised a hand to her face where even now the skin was beginning, ever so faintly, to discolor. Then she dropped her arm and looked at him sadly, a sadness that shook the dream-mad coffin maker from the Other World like a man taken emphatically by his collar and told the way of things.

"Kindle, I, I didn't mean to, I was, I was..."

"You were delirious."

He nodded and with an unnatural, seemingly great effort, as if he moved through some viscous sludge that had vehemently congealed round his shivering frame entire, rose to her.

The moon was high and silver; shining in through the low boarded windows like fingers from a snooping deity of night, and light peering through the fickle curtain of the world into the next. He pushed himself up from the ground and looked round like one whose blindfold has just been removed, slowly but surely taking in his surroundings.

"Come here, please."

She slowly came forward and felt his face, unable to take her sympathetic eyes off of him. "Are you all right now?"

"Yes."

He embraced her as the response fell gently from between his mouth like satin feathers on a silken mattress. So sure was she of violent intent in his movements that she inhaled sharply as his arms came full and fast around her.

"Don't fret. I would... I would never harm you knowingly; you know that, don't you?"

"Yes."

As she replied she slipped her slender arms round him, and there they swayed in the soft embrace, full with pale moonlight like figments of some romantic novelist's idle imaginings.

He released her and moved away before she disentangled herself from the carpenter, staggering slightly away as he began walking.

"What happened?"

"What do you mean?"

"In your dream, what happened? You were so frightened... and don't try and be proud and manly and tell me you weren't!"

"Why would I do that? It's like you don't know me at all. I was scared shit-less, I believe the saying goes."

He cracked a sly smile as she laughed and breathed in the chill night air; the scent of flowers and wild things less subtle and fair.

When their mirth had subsided, she assumed a serious air about her which, to Eisen, was dreadfully uncharacteristic.

"What is it?"

"It's just..."

"Yes?"

"It's just that I don't think they like us."

"The townsfolk."

"Yes."

"Some of them don't."

"Except the puffy-man and his friends."

"Puffy? The preacher?"

"Something like that – apparently he talks to God, you know that?"

"Well, I fancy he certainly thinks he does. I had meant to ask you about him, actually. What was it like in the church?"

"Spooky."

"Yeah, that was my reaction too. It's all those statues... like they're staring at you."

"Yeah. But the people were nice. I've never had so many people being so nice to me before, but they did confuse me a lot. They kept talking about some book I ain't never heard of and all this stuff what happened in the past. They were very adamant on it, kept saying, 'We are a people of one book.' Didn't make no sense."

"They must hate libraries."

"What's a lie-berry? Do they grow round here?"

Eisen raised a brow, smiled slightly and then shook his head. "No, never mind. But what of the priest?"

"Who?"

"The preacher, the puffy man. Luce."

"Oh, he was the nicest of them, him and his son, Michael. First the preacher came on and said to them to stop spreading rumors about you and that he had never said anything bad about no coffin maker whatsoever."

"Really?"

"Yeah. Guess you're quite popular."

"I guess so. Don't know why."

"Because you're 'Ever so charming,' that's what Jen kept saying, she was very keen on meeting you again."

"We did meet again; I think I made her angry. I don't know why, though."

"Better not let Jen know that, she'll think you don't know much of anything, what with all the times you've been saying, I don't know."

"Don't, not really. The only thing I know how to do is make coffins and all that's required for that."

"Oh I was only joking, you're so serious all the time. It's excruciating."

"You speak very well for someone who has been living in the woods all her life."

"Well, I haven't been living in the woods my whole life, just most of it; all that happy green and bountiful gold, it's like a sanctuary for my soul."

"Then, if you don't mind me asking, how did you learn how to speak with such eloquence? I mean no derision, only that I've heard stories of people in such situations as you and they have always been unable to muster a coherent sentence, much less use words like 'excruciating.'"

"Can we speak of it another time?"

"Another time?"

"Yes."

"All right. I didn't mean to impose."

"Oh no, it's not that, it's just..."

"It's all right. Tell me about Luce and his son, didn't know he rightly had a boy at all, not that there is any reason why I should have to begin with. Tell me about this... Michael."

"Oh, well, he's very serious, like you, not at all like the puffy man, he was always so jolly, always smiling and laughing and moving about while his son barely seemed to breathe. I swear if he had only kept his eyes closed I would have thought he was dead; then you could have put him in one of your creepy boxes."

Eisen smiled and sat down at the table and motioned for her to sit down beside him. When she had, he rose and put a kettle on the stove.

He worked at their tea all the while she was talking, chattering away like a school child that had partaken of far too much sugar, but then, that was how she always talked.

"The puffy man gave a big speech, I didn't understand much of it, well, most of it, actually, but he seemed very intense about it, as if it was something terribly dire. Thinking back, he did keep going on about 'Brimstone and fire,' so I guess he was paranoid about that drafty old building catching fire. Silly, if you ask me, I mean, it was made entirely of stone. Stone don't burn, whoever heard of a stoneburner? I didn't mention it. I figured that they would work it out eventually. He was very talkative, the puffy man, never stopped talking, but after his speech he only said pleasant things and he said them to everyone. He seemed to know them all like family, and they kept calling him 'Father,' though I had no idea why, I mean, he couldn't really be the father of all of them. Then we ate some bread and some wine that he said belonged to some dead guy, only that he wasn't dead and that this dead man who wasn't was his own father as well as his son, or it was something like that. It didn't make any sense to me. He started speaking in Latin and then my attention wandered to his son who stood beside him like an icon. He was a statue; you couldn't have moved him with a crowbar.

Hands always folded in front of him just like his father, only more firmly, eyes fixed straight ahead like he was lookin fer something that nobody else could see and not finding it. He was kind of scary at first, actually, but he noticed me halfway through his father's squiggly speech and came to speak to me."

"What did he say?"

"Well, I wasn't quite sure at first. He spoke so quietly and gently it was hard to make out his words in such an echoing place. But when the puffy man was through and everyone had eaten and drank the dead man's food and sat back down, I could hear all right: he asked me if I was new to these parts. I said I wasn't but I was new to the town, and he nodded as if he already knew that, and for some reason I don't doubt that he did. Then he turned to me and put his hand on my shoulder and asked if I was right with the Lord. I told him I didn't know what Lord he was talking about, and he looked hurt. Then he told me that the Lord was their god and that he looks out for us and loves me, and there was something about... about his voice when he said it, something in his eyes and his words. It was like he was overcome with this unbearable... passion and he just couldn't speak through it. Anyways after he got a handle, he said, 'Would you like to be part of our flock?' and I asked him where he was flocking to and if he thought I was a bird. He got very angry for a moment until he realized that I wasn't making fun of him, and then I think he felt bad because he apologized and walked away with his fists clenched tighter than dry bark on a windy day. I didn't see him again after that. Kinda wish I had."

Eisen had been listening with subdued intensity, his attention split, fairly disproportionately betwixt the steaming mint tea on the stove and Kindle's fragmentary tale.

"This lad intrigues me; do you think he would see you again if you went to him?"

"Don't know, why?"

"I need to meet with his father, and I thought as long as I'm there, I might as well meet this zealous youth, Michael. I'm going into town tomorrow and you can come with me, all right?"

"All right."

"Goodnight Kindle, thank you for all the... for everything."

She blushed and hurried away up the stairs in her flighty fashion, eager and hesitant, paradoxically she moved; with firm intent, he watched her go, thinking and thinking all the while.

Chapter Ten

The Circus

In the morning they ate a light breakfast which Kindle had fixed (being the perpetual early riser) of blueberry hot cakes and blackberry tea and left for town.

The day was blisteringly heated and the air was heavy and malign with it. Vultures turned above them, queer looking, those followers of death, near so much that was living and green and vibrant. They shrieked and cawed, then flew off suddenly with great animation as if swept from the sky by the hand of some devious djinn.

The travelers, upon seeing this strange sight, paused and listened with great focus; there was a building murmur in the distance, far off fluttering and the cawing of a vast multitude of avian.

Then they saw them; hundreds upon hundreds of crows, great black shapes like solid shadows in the sky, untouched and untouchable by the light of the sun and all but threatening to blot out its very existence. They came all of a sudden and with great direction and gesticulation, as if they had been forced through some great and harrowing passage, a pressurized vortex that eyes failed to perceive.

Kindle's curious eyes glistened with an eldritch shine as she raised them to the silent blue and the deafening black above.

"Oh, Eisen. Aren't they beautiful?"

"Very. I've never seen this many in one place before. Have you?"

She spoke not a word, too transfixed with the whirling black wonder before her to adequately respond. After a few moments she tore herself away from the fey vortex of wings and wind to shake her head back and forth in a most decisive manner. Then she turned back to the seemingly endless mass of birds, too many to count, too many to believe, too many to imagine.

The army of black wings rushed past them without pause and swept ominously over the town, and then turned up and arced above Ledru's stately manse before vanishing from sight into the deep, deep reaches of the misty mountains, far-painted in the distance.

"What do you think that was all about?"

"What do you mean?"

Eisen raised a brow slightly, as was his fashion when he knew he was about to hear something he would regard as absurd. And, given the torrential amount of absurdity that existed in existence, this was a gesture he had grown quite partial to.

"The crows; do you think it was an omen?"

"I think it was crows. Lots of them perhaps, but just crows all them same. We are ever ready to impose the purpose we create upon that which has none at all save its own."

"But it was so strange! It had to mean something!"

"Why? Rarity isn't evidence of magic, just rarity. Or do you really think that the crows took the time to assemble themselves before so as to warn us foolish mortals of some dire and impending situation? Which seems more plausible to you?"

"Oh, you're no fun at all."

"It's not about fun, it's about the truth; now which of the two is more steadfastly important?"

"I don't know."

"Sure you do. Falsity in the long run is almost always bad. In fact, I can't think of an example where it wasn't and in the worst possible way. Can you?"

Kindle tilted her head in that strange fashion then cupped her chin meditatively and thought about it for several moments, all the while silent and introspective.

Finally, she turned to him and shook her head vigorously, saying, "You know what, I can't. I can't think of a single thing like that. I think you're right."

"I certainly hope so."

"Why is that?"

"Because otherwise I've been misleading people for quite sometime, and that, well, that would be falsity over the long run, wouldn't it. I suppose then I'd be the hypocrite."

"Well, you should just have some more faith in yourself, that's what the puffy man kept saying at the church, 'Have faith in God, and God will give you the courage to have faith in yourself.' He said that twice, that's why I remember it, must have been important."

"I don't have faith in anything, only reasonable expectations."

She looked at him a moment with something like uncertainty, not saying a word but moving her lips ceaselessly, as if such movement would assist her in articulation. But then, as if she had decided to drop the subject, she pressed her lips together, nodded and went on as before. Eisen found this kind of thoughtful acceptance peculiar, and due it, he studied her quite intensely for a while thereafter. Such an attitude was as foreign and distant to him as wooden clogs, square dancing or the Russian tongue.

They arrived uneventfully at the edge of town some half hour later, and it was as the quiet before the storm.

For suddenly there came great fanfare, a boisterous cacophony of strange and familiar sounds, dually delightful and dire. And behold, wonder of wonders, a circus had come to the lonely little town, all bright lights and gaudy makeup, keen eyes and empty purses.

The band of traveling performers moved in caravan fashion, a long single file that stretched back for several hundred feet. They came along steadily with great merriment and jubilation, whether it was from the prospect of a new performance, gold or merely to escape the blazing heat of the sun, none but the members of that outlandish troupe knew.

GRAVE.

The road which Eisen and Kindle had taken was such that it ran counter to the dusty town's main thoroughfare, meaning that they would, if they had continued in such a fashion, walk directly into the path of the oncoming parade.

Eisen adjusted his hat against the baleful blaze of the sun and slunk into the shade of the nearest building, a shoddy tannery. Kindle stood like some deranged bird watching the colorful company; her neck craned out with much exertion, and her eyes wide as if in the throes of some shocking hysteria.

The people of the town gathered with a heterogeneous soup of sentiments at their behest, a mix equal parts xenophobia and fascination. Thronging either side of the streets the more wary among the rank and file of the onlookers crossed their arms and glared, some even spat at the feet of the sun-stained wayfarers.

Some of the children (those of a clever, if somewhat mischievous, inclination) in the crowd were able to break free of their respective retainers and chivy about the skirts of the performers like restless mayflies round a pond.

They continued on, that odd and motley congregation, same as any that never were, finally coming to rest in the small stretch of the town square whereupon a man appeared from one of the wagons toward the rear of the assembly. He was extraordinarily tall and impressively stately in his bearing.

"Your attention, good people. Your attention, please!"

So sudden and booming was this outburst that the murmuring, both amongst the circus folk and the townspeople, died instantly away. This bold, blond, tall and stately man leapt upon the nearest bench as if he would attack it; rearing up with theatrical poise he called again in his heavy, arresting voice, "Have you a mayor present, oh, my dear people? Have you?"

A man that Eisen had never seen before emerged from a nearby dry goods store, pocketed a pack of expensive-looking cigarettes and then addressed the circus master.

"My name is Caldwell, Elis Caldwell, and I speak for Ledru Monteblanc, the mayor of this fair city. What is it that you wish to speak with him about?"

"What do you think, my good man, about THE SHOW?" asked the ringmaster.

"You want to know if you can perform?" asked Caldwell.

"What else do performers do?"

"Here?"

The blond giant laughed. "Where else?"

"You want to perform in the city square?"

"You're not as slow as you look and only half as fast as ya talk, ain'tcha."

At this the circus folk burst into howls and cackles that reverberated all throughout the square whilst Caldwell, though quite obviously put off and mildly confused, made a show of his shaky stoicism. "You'll have to arrange a meeting with Mr. Monteblanc to get your papers in order."

"Papers?"

"Yes. Papers. Like what comes from tree pulp," said Caldwell.

Now it was the townsfolk's turn to laugh at the circus master. He laughed right along with them.

"Sharp lad! I can tell I'm going to like this town already. Well, when can I meet this mayor Monty of yourns?"

"I don't know. I'll ask him when I can spare the time, but I'm currently engaged in a rather pressing affair."

"Mustn't press pressing affairs, that'd be right terrible. Well, that's fine, we don't mind waiting here," said the ringmaster with an added wink.

"I'm afraid you can't do that."

"Why the devil not? Isn't it public property?"

"No, it's private property, leased to the town through Mr. Monteblanc, even the initial construction work was financed by him. So, in short, no, and no, you can't stay here."

"Have you any idea how long we've been traveling?"

"No, and that's none of my concern anyway."

"I bet it bloody well would be if you were near dead with the heat and full and sick with it!"

It looked, to Eisen at least, as if the blond giant would in his sudden and terrible anger, fly down and throttle the apathetic

Caldwell right there and then as one might strangle a cat that bites one time too often.

At that very moment the priest, Montferiat, intervened with that unconsciously condescending smile and his long, pale hands up thrust in gentle entreaty.

"Gentlemen please, please, calm yourselves. It's downright ungodly, it is! All this shouting and fussing!"

"I don't see how any of this concerns you, preacher," said Caldwell.

"Please, call me father, my son."

The ringmaster seemed intrigued, and it was only then that Eisen noticed the rosary he wore at his bullish throat. "You're the local priest?" said the ringmaster.

"Yes. I suppose it will do, if you want to call me that, my son. But to answer your question, my son," with every "my son" Caldwell flinched as if recoiling from some venomous serpent, "if what you say is true and Ledru has taken it upon himself to dictate even where weary travelers may and may not rest their heads... Well, I say down with all of it!"

"And you are welcome to say it as much as you like, but the point is that you didn't pay for it, ergo, you have no stake in the final say. This is a capitalist society last I checked. Mr. Monteblanc has done a lot more for this town than you ever have, preacher, and all you can do is spit venom. Well, that's just contemptible and I don't mind saying it. I expected better of a man of the cloth."

"Better? Fie on your bureaucracy and coin! This man merely desires shade from the sun, and here he'll find it, so here I say he should be able to stay! And it was my idea to plant trees here in the first place, not, I fancy, Mr. Monteblanc's!"

Eisen noticed a number of vaguely familiar faces behind the preacher, namely the man Kindle had described, Michael, Luce's son. At the utterance of their idol's indignant words, his congregation nodded gravely in staunch support, much to Caldwell's ill-concealed chagrin.

"As I said, you don't get the final say," Caldwell replied.

"You're right, my son, I don't, you don't, even he doesn't, it is God Almighty to which we turn in the end! Would our Lord turn away weary strangers if they desired his harbourage?"

"I don't know, nor do I care. Rules are rules. I don't make them, I just follow them."

"Whose rules, Caldwell? Yours? Monteblanc's? Mine? NO! And again, no I say! The Lord, our God, Divine Lawgiver; it is He who writes His will upon this world, upon the skins of us ticklish humans, yet you would deny them, these bone-worn travelers, this paltry gift so painlessly spared?"

The preacher had worked himself up into throes of such fiery vexation that he threw his hands up into the air and gesticulated wildly as he spoke, his eyes fairly bulging and the muscles in his neck taut, even against his plush, puffy skin, standing out like monks in a flophouse.

Caldwell slowly produced one of his expensive-looking cigarettes and methodically and most artfully lit it, much in the French style, though he had not the clothing for it. Placing the white and smoldering cylinder between his muddy-colored lips, Ledru's avatar spoke icily and with great precision.

"If I can, if even I can deny such a gift to these people, our Lord must be a terribly incompetent fellow," said Caldwell.

Both the preacher and the ringmaster recoiled as if burned at this cold and callous blasphemy.

Without waiting for a reply Caldwell sauntered away, puffing haughty circles of smoke above his slick and subtly balding crown. There was smugness in his languid movements, though this was not quite the right word, for he didn't seem invested enough in anything, even his arrogance, for it to germinate properly. The circus folk watched him go with contempt and derision, some even shouting at him or proffering rude gestures in his direction. Yet he remained almost completely unemotional throughout the entire maelstrom of outrage and scorn. His cold, distant face turned back once and something like irritation flashed in his hard black eyes, and then was gone with the rest of him.

Caldwell turned a corner about the dry goods store from whence he had come, still languidly set at his smoke and the circles thereof, and vanished from view.

The preacher watched him go, grimacing and grinding his teeth, whilst the ringmaster, red-faced and tight-fisted, howled, "Bastard!" with such profoundly cartoonish gusto that Eisen couldn't help but chuckle. Thankfully, no one but Kindle noticed this covert display of humor.

Eisen, his interest piqued, sidled up beside the preacher as he walked back to his congregation who eagerly awaited his return.

"Ah! Mr. Torquiam. How can I help you?"

"Who was that man?"

"Caldwell?"

"Yes."

"Elis Caldwell, the local printer, he runs the press almost as much as he runs his lying, albeit silvered, tongue. He's also a lawyer; represents Ledru and Statletter whenever they get into land disputes. In other words, whenever they want to steal somebody's land they give Mr. Caldwell a call and it's done, and him's the one what does it."

"You sound bitter."

"Mortal failings, perhaps?"

"Perhaps."

They shared hopeful smiles and parted ways, with Eisen giving the puffy-faced preacher one final wave goodbye which was amply returned in response and thinking that the puffy-faced man wasn't so bad as he had thought.

Behind him as he walked, the crowd, both old and new to the town, murmured and stirred, a strange energy building therein like power in a Tesla coil.

There was a tug at his sleeve at which point he turned to behold a very agitated Kindle motioning in a panic with her large, owlish eyes. He followed her gaze into the circus assemblage and perceived a man about his own height staring back at him from behind a most singular mask. The man wore a long cloak of ragged quality above drab jester's clothing.

His mask was bone white save at the eye holes, which were rimmed with black, and the mouth, which was deep blue and curling about in a monstrous and horrible smile. The grotesque artifact was secured to the man's head by way of a length of shimmering silver silk. His hair was all in disarray and stuck up in wild shocks about his skull. His hands were veiled in black gloves, and on his feet he wore exquisite riding boots.

It was the gaze of this most extraordinary man that struck Eisen above all this mysterious being's characteristics. It was a gaze that seemed to have been ripped from the very heart of a grand and searing volcano, burning with every flickering in his glance.

Upon noticing that he had been observed by his quarry, the masked man gazed fixedly awhile longer and then turned his regard slowly from Eisen as if to say, "I know you've seen me staring at you – but what can you do about it? What will you do?"

Slowly the coffin maker returned his attention to Kindle, who still clung to his sleeve like a lost child in a foreign market place. She was paralyzed with fear, down to her very quintessence full of it. As stiff and still as the boiling, acrid air, as the dead grass at her feet, as the stucco houses peeling with the malice of the sun; their chipping paint like the skin of some bloodless aberration.

"What is it, Kindle? Goodness, you're shaking!"

"That man, he... come on, I want to leave, let's leave. I don't like it here."

"What is it? What is it about that man?"

"It's nothing. I just, I can't explain myself!"

"He's only a jester."

"I can't abide jesters!"

Unable to comprehend such sudden profundity in his wild companion, the hapless coffin maker could do naught but acquiesce. Gently, he took the shaking woman by her sinewy arms and led her from the square and the crowds, the ringmaster and the man with the smiling mask.

GRAVE.

Eisen chanced a single look back for the masked jester; he was gone, vanished like a whisper in the night. Liken more to a phantom than any mortal man.

Perhaps, thought Eisen, he was something more than a mere jester after all.

Chapter Eleven

Shadows of the Past

He steered her into Arrgilius' inn, where the rumor-herding barkeep greeted them with two frothing pints of mead. There the coffin maker set himself down at a rickety table (though it should be remarked that all of the tables were rickety and seemed as if they would collapse at any minute) in the middle of the room and waited for her to do the same.

At length she did so but seemed very displeased and panic stricken with it all. The place was fairly packed and a heavy, gleeful din surrounded the two friends as they adjusted themselves in their puckish chairs.

In the far corner, a little man was playing at a poorly tuned fiddle. His rosined bow shrieked as if torn slowly across the strings much to the dissatisfaction of the merry drinkers ringed round him. In the opposite corner, farthest from the door, there sat three middle-aged men in dark suits; they said not a word to anyone and drank their brews with dire expressions.

Constantly did the little waif kept shooting wild and worrisome glances all about the room, as if the jester would, at any given moment, leap suddenly at them from the shadows, maul her and drink her blood or some other such monstrosity.

So taut and paranoid was she, that after several rather grave moments of intently watching her, much to Eisen's chagrin, he was beginning to cast his eyes warily about as well; looking to every corner for the faintest flicker of movement, for the shine of a blade or the hiss of malicious breath. Yet all he heard was the pounding of his own heart, the piercing rhapsodies of the fumbling fiddler and Arrgilius' footfalls behind him.

He slapped the table with the flat of his hand, an unusual gesture for a man of such distinct reservation.

Kindle fairly imploded, inhaling sharply as the table shook before her under Eisen's forceful blow.

"Damn it, Kindle, you're making me paranoid! That was more than simply a mere dislike of jesters. Now what was all that about? You are well and right to desire privacy and keep it for its own sake, but if you are going to be staying with me for any length of time, I'd prefer if you could trust me a bit more with your past, and obviously something in it is causing this. Did you know that man? The one with the mask?"

"No. Or... I mean, if I did, I'm not sure, I couldn't say, it could really be anyone, couldn't it? With a mask, it could be anybody at all. Or maybe nobody. I must be hallucinating. Maybe I was confused? That must be it."

"No. You're quite clearly not confused or hallucinating. Unless I am as well?"

She shook her head and inhaled the brew-laden air and the wet stone, aromatic wood, dirty cloth and stale sweat.

"The only thing you are confused about, Kindle, is your own confusion."

Arrgilius watched with great curiosity and failed concealment from the bar where he busily shined the wood and cleaned the mugs with mechanical precision.

"That man is watching us, Eisen!"

"Who? Oh, Arrgilius, yeah, he watches everyone. It is his place after all, but he's all right, just a bit too nosy for this town's taste. Don't let him concern you. Now, will you tell me what's bothering you? I can't very well help fix something if I don't know what's broken, can I?"

What came next was so abrupt and horrible that Eisen could scarce believe what he was hearing. He recalled her words and wondered similarly if he himself were now prey to her internal illusions most foul.

"My parents were... murdered... by a man with a... mask, a mask just like that, like the jester's... he had a steak knife... they had invited him to dinner, then he just started slashing at them, over and over and over... there was blood everywhere... so much blood, you wouldn't think they'd have so much in them... especially my mother, she was ever so pale and thin... but there was so much in her and it just kept spilling out like a broken fountain. The man with the knife was laughing all the while and he kept looking back at me and saying, 'Lucky girl, lucky girl!' And when he was finished with them he took me by the throat and bent me over the table right in my mother's blood and then he... he ripped off my skirt and he..."

"That's enough, Kindle!"

She was near tears upon the telling of her tale, but Eisen's sudden, impassioned outburst sent her over the edge; she broke down there in greatest agitation and began, to everyone's mortification, to cry as if she had been told she was about to die.

"That's enough, Kindle."

"Get a hold of yourself, woman," someone cried from the corner.

Other voices soon joined the cacophony, though half the room didn't seem to notice the poor girl or just pretended not to, or simply didn't care.

Eisen turned in his chair and spoke to the first and most verbose heckler. "Silence your tongue before I cut it free of your filthy mouth."

The heckler shut up and turned round quite promptly to the jeers of his fellow toughs.

Quickly the girl, the threat, everything was forgotten, and the bodies therein reverted to the ebb and flow to which they had there become so accustomed.

Eisen repeated his words once more, softly this time and with a subtle tone of self-denigration, as if he were speaking to his own raging emotions as well as to hers. "That's enough, Kindle. Let's go, come on, let us go. We'll take a walk. It's a beautiful day, would you like that? Would you like to take a walk?"

She said nothing, only nodded her head very rapidly, shaking the tears from her wide, deep eyes; such depths as had never been exposed before, and, perhaps, never again.

Calmly, but sternly, Eisen told her to wait for him outside on the porch and not to stray, that he had to speak with Arrgilius and then would return to her and together leave.

She acquiesced, left hurriedly and sat utterly motionless upon an overturned barrel near the far left side of the porch behind a stack of crates that smelled faintly of ale. Sitting all a huddle, her eyes dreadfully blank, downcast to the dusty wooden planks in something like shame, as if the wild girl thought the grotesque clockwork of events that had wrought her family's demise had somehow been set in motion by her very hand.

As for Eisen, he stood with his usual luxe poise, elbows upon the shining mahogany counter and a dire look in his eyes that would have been as a magnet to men, but whether for their repulsion or attraction or both, none could say.

Arrgilius leaned in close to better hear the younger man's words, for he spoke in a tone that was barely above a whisper.

"What?"

"I said does the preacher's son stop in much? On the sly, perhaps?"

"Look, now, well you know I like you, and it ain't nothing personal, you know, it's just that I can't talk bout that... wouldn't be, ya know, wouldn't be– "

"Proper?"

He nodded his furry, weathered head vigorously, much like an animate bush gone wild; the regretful firmness of the gesture disclosing all that Eisen needed to know.

"Possibly you are right, Arrgilius, but this matter could well be the difference between life and death."

"For who?"

"Can't talk bout that, wouldn't be proper. You know how it goes."

"But this isn't fair now; you can't tell me something like that and then not elaborate on it!"

"Apparently I can. Funny how things work, isn't it?"

"Cruel! Downright malicious! You're offering me a trade, aren't you. Blackmailing me is more like it!"

"You're the only person in this town as curious as me. It seemed fitting."

"Blast you for breathing!"

"Are you going to tell me?"

"Yes, damn your eyes. Damn mine as well. If the lad gets wind of this, he'll never forgive me! And if his father hears it, he'll never forgive the lad! Oh, damn my eyes!"

"Just as I thought. But really you should be damning your tongue."

"How is it that a coffin maker can be so damned insidious?"

Eisen smiled like the hound before the hunt and leaned in slightly closer as a group of Ledru's teamsters passed by with inquisitive looks from above their bristling mustaches.

"Insidious? My, oh my, Arrgilius, how you have a talent for embellishment."

"Hmph."

"Now, if you see young Mr. Montferiat, would you tell him that I am desirous to speak to his father?"

"Aye, I will, if'n ya be telling me bout this hoopla."

Eisen shot him a pleading and obviously overacted look, but the barkeep merely folded his beefy arms sternly across his breast and squinted disapprovingly.

"Tut, tut, but then, a deal is a deal, after all. You know Daniels?"

"James Daniels?"

Eisen nodded.

"Course I do. What of him?"

"It's his life that's in danger. You must have heard what happened to his friend."

"You're not tellin me that he's planning on going after him?"

Eisen nodded again and turned to look behind him in his subtle manner; there was no one close, a few newcomers but no one within earshot.

"I'm trying to stop him, that's why I need to speak to the preacher."

"Ah, Daniels used to be part of his congregation, was a man of tremendous faith, if'n I recall right, and I always do, save when I don't. Yeah, that might work, even with their recent fallout."

"Now listen, Arrgilius, this is very important. As you well understand, you can be sure, as much as I, that a man like Daniels will drag his fair share of others down with him. He's planning on rounding up a posse of his friends, others who have been wronged by the gang. A lot of people could die and this town could erupt into a bloodbath, so when I say that this is something you should keep to yourself for the moment– "

"I understand. I'm not the flapjaw they make me out ta be, laddie. Naught tat all, you'll see."

"I will indeed. Take care, Arrgilius, and... thanks for all your help."

"Don't thank me yet."

Eisen released a wry, subdued laugh and then departed from the inn with the weathered barkeep watching him all the while.

☼

Kindle was just where he had told her to wait, her eyes still low and her body hunched as if she were afflicted with some grotesque ailment. Her face was wan and yellow, and her lips twitched strangely as if she were working up the courage to say something dark and terrible.

"Kindle?"

"Oh!"

She leapt from her seat as if she had been bitten on the heel, a look of impressive shock registering on her slender, elfin face. Clearly she had been so engaged and distracted within the realm of her own thoughts that she had no concern for the realm without.

"You look unwell, shall we leave?"

"No, I'm feeling... much... better."

"Um, well, all right. I'm going to the church. I need to find the preacher."

"Who?"

"The puffy man."

"Oh. Can I come?"

"Yes. Actually, I've only been there once, and this town is a bit bigger once a body is in it than it looks from without, so I was wondering if you would show me the way. You're good at that kind of thing, right?"

She nodded but without her usual exuberance; obviously the day's events still bore down upon her, consuming her near entirely.

They started off at an easy pace down the main road toward the church. The roads were full of workers, either on break or leaving for the day, coming away from the oil and the sweat of the massive derrick set far off in the eastern fields at the opposite side of town. Henry Collins was amongst them and gave a hearty wave as he approached his friend.

"Well, it's been sometime, Mr. Torquiam!"

"Indeed it has. Well met, Mr. Collins."

Quite unexpectedly another man emerged forcefully through the throng of workers, none other than James Daniels himself.

"That's enough chatter, Collins!"

"But it's the lunch break!"

"I don't give a good god damn, if ya'll want to continue to work for us, then ya better shut that oversized mouth a yours."

Eisen stepped in between the two men who stood glaring fiercely at each other and spoke in the gentlest of tones.

"There's no need for that, Daniels."

"I don't believe I was addressing you, outsider."

"I never said you were, but I am certainly addressing you."

"You better watch it around here from now on."

"Why? Because I refused to help you commit a murder?"

Collins grinned with obvious spite while Daniels' men murmured amongst themselves in a mixture of equal parts outraged surprise and utter bewilderment. It was apparent that few of them had ever seen a man dare talk back to their fiery leader in such an offhanded fashion.

"I told ya ta watch it once, I ain't gonna do it again."

A look of faint triumph shined ever so subtly on the coffin maker's pale, angular face.

"It appears you just did."

Daniels took two steps forward, dust rising heavily with each footfall like tiny hurricanes, now no more than a boot's length away from the calm-eyed craftsman. Eisen tilted his head upwards challengingly, a gesture Daniels mistook for arrogance. A gesture that, having been thus interpreted, wholly solidified Daniels' vengeful rage.

Stepping away, Daniels wordlessly drew back his left arm and struck Eisen full across the face, as if challenging him to a duel. Before Eisen could properly react, Kindle charged head-on into Daniels, tackling him painfully to the ground, whereupon she began hammering her knobbly fist into his face. Two blows into the fight and already she had drawn blood, spattering her shirt in misty, sanguine geysers.

Daniels was, at first, so shocked and stupefied by the whole bizarre twist of events that he could scarcely comprehend his situation, much less react to it. When finally he came to his senses, the feral girl had nearly beaten them all back out. He threw up his arms as she continued to punch savagely into his face; the workers all unsure what to do, some were laughing while others looked on with grave, disconcerted faces.

With considerable effort and much up-thrust dust, Daniels managed to grapple her hands away from his head and bind them in his superior grip, upon which point Kindle only howled and bit fiercely into his throat. Daniels screamed and threw her from his wounded and withering body.

Eisen leapt forward and pulled her away before she could sink her canines into Daniels' veins again. He was surprised at how uncannily strong she was, for she looked to all to be the picture of utter frailty, yet he could barely detain the waif. Holding her at the waist, it took all of Eisen's formidable strength to stay her fury; every tendon in her lithe, thrashing body seemed to stand out in stark relief amidst the radiance of the relentless sun.

At this point in the skirmish a seething crowd of onlookers had gathered on either side of the street, pointing, shouting, some even chuckling and jesting, all of them gawking wide eyed at the young woman's animal vehemence and the wild spectacle it had caused.

"Help him to the doctor, Collins. Hurry, you men, help, Mr. Collins."

One of the workers turned to Eisen with unconcealed indignation and spoke from behind an impressive beard.

"Now who the hell ya think yar to be givin out orders?"

"Your friend is bleeding quite badly. He'll only get worse without a doctor's attention, unless you would like to assist him yourself."

"It should be that beast there that is doing the assisting! She should be burned with iron, the devil!"

"Enough. Now, do as I said."

The coffin maker said the words quite calmly, icily even, yet loud enough so that all present before him could hear. So impressive was his tone that even the bearded man almost instantly bent to Daniels' much-needed aid.

"Come now, Kindle. We should leave, come."

She was breathing heavily but she seemed to have regained most of her composure. Yet before she allowed Eisen to lead her off, she spit on her downed and bloodied foe with such all-consuming hatred that the entire crowd fell utterly silent. It was as if some malign apparition had stolen their tongues for some wicked game, twisted the things and put them back perverted and grotesque.

As he walked away with the young woman at his side, Eisen swore he heard someone mutter the word "demon" behind him. He paused and heard it twice more; there was much babbling and chatter of possession and dark magic, curses and every sort of fanciful absurdity imaginable.

He steeled his nerves and walked on, the blood afire in the throbbing rivers of his veins. They followed the drab and dusty street a little way until they came upon the dry goods store from which the apathetic Mr. Caldwell had so infamously emerged earlier that day.

Eisen, so consumed with the immediate and violent events outside of the inn, completely forgot his companion's troubles and turned at the corner of the store and followed the little stone pathway that led into the town square.

As soon as Kindle, who had been gazing fixedly ahead, silent all the while, saw the colorful ribbons of the circus, she screamed and ran back the way they had come. Away from the disheveled jester with the freakish mask.

Eisen took off after her, cursing under his breath. His boots echoed dully off the wind-worn stones beneath him, dying away amidst the dirge of a newborn gale. A storm was building off in the distance, and such winds were its wild, searing harbingers; voiceless servants to a merciless Lord sallying forth on an endless quest.

He exited the narrow alley, crossed the street and entered another alley, this one longer and dimmer than the other, that lay directly adjacent to Arrgilius' inn. Old crates and broken bottles adorned that tight, stony pass; a cat jumped and scurried away at his approaching footsteps.

Shuddering, he found her hiding behind a stack of ancient crates, one of which she had draped over her trembling knees like a blanket. Cowering with her head in her hands, she refused to speak, refused even to look at him.

The coffin maker slowly lowered himself to the filthy ground and sat staring at her until her tears had subsided, at which point she embraced him with a deep exhale. Once more she was quaking all over, as if in the grip of some terrible palsy.

With his usual reserve the coffin maker methodically wrapped his arms round her. He pressed her warm beating heart to his own until her tremors had passed, and then he released himself from her grip, whispering, "You're safe, you're safe now. Come, let us be away. Let me take you."

She did, though with a sombre reluctance that seized from Eisen's heart all its vigor and strength and dashed it, as one might an egg upon a cinder block, wholly and thunderously. It took every ounce of his considerable will to keep from crying at that moment as he gazed at that unfortunate form huddled so despairingly and pathetically against the whirling dust and grime. Extending his hand she took it, and he helped the feral girl to stand, then they turned their backs to the wind and left.

Realizing that he couldn't possibly go anywhere near the city square, Eisen decided that there was nothing for it save to go the long and only way round to the cathedral. This meant winding up into the mining hills near both Ledru's manor and the ramshackle hovels which housed the cats that Statletter had so warmly remarked upon.

At that moment Eisen was gripped by a sudden and peculiar thought, and he wondered just how there came to be so many felines in such a place. For some reason this gave him a jolt of exhilarating joy; he smiled. Perhaps it was because of their endurance, for if a cat could exhibit such resilience in realms as inhospitable and cruel as these, certainly man could as well. But it was not enough merely to flourish; the vine flourishes, but it chokes out everything round it in its struggle for existence.

Eisen murmured to himself as he looked out at the passing hovels and the shocks of black and gray fur that skirted round them, mewing and hissing.

"People are going to think you madder than they already do if you keep on mumbling to yourself like that, Mr. Torquiam."

The intrusive new voice was so unexpected and the previous mood one of such immense oppression and contemplation that both Kindle and the coffin maker fairly jumped out of their skins. Eisen was the first to perceive the speaker, tall and thin, sitting on a dilapidated porch, surrounded by cats. They all sat perfectly still about him like a regimented vanguard, their ears and tails the only movement in their sinuous forms.

"Hello, Mr. Statletter. You seem to have made some new friends."

The blind man smiled faintly and spoke without turning his attention from the feline in his lap, purring like a broken motor.

"You're not the only one; aren't you going to introduce me?"

"No, I'm not actually, she's not feeling very well and– "

Rather imprudently Kindle nearly shoved past her boon and marched solemnly up to the porch and with a bow said, "My name is Kindle Fontaine, it's a pleasure to meet you."

"Fontaine?"

"Yes."

Eisen himself was about to pose the exact same question, for this was the first time she had spoken of her family title.

"That's quite impossible, my dear."

She was silent. Grave and silent.

"The Fontaines are all dead; butchered, I hear, in their own house no less, terrible business. Yes, I know the records for these lands fairly well, they don't go that far back, but Fontaine... well, they used to be one of the biggest cattle families around. Why, in their prime they could have bought and sold even Mr. Monteblanc. But this is really quite extraordinarily! Are you telling me that you, yourself, are the only surviving member of so distinguished and prominent a family?"

She nodded.

With another faint smile Statletter removed his thick-lense glasses and cast his head about all the better to hear, turning from one ear to the other.

Gasping, Kindle nearly stepped back.

"Oh, don't be frightened, my dear, I'm not nearly as bad as I look. Though, I fancy I can never say the same for another!" He burst into a volley of subdued laughter then, even going so far as to slap his knee, only this knee happened to have four legs and a tail.

The cat shrieked and hissed under the unintentional blow and then leapt from his lap and slunk angrily away like a sullen child deprived of its sweets.

"Oh, dear, I must be more careful. At any rate I presume, my dear, that you were nodding before, but given my situation, you'll have to put that gesture into words, so I'll say again; Are you truly a Fontaine?"

"Yes."

"Marvelous! I can scarcely explain my delight."

Eisen, with furrowed brows and disconcerted steps, approached with a question tingling his tongue.

"Why is that, Statletter?"

"Why? Why!"

"Yes, why? Certainly that's not too hard to explain, is it?"

"Oh, no. Forgive an old man his excitement, will you."

"Certainly, if you'll get on with it."

"Well, I forget that most others are not so informed as I in such matters, so again, forgive me my folly. It's only that the Fontaine claim would completely change the... ah, but I'm getting ahead of myself. You, my dear, wouldn't know, would you? No, no, I fancy you would not, your movements give you away; lose one sense and the others compensate. But now, to the point: The Fontaine estate, though rumor and records suggest they knew nothing of it, sat atop the largest oil reserve in this whole forsaken country! It was a veritable gold mine! The claims that there was oil there started as nothing more than idle talk; you know what I mean, an old hunter says one thing here, a traveling busker says another, all corroborate each other, but all are suspect. No one believes it very much, but they try their hardest to pretend so as to keep their excitement intact. Well, recently Ledru and I have been doing our own studies, and to cut a long story short, have confirmed to our own satisfaction that all the stories are absolutely true. All of them."

"You greedy fop. Is that all you can think of, oil and the gold it will bring! She's lost her family; it should belong to her, not to you or anyone else."

Eisen had moved even closer than before and now stood upon the bottom step in front of Kindle in extreme agitation, his shoulders set wide and his jaw squared, as if shielding her from the blind man.

"Calm yourself, please sir, it's most undignified! You misunderstand me, whether through designs of your own or sheer incompetence I cannot say, but I'll not push my chips on you, Mr. Torquiam. You are a subtle serpent if ever I heard one! Nearly, did I say seen! But I'm rambling, you asked for answers; yes, it is the gold that our oil can bring which I am interested in, but, no, not because I'd like it for me. This town is dying, you can see its death throes all around you, that derrick is drying up fast and Ledru is getting anxious– heck, I'm getting anxious about it. Once the oil stops flowing, this town stops flourishing. Once it falls, it falls forever. It'll end up like every other prospecting town that's ever been tried, an empty shell, full of ghosts and broken dreams, forgotten hopes and fractured lives."

"I apologize, I didn't think it through."

"Clearly, Mr. Torquiam, but all this talk of forgiveness and apology is becoming unbearable; it's turning into one of Luce's sermons. Come, let's forget the whole thing and be done with it. On another point, Mr. Monteblanc would like to speak to you."

"What about?"

"One of the servants has passed on, he was very old and, well, very dear to Mr. Monteblanc. Now I'm not one for ritual and tradition myself, but Ledru, well, he'd give almost anything to make sure Old Turpin got a burial to put the ancients to shame."

"I understand, yet I am currently preoccupied, tell him I shall be here tomorrow unless that is unacceptable?"

"No, it's fine, perfectly fine, I'll be waiting right here. You meet me here and I'll have my carriage ready with some chilled Bordeaux. What say you?"

"All right."

Without saying goodbye, Eisen departed.

Kindle hung back a moment to bow, very elegantly and deferentially, to the blind man and then, remembering his condition, rose, rather red in the face at her folly.

"Um, take care."

"You as well, Miss Fontaine."

She left hurriedly, stumbling and nearly falling more than once. When she finally caught up with Eisen, her mood seemed to have changed, though he couldn't tell if that change was for the better or for the worse.

The broken houses that dotted the landscape seemed too dilapidated for any sane human being to try and occupy, and yet several dusty and disheveled people had gathered near their windows, moving aside shattered shutters and ratty blinds to better view the duo.

To Eisen, they looked much like Kindle had when he had first awoken to her mad dancing, only there was missing, in their eyes, that spark of wonder and bountiful energy. They looked as dead souls and moved likewise, with a listless shuffling gait, joints stiff with the weight of their lives; the hovel of their circumstance more than all the ratty timber above their skulls.

"Why are they staring at us like that?"

"It could be for any number of reasons, but probably because they think we're going up to Ledru's mansion. People such as these disgust me almost as much as pompous hoarders like him. Too weak to rebel from their situation, from their wage slavery, only strong enough to hate. It is the lowest kind of strength."

"Let us leave, I don't like the way they're looking at us."

Eisen nodded and they cut out of the narrow row of houses and tramped up a stony, barren hill, dotted here and there with animal skulls that seemed almost to be intelligently arranged in a large circle in the center of which was but a single black feather. As Eisen gazed on it he was struck by the blood that had been splattered about on the ground, yet none of it touching the feather. Some unholy ritual. Some sinful sacrifice. And that feather motionless in the windless world, a dark effigy of violence and death and all that followed with it.

Kindle hadn't seen the strange circle nor the macabre token within. Eisen didn't see any reason to disturb her further; he said nothing and went on behind her. All the while he walked, from that circle of bone to the church, so far flung from the city's hissing heart, never did that feather nor those drops of blood leave his mind and all that such ominous omens implied.

Suddenly he was overtaken with great anxiety, and visions of that dark night of death came to sunder his being on silent wings.

He stopped in the middle of the street, clutching strangely at his kettle drum heart; there was a sound in the distance, quickly closing.

"Eisen!"

Abruptly he was torn from his reverie as Kindle lunged forth and with all her might hauled him straight off his feet backward into a puddle of mud as an enormous horse came thundering down upon where the coffin maker had been standing.

"You should be more careful, laddie."

Eisen recognized that voice, recognized it at once, but could not place it, yet it was unmistakably familiar to him. He looked up and beheld the circus jester with the grotesque mask whom he had previously encountered in the city plaza; that peculiar facade ever smiling its disturbing smile.

"Me or you?"

"Oh! Cagey! I like that! Lots of fun for a wretched one, what has no time for convention; and so, with the very greatest attention I proudly shun its very mention!"

"Riddles?"

"Oh yes! For the giving or the taking, or even, if milord so verily wishes it, the merry making!"

Kindle shrieked wrathfully, "You're mad! You're mad!"

"Methinks the lady muddles in malaise. But I tarry not and thus hasten far! Know full well whom your masters are!"

Laughing manically, the mad jester touched up his horse and rode away toward the city square, riding with but one hand and slapping his knee with the other in his bountiful, disturbingly childish mirth.

Eisen rose first and held out his hand, but Kindle didn't reply. She seemed under a powerful spell, some cruel hypnosis; staring with mortal dread after the masked man, she moved not a single muscle and breathed hardly at all. It was as if the whole of her consciousness had been shut down, replaced with a stifling terror that reverberated to the marrow, down to the bone.

"Kindle, come. Let us go. He's gone, see, you're fine. Let us go. Come now, come on. Kindle."

She did not respond. Gently he bent down and touched her shoulder, then he rocked her lightly at which point she finally turned and nodded vacantly, as if under the sway of some potent tranquilizer. She rose and followed the coffin maker to the church like one in a fog, moving like a sleepwalker.

The massive doors to the cathedral were closed but not locked. Without knocking, Eisen let himself in whilst Kindle continued to follow him amidst the daze of her catatonic stupor.

He wanted to shake her, to scream for her to awake from her fear, to free her from the terror, but, knowing full well the futility of such efforts, he did nothing.

Chapter Twelve

Michael

The church was empty, save for a few visitors who came, one could only assume, quite regularly, to pray in the midst of their collective solitude. One old man nodded reverently toward them and then turned away without waiting for them to reciprocate his cordiality. He was speaking very rapidly under his breath but had to stop, coughing violently, and with every expulsion from his throat his whole body shook and trembled.

Eisen was on the verge of walking over to ask if the old man needed assistance when the very man he had been seeking appeared with great solemnity.

"You have not seen a doctor as I advised?"

The old man turned toward the preacher and with a strange mixture of expressions, he looked toward Luce willfully, not blinking once. The elder man leaned slightly forward with his hands clutching unto both his own pew and the back of the one before him. It seemed as if he were exerting all of his energy to merely pull himself forward.

"What you and I will is as nothing compared with His, the will of Our Father, and if'n He wills that I should feed the ground in this selfsame hour, then so it is written. Ain't no doctor under the sun what can change that. No, you shouldn't look at me like that, I'm well prepared; I've lived a good life, I'm ready now." The preacher, surprising Eisen profoundly, looked extremely concerned with this peculiar outpouring; he began rubbing his long, spindly hands together in great agitation and then let them fall limply, shaking his head as if the circumstance was too grave to be considered.

At length he finally spoke and when he did, it was with a heavy heart and a sombre, hushed tone.

"Has my son been speaking to you again?"

"Why, yes. Not but two days ago, a day after we last spoke. But what is it, Father? Surely ya don't disagree wit the boy?"

"I do not; I merely disagree that he can interpret the will of Our Lord. Perhaps it is His will that you visit the doctor and get this illness taken care of? Who can say? I, for one, cannot."

The old man raised his head, pushing himself farther upward on the pews and opened his mouth to speak, but was at that moment struck with yet another coughing spell, this more dire than the one preceding it. He heaved suddenly and spat blood and bile, the foul debris speckling the preacher's pristine suit; a soiled canvas with wide eyes.

"Robert! Someone help! Robert, steady man!"

Eisen rushed up then as the old man collapsed in his pew and slumped to the floor barely conscious, wheezing and drooling blood. The coffin maker bent down and rolled the old man over. The elder's eyes were glazed and steady, strange orbs looking out into a strange world, one that had ceased to carry the accumulated weight of his spirit, marrow and bone; Indian giver; treacherously indifferent.

Eisen reached for the back of the man's head to shift him to a better position, but the old man stopped him, grabbing his wrist and shaking his head feebly.

"Let me be... I'm ready, I'm ready..."

It was too late for the doctor, too late for anything, and very shortly the old man coughed heavily once more and lay still. Eisen rose slowly from the corpse; pale, silent and horribly affected.

He turned to the priest who made the sign of the cross over the dead man, bent down and closed his eyes.

"Rest easy, my friend. Your troubles are over."

"So are all his pleasures."

"He knew well what you still ignore and disregard!"

"And what is that?"

The preacher rose up to his full height with flashing eyes and a certain measure of subdued severity. He looked poised to strike, but with great effort he stayed his tightly clenched hands.

"That these earthly pleasures are but the devil's lure! He, the great fisherman and you, the willing minnow, willing to cast yourselves unto his frying pan with even something like gusto; with mirth!"

"Luce Montferiat, you're a comedian."

They locked eyes, both men standing quite still as if mutually immobilized by their antagonism.

The preacher stormed away without another word. Shortly thereafter two men, who looked to be monks, appeared and carted the body away with merry expressions; for all intents and purposes, one observing would think nothing could have made the carriers more happy than for all the old men in the town to begin dropping like flies.

All the while these events had been occurring, Kindle stood off in the corner not paying attention at all, a little glass-girl cast upon a stone sepulcher. She hadn't heard the old man hit the floor, for her the only sound was the jeering voice of the jester and his insidious laughter; mocking, everything and everyone. There was no longer even the concept of sound, there was only the laughter of the fool and the horror it instilled in her marrow, her blood and her soul. Trembling ceaselessly, she lowered herself almost unconsciously into the nearest pew and slumped her upper body over her knees like one about to vomit. Her humors blacker than the darkest night.

Footsteps and a firm white hand upon her shoulder.

The stoic, unblinking face of Michael Montferiat gazed down at her with something like pity imprinted and reflecting there in those mysterious depths.

She began to pull away, but upon recognizing the young adept's face, she smiled and reached up and touched his hand gingerly.

"Are you lost?"

"What?"

"Your soul, does it feel... lost?"

"I know nothing of souls."

He nodded.

"Come with me, come away from this tragedy."

"What happened?"

"You didn't see?"

She shook her head.

The young man straightened up with a look of furthered apprehension and then took her by the arm, exuding a firm, yet gentle resolve. At first the young woman nearly pulled away but then allowed herself to be led with something like curiosity.

Eisen hadn't noticed any of this until the pair were nearly out of the room, at which point the young coffin maker quickly trotted over and blocked their path.

"You are the preacher's son?"

"Yes."

"Where are you going with her?"

Eisen turned to her.

"Kindle, where are you going with him?"

"I don't know."

Eisen returned his gaze to the other young man, expectant, severe.

"She is ill, you have been neglectful and unobservant, otherwise you would have noticed this yourself."

"I have noticed. I can handle it."

"Handle it?"

"Yes. But I appreciate the incentive."

"What incentive?"

"Yours."

"Mine?"

"Yes. Have I offended you, Michael?"

"Frankly yes, but it isn't your fault."

He sighed and guided Kindle toward her friend with a sad expression.

"I understand."

"What?"

"The old man, he was a friend of yours, yes? That would rattle anyone."

The young acolyte nodded vacantly and raised his head to look into the coffin maker's eyes. Blue into green, green into blue.

"You have lost someone as well."

Eisen flinched, finding it strange that the acolyte's words were not formed in the fashion of a question so much as they were a simple statement of fact.

"Yes. I have lost someone, someone very dear."

"Wages of sin, my father says, so complacent is he in his belief that if the world were to burn before us all, he'd raise his hands to the skies and dance with jubilation, praising God for sending us to heaven so much the faster."

The young priest laughed to himself, a cold, humorless, spiteful gesture.

"I see you have a weight upon you, would you like us to go?"

"No, please, forgive my deplorable manners. I'm not really so horrid once you get to know me."

He held out his hand to the coffin maker and smiled thinly. It was a motion that didn't seem to fit him, an awkward and forced pleasantry.

Eisen took the other man's thinner, weaker hand and shook firmly and mannerly; it was only then that he realized the ring, pure gold and elaborately inscribed, reading 'Let the hearts of the wicked tremble at the sight of my brand, the judgment of Heaven.'"

"A gift from my mother, she always thought I'd grow up to be the hero of the town, God willing. That's what she used to say, anyhow. But I have no doubt that you grow weary of my verbosity."

"Not at all, you are an interesting man."

"Man. I haven't quite got used to it. But please, won't you let me get you something, both of you, if not for yourselves, then for me, some company would do my nerves good."

Eisen looked to Kindle; she nodded vacantly, almost dismissively.

"Certainly. Lead the way."

The young acolyte smiled his hollow smile once more and then turned back toward the doors before which the small party stood. He produced a little set of keys, unlocked the doors and disappeared off down a corridor with high ceilings and low lighting; the smell of moist stone, mold and incense wafted throughout.

Eisen followed the young man at a polite distance with Kindle slinking furtively behind him like a frightened weasel seeking shelter from a storm.

"It's not that far to my father's study. We can go there, he rarely uses it anymore."

Strange and fearsome effigies leered out at them from the shadows, cold eyes, unmoving hands, frozen cloth. Gargoyles and stranger beasts; finally the stone busts of men, solemn and severe.

"These are the statues of all the previous priests who have presided over this church since it was built 357 years ago. It always seems strange to me that with our lives seeming to take so long, so painfully long, that there could ever be this many statues, so many souls lost to the sands of time, never to be reclaimed."

"That's not what I was expecting to hear from a man of the cloth."

The preacher's son stopped dead in his tracks and swung his head out above his shoulder with a patient waiting in his gaze.

"And what were you expecting, Mr. Torquiam?"

"You know, you're one of the first people to pronounce my name right in a very long time."

"Should I feel honored?"

Eisen at this point had reached the preacher's son, standing beside him with a slender smile and a silent breath; he shook his head ambiguously and spoke.

"I don't know? Should you?"

"I don't know. Should I?"

They exchanged smiles and then set off at an equal pace, walking amiably side by side like old friends newly united.

"It's right up these steps."

"I haven't properly thanked you for looking out for Kindle."

Michael looked over his shoulder once more at the morose figure gliding silently behind them, more like the statues that lined the hall than a human being.

"She seemed..."

"Lost?"

"Yes. She said as much. Where did you meet her?"

"In the forest at the base of the mountain."

"Near where you lodge, yes?"

"Yes."

"Collecting firewood?"

"You have a future as a detective."

"I have heard as much of you, Mr. Torquiam. They say you can cut grain with your wit alone."

"They like to talk."

"Not as much as you, I fancy."

They laughed once more and ascended the stair, their polished shoes clacking strangely off the unyielding stone beneath them as amber sunbeams whirled through the air like the filaments of some sun god's newly donned jerkin.

Behind and subsumed beneath them, Kindle stared up through that lightless portal at the base of the stair, a portal that seemed to bespeak of other worlds, darker worlds, grander worlds.

Upon reaching the upper landing, the preacher's son strode to the nearest window and raised his hand to the shimmering path of the high, narrow windows of regal and elaborate décor. He stretched his digits askew with force, pale forks seeking the unseen; eyes shining feverishly, were that they could sear the stone of the cathedral entire, they might nearly have done so.

Michael stopped and spoke then with great solemnity. He looked not at all to his companions but kept his head upturned to the light as it drifted about his hand.

"Grandness guised as glory flickers the flame of sacrament, threatening its demise; destruction of the holy temple that is the soul. And those who would feed those flames cast their hooks into the edifice of complacency and call it the Will of God. My path is a higher path; my goal is a nobler goal."

Eisen picked up the chant.

"My wings are the wings of a beast, dissilient and invariable as the raging heat of the sun. 'Requiem,' chapter 2, verse 3."

Surprise showed clear as an impending thunderhead upon the visage of the youthful acolyte. He lowered his hand from the radiance of the glass-filtered light and turned to the coffin maker with an expression of sudden and profound joy.

"So you are familiar with the work?"

"It is one of my favorites."

"Truly?"

"Indeed."

"Yet you put no stock in a higher power?"

"Certainly I do. Floods."

"What?"

"Earthquakes, solar flares, tsunamis, and the occasional errant banana peel; but in gods? The romantic ideal of a god is the supreme artist, he that creates for the joy of creating, magnificent in his accomplishment thereof. But the truth of gods is that they exist for the sole purpose of torturing their creation as a bitter prelude to its collective destruction."

"Certainly you jest."

"You would think so."

"Why do you speak so? I know you are an intelligent man, yet you speak madness from the fountainhead of delusion."

"I speak only of the predisposition of feral beasts. Man is no more elevated in his quest for self preservation and dominion then the most viscous arctic wolf."

"I didn't peg you as a nihilist, even now I am sure you are not, for no violent anarchist could fully appreciate a work as profound as 'Requiem,' yet in all truth you speak as one, distinguishable from their ranks only by the refinement of your speech."

"Your lack of pegging was correct."

Michael looked fixedly at the coffin maker until Kindle crested the stairs and emerged like a tranced ghost upon the landing.

The young acolyte walked purposefully forward, took her gently by the arm and led her away down the hall.

Eisen followed them a ways, past several doors, all of them closed and forbiddingly so, until at last they came to the end of the hall and disappeared into a room with a door which was twice the size of all the others before it.

Peering tentatively inside, Eisen beheld a room of stunning aesthetic contradiction; for the floor and walls and furniture were all of the utmost austerity, rigid, firm, hard and unyielding as steel. Plain in their construction and utterly devoid of superfluous decoration, save one magnificent arm chair. Yet at the very back of the room, upon the upper middle of the wall hung a massive golden cross, set above an impressive throne-like chair; dominant and oppressive, lording over the rest of the room with unmatched zeal. There was little enough to lord over, save one small wooden writing table accompanied by the aforementioned high-backed chair of impressive quality, two spindly, antique lamps which stood like dutiful soldiers, one at each side of the room, nearest the door, a lamp and various writing oddments, one stiff-looking red couch, tearing at the seams but comfortable looking, one book shelf, completely full (mainly of theological text) and one dwarfish, awkward stool set before the desk as if in afterthought. Aside from this assortment there was nothing else in the room.

"Please, Miss Kindle, take a seat."

Michael motioned cordially to the soft, sanguine sofa. He darted behind the desk and began rifling through the contents of the drawers. Shortly thereafter he returned to the young woman and, finding that she had not moved, furrowed his brow and guided her to the couch. He returned to the desk, pulled out a bottle of brandy, three shot glasses and an ice box, which must have been concealed in some lower drawer, and departed to the shaking female a full helping of the glistening brew.

"Drink this; it'll ease your nerves."

He pulled from the back of the couch a thick, elegant wool blanket of azure and draped it round the poor girl's shoulders like a tender mother catering to the needs of a sickly child.

"Please lay down, as I observe that you are shivering."

She did as he instructed, setting her empty glass aside wordlessly upon the hardwood floor and within moments was snoring peacefully with her limber limbs all askew upon the soft fabric of the sofa.

Eisen watched these events occur with a calm, quizzical expression upon his keen, sleepless face.

Waiting.

After he had watched her lazy breathing, the acolyte rose, fixed his suit and ambled to the high-backed chair, lowering himself down into it rather awkwardly. He folded his hands about each other as if in prayer, his eyes shooting up and out and over his rigid, bloodless knuckles, white as sun-worn shale.

"So, I hear you desire to speak with my father and me."

Eisen was surprised but he didn't allow it to show. Yet when he realized he was conjuring up a mask for his host, he felt a heavy pang of guilt slither through him like the cephalic groping of a hundred hateful beasts. Instantly, did he seek to rectify this laxity of principle, this inexcusable lapse of character.

"I am surprised; you are very well informed."

"Surprised? You don't look it."

"Don't I?"

"Cease your jesting, please. I hear... I hear talk that you're not right with the Lord."

"I don't really care about being right with your Lord or anyone else's; I care about these seditious rumors that are circulating around town about me. You've been spreading them, haven't you? I know it wasn't your father, not from the fact that Kindle over there heard him say as much, but because he is the kind of man who figures his god will deal with me in his own good time. I know this is so from seeing him, speaking with him and, lastly, from hearing you speak of him. I know something else as well, you're not the kind of man who would just wait around for divine justice, are you, Michael?"

Michael looked as if he had been branded, but he quickly regained his composure. His knuckles, however, became even more starkly white.

"You seem very sure of yourself, Mr. Torquiam."

"That is because I am."

"You didn't, at first, strike me as arrogant, either."

"Perhaps you should leave the profiling to the psychologists."

"You don't like me, do you, Eisen?"

"I only just met you. I can't say whether I do or I don't yet. What I can say with utter finality, however, is that I don't like people spreading incendiary lies about me all over a town I have only just arrived in."

The priest nodded vacantly, his eyes sliding to one side, his thoughts clearly upon other matters than the one immediately at hand.

"Why do you think I would be spreading these rumors you speak of? As you say, we only just met."

"That's what I'd like to know. Why would you?"

Michael shook his head and placed the palms of his hands down upon the table and then stood slowly but impressively.

"Much like yourself, Mr. Torquiam, I don't like being accused of things that I didn't do."

"You deny it then?"

"I don't know what I'd have to deny to begin with. I have no idea where you came up with these ideas. It was my father who has slandered you. I don't think he much cares for you."

Eisen nodded with dark humor, then he smiled.

"Well now, that's not very priestly of him, is it?"

"What is it you want me to say, Mr. Torquiam? Do you want me to confess my guilt to a crime I didn't commit? Is that what it would take to please you?"

Eisen rose and walked to the bookshelf and ran his hand across the myriad spines as he spoke; a lustrous shine and superb gilding slipping easily beneath his supple touch.

"I am no psychologist, but I know well enough when a man has principles he would sacrifice his life for, and you are such a man. If you would deny this, then I was clearly mistaken and I shall apologize immediately. So, was I?"

Still straddling the gray space between indecision, indignation and something else less amenable to the observations of the coffin maker's discerning eyes, Michael clenched his fists, realized the motion all too late and quickly relaxed his entire body, but not quickly enough to keep from giving his mind away.

"I thought so. Tell me, Michael, what's your game?"

"Since I see that here deception would fail me, I'll tell it to you straight."

"How I wish you would."

Michael turned to the crucifix upon the wall and motioned to it as might a page introducing an incoming magistrate, a movement fine and fair, harbinger to a beatified resplendence.

"My grandfather put this here when he first arrived to this holy place, consecrated with the blood and sweat of better men than now here reside. My father wanted to take it down, he said that the Lord would provide whether one touted his ensign or not; the fool misses the point completely. Does not the lover carry some token in thought or flesh of their beloved? A lock of hair or necklace or handkerchief. It matters not, what matters is the sentiment and the ritual power thereof. Men are nothing without their ceremonies, even memories fade when the ritual of remembrance is done away with. Our Creator knew this well and provided the greatest of all possible rituals for the lowest of all possible creatures: Loving praise for its own sake. True, the execution of this deed, this holy promulgation, is the highest a man can hope for, needing nothing further, nothing more. For his love of the ultimate makes his love for the most pathetic all the more powerful. Love, like a muscle, is apt to wane with disuse and wax with the proper exercise. But do men not all build monuments to their own selves, to their bodies, to their disgusting perversions. Yet to this my father turns as if into the darkness of a moonless night, saying nothing, minding naught!

And he calls this sacred! Inaction. If men can build monuments to themselves, raise their flags of greed and war in their own name, how much more satisfying must it be to raise that banner in the name of one beyond oneself; to vest one's life in a cause that transcends blood and flesh and earthly despoilment? That is the purpose of this cross. That is my cause, the cause you seek to wreathe in the flame of your words."

"There's really no need to get so overexcited."

"You test me, carpenter!"

"Obviously."

"Mockery?"

"One thing I'll tell you is that I have absolutely no interest in wreathing anything in flames. I am not this world's enemy, nor your own."

"Denial will not avail you here, Eisen. I have many confidants all throughout town, more even than my father himself. I hear well enough what you have been saying, about him, about these good people, about our faith."

"Man's allowed free purchase of his tongue."

"Blasphemy."

"Well, like father, like son."

"Still your tongue before I cut it from your head!"

Eisen furrowed his brow and shoved his hands in his pocket. Inhaling deeply, he about-faced and shot his adversary a quizzical expression.

Their eyes met as raging lava hailing the screeching sea, a war in a whisper, a whisper in the head. Silence fell.

Rather suddenly the acolyte dropped his gaze, his face falling from the highest heights of hatred into the lower depths of shamed dejection.

"Forgive me, Eisen."

"There's nothing to forgive, forgiveness begs transgression; how can the baring of one's mind be so misconstrued? No, there's nothing sorry and shameful about being honest, even violently so. For he, compelled by his foes, former friends in masks of light, took flight from even the water and the wind in the throes of his ignominy. But lo, he was deceived and the deceiver was ever smiling; the smile a folly of an age."

A tinge of humor so slight it wouldn't have been perceived by a less astute observer spread like quick flame over Michael's brooding face; he looked up at the coffin maker and nodded respectfully. "'Requiem,' act 2, verse 9."

"Very good."

"I shouldn't have allowed my anger to get the better of me like that. Please understand that my relationship with my father goes deeper than appearances attest."

"So I had gathered."

"Perhaps I should leave you two. When she wakes you can... perhaps I should go."

But before Michael could leave the room, Eisen walked to his side and clapped him upon the shoulder with good humor and a friendly smile.

"My good man! My dear chap! Calm your nerves; it was nothing, nothing at all. Sit. Come now, don't get so flustered over trifles."

Michael looked with bewilderment at this sudden display of kindness and affection as if it were a fever dream delusion. Then, very slowly and solemnly, he nodded his head.

"Yes, yes you're quite right, Eisen. Thank you."

"Don't thank me yet."

"What do you mean?"

"You've yet to answer my question."

"Ah, I know you may not believe it, but it wasn't I. I find gossip indescribably distasteful."

"Well, at least we share that in common."

"Indeed. Look, I have to go attend to the old man's family. I just wanted to make sure that your friend– "

"Kindle."

"Yes, that Kindle was looked after, she's a lost sheep; don't let her wander."

"You don't know her. Only a half hour ago she was taking care of me, but that's another story for another time."

"I'm glad I was wrong about you, Mr. Torquiam."

"Goodbye, Mr. Montferiat."

"God bless you."

"Well, my own blessing on you then. Whatever a coffin maker's benediction might be."

They shook hands and the young acolyte departed hastily, walking, as he always did, in a very austere, impressive fashion, as if he were entrusted with dangerous knowledge of the greatest moment and gravity that both burdened and privileged him.

"Liar," Eisen uttered the word with dreadful finality as the acolyte's footsteps faded away into the awkward nothingness of distant things that may or may not be where one thinks they ought not.

What designs have you against me, Michael Montferiat?

After watching him go, Eisen walked round the plain writing desk and took a slumped seat on the throne-like chair, tired with the weight of recent events; he felt worn to the bone. He gazed at the fixture that cradled him, strangely gaudy in comparison to the rest of the décor, much like the effulgent crucifix that burned radiantly upon the wall as if in silent challenge to the spent mortals below. To the coffin maker's sensibilities it seemed as if both the chair and cross belonged in a different setting entirely, perhaps next to a pipe organ in a mighty Roman basilica, grander than this decaying edifice; so starkly did they protrude to the forefront of any spent attention.

Chapter Thirteen

An Appearance of White

It was an hour before Kindle woke, groggy eyed but apparently much relieved of her previous burden.

Eisen knew better, he knew that the terror had wormed down into the deepest reaches of her heart where no soul could touch it, where it would fester like an open wound, reeking and malign.

He approached the couch and knelt beside her, feeling her forehead gently.

"Feeling better, Kindle?"

"Much. Where did stone face get to?"

"Stone face? Oh, you mean Michael?"

She nodded, looking about as if expecting him to pop into the room at any moment. Her expectations, however, were not to match up to reality.

"Yes."

"He had to go attend to church business, or so he told me."

"You don't believe him?"

"I believe that."

"What don't you believe?"

"A whole lot, but you mean about Michael?"

"Yes."

Before he could answer there came a great and unaccountable commotion from downstairs; the sound of rushing feet and raised voices crying out in great excitement.

"I'll tell you later."

Eisen leapt up and dashed into the hallway toward the nearest window from which he scanned the green and swarming ground below, heaving with the wind like a stomach-sick babe.

Four men approached the church bearing a corpse between them on a stretcher, his face horribly mutilated, as if by wild beasts, his skin wormy and worn, bloody and stiff. There was something terribly familiar about the man, but Eisen couldn't quite place it.

The pallbearers were but twenty feet from the church when a devious wind came spiraling in and snatched the largest of the four's hat from his bulbous, craggy head and sent it dancing on down the cobbled lane.

It came to rest at the feet of another man who stood perfectly still in the far corner of the church yard dressed in an odd patchwork suit.

This apparition carried an umbrella over its left shoulder, similarly white, holding it at an extreme angle such that it shadowed his face utterly from view; a mask of splintered darkness.

Eisen had but glanced at the queer specter when the lone figure ever so slowly raised the umbrella and gazed up at the peering coffin maker, eyes colluding in shadow, tenebrous smoldering pits, a faint sparkling therein.

Diamonds in the dark.

So startled was he by this unexpected and somewhat arcane perception that he drew back full from the window with a sharp inhalation of air, losing sight of the man with the albescent canopy.

When he had regained his composure a few moments later, he looked out the window once more, but the man had gone. Where he had gone was a great mystery, as the church yard was flat and bleak as any Scottish moor; consisting of only the cobblestone path, two thin, withered trees, which stood at either side of the entrance to the yard and looked as if they were about to embrace one another, and a few tiny, haggard, leafless, dying shrubs. Aside from this, the landscape was covered by nothing but a few swaths of mud and dirt and the sickly yellow-green grass.

Eisen felt a strange tingling dancing about his flesh, like electric centipedes beneath his skin.

He looked both east and west, and up and down, but the man in patches was nowhere to be found.

Eisen stood for a moment, paralyzed by the queerness of the situation. But then, remembering the corpse on the cart, he pulled himself away from the window with one final wary coup d'oeil.

As he hurriedly walked down the stairs, Kindle poked her head out of the room and then fully emerged with an expression of curiosity.

"What is it?"

"Someone has been killed."

"Who?"

"I have a suspicion, but I'm going to see. Why don't you stay here, you'll only distress yourself further by viewing a corpse."

She nodded, a motion barely perceptible, not as if she agreed but that she would respect his wishes regardless.

Eisen noticed it nonetheless and nodded once with finality, and then continued on to the bottom of the stairs. He quickly trekked back the way he had come, the objects flashing by as he passed, the reddish-brown of the doors, the gray-blue of the stones all passing like a photo reel gone mad. When he got near enough to the end of the hallway, he could see that a large number of people were darting about anxiously just beyond the sanctuary of the corridor, though he could not see the cadaver nor the men who had been carrying it.

As he emerged into the chapel proper, moving through the softly shadowed light and glimmer-dappled stones, not a soul was to turn nor eye to see this solitary figure, so enveloped in curiosity did they remain.

The dead man lay stretched out upon the middle of the aisle surrounded by churchgoers who mostly gawked and gossiped amongst themselves as any group of school children might.

Cocking an ear, Eisen caught enough disparate snatches of conversation as to paint a conclusive whole, the collective mind of the mob. They spoke and whispered in hushed, but giddy tones, like ones whom quake and cackle of ghosts and demons all in the same excited breath.

Children indeed, the coffin maker thought dimly to himself.

That very moment a young boy emerged from behind the altar, guiding none other than the preacher himself who, upon drawing near the fetid husk, was so overcome with emotion that he covered his contorted face in his wide, shaking hands as one might that has just lost a lover.

"What has happened? What manner of devilry is this?"

One of the pallbearers, the large craggy-faced man who had earlier lost his hat to the wind, came forth and shook his head, his expression utterly grim.

"Don't rightly know much but that he was murdered. We thought you and your son could call the congregation together, as he is, none of us can tell who he is... or was."

At this time Michael came marching up the aisle, evidently having left the church for an errand and only now reentering it.

"Is there a problem?"

He froze when he came upon the body, and then, very slowly, almost reverently, he knelt down before the man, gazing with wonder in his fiercely shining eyes. A hush fell over the crowd and Michael nodded sorrowfully.

"I knew this man. His name was Adams, Frank Adams, he lives... lived with his wife on the other side of the forest, he'd come into town sometimes for food, to pray at the church. What happened to him?"

No one answered. The crowd remained silent and apprehensive.

"What happened?"

The large, craggy-faced man whom had previously spoken, turned to the preacher's son and shook his cropped and chestnut-colored head.

"No one knows."

"I do."

With unnerving synchronicity, every head of every present body turned upon the coffin maker who had just made the aforementioned statement.

Michael took several steps forward and bent toward the coffin maker with solemn reservation, though all could tell that a great curiosity was upon him.

"Well, what happened, Eisen?"

"I killed him."

Several people gasped; the crowd struck up a simmering murmur.

Michael just stared with discerning intensity whilst Luce rolled his eyes and shook his head; it was he who next spoke with fiery indignation.

"This is no time for jesting!"

"I agree wholeheartedly."

"Explain yourself, Eisen, but before God and this company, do not lie."

"I don't lie."

Reallocating his attention from the father unto the son, the coffin maker inhaled meditatively as he prepared his tale.

"I was traveling with Kindle through the forest, and this man here," he gestured to the corpse carelessly, "assailed us, alongside two confederates whose identities are a mystery to me. I told him not to press us, but his heart was filled with savage intentions. He heeded me not, so I defended myself and killed him. Seeing the look in his eyes as he drew his knife, I knew then, as I know now, that no misstep on my part was made."

Eisen paused then and looked about as several exclamations emanated from the throng like the baying of beasts long mind-struck with heat.

"Kin ya prove it?"

"Yeah, what evidence do ya have?"

"Well, I ain't no fool; lying out his teeth, the rogue, lock him up, that's what I say!"

"Murderer! Lying in the house of God, you should be ashamed of yourself!"

"Some say the devil walks with him. I think he's lost it."

"I knew Adams. He was a good man; I say hang the bastard!"

"He's crazy."

"I hear tell that girl he's with is touched by the devil's own hand!"

"Why just today I heard someone say she attacked James Daniels, just up and attacked him for no reason at tall! Now who'd do such a thing? How'd you explain it cept for devilry?"

"That's what it is."

"That's all it is!"

In a thundering voice crafted from a lifetime of sermons and ecclesiastical showmanship, the preacher intruded upon the din like a maelstrom upon a placid lake.

"Silence, I beseech you, my brothers and sisters! You must let this man speak. You must let him have his say! We are not as a wild rabble, frantic as rabbits and wide eyed as a feral doe, are we, oh, my brothers and sisters? No! No, I say! My son, go fetch the sheriff, he must be informed. Bring him back here as soon as possible. Eisen, forgive my flock, they are unnerved by this horrible tragedy. I believe your story but they are right, can you prove your words?"

"Indeed. Michael!"

His call stopped the preacher's son just short of the church's massive doorway. The latter turned back inquisitively as the light enveloped his body in a golden aura, looking now less man and more some ethereal being, less of the earth than of the firmament he so desired.

"Yes?"

"You will doubtless recall that upon Kindle's body there were a number of bruises, most prominently borne on her face, upon the left side. Correct?"

"I reckon so."

"Then there is your proof; a closer inspection upon your part would have revealed that it is indeed the kind of bruise a fist would create, and it is far too large to be my own. Is that satisfactory?"

Once more he looked round expectantly. His tone was even and decisive and emotionally reserved, which doubtless angered the seething throng far more than any indignant outburst ever could have.

Michael looked suspiciously into the windows of Eisen's face before turning about sharply and vanishing into the brilliant, consuming sunlight.

The preacher walked up to Eisen and nodded firmly. "If the facts should align with your words, and I do not doubt that they shall, then you will be exonerated from their ire. But for the moment I must detain you here."

"Until the sheriff arrives."

"I'm afraid so."

"That's strange," said Eisen.

"What is?"

"You don't look frightened."

Luce squinted at the blank-faced craftsman in a vested attempt to discern whether or not the man was being sarcastic or not, but the effort yielded no results.

Eisen tilted his head down and looking up from under his brows peered up over his tinted glasses with an arched brow.

"Have I something on my face?"

"What? No. Why do you ask?"

"Is there a reason I should not?"

"I don't know. No, I suppose not."

"Then it doesn't matter, does it?"

"I'm not sure I understand."

"Nor am I, but that alone will not blunt my zeal in the trying."

"Have you and my son become properly acquainted?"

"Yes."

"You speak like him. He'll like you, I imagine."

"I'm not sure of that, but he did say you didn't much care for me."

"My son said that I... what now?"

"That you didn't like me, is that so? I ask only out of curiosity, not out of utility or some twisted attempt at spite."

"I can never tell, Mr. Torquiam, whether you are being honest or just sarcastic."

"Don't be so suspicious."

The priest made as if to turn away, his whole countenance one of great confusion. He was stopped short of turning his entire back to the elegant, young craftsman by the latter's words.

"This situation is quite convenient to me. While we wait for the sheriff, we have plenty of time for talk. At any rate, there is something I would like to speak with you about if you would indulge me. I understand you didn't appreciate what I said about that old man, and I should feel very much the same if he were my friend, or perhaps not, but at any rate I would not allow death to cloud my reason."

"What is it?"

"James Daniels."

"Ah, yes. I hear you've had some trouble with him. A nasty run-in."

"Me? Hardly, it was Kindle that really crossed him. Course if she had jumped on me and bit me, I imagine I'd be a little put out as well."

The preacher whirled full around, eyes wide and breath sharply inhaled, his voice distorted and his brow deeply furrowed.

"She bit him?"

Instantly, Eisen realized he had made a misstep. The crowd pressed slowly upon him, smelling blood in the water. It was not in keeping with his principles to lie, but when he thought of Kindle and the dangers and humiliations which might well befall her from his honesty, a vile indecision crept then into his brain and lay waiting like a hungry lion. No, he thought at last, it was not his failing, he had nothing to hide, and even if he did, he'd not conceal it. Such was his conviction and thus his action.

"Yes, he struck me," Eisen turned his head and moved into one of the overwhelming rays of hard light that fell from the cathedral's high, looming windows, "quite forcefully. Impertinent but understandable; she was merely trying to protect me as you would have done for your son where the two of you in such a situation."

"I would have done nothing of the sort!"

"Truly? Why not?"

"Violence is utterly abhorrent to me."

"Yes, but your son's safety, his life, is surely worth the burden of that repugnance, is it not?"

The preacher was silent and considerate a moment, and then a peculiar look of resolve fell about him before next he spoke.

"If God should ordain me or my son to die, then we should take joy in the working of His will, for it is for the betterment of all things, in Heaven as on Earth."

Several members of the crowd crossed themselves and said, "Amen," reverently as Eisen moved out of the light so that none could well see his face and the disdain written plainly upon it.

Addressing Luce where he stood in the wide ray of light which the coffin maker had just left, Eisen spoke with cheerless reserve and subtle forewarning, "I do not believe you would do as you say."

"If that is the price, then that is the price."

"You have considered the price, but not the cost."

"You speak in riddles."

"As does every man. It is the gods that are silent. One in glaring particular."

"That is not so. Now really, one shouldn't say such things!"

"Why? Did your god reach out his hand to help that old man, your friend? Or Daniel's friend, slain by the bandits who, for months unheeded, have besieged this town without the slightest trace of divine intervention on your behalf? Or him lying cold and unmoving there before you, was he spared or saved or set straight by your will o' wisp, your celestial sphere? No. You wail at phantoms."

The preacher thundered and boomed with outstretched hands, looking very much like he was about to cast some strange spell over the defiant craftsman; as if he expected to sunder the coffin maker with the sheer force of his voice alone. All he did accomplish, however, was to hurt Eisen's ears.

"Enough!"

The crowd had fallen silent once more and looked on with bated breath; they waited, not with fear, but with eagerness. They could sense a conflict brewing and awaited with a savage yearning, the longing of the mountain lion for the blood of lambs.

"Enough? Enough! You just told me that if your fantasy desired to take the life of your son, you would rejoice! Seldom have ever I heard such disgusting, loathsome words! And none more delusive. Were I you, I would hide my face from the hideousness of my shame! Even if I knew for a fact that such a being as you speak existed and He then demanded the life of my son, I would bury my blade in his breast with the greatest of pleasure."

So shocked was the preacher upon hearing this language that he could scarcely utter a sound. It was as if Eisen's very words had shriveled the cleric's tongue as it had confounded his brain. And at that moment his son returned, stony faced as usual with the sheriff dutifully in tow.

Eisen scrutinized the lawman from the corners of his eyes. He was large and burly, with his bright, golden mustaches all bristling like the spines of a wild boar. His clothing was utterly singular, and it suggested that he thought very highly of his sense of fashion. A little too highly. He wore a Stetson with a band of rattlesnake skin strung round the innermost section of the top of the brim, an alligator skin vest, very fine riding boots and heavy leather bracers. Red was the color of the neckerchief that functioned as sling and cradle for the burly man's left, and broken, arm. His face was jolly and open, but he kept scowling periodically as if he, too, realized this and, disdaining his own amiability, sought to erase it with, every now and again, an injection of forced imperiousness and venom. However, this only served to undermine his authority even further and make the whole of his facade rather clownish and farcical.

Before either addressing the crowd, Eisen or Luce, the sheriff walked to the body, knelt to make observations, then rose and turned slowly about, regarding every present face, save his own.

"Michael hasn't told me much. What's all this about the coffin maker being a murderer?"

Eisen drew himself forth and addressed the sheriff directly. "A killer I am, unfortunately, but not a murderer."

"What do you mean, Torkey?"

"It's Torquiam."

"Don't sass me, boy. Out with it."

"He attacked me. I have already told Luce and his son, and everyone else here, that I can present evidence of it."

"Oh, ho ho! Indeed?"

"Yes, though I clearly see that you don't believe me."

"And why should I believe ya?"

"You can hardly expect me to know why you don't believe what I say, but once you tell me, I shall inform you directly."

"Saucy, ain't ya! Well, Torkey, if ya smart, and ya don't look it, ya'll learn ya one better than ta sass me."

"Sass?"

"Now why don't you tell me why I should take the word of a killer?"

"It strikes me as noteworthy that you so easily accepted the idea of me killing him, yet you'll not even allow for the possibility of granting me nobility of motivation. Is it not curious to you, officer, that you've no more evidence of me killing him than you do that I committed the act out of blood lust rather than self-defense?"

The lawman's mustaches twitched apprehensively.

"Why would anybody make up such an outrageous lie?"

"Any number of various reasons, attention maybe, regardless, I only bring this up to illustrate the fact that your preconceptions are biasing your every move. If a man isn't dancing to the rhythm of his own tune, then another is playing it for him. Their fingering could well be wrong. Perhaps I do not want to dance."

"Well, it's the law what's playing this tune, son."

"The rule of law is worthless if it's irrational."

"You saying I'm not making sense, son?"

"We're wasting time talking, come with me and we'll go to Kindle, she and her bruises can collaborate my story."

He began walking off but then stopped and turned around.

"Coming, officer?"

The sheriff looked uncertainly toward the callous and determined young man, as the matador might look to the bull asking all the while, Would his sword be enough?

Quite unexpectedly, the lawman turned to the preacher's son and formed for him a questioning look.

Eisen flicked his eyes from one to the other and watched as Michael nodded faintly and finitely. It was a gesture of a very strange kind of high-handedness, one which the coffin maker could not wholly place within the realm of his experience. Nevertheless, it instilled in him an undeniable sense of unease.

The moment that the sheriff received these unspoken commands, he turned and left with Eisen at his side.

Michael accompanied them. Together the solemn, purposeful trio made their way hastily to the preacher's chamber. But when they arrived, they could not find Kindle; she had simply vanished as if the woman had evaporated through the very walls.

A face flashed through Eisen's racing mind, or rather, an imitation which the man with the horse had worn. The man whom, according to Kindle, had been the harbinger of her family's demise and her own unspeakable torment. Had she been correct? Was it indeed the same man? If so, had it been him who had made off with her? Was he even now, Eisen shook his head and inhaled the cold heavy air, feeling only the most intense sense of immovable dread.

"There ain't no one here!"

Eisen turned with a sour, mocking expression which he displayed proudly, garishly, addressing Michael in caustic tones.

"He's a sharp one, your sheriff."

Michael's face twitched with the faint trace of a smile as he spoke, cutting off a shout of outrage from the belittled lawman.

"I assume from your somewhat frantic expression, Mr. Torquiam, that she did not tell you she was leaving? Is that so?"

"It is. Come."

Eisen darted out of the room and went tearing off down the corridor like a man on the lam with Michael in more reserved tow. The portly sheriff threw his hands up and shook his head before slowly wheeling about and stumbling on down the hall after them like a clumsy circus oddity.

They searched the whole of the massive building, but there was no trace of Kindle to be found. On the highest floor Eisen suddenly stopped and turned to Michael.

"The bell tower."

"What of it?"

"Can we access it?"

"You mean can you walk up on it?"

"Yes."

"Certainly, if you're suicidal."

"Only in the morning."

Michael, furrowing his brow, studied the impassive face before him in perplexity.

The coffin maker dashed to an old battered door of black lacquered oak and pressed a worn, callused palm to it.

"Is this it?"

"Yes, but it's always kept locked so as to prevent any children from playing up there. As I said before, it's dangerous."

A place for children to play. Yes, she probably is up there.

"May I have the key?"

"I'll open it for you."

The preacher's son produced from his waistcoat a small ring, full of keys, and began flipping methodically through them.

Eisen hastily flexed his hands, as if spoiling for a fight. He wondered at this sudden, crushing anxiety which he felt with every fiber of his being. He had felt it when he had met the masked jester and when he had seen the man with the white umbrella, but what was it? Why did he feel such fear and hopelessness? He could not say. The uncharacteristic nature of those feelings bit deeply and held him in their sway. He felt as he did in his dreams, in his night terrors, dangling head-first over the maw of an inexplicable void without escape, without respite, with horror as his only companion.

When the door was finally opened, the coffin maker tore through its portal with such speed that both Michael and the sheriff assumed looks of astonishment and shock.

The stairway was narrow, too narrow for two people to walk up it side by side. The higher he rose, the more cramped and cloying the space about him felt, as if with every step the walls drew upon him, as if they sought to crush him and wring from him a bloody rheum to slip and splash down that darkened way. When he finally reached the top of the cloistered stairs, the first thing to strike him was the sound of birds.

Squawking.

Singing.

The flutter of ascending wings, the silence of falling feathers.

The bell tower was perfectly square and covered by a high spired roof, held up by four enormous columns, from which the four massive iron bells hung like the severed heads of faceless giants. Ringing round the full length of the small platform was a decaying stone wall, waist high and beautiful even in its pitiable current state. It was directly before Eisen, near the northernmost wall where Kindle stood with her slender back to him.

"Kindle, what are you doing up here?"

"Looking."

"At what?"

"Everything."

A bird rested magnificently upon her shoulder, naturally, like an ornament, looking as at home there as it doubtless would upon the branch of any given tree. Several other birds had gathered round her, some near her feet, others flitted lazily about her head forming a kind of shifting, feathery halo.

The animals were completely foreign to him, reddish orange and redder, and more orange still due the slowly sliding light of the dying sun, bleeding colors like a wounded man bleeds blood.

They flitted away briefly and mockingly as Eisen emerged full and wide eyed from the stairwell, as if they were not afraid at all but were by some other mind compelled to such pretension.

He was strangely moved by the stillness of the scene upon which he had so swiftly burst. He felt as if he were in a dream made flesh and stone and beautiful feathers and flowing hair.

"How did you get up here?"

Without turning or frightening the birds, she withdrew from her left pocket a small set of keys and jangled it as if in triumph. She laughed sadly and quietly as she did so, as if the gesture cost her some kind of internal strength.

"It was in the preacher's room?"

She nodded and pocketed the key ring, her back to him all the while.

"Is something the matter?"

"I thought of that man and I, I had to get away. I just had to."

"The jester?"

"Yes."

"I won't let anyone hurt you, I promise."

"And what if you can't keep that promise?"

"No one ever knows to a certainty whether or not they will be able to keep a promise, the only thing that matters is trying. Trying to keep it. And I will try."

There was a sudden, heavy stillness in the air, as if the very lungs of the earth had been punctured. The next voice that spoke belonged to Kindle, and it was open and unstressed, strangely devoid of emotion.

"I was going to kill myself, that's why I came up here. I thought of doing it many times before. Everything was too much to endure, too much. I got up on the barrier, climbed right up and stood there. Then I thought of you and of all the nice people I've met and the flowers in the spring and the little hats and snails that sleep beneath them, unnoticed but noticing, and I couldn't do it. I didn't know what I was doing anymore, didn't know what was wrong with me and then I half lost my balance and nearly fell straight off."

She began to laugh nervously; it was the laughter of a frightened creature that no longer knew what else to do.

Slowly the coffin maker walked up behind her as the birds cocked their heads in strained jittery motions.

She turned and as she did so he backhanded her in the face.

Neither of them said anything, they just stood looking at each other. His eyes burned intensely as the fires of a steel furnace while she quivered on the edge of tears. Then, quite abruptly she averted her eyes, then turned her face away from him as a slight trickle of blood ran placidly down the right corner of her mouth.

"You'd just give up? Give in? Forsake yourself to weakness?"

She nodded her head; he struck her again, harder this time, without remorse or hesitation. What birds remained scattered to the pillowing winds, shrieking as if it was they themselves that had taken the blow.

This time she could no longer contain her tears, and they fell from her eyes even as she fell to her knees.

He looked down at her with a curiously opaque expression and commanded her movements in a flat, but imperious tone.

"Get up."

"Leave me alone!"

"I said get up."

"Why do you even care? Why? Tell me that!"

"Because you are dear to me! Because you have potential, because you are fair and beautiful, because you're kind! Because my heart overflows with love for you as a brother would for his sister! Can you not understand that? Have the wilds stripped from you even that inheritance? Speak!"

Never before had Kindle witnessed from Eisen such a wild outpouring of emotion; his face had contorted into a grim diagram of despair and anger, and he had turned quite pale.

"I feared you'd pity me."

"There is no pity in me."

He spoke quietly and contemptuously in measured tones and then turned his back to her, gazing out into the rimless distance.

His hands were clenched tightly, and his whole body shook with uncontainable fury.

"The man of which you spoke, the jester, he has taken your family and your chastity from you, yet he spared your life and now you'd throw it away like any filthy rag? Your weakness disgusts me."

And with that he stiffly descended the stairs, slamming the door behind him furiously, leaving Kindle weeping upon the cold and uncaring stones as the little red birds whirled high up above like drops of blood against the waning sky.

Chapter Fourteen

Captive

Eisen didn't stop for the sheriff's questions, neither did he let the intent and suspicious looks of the congregation give him pause. He left the chapel and continued on his way, oblivious to any passers by, oblivious to the heat and the sharp rocks under his feet, oblivious even to the distant form of a man with a white umbrella standing in the shadow of the alley of the plaza-bound dry goods store. He didn't stop moving until he was seated comfortably within Arrgilius' inn. Only then did his senses fully return to him, all at once in a white hot rush. His mind swam and his head spun, his vision blurred and starbursts and wild flashes of light exploded in his eyes.

The inn was brimming with folk, full to bursting with their raucous voices and mad, strike-stomping. Eisen threw a quick glance about the pinewood place and the whirling, boisterous figures within it; they were singing and dancing. The merry makers took no notice of him and he was glad, for if they had, he was certain they would ask him to join in their party. But if they did, he knew he would deny them; there was nothing to celebrate upon this day. He felt drained and wanted nothing more than to let his head fall upon his arms and lay upon the table in a pitiful slump. But he refused to let his weakness overcome him, so he sat up ramrod straight and called for Arrgilius, who was talking to a young, redheaded woman.

Arrgilius saw Eisen, waved and smiled, his nose and cheeks touched up fine and ruddy by his bottle. The barkeep poured a frothing pint upon the counter and then took it in hand and made his way to Eisen's table. The redhead to whom Arrgilius was previously speaking turned around to see where her friend was going.

It was Jen Arlington.

Her eyes grew perceptibly wider and then narrowed suddenly. She turned her nose to the air and whirled quickly back around, leaning upon the counter as she had when she was talking with Arrgilius. Eisen continued to watch her in between the gaps of motion. He could perceive a certain tensity about her stance that had not been there before, but with every passing second since she had glimpsed him, it seemed to grow only more prevalent until it was the single defining feature of her stance. The whole of her physique, one shining monument to fragile rigidity; he was reminded of some ancient effigy, a statue perhaps, a tribute to a goddess. The static white of her skin like polished marble, unmoving but coiled, reading to strike, to sunder anything before her, the red streak of her hair blazing like molten copper in the spattered lights of the rowdy hostel.

She wore a white duster, beige cotton work pants, and heavy traveling boots. Were it not for her hair and the undeniably feminine curve of her body, one passing would have mistaken her for a man. The coffin maker thought that though the clothes were not tailored for her gender, she wore them so confidently that they only served to further accentuate and heighten her exceptionally maidenly aspects. She had first glanced at him over her right shoulder, as Arrgilius arrived at the coffin maker's table with a blustery, "Ello!" She looked back again, but this time over her left shoulder. As she made the movement, he caught sight of a blackened bruise over her eye and forehead, no token of an idle knock, but a remnant of some furious, rage-fueled blow. He wondered at that and at the peculiar change in her wardrobe and the fact that she was spending her time in such a fastidiously traditional town at the local bar.

"Eisen?"

"Huh?"

"I said how ya been?"

"Oh. I've been fine, but I could be doing better."

"Couldn't we all!"

"What's got you in such fine spirits?"

"Ah, the carnival! It's wondrous! Never seen anything like it in all my days. They've moved out of the plaza and started setting up in the edge of town near the forest, some of um anyhow, looks like the leaders wanted to stay and hash out something with Ledru. Anyways, it's just what this town needs right now, a little more festivity, what with all the bad things been falling upon our heads, and here our plump little master n' chief wants um gone! Ridiculous."

"You mean Ledru?"

"That's right."

"He is the one that hired me, the very reason why I came all the way out to your interesting little town to begin with, and I've gotten to know him some. I could talk to him if that would please you, as I know very well that it would please those performers. I've been around enough to know that traveling circus men are a fast-dying breed – it's a hard life. Besides, I've a more selfish motive as well for wanting the carnival to stay."

"And what might that be then?"

"I've yet to see them perform."

Arrgilius gave a hearty laugh and set the frothing pint of mead down before the young man with such exuberant gusto that the coffin maker could do naught, but accept it. Engaged in conversation almost as much as he was with his brew, Eisen failed to notice that Jen Arlington had approached and now stood directly behind him with a wistful expression.

"Ms. Arlington! Eisen, let me introduce you to the lovely--"

"Yes, we've met previously. How do you do, Ms. Arlington."

It was not a question; he knew exactly how well she was doing from the bruise on her face and the lost and dejected look in her eye.

"Call me Jen, please."

"How do you do, Jen?"

"May I sit?"

"I couldn't say, I don't own the table."

So violently did she react to this little quip that Eisen was certain he could see the spines bristling on her back until he remembered that she wasn't a porcupine.

"Why Jen! You're practically bristling."

"Shut up!"

Arrgilius attempted to intervene with a pleading look and the merry tone of a festival goer.

"Now, now, Jen, girl, don't be that way. It ain't civil."

"Shut your god damned mouth, the cursed both of you! To the dogs with your civility! The devil take it like a whore!"

The coffin maker wondered if she had begun to wander slightly outside the grounds of sobriety or if this was just her usual manner.

Jen looked then, in that moment, which seemed to hang potently beyond its expected duration, as if she would seize the ruddy barkeep and dash his head against the table until his brains ran upon the floor like spoiled jam. Instead she merely tightened her jaw unconsciously, heightening the sense that this woman was something sleek and volatile.

In that space of time as he watched her with keen interest leering from behind his form of slumped passivity, Eisen was reminded of Kindle and her altercation with Daniels earlier that day. The fiery unpredictability was there in them both, but what drove it in one was something completely different in the other.

"Arrgilius, might you leave us for a moment? I desire to speak with Ms. Arlington alone, as I believe there is a matter that needs sorting between us."

"Yes, I can see that."

Turning to go, the portly barkeep turned round and wagged his finger at Jen disapprovingly in a gesture that was meant to instill humor into the rather tense situation. She shot him a glare that, were it flame, would have scalded him from his skin to the bone.

She flung herself down into the chair farthest away from the dispassionate craftsman and threw her feet up to rest upon the table with pointed exuberance.

"Are you trying to prove something, Ms. Arlington?"

"Why the hell would you ask something like that?"

He motioned to her elevated feet without taking his calm, stormless eyes off of her intense and darkening ones.

"See! That's why no one around here can stand you, Eisen, the fucking nitpicking! Makes everyone realize the quicker just how much of a prick you are."

"You're drunk."

"Oh? I hadn't realized, wonder why I came to the bar to begin with? Ya know, ya'll a sharp one. I'll make sure ta tell Ledru to hold on ta ya!"

"Sarcasm ill becomes you."

"Oh that's rich."

"No, I don't think it is. At any rate, I didn't wish to speak to you so I could work on sharpening my sense of spite. I just wanted to– "

"Apologize?"

"No, last time we spoke, at my house, what I said was the truth, so there is nothing I feel I need apologize for. I just wanted to tell you that, with the hope that you value what is true more than your preacher. I really do hope. For in such a place as this, I fear that hope is misplaced, I fear it with every fiber of my being."

He spoke with such a sudden solemnity and abject gravity that she couldn't resist the uncoiling of the serpent within her, the softening of her gaze, the concern in her every movement.

He saw none of this. He did not look at her at all, but rather gazed off at the far wall over her shoulder, though he didn't see that either.

"Ya all right?"

"Huh?"

"You drifted off."

"Did I?"

"You aren't all right."

"No. I'm surprised you care. What happened to the fiery creature that was intent on drawing down a rain of blood?"

"I guess I overreacted some, I just..."

"What?"

"I just really liked you. If Tavis had said that, I wouldn't have given a shit because he's a jerk, but you've been nothing but cordial to me. I suppose I'm the one that should be apologizing."

"I don't dwell on trivialities, so don't trouble your pretty head over it."

"Ya'll really think that?"

"Huh?"

"I mean about me?"

"I don't follow."

"And here I thought ya'll were supposed to be smart."

"That's quite an assumption, milady. But what is it you want to know if I think?"

"If I'm pretty."

"Why should it matter?"

"It doesn't."

"Then why do you ask?"

"Why ya have to be so god damned circular!"

"I'm not even sure what that means."

"Yeah, well, sarcasm doesn't become y– "

She stopped suddenly, looking intently at his face, realizing that he wasn't being sarcastic at all, but wholly earnest.

"I take it back, what I said earlier."

"About me being a nitpicking prick?"

She suddenly burst out laughing, shaking her head bashfully.

"I am a little drunk."

"So I observed. You were saying?"

"I was saying I take it back cuz that isn't the reason the townsfolk can't stand you, it's not nitpicking, it's honesty. If there's one thing that civilized people hate, it's the perfectly honest man."

"That's what you think of me, is it? That I'm perfectly honest?"

"Aren't ya?"

"Well, I lied once when I was seven."

"How scandalous."

"My mother asked if I'd said my prayers and I told her that I had, but the truth was they gave me the creeping willies; I was eating cookies instead, used to hide them under my pillow."

Jen smiled and it was like the smile of a child in the midst of a beautiful summer day, utterly taken with the mere fact of her existence, and not mere in the slightest; feeling nothing but the profound joy of being alive and the additional pleasure of sharing that sense of mirthful profundity with another living being.

"What makes you say that the one thing that civilized people hate is a perfectly honest man?"

She flung her hair brazenly from the nasty welt upon her face, despoiling her youthful beauty like mold stealing from the fresh apple its soft and silver sheen.

"You see this bruise, of course you do; token of a father's love."

"Your father did that to you?"

"Had you assumed it was my mother?"

"There's no need for animosity."

"Well, I told him that I had been having notions about a man, and I guess I got a bit overly descriptive. He told me I was a whore and hit me with a rolling pin. A fucking rolling pin. Told me I was going to hell. I said I was glad of it if it meant I'd be away from him."

"Did you mean it?"

"Yes."

"You despise him that much?"

"I do."

"And yet I fail to understand why, don't you believe as he believes? You are a member of the church, after all. By every standard which I know, such people as your father and Luce to hold your... desires, should be held in the greatest possible contempt and resentment."

She flung her legs down from the table and glared at him as a prelude to her indignant words.

"How can you say that?"

"Because it's true, but do not misunderstand me. I do not mean that I agree with them. I don't."

"That's what I thought you meant. You could be right about them despising what I think. It's been my fear all along, why I don't talk much to anyone but Tavis. He might be a jackass but he listens, I mean really listens, when you talk to him."

Eisen burst out in a sudden spasm of mirth that was so unpredicted by the young woman that she didn't know whether he was laughing at her or at some sudden thought all his own.

"What's so damn funny?"

"A great many things. Don't let me incommode you."

"Incca-what?"

"Put you out."

"Huh?"

"Trouble you. Don't let me trouble you."

"What the hell were you before ya came here, an English teacher or something?"

"I've been making coffins most of my life."

"I don't know if I could stomach that kind of work."

"Well, it is a little different than working in a morgue."

"Yeah but, I don't know, I think it'd creep me out."

"Well, of course it would, you are a woman after all."

She chuckled at his jest, but then assumed a grave countenance.

"That's pretty much what most folks ere think; same reason why no one'll make a fuss about" she gestured hesitantly to her face, "cuz I'm just a woman and a woman needs to know her place, which is either as a house slave or whore," she sneered suddenly and spoke with vicious relish, "and apparently there ain't no other fuckin options."

"Jen, may I ask you a question?"

"Well, I don't think I could tell you until you ask it, but go ahead."

"Who was the man you were thinking about? The one you had been having, notions about?"

"Nobody."

"So you lied."

"No."

"Then who was it?"

"It's not really that important."

"Then why would it matter if you told me?"

"Because it was you."

He was silent for a moment and then smiled slightly in something like subdued triumph.

"Why?"

"Because you're the first man I've met around here aside from Arrgilius and that snake Caldwell that has a fuckin brain."

"You had naughty thoughts about me because you admire my intelligence?"

"Oh god! Why am I telling you this?"

"I appreciate your honesty, but you're clearly not thinking straight. You've crawled a little too far down that bottle, I think."

"Yeah. I should probably lie down. Eisen?"

"Yes?"

"Thanks for listening to me. It means, it means more than you know."

"I somehow doubt that. Arrgilius!"

"What is it lad? Have your pants caught fire or what! Howling like a banshee bitch in heat."

Jen and Eisen erupted into violent convulsions of laughter as the ruddy barkeep appraised them kindly and proudly.

"Seems you've worked those kinks out. Earlier I was afraid to leave the two of you alone, as I figured if I did I'd be cleaning blood stains off my floor for the next few weeks."

Arlington looked up at the barkeep with a countenance of resolve and self irritation.

"I wasn't thinking straight. That's all. Did you get a haircut?"

"No, good Lord, Eisen, did she drink the entire bottle by herself?"

"I'm afraid so. I think we had best take her upstairs before she collapses on some hapless, unsuspecting patron."

"Yeah."

Jen looked from one to the other and then wagged her finger before their faces.

"I'll collapse on yourn's unsupeaking paton!"

Arrgilius shook his head and took her by the left arm. "Come on, my dear."

Eisen rose and took her other arm in his own, and together the two men carted her up to one of the empty bedrooms where they deposited her on an empty mattress like a sack of potatoes.

A voice called from down the hallway for Arrgilius who looked to Eisen, pointed out the door and shook his head and diverged.

Eisen was left alone with the young woman. He stood over her without the faintest suggestion of movement in the entirety of his form. He didn't know what held him to that spot, didn't know what instilled such precision and focus unto his actions, didn't mind. He felt completely and wholesomely relaxed.

A few moments later she rolled over on her right side and lay there, blinking her eyes in dazed confusion. Then slowly, but steadily, something else began filtering its way through the fog of her gaze, something feral and hungry, something which Eisen had experienced the very first time he had met her.

Something that unnerved him as deeply as it excited him.

"You've got handsome eyes, Eisen. Any gal ever tell ya that?"

"No, just a couple of men."

She chuckled a little and then resumed her piercing, serious expression. She seemed straining to retain a dire focus through the haze of alcohol and weariness.

"Jen, I have to go."

"Why?"

"Because... I don't know."

"You been drinkin too, better lay on down fore ya fall down."

"No, I'm fine. It's you who've drank too much."

He began turning to the door, but was stopped by her suddenly shrill and panic-stricken voice.

"Please don't leave me. I don't want to be alone tonight. I know I'm surrounded by people, I always am, but the bigger the crowd, the lonelier I feel. I don't know why. Can't you just sit for a while? It's sure nice to talk to such an awful good listener, maybe that sounds dumb, but I don't care, it's true."

"All right."

He sat down like a man awaiting his execution, his face completely devoid of emotion and his poise stiff and awkwardly solemn.

"What did you want to talk about?"

"You."

"What about me?"

"How should I know? I ain't you, am I?"

"If you're this clever when you're drunk, I can't and won't even begin to fathom the depth of your sarcasm when you're sober."

She giggled.

"What?"

"You talk so funny."

"Why are you so giddy?"

"Because, I like you. Like talking to you, I mean."

"You don't even know me."

"You're right. "

She rolled over to where he sat, wrapping her arms about his waist as she did so.

"Let's get acquainted."

"Wha?"

"Intimately."

Pulling a face of utter bewilderment and perplexity, he shot up like a man afire and wordlessly left the room, knowing full well he should have left far sooner.

"Eisen? Eisen! Where are you going? Eisen?"

He didn't slow until he reached the bottom of the stairs where waited a disconcerting silence, followed by a small group of ragged-looking toughs who had been awaiting his descent.

The first man to break the silence was a beefy, red-faced, weather-worn man of about five and forty who wore a bright red bandana about his peculiarly squarish skull. He sat at the table closest to the stairwell and had his feet propped up on a stool which he had apparently stolen from the bar.

"Hey, boy?"

Eisen turned to the man without speaking.

"I said, 'HEY, BOY!'"

"You may enjoy repeating yourself, but I assure you, whoever you are, I do not."

"The sheriff was right, Pete, this one ain't nothing but trouble, mouthing off at ya like dat, ain't civil it ain't."

"No sir, Jimmy. No sir, it ain't. You want everyone here to think ya'll ain't civil, boy?"

"You can think what you please, but I'm going home."

"Oh now, that's where you're right and where you're wrong. I can think what I please, and I'm gonna, but you sure as shit ain't going home."

"And why is that?"

"Why don't you tell him, Jimmy, boy seems a little slow."

Jimmy approached with a haughty, ugly swagger, his lank arms swaying limply at his frayed, leathery sides like dead, emancipated boas. His knobbly, oversized fists like the knots of some malicious old willow tree.

"Well, ya see," he lurched forward and decked Eisen in the face, dropping him to the floor, "ya'll under arrest for the willful murder of Frank Adams, you smart-mouthing sumbitch! And we ain't gonna ask ya ta come peacefully, cuz honestly we don't give a good god damn bout asking ya nothing."

They scooped him up off the floor, the thin tall one and the boss with the red bandana, and carted him outside. Faintly aware of motion and a warm trickling from his nose, Eisen waited patiently, too weary and beaten to muster up a fight. Serves me right, he said to himself, under his breath, inaudible to anyone else. Serves me right for hitting her, serves me right.

Then, quite suddenly, he was acutely aware that his nose was gushing blood in heavy snaking torrents that plopped down upon his shirt and vest.

White cloth and skin, red sand and blood.

The sheriff was waiting for them in front of his desk, arms crossed and his fat, ugly lips working anxiously, like two ungainly brown slugs fighting for supremacy upon the bloated plane of his face.

When the portly lawman saw what his two deputies had done to the young coffin maker, he fairly flew out of his blotchy, sunburned skin. Eyes about to pop free of his distended skull, chin fat swiveling like falling yogurt, complexion fading from red to white.

"What in God's name?"

The skinny one, Jimmy, that had struck Eisen, threw him down at the sheriff's feet with as much unnecessary force as he was able to gather.

"You said ya wanted him brought in."

"I did Jimmy, but – Peter Joshua Logan, what the hell is the meaning of this?"

"We deputies, ain't we, he was resisting arrest."

Eisen, having struggled to a sitting position, flung his arm up over his left knee and let it dangle limply as he looked up in perplexity at the two roughs and their employer.

"Yeah, resisting arrest!" Jimmy put in heatedly.

"No, I wasn't."

"Shut your cock-sucking mouth, boy!"

Peter looked to his foul-mouthed partner with one eyebrow raised and shook his head almost imperceptibly, saying nothing.

Eisen rose to his feet, his eyes fixed on Jimmy who drew back and then, realizing that this was unacceptable behavior for the kind of persona he was attempting to project, drew forth once more with great agitation.

"Don't you eyeball me, you sumbitch!"

"Enough, Jim."

Jim and Logan turned to the sheriff who had last spoken, hesitant but not particularly concerned by his presence.

"Sheriff," Eisen began, "I take very little pleasure in violence and am most happy to avoid it, if able, but if your man here," his eyes were still fixed on Jimmy so he didn't bother to point "strikes me once more, I shall be compelled to offer my less than humble services to his family, free of charge."

"What's that, dick-shit?"

Jimmy advanced once again, now standing scant inches away from Eisen's sanguine speckled face. The coffin maker's eyes shone through the blood like emeralds through a ruby mask.

Logan shook his head again and chuckled to himself, walking off into the far corner of the room, opening a bottle of whiskey and storing it away as if it were lemonade.

The sheriff tensed visibly, but said nothing.

Stillness.

Then Jimmy swung, hard.

A blow that never connected with anything but Eisen's fleet and enduring palm.

Without further warning or visible effort, Eisen snapped his adversary's wrist as a child might snap off the head of a dandelion. His face expressionless, the coffin maker watched as the tough slid to the ground howling with such intensity that one would think he was trying to erase silence forever from the vast weave of the earth.

In the corner Peter Logan shook his head as he took another gulp of whiskey, the glass shining nearly as intensely as Eisen's eyes.

The sheriff looked on for a brief moment and then, regaining his composure, shouted "God DAMMIT!"

"Sheriff, he hurt me bad!"

"It's your own damn fault, you dumb hick," Logan taunted from the back of the room.

"Shut the hell up! Do something, Sheriff! Fuckin kill the bastard!"

"No one's killing anyone. All right, Eisen, get in one of the cells."

"Why?"

"Now don't make me– "

"Make you what?"

"Let's all just try and calm down. Damn!"

"He broke my fuckin wrist!"

Eisen, finally breaking his gaze from the pathetic creature withering in pain before him as before a king, begging to be spared the guillotine, turned slightly toward the quaking sheriff, looking at him solemnly.

"I am calm." And he was. Realizing that, the sheriff became even more unsure of himself and frightened of the coffin maker, turning toward Logan as if in expectation of some kind of guidance.

"What the hell you looking at me for, it's your jail, your mess. I was just following orders, like you said, it's Jim went off the hook."

The sheriff paused briefly, sweating and turning very pale.

"Now listen here, Eisen– "

"I am always listening, officer." He drawled the last word derisively.

"Yeah, well, you gave the confession. Everyone heard it, you murdered him."

"No."

"What the hell you mean, no?"

"I mean that I didn't murder anyone. I killed him in reasonable self-defense, and I don't feel the least bit bad about it. He and two other goons attacked me and my friend, this... Frank Adams, pulled a knife, I reacted. I tend to do that as well, I imagine, as you yourself might. You asked Kindle about what I had mentioned, I take it?"

"Yeah, about that. Her, we checked those bruises and, well, they were there, but there were also fresh ones as well, ya'll want ta explain dat?"

"Didn't she?"

"She wouldn't say anything. Now, ya wanna explain it?"

"No, but I shall do so anyway. I struck her, twice. I back-handed her for what she was about to do."

"And what was she about to do?"

He paused for a long while and then spoke solemnly.

"Kill herself."

The sheriff looked as if he had been struck harder than Jimmy, who had limped away to the back of the room, silently nursing his broken wrist and cursing under his wretched, whiskey-laden breath.

"I suppose you don't feel bad about that none, either?"

Eisen turned to the low, harsh voice rising up over the whiskey glass.

"No, Mr. Logan, I don't."

"Hell, Sheriff, don't lock him up, I like this one."

"Shut up, Logan!"

"Logan, Sheriff, you had better get this man to the doctor to see about that wrist."

The sheriff flung up his hands and began massaging his left temple, "Both of you shut up, I need to think."

The lawman then walked around his desk and sat down heavily, the chair creaking ominously beneath his considerable weight, and commenced thinking (or at the very least, attempted to).

Eisen surveyed the three men each in turn: Fat, thin, athletic. Then again, only more perceptively: Confused, foolish, and cunning.

Out of the three, only the latter was of any interest to the bloodied coffin maker. He directed his calm-eyed gaze toward the weathered face, impossibly contorted through the fun house facade of the shot glass.

"Tell me, Mr. Logan, what is it about me that you like?"

"Your honesty. Anymore a body cain't even find honestly dishonest folk."

"Honestly?"

"Honestly. You're not gonna hold nothing gainst ole Jimmy here for, well..." he gestured to Eisen's messy clothes and blood-speckled face "all that, are ya?"

"No. Not in the slightest. But next time you decide to apprehend a suspect, just ask them to come along before you decide to beat them."

"Didn't spare no time attacking me, didja?"

Eisen turned to Jimmy with a deadpan gaze and a brow so subtly arched as to not be arched at all.

Under this renewed disapproval, Jimmy fell silent once more and averted his eyes to the ground, his filthy, tattered shoes, anything but Eisen's disturbingly immobile face.

"No, Jim, I didn't."

Logan laughed.

The sheriff looked apprehensively about and then slapped his desk.

"Come on now, Dawggoneit! All right, Eisen, we'll call in Kindle, and if'n ya story checks out, you can both git."

"What do you mean, both?"

"If I find out she's been lying for ya, I'ma gonna lock ya both up, ya understand?"

"Yes. Perfectly. But to tell you truthfully I don't think she knows how to lie."

"Now what the hell does that mean?"

"Never mind."

"All right. Logan?"

"Yeah?"

"Go find the girl, bring her back ere. Jim?"

"Wha?"

"Go find the doctor for that hand of yours and keep sober."

"I will if'n you will."

"What's that?"

"Nothing."

"All right then. Mr. Torquiam, step into one of those cells, you'll be staying with me until we get your girl."

Eisen turned back to the fat lawman and held his gaze until the sheriff averted his eyes, speaking hesitantly and quickly.

"That is, if you want to. I mean, don't make no difference ta me whether you sit in the cell or one of these chairs."

Logan chuckled, still shaking his head and left the building, followed shortly thereafter by his morose and brooding partner, still cradling his damaged wrist.

Eisen watched them go and then removed his hat and walked up to the sheriff and placed it on the officer's balding, naked head.

Wordlessly the coffin maker stepped away.

He walked easily into the third and last cell, feeling the cool, soothing bars of metal against his warm, rough palms and sat down on the ratty cot. There was nothing on the hard dirt floor, save for a couple of stones and an empty, old wooden bucket. "Hold on to that for me, Sheriff, it has sentimental value. Not much else, but it'll do for me... like as your badge does for you."

The sheriff didn't know what to make of that, so he tried to make nothing of it at all. He waited until Eisen lay down on the cot and then removed the handcrafted hat and gingerly hung it on the coat rack to the right of his desk. Then the fat man sat down, looked at his prisoner, sighed and rubbed his temples again, starring at the huge pile of papers set upon his desk.

☼

It was nearly half an hour later when Logan finally returned, alone and somewhat put out.

The sun was setting behind the town, filtering in red and luminous like the blood of some dying god through the high, iron-barred windows of the jail. Logan and the sheriff were masked by deep, dancing shadows, the former sitting before the latter and shaking his head as Eisen, effulgent as a fire-bound martyr, watched from the cot on which he calmly sat. His bright, shining eyes weaving to the ebb and flow of the dying light, the bend and turn of the conversation, the to and fro of people outside going purposefully about their daily business.

"Well?"

Logan sat down and poured himself a generous helping of whiskey before he answered his employer.

Over the rim of the shot glass he said, "That prim little bastard has her."

"Who? What bastard?"

"Michael."

"What?"

"The preacher's son."

"I said, what, not, who."

"Yeah."

"I know who he is, Logan; what do ya mean, he has her?"

"I mean just like I say. He's keeping her at the church, tells me it isn't safe to let her out, that she's spiritually imbalanced, whatever the fuck that means. All the people were with him on it."

"Well you should have reminded him that we're the law round here; should have just taken er."

"I tried and I nearly had a mob at my throat for it."

"But we're The Law!"

Logan chuckled in his acerbic, nihilistic manner, shaking his head.

"That's what I said, Sheriff. And he said, 'I abide by a higher law.'"

The portly lawman nodded his head solemnly.

"I suppose it isn't our place ta question that."

Tersely Eisen began to laugh, deeply and bitterly, a sound mocking and completely devoid of any touch of mirth or humor.

The sheriff spun round as if he had been branded.

"What in hell is so damned funny in there?"

"Absolutely nothing, your highness."

"Don't get tart with me, boy!"

"Or what? You'll send Jim in after me?"

"Logan, you better teach that boy a lesson in manners."

Logan slid his hollow, glinting glass hesitantly across the small, messy surface of the wooden desk, a crisp cylinder of diamond, and then leaned back idly and wagged his finger at Eisen as one might gesture to a naughty child, saying only, "Bad. Stop. Sit. Roll over, good boy."

The sheriff waited tensely for further action.

None came.

He burst like a lanced cyst.

"This is serious, hang it all, serious, Logan! Ya understand! Do ya?"

"Yeah, sure. Not really. What's so serious about it?"

"He's a murderer." He was whispering now, leaning toward Logan tautly. "A murderer, Logan, in my jail."

"Yeah, in ya jail." Logan made no attempt to lower his voice, even glancing briefly, impassively at Eisen; once, twice.

Eisen leaned out from the shadows, grinning playfully, "Yes, I'm getting rather to like it here; cozy. Snug, even."

"Shut your damn mouth!"

"My dear sheriff, is that any way to terrorize a suspect? A paltry performance, you're not going to scare anyone with that act. Not a one. What you need is a blade, something vicious and wicked, like what so handsomely adorns Mr. Logan's belt there, something to really put the fear of death into the helpless and the innocent. Now that'd get your blood going, wouldn't it?"

"Innocent? The hell ya innocent!"

"I didn't say me. Though whatever I am, I'm certainly not guilty."

The sheriff studied Eisen's face, a face without pain or guilt or fear. A face like a marble statue made flesh and a mind behind it more immovable than any statue what had ever been wrought by mortal hands. With a jolt of panic the sheriff spun quickly around, too quickly, and set himself to inspecting his papers, pretending to be diligently working so as to distract himself from the terrible apprehension which now powerfully gripped him in a way he could not entirely grasp or define. With a sinking heart he came to the realization that this incompetence brought him lower still. Down into realms of descension. Where men met themselves and were made.

Or unmade.

As the lawman retreated from his pose of fragile hostility, Eisen languidly withdrew, once more, into the shadows of the prison cell, now enveloped in darkness so thick one could nearly taste it upon the tongue.

"GOD DAMN SHITS!"

The heads of Logan, the sheriff and Eisen all turned in perfect unison as to have been prearranged to the raging violence of the voice which had suddenly and completely shattered the fragile patina of silence permeating the dingy, ramshackle jail.

In the doorway a figure swayed momentarily and then nearly fell through the threshold.

It was Jen Arlington.

Bottle in hand and as drunk as a love-sick sailor.

There was a look of such extreme and uncontrolled rage set upon her face, that for a moment her presence silenced the tongues of all the onlookers in the room.

"Wha in hell is going on here! Whyiz e ina ya jail! You tell me now, Sheriff! Right god-damned now!"

"Miss Arlington, calm down now."

"The hell I will!"

She lumbered forth, raising the bottle over her head and smashing it upon the sheriff's desk; glass and whiskey went careening about the room like so many meteorites.

Logan shot up from his chair and took her by the arm, twisting it firmly and causing her to wince with the pain.

"You better come along out of here and not make no more of a fuss n you already have, Jen."

"Or what, whiskey breath? Ya'll arrest me for insulting an officer? Destruction of private property?"

She broke free, kicking her former captor in the left shin with as much force as she could muster and then whirled on the sheriff, a dire look in her young and fevered eyes.

"You let him go you fat, scheming bastard! Let eim go right now!"

Logan, having recovered from her blow, grabbed her about the waist and lifted her up over his broad shoulders and carted her out of the building saying only, "Whiskey breath? That's mighty funny coming from you, miss, mighty funny."

Eisen watched these events with a look of bewilderment and sadness; bewilderment because he couldn't understand why she had become taken with him, and sadness because he knew that her outburst in his defense would not be forgotten. And that such memories would bear foul of her fortune, sooner or later.

Half an hour later this notion was wholly validated when a man the coffin maker had never seen before entered with the trim, tidy, cigarette-poising printer, Elis Caldwell.

The man, who walked before Caldwell, was tall and stately in his bearing and, despite a pronounced limp, carried no cane. He wore a fastidiously immaculate trench coat of the highest quality over a well-tailored suit of black, large, well-groomed mustache and slickly parted hair. His face was long and proud, and sad and tinged about with strange little blotches, sun spots perhaps.

It was this man who spoke first.

"Where is my daughter, Sheriff?"

"Don't know."

"She was here though, yes, Hanes?"

"What makes you think that?"

"She's done run off again, and every time she does I find her down around here consorting with the despicable rabble you seem so fond of employing."

Looking utterly cowed, the sheriff shook his head and stuttered out a string of half coherent words in his feeble attempt at defense, raising his good arm up as if he expected the old man to lash him for his incompetence.

"I-I'm not fond of employing r-rabble! See here! If'n they turn out ta be, what kin I do bout it?"

"Fire them."

"Fire them? They lawd above! Wouldn't be godly."

"Wouldn't it?"

"I don't know."

"Sheriff, you are wasting my time, and I've little enough left to spare you, let alone my poor, feckless daughter. I just want to know where she is."

"I already told you, sir, I don't know. Logan carried her out of here not half an hour ago."

"What?"

"Er– "

"He carried my daughter out? I'd like you to explain yourself, Mr. Logan. What is the meaning of this?"

"She came in here cussing up a storm and drunker 'in a skunk. Broke a bottle over the sheriff's desk, poor man. Nearly pissed hisself."

"Logan, now you watch it, boy!"

Peter Logan, who wasn't even remotely boyish, merely grinned defiantly and leaned back in his chair, eyes darting back and forth between Mr. Arlington and Hanes.

Rather abruptly Elis Caldwell, who had until this moment not spoken a single, solitary word, cut, with forceful reserve, into the middle of the tiff.

"Gentlemen. And I use that term loosely. Tell us where she is."

Peter Logan glared up at Caldwell for a moment and then took a deep breath and pointed to the inn across the street.

"She's at Arrgilius'?"

"Yeah, Caldwell, that iz were I'z pointin, ain't it? Told him to keep an eye on her till she sobered some."

"Your sarcasm, as always, Logan, is much appreciated."

And with that the two men disappeared into the settling middle-dark that fell as a giant's shawl across the wide lane of dust and dirt and the bones of beasts and men among them far below, all along the open and outer space beyond the jail.

"He beats her, often, harshly. Someone should do something about it."

The sheriff got up and poured himself a drink, pretending not to listen. Logan perked up and leaned forward in his chair, craning his head toward the vague, near formless shadow shape of Eisen de Torquiam.

"Who beats who?"

"Don't listen to him, Logan. He's just trying to stir things up."

The voice in the darkness spoke once more.

"Mr. Arlington, he beats his daughter, not that such a tradition is particularly surprising in such a town as this... if the word even applies."

This flippant remark hotly incited the sheriff's ire, however lukewarm and feebly it was distilled.

"And what is that supposed to mean?"

"It is supposed to mean exactly what I think you think it does. If I had intended it to mean more or less, I would have held or stretched my tongue accordingly."

"You've got quite a mouth on you, boy."

"Do I? Is it pretty?"

"What?"

"No? Not a come-on? Oh. My mistake."

"I can't deal with this now. You handle him, Logan. I need... something."

The sheriff hurried from the jail to the inn like a fish too long deprived of water, and gasping and shaking with the force of his privations.

"Souse-soaked slag. How do you know what ya claim, Eisen?"

"That Mr. Arlington abuses a member of his own family?"

"Yeah."

"I don't know to a certainty, but I'd wager strongly upon that being the most likely conclusion one can draw from my inferences."

"What inferences?"

"The standard ones."

"Which would consist of what?"

"When I observed her earlier today, at the inn, she was hunched up, brooding, clearly in the deepest of fashions, and when she turned round she had a fading bruise upon her face, the left side. I have no doubt that were you to examine the rest of her body, and were she to allow you to, which is quite doubtful, you would discover several more such blemishes. Poor choice of words perhaps. Blemishes, that's almost funny."

"What makes you think it was her old man?"

"She doesn't have a boyfriend."

"So?"

"And she told me."

"What?"

"That he did it."

"Who? Her boyfriend? Thought ya said she didn't have one?"

Eisen tilted his head, waiting for the inevitable punch line.

"Nah, I'm just messing with ya."

"I think I now understand the basic concept of Logan."

"Whaddoyamean?"

"I mean you're chuckling not because you actually find it funny, a father savagely striking his daughter, but because you find these situations extremely discomforting because you don't think there is much you can do about them. So you pass your anxiety off as a joke, albeit, a blackened one at that."

Logan was silent a moment and then, "Whatever helps you sleep at night."

"It is not I that will have trouble sleeping this night, Peter Logan, not I."

Then Eisen laid down upon the tattered cot within the cell and fell into a deep sleep populated by strange wonders and foul aberrations.

☼

Out along the plane of bleak ash, endlessly gray, there jutted bizarre constructs that framed the sun, or whatever remained thereof in that pallid, sterile expanse. For the brilliant, gaudy sphere, that golden globe of radiant salvation now but a shadow-shell of its former self, hung like a desiccated corpse from the salivating tendrils of the sky, held there by slender chains that rattled like a battle cry of the shackled and dispossessed.

It took Eisen a moment to realize what the peculiar jumble of unadorned monoliths really was – a town.

A town without color, or vibrancy, without sound or the festivities of a merry heart beating therein.

A town of gray, phantasmagorical shapes.

Wraiths and hollow-men, as empty as the buildings they failed to inhabit.

These wayward shapes being both form and function, both the living and the dead and that which had never lived at all, and that which, thus, could never be expected to die, only decay.

In the very center of the phantom metropolis there loomed the largest tower of all. So massive was this harrowing edifice that its shadow lay long and thick and cloying from its base all the way past the edge of the horizon. This grand and enigmatic construct did not rise up from the dust, there implanted, like all the rest, but rather seemed as if it had burst from the very bowels of the earth. For it stood full from and within a seething crater of boundless fog and endless depth. Fearful reaches unfathomable. And it was upon the edge of this crater that Eisen stood, looking up at the tiny stone windows or doors or arrow shafts that riddled the surface of the lifeless behemoth, such as pores might the skin of an old man, impossibly weathered and feeble, yet enduring, undying, immortal by sole sanction of his will alone and no other.

A will with which no other could contend.

The base of this structure, fettered ever in a thick pall of swirling mist, was so thin and brittle looking that Eisen wouldn't have believed that such a column could support even a quarter of the top of the structure had he not seen it suspended there himself.

Not 300 feet from him, emerging from the dust unto the fog, there shambled a bizarre procession of figures. Men and women, all solemn and badly burned and cloaked in mangy furs and bloody wraps. Their feet were bare and bleeding, their eyes feverish and wide, seeing nothing that was before them, behind them, observing only that which existed within. Indeed they seemed fairly blind, for they groped languidly before them, some carrying canes or staffs, pounding the dirt and dust with them and all seeming grave, yet eager with some kind of rare sense of anticipation.

In the center of their ebb and flow there walked a little girl, moving as if in a dream, sure in her movements, yet unsure whether there was really movement at all. This perfect little creature, sun-kissed and pure, had large blue eyes that looked up from hair so pale blond it appeared nearly white and seemed the entirety of all that the town had ever lost or never had at all.

Her garb was different from her escorts; a long silken dress with a wide hood from under which she gazed with unaffected tranquility. She walked without assistance, sometimes looking to the high faces about her; they never looked back.

As Eisen watched them he drew back gasping, realizing with sudden terror that they were trekking straight to the edge of the cliff, straight into that dark, unending maw. For all appearances it seemed as if the procession remained completely unaware of the danger to which they approached with such stalwart determination.

Shouting at the top of his lungs and waving his arms above his jumping form, Eisen waited for them to make some sign of acknowledgment, some cry or movement.

There was none.

None at all.

It was as if they could not hear him, or if they could, merely ignored him. Only the little girl turned and held his gaze, a motion of the greatest brevity, as she stepped from the edge of the world and vanished into the whirling depths of the fog. Eisen screamed, rushing forward, fearfully, futilely.

Rushing.

Though there was no wind, the fog continually spun round the base of the great edifice, as if by some volition or desire of its own. Moments after the grim procession had vanished, the curtain of cloud, which had previously shrouded them, parted as if for the prelude to a play, revealing a checkered bridge of black and white that hung suspended by some force at which even the greatest intelligence could only guess. The tattered and dull-eyed travelers moved upon that bridge, held aloft from the fevered, flowing world beneath them, moving toward the tower. With slow sluggish steps the coffin maker approached the hovering span of the chess-textured construct, his eyes rarely leaving the travelers. He could no longer see the little girl.

He inhaled deeply, and it was as if that breath and the depth thereof and its consequent expurgation were the summation of his fears and the soothing erasure thereof.

Silence, and the form of a man that appeared as a loathsome, eternal adversary, rising from the riven breast of the planetary, rising from a sea of fog like bitter words as radiant brands through the fabric of scuttled dreams.

Silence, then the sound of footfalls on an unbound bridge and that form crossing it like the crossing of one idea to another. A transfer of conviction in the sound of heels and soles and the grinding of stone. A solidification of conviction.

To Eisen it seemed almost as if he had been walking for nearly a week entire before he came out full and unscathed upon the other side of the bridge. Before he emerged onto the grim monolith, he heard a fell voice taint the air like blood muddying any sullen pond.

Then two.

Next three.

Now forty.

Maybe more.

The ground beneath him seemed to have been crafted of the bones of great beasts, the milky white of their forms impossibly fused and molded as easily as wet clay to create a landscape of pitted divergence. Looking about himself directly, he seemed to be standing in what had once been the jaws of some great and fearsome predator, but where the mandibles ended and the rest of the tower began, he couldn't quite tell. He moved beyond a cluster of what appeared to be a myriad of horribly contorted spines in just enough time to discover the members of that inexorable procession disappear up a stairway of enormous hands, fleshless and frozen.

Beckoning.

There was then a fire in the sky, the shell of the sun but a pale remnant in comparison, bursting and fuming as if to birth a galaxy or consume another. A rain of ash rained that day, and the coffin maker moved beyond the earth, ascending the hands, as the walls closed in upon him faster and faster.

Faster still.

A pinpoint of light so blue and pure as to nourish the soul, were man to have possession of such a contrivance, appeared suddenly as he wound higher and more hastily from the dismal confines of that blasted heath. And in it, upon it, and round it he emerged, gasping and stumbling into a circular room as colorless as the wasted town-land beneath it.

Gray walls and gray lives within it.

An altar rose up upon a dais from the perfect center of the cell and the relentless procession of travelers ringing it round.

There appeared to be something upon the dais.

He moved in closer to see what it was. Gasping, he drew back.

A little girl lay nude upon the stone, the robe discarded upon the cold floor and her face devoid of emotion, a dagger clutched in her pale, delicate hands.

Shouting at the top of his lungs, Eisen approached this grotesque carnival with repulsed incredulity, addressing them with terror and rage.

"What is this, this... madness?"

None turned.

None spoke.

None moved.

None heeded him at all.

He tried to approach, to intervene in whatever impending travesty was about to befall that fragile little life, but the floor rose to his impediment, fangs and claws of bone and bane rising to strike him down.

Brought full to his knees, bloodied and bound, he looked up and then averted his gaze at what he saw, so dense and crystalline was the dark revulsion before him.

A creature appeared in the chamber, tall as three men entire and thinner than a starving child. It was garbed in an elegant robe of purest white cloth. It had no face at all nor any hair upon it, and its hands had but three fingers each, without nails or discernible joints of any kind. This foul aberration loomed above the girl, running its disjointed limbs over her pale body as if in arcane consecration. The members of the processional raised their hands into the air, shrieking with sudden fury that blood began to pour from Eisen's ringing ears like so many serpents struggling for an exit from that spherical dark.

The girl looked to the creature with serenity clouding her eyes. And then drove the dagger down into her heart.

He couldn't speak, couldn't hear, couldn't move. All the coffin maker could do was think, and he didn't want to inflict that upon himself, either.

He shut his eyes against the furious strain of the horror of that unspeakable act. When he opened them, he moaned and began to cry. For the monstrosity that had so tangibly coaxed and soothed the girl had now assumed her visage, its blank, faceless head slowly dripping away like burning flesh and melting wax to reveal the stark blue eyes of the little girl. The button nose, the pale blond hair, the soft, healthy lips and the curve of a small delicate chin.

The abomination turned to Eisen.

A meeting of eyes.

Child's to a man's.

Then the face distorted once more, and it was Eisen staring back at himself.

A feeling.

Dire sensation.

Something warm and wet. Sticky.

He looked down at his hands which had previously been pinned to his heaving chest; they came away slick with blood.

His eyes widened as he realized that the dagger the little girl had previously buried in her chest only moments before was now protruding from his own.

Gasping and spitting his life's blood upon the floor, he saw a shadow pall his vision.

He looked up and beheld an umbrella.

An umbrella of starkest white and a man with a crescent moon smile and eyes nothing but hollow pits of shade, deeper and darker than any infernal dog that had ever sucked the marrow.

As Eisen's skin split and ruptured like overfed maggots dangled above a furnace flame, the man with the albescent umbrella laughed.

And it was a laugh that shook the earth and split the sky.

GRAVE.

Weakened strands of daylight spilled over the unnerved sleeper's contorted form as his eyelids quivered and then retracted. He looked about through the rusting cell bars, breathing heavily, his heart beating like a madman's tympanum. Neither the sheriff nor Jimmy were anywhere in sight. Only Logan still resided with the attentive prisoner. Judging from the quality of the light and time of year, Eisen approximated it to be around six or so. He had hoped and counted on sleeping more and better; so tired was he still, in addition to the weakening effects of the dream, that he could scarcely bring himself to rise.

When finally he did so, his cot creaked loudly, shaking Logan furiously from the throes of a restless sleep.

Their eyes met.

"It appears I was wrong, Logan."

"Manly of you ta acknowledge the corn on that."

"Oh? At any rate it was not pangs of conscience that kept me fettered to the waking world."

"And what did?"

"Dreams."

"Nightmares?"

There was a long, dense, uninterrupted pause. Eisen looked off toward the corner of the cell, a flash of pain in his eyes, with stiff, heavy, languid movements, as if he were struggling through a rising wetland of consumption.

He looked back very slowly at his jailer, his face returning to the shelter of darkness cast by the high walls of the Spartan compartment.

"Yes. Nightmares."

"You have them often?"

"Yes. Very often."

Eisen shook his head and rubbed his foggy eyes with the heels of his hands.

"Almost every night. And you? Do you dream much, Logan?"

"No, not hardly at all, probably I drink too much."

They both chuckled strangely as Logan set two glasses upon the table. He had rather arrogantly usurped the absent sheriff's chair and had set to lording over it like a king, his feet thrown haughtily up on the right corner of the desk. Diving into the ice chest, he produced a bottle of spirits and poured both shot glasses half full (his, admittedly, higher than Eisen's) and then rose and, with glasses in hand, ambled to the bars. He extended his left hand unhesitatingly through the divide, not in the slightest concerned about the prospect of violence, and proffered the glass to the shadow-masked prisoner who smiled faintly and took it with a respectful nod.

"Logan, when you were at the church, you said that Kindle was there with Luce, yes?"

"Yeah, Luce and his son, Michael."

"And did you see her when you were there?"

"Well, no, actually. They said she weren't feeling aright, and I mean what with all that had happened, a body kin understand. Now you tell me something."

"All right."

"Y'all really don't feel bad bout it?"

"What is it?"

"You know what I mean."

"There are two things that spring to mind, but no, I don't."

"About hitting her."

"I thought you meant the man that attacked me."

"Hell no, he was violent and reckless as they come. If you hadn'ta finished him, someone else would have, sooner or later. I had always thought the same would happen to me."

"You're still young, give it time."

Logan laughed, at first mirthfully, then ambiguously, finally sadly, dryly, darkly.

"You may be more right then you know. You still haven't answered my question."

"No. I haven't. But I will. First, however, I want to ask you one more question."

"Shoot."

"What, to your mind, is the best single word with which to describe the moral code of most cultures?"

"What kind of question is that?"

"A very hard one. Concentrate."

"Can't rightly say. I just don't know. What word are you thinking of?"

"Sadistic."

"Sadistic?"

"Yes, as in the Marquis de Sade."

"The what?"

"The Marquis de Sade."

"Who?"

"Never mind. The important thing is that you know what the word means, and what it means is precisely what most people mean by 'morality.'"

"I'm not following. But I am feeling a speech coming on."

"Ah, but that is the difference between me and most of the people in this town; I speak, they preach."

"What's the difference?"

"If you don't know, then you're not the man that I had you figured for."

"I don't understand what exactly you're trying to get at, cuz you didn't exactly strike me as the kind of man that was stupid enough to try to bribe ya way out a here with flattery."

"Bribery! How despicable. I'm insulted. Take it back."

"I kin never tell whether ya being serious or just damn snarky."

"Why does everyone keep telling me that?"

"Probably, cuz it's true."

"Am I really so mysterious?"

"I'd say so."

"That's certainly very queer."

"Why?"

"I've endeavoured all my life to lay bare the complexity of nature, especially my own. To expose the unknown for what it usually is: Cowardice in a charlatan's dress."

"I was about to ask you whether you used to do stage work, but I figured ya'll been asked that before."

"Only every other day."

Logan nodded, suppressing a smile and finishing off his glass.

Eisen watched him with a focus that was born of some powerful inner desire, the shadows twining about his hair like so many macabre tendrils; the light chasing them away with every turning.

"Logan?"

"Yeah?"

"You said you knew the man I killed. Would you speak on my behalf, or would the precarious position of your paycheck mute your tongue?"

"Ta be honest, I got no reason to care, one way or the other."

"If that were true, you would not have gifted me with a glass."

Eisen then held his still-full drink up before the older man's eyes; it glinted in the sunlight like liquid gold or so much fire.

The coffin maker swilled the beverage playfully, tauntingly, within the bounds of the tiny glass and then poured it down his throat; gulping, grinning.

Unfazed.

"You're not such a whelp after all."

"If I were a whelp, I would have let your friend have more fun with me."

"Good point."

"I don't endeavor to make bad ones."

"Your jaw's oilier than a toad's backside."

Eisen's brows nearly scratched the ceiling so high did they archedly purport themselves.

"Is that a compliment?"

"That's for me to know and you to find out. Look, I'll do what I can. He had it coming. I don't know you well enough to say whether you have or not, but frankly, I'd wager against it."

Eisen smiled.

"Thanks."

Chapter Fifteen

Freedom and Proposition

In the morning the jail received another visitor, one of more portly countenance and garish disposition than those preceding him.

None other than Ledru Monteblanc himself.

"What is this here? I was sure it'd just been a rumor that you had been locked up!" Even though it was plain for everyone to see that he was lying through his oversized and slightly crooked teeth.

"Why do you think that, Ledru?"

"Ah, how very impertinent to address an employer by his first name."

"Are you being serious?"

It was readily unclear whether Ledru Monteblanc was sure or not himself, so he merely changed the subject.

"Logan, where is our dear sheriff?"

"Out."

"Out where?"

"Donno, just out."

"That doesn't help me."

"Nope. Guess it don't."

"Well, then, Mr. Logan, would you care to explain why this kind young man is locked up?"

"Cuz it's the law."

"What's the law?"

"You mean you haven't heard bout it?"

"Bout what?"

"Why, he kilt old Frank Adams."

"Who?"

Logan merely frowned and shook his head.

"You don't mean to tell me, Mr. Logan, that Eisen did this!"

"Yep, actually that's exactly what I mean to tell you. Ask. Go on."

"But..."

"No buts about it, ask him. He'll tell you, he told the preacher readily enough."

"A confession?"

Eisen walked to the bars, grasping them authoritatively.

"No, Ledru, an explanation."

"Would you care to give me one as well?"

"Certainly. I did in fact kill this... Frank Adams, but the matter is not so precisely drawn as Logan has stated. I was assailed, attacked by Adams, disrepute, I am told, and a violent man, both black marks against him and for my favor. I was attacked and I defended myself and my friend. Simple as that."

"There was a witness to this grave business?"

"Three actually, only one, though, will be of any immediate use to you."

Logan cut in rudely, suddenly.

"It's strange to find you only just now hearing bout this, Mr. Monteblanc."

"Yes. Well, folk don't speak as freely as they once did, after..."

Eisen poised a question with a challenging gaze, "After what?"

"Nothing. My thoughts are scattered like so many leaves. I believe you were going to explain this rotten affair to me. And I wish you would. How would it look for me if folk began to think I had a penchant for killers and toughs?"

"I am a killer. I will not apologize. He should have stayed his hand; he didn't, so I did as much for him."

"Why this is extraordinary! Logan, why didn't the sheriff inform me immediately?"

"You ain't the mayor here, oilman, no matter how much you may think you are."

"We shall just have to change that, shan't we?"

Logan merely shrugged and sipped from his glass.

At that moment something peculiar occurred. The sheriff came fairly hurling in through the doorway with someone close behind. This someone turned out to be none other than Ledru's blind partner, Statletter.

The sheriff spoke to Eisen with something like despair. "You're free to go."

"Why is that?"

"Now you listen, boy, an you listen good. You leave for I change my mind."

"Why do I get the feeling that it wasn't you who changed it?"

The sheriff shook with impulsive rage, but was quieted by Logan who languidly stretched out his hand for the cell key.

Logan opened the door and, smiling slightly, handed the young coffin maker his personal effects. Then he resumed his seat as if nothing whatever had happened as Eisen meticulously inspected his hat, checking for signs of damage. Finding none, he placed his most prized possession back upon his crown, straightened the brim and lowered it just above his eye line. Then he looked to the image of silent screaming fire outside the enclosed dimness of his surroundings and put on his glasses.

Statletter turned and left whilst Ledru waited for the former prisoner with a smile that was a bit too big and bright to be believed.

"Shall we, Mr. Monteblanc?"

"After you, sir, after you."

"All right."

Once the trio had all properly emerged from the jail, Eisen whirled on Statletter with squinting eyes and a certain strain to his voice.

"It was you, wasn't it?"

"Yes."

"How honest of you."

"I don't lie to folk what will know it when they hear it."

"I take back my former comment."

"You seem angry over it."

"No, I'm off-put over it."

"Why?"

"Because when people pull strings for you, especially these kinds of strings, it's rarely because they like your face."

"Ah, but I do like your face."

The old man laughed as Ledru jabbed the ground beneath him impatiently with the tips of his mirror-finished shoes. He was clearly putting off a lot to be where he was and trying ever so hard not to let it show. Trying, but failing.

"Ledru, is something on your mind?" And upon closer inspection, the ruddy-haired gentleman did seem to be deep in the folds of thoughts both dismal and dire.

"No, no, just this wretched business – a killing! A killing in this town! Extraordinary! Absolutely extraordinary! And what with them telling me I've no say about it! No respect! None atall! Without me, this town would be nothing but a church and a graveyard and the two or three people that such embellishments require! This town wouldn't exist as it is without me, and what do they do? What do they do? Spit in my face. I've tried and tried and tried, but they just won't accept me. Whatever I do, they turn their backs to me!"

"Once a few of the rougher, rowdier boys even tried to run us out of town. Isn't that right, Ledru?" said Statletter.

Ledru nodded his bulbous and volcanic head slowly, mournfully. Clearly it was a painful memory. In fact, he seemed more disconcerted by the town's rejection than he did of the killing. Eisen didn't know what to make of that.

Eisen turned back to Ledru and began walking away from the ramshackle jail. The blind man perked up his head, cocked an ear and began to follow, ready for the questions he knew would soon emerge.

"Well, what happened? Clearly they failed to run you out of town."

"Tell him, Ledru."

"No, you're the storyteller. I haven't the tongue for it."

GRAVE.

"Very well. Our mutual friend behind us thought it was best just to leave. Violence has always turned his stomach, you see, and though he could have easily brought them down with the servants, or hired personal security to do it, and with proper cause, I might add, since they were throwing rocks through his windows and mashing up his property. But no, he decided that it would just be better to pack up and leave."

"You make me out to be a coward!"

"I never used the word."

Eisen intervened firmly, "Go on with the story, Statletter."

"Right. Well, I talked him down out of that flighty tree and he decided against his instinct – and really it's been all for the best – but since that time, the mood of the people has darkened against us, quite markedly."

"Why?"

"We had to shoot one of the vandals."

"What? Who?"

"A queer question coming from you, Mr. Torquiam. You wouldn't know him and he is long since dead. At any rate, he was a good friend of the preacher's, a devout member of the church. You know, didn't work on Sundays, fasted, prayed three times a day, that sort of thing."

"I would assume that such a horrible event would conjure up some unpleasant emotions, for both of you. Even now."

There was a curious exchange between the two, and then Ledru broke in rather too tersely.

"Oh... well, not really, onward and upward, that's what I always say."

"Indeed? I concur. Well, Statletter, what happened then, what was this man doing that forced you into such a corner?"

Statletter smiled humorlessly and twirled his cane rhythmically at his side.

"Well, it wasn't me that was forced, and even if it were, my marksmanship was dreadful even before" he motioned to his empty sockets, "the incident."

"You know what I mean."

"Do I? Yes, I suppose I do. He, the man Ledru shot, broke into the manor. He had a knife. A big one. A big one which the ruffian threatened to use on our mutual and portly companion. Ledru picked up his rifle and shot the fool dead before he could do any more damage."

"Any more?"

"He stabbed one of our servants, nearly killed him. The bloke survived, thanks to Mr. Monteblanc."

"You seem quite the hero, Ledru."

"Not at all. Pish posh! Ha! A hero... how absurd. Businessmen aren't allowed to be heroes. It's an unwritten rule."

"Is it? Well, at any rate, you gentlemen have not yet told me why you are both willing to go to such lengths for me."

Ledru looked uncomfortably toward his partner; a silent, wary exchange.

"Come now, young man, you're not as slow as all that."

"No, I'd imagine I'm a might bit slower. So you tell me."

Statletter smiled deviously, his delight obvious.

"Our friend Ledru is ever the soul of delicacy. He has always been sensitive to scandal, overly sensitive if you ask me, but of course, you didn't. What you asked me, us, really, was why we are showing you such kindness. Well here's why, my friend. We brought you here, hired you as it were, not for your wood work, but for the talents of your tongue."

Ledru was aghast and made his apprehension known.

"Percival, this isn't the place for this kind of discussion."

"Why not, no one's listening."

And indeed the street was practically deserted. The few that still occupied it strolled about absently, paying the trio no heed whatsoever.

"Go on, Statletter. What do you mean, the talents of my tongue?"

"The reason I was pleased when I first spoke to you was because you were honest, direct, and most importantly, clever. It is cleverness that is lacking, and cleverness which may yet save this town."

"You mean you wanted me to smooth things over for you and Ledru with the locals?"

"In brief, yes."

"And you're telling me all of this because your plan has fallen rather flat."

"As flat as possible, really. What on earth have you been saying to garner such vehemence? You're even less well liked than Ledru, and you haven't even been here a month!"

"Ha!"

"Do you think this is funny?"

"Yes."

"This is a very serious matter, Eisen."

"I can see you certainly think so."

"Will you help us?"

"I will do exactly as I have been doing."

"Am I to take that as a no?"

"Take it anyway you like. I'm only stating that I was hired for a job that I intend to do for as long as I stay here. No more or less should you – can you – expect from me."

"And what if we were to pay you for another job?"

"Which would consist of?"

"Percival!"

"All right! Damn it all. Eisen, would you accompany us for a little while, so that we may continue this discussion in private?"

"Sure."

He followed them to a four-man carriage helmed by none other than the glum, sunburnt and terminally pea-coated servant, Sievers, who mumbled something frenetically under his breath as Eisen passed. The coffin maker was all but assured that the utterance was anything but friendly and most likely obscene.

He said nothing.

A few moments before Eisen was even comfortably within the four-in-hand, Sievers raised his whip and lashed down upon the hapless animals before him with all the increase of a savage thunderhead, unbound. The carriage jolted fitfully forward over the rough and sand-strewn terrain and they were off, clacking and clattering down the road like a doll cart in an earthquake. They continued along for some time with only trivial, passing comments breaking the peculiarly noticeable silence. After about twenty minutes of this tumultuous traversal, Sievers pulled the rail-coach to a sudden stop.

Eisen had been so intent upon his suspicious companions that he utterly neglected his surroundings during the short trip. Having stopped, he instantly regained his bearings, peering with his keen and consuming eyes through the small carriage windows, caked with an unseemly accumulation of cigarette and cigar resin. The fruit of his endeavor was revealed in the peculiar image that presented itself to him.

The tower which rose out of the bloody alcahest, the pitted skin of the world, was liken to the tooth or fang of some near unimaginable entity from times long since forgone. Some monolithic metal monstrosity, and yet for all that looming structures grotesquerie, it retained a subtle shimmer of industry, of promise, of hope. A dark and smoldering ember thereof, but an ember of hope nonetheless.

"Do you know what that is, Mr. Torquiam?"

"It's an oil tower. Your oil tower, Mr. Monteblanc."

"That's quite right."

"Indeed. I know you didn't build it yourself, but I hear you worked on the initial designs, drew up the plans. I know Statletter didn't." The blind man smiled ambiguously. "And, seeing it up close, it's really quite something. Impressive. Worthy of commendation."

"I'm glad you feel that way."

"Though it is oppressively ugly."

"Oh."

"Don't let my lack of aesthetic appreciation deter you, Mr. Monteblanc. There is a reason we are here, let us be to it and be done with it."

"He so reminds me of you, Percival! Striking. Simply striking."

"I don't see the similarity."

"Gentlemen, come to the point!"

"Goodness!"

"It isn't good at all. It's bad. Bad manners. Now I've been very patient, that which I do consider a cardinal virtue, and I don't mind waiting if there is a reason to. But now you two are merely stalling and I will have none of it. Tell me."

"This insolence does not become you, Mr.– "

"I frankly don't care. Answer my question, Ledru."

"Stop this squabbling, both of you!"

They both turned to the blind bookkeeper.

"He's right, Ledru. You're stalling. We both are, I suppose. I understand why, but it really is bad form, old man, it really is."

"Well. Yes. I see that now."

"Good. Now, let's get to it then, there's no point in keeping him in the dark any longer, and we should, at the very least, apologize for jeopardizing both our positions."

"What do you mean?"

"Quite simply this, Mr. Torquiam; that we never should have brought you to the manor."

"Ah, now I understand."

"Yes, we are partly, and perhaps more than partly, to blame, I fear, for this black disposition which has risen up against you. Borne also out of bad religion, ignorance, superstition and the errant xenophobia that inevitably follows. But still, we must take the fall insofar as is truthful. Now, unfortunately, we cannot repair this damage, but I think, very confidently, that you can."

"How?"

"First I want your word that you will help us with our cause."

"And what, Mr. Statletter, exactly is your cause? I will not devout myself to a mystery, only its unraveling."

The blind man reached up with his free right hand and placed it upon his partner's thick and fleshy left shoulder firmly, as if to flaunt some noble and dramatic bond.

"Our cause is simply this; the preservation of the corporation. It really is as simple and, yes, selfish, as that. It is a necessity. If we go down, so does everyone else. You must see this. And it wouldn't be out of spite that they fall, nor baneful impulses on our side. It wouldn't be wrought by our intentions at all, but by the principles of supply and demand. By the laws of economy. By the very laws of nature. This place was nothing more than a barren, starving lump of hovels before we arrived. If we disappear, so it will be again."

"Why are you so sure? Could they not prospect and drill on their own?"

"You've seen these people; do you honestly think they have the capacity?"

"Under the right circumstances, certainly. Desperation is a universal incentive."

"Well, there we must disagree."

"If we must. But I think you're jumping too radically and quickly to a single conclusion."

"I think not. I'm talking probabilities, not certainties."

"So am I."

"Well, even if they could do all that, they still couldn't do it for very long; they've no funds for it."

"Lumber."

"What?"

"The forest. All that verdant lumber, that forest is ancient, it would sell marvelously well."

"Were it not for Kallista, what you say would be true."

"There's that name again, following me like some malevolent ghost."

Ledru leaned in keenly.

"I hear you saw him. Is that true?"

"Partially."

"What do you mean?"

"He was wearing a hooded traveling cloak, much in the fashion of the Bene Salam of the East, so as to shield himself from the sun. So I only saw part of him."

"Ah."

Statletter cut abruptly back in.

"Will you help us?"

"What you are asking of me is impossible."

Statletter was utterly aghast and grasped his kneecaps fitfully in his trepidation.

"Why?"

"Because you're asking me to chose between complete loyalty to you and Ledru or to the town. I own such absolute allegiance to no one, not even myself."

"You have misconstrued my words."

"Then clarify."

"Very well. I'm only asking that you help us to build... credibility among the townsfolk. We are facing a crisis of derision which is so reactionary as to be a matter of life and death, and I do not jest nor exaggerate."

"I did not say as much. You've faced that kind of hate first hand."

"Yes. Better that a man grow cold as a corpse than be filled with such fire."

"I nearly agree."

"Again I ask. Will you help us?"

"If it is only a matter of PR, then certainly, but I fail to see how I could possibly be of assistance."

"Ah, then let me get to it. A bird tells me that you have become quite familiar with young Miss Arlington. Is this so?"

"Yes, in a fashion. But I fail to see– "

"I also hear that she has taken quite a liking to you."

"She has, but the answer to the question you're going to ask is no."

"You haven't heard me out."

"I do not need to; I well enough foresee the direction you desire me to take. That course of action is inexcusable. I'll have no part of it. I am a coffin maker, not a succubus."

"That is most disappointing."

"It is disappointing that you even asked."

"Eisen..."

"It wouldn't have worked anyway, her father has no great love for her, I saw the bruises, and she told me of his brutish ways."

"I imagine she did. Her father, however, has never laid a hand upon her, not in violence anyways."

"What do you mean?"

"She lied. She's a liar. A leech of sympathy. If she does not have something to present which will elicit the desired response, she has no great difficulty in manufacturing one."

"Why are you so certain?"

"Why are you that I am not?"

"It is not merely solipsism when I say that I have long been as good a judge of character as any I've ever met; so she either wasn't lying or is pathological."

"The latter, I'm afraid. And, well, I've contradicted you so often in this little discussion it seems like I'm doing so out of sadism rather than honesty. But her father respects her above almost any other. He is stern, and somewhat cold, but she has his ear and his heart as sure as the sun will rise."

"This, if true, is a revelation, Mr. Statletter."

"Let us make a deal."

"I'm listening. I always am."

"Investigate. If you discover that the information which I have provided you with is true, then you will help us, and if not, then not. Agreed?"

"Agreed. Now I have something to ask in return."

"Very well."

"Kindle."

"What of her?"

"I want her kept from the preacher. Her mind is in a very delicate state, and the last thing on earth that she needs is his incessant, though good natured, rambling of hell and fire and eternal punishment and so forth."

"A delicate state?"

"I would prefer not to name the particulars, as it is not my business to dispense with. I don't know if she would want me to. I trust you understand this sentiment."

"Certainly I do. I could tell when I first met her that there was a certain... fragility to her nature."

"Good. But there is one more thing."

"Which would be?"

"If I do as you ask, I want a house built for her. A house, you understand?"

"You must be joking."

"Not in the slightest. I want a house built for her on a plot of land she designates, paid in full with a title to the deed. It isn't as if neither of you have the money such a project would require."

Ledru, who had until this point been uncharacteristically silent, boomed suddenly and warmly, "Done! It's a gentleman's prerogative, it is!"

"I'm glad to hear it! Let us shake on it then to seal our agreement."

Eisen held forth his pale, dexterous hand which was quickly embraced by Ledru's red, doughy one. They clasped and shook hands with such sudden and furious brio that neither could help but smile. Throughout the whole of it Statletter sat silently with folded arms and a peculiarly opaque expression. A little too opaque.

Eisen noticed this slightly startling reticence, but said nothing, merely observing instead, leaning back upon the plush red seats.

"Well, before we depart I have one more question for the two of you."

"And what would that be?"

"Why haven't either of you asked about Adams?"

"Who?"

"Frank Adams. The man who attacked me, the man I killed."

Upon hearing the word "killed," Ledru visibly burred with agitation whilst Statletter's face grew only more glaucous. Eisen commented on none of it. He rubbed and then clasped his hands together, bending forward with a hawkish intensity, head tilted to the left, eyes slightly too wide for those reflected therein to remain at ease.

Ledru began stuttering something meekly, but Statletter cut him off with a wild gesticulation, his cane splitting the light.

"Eisen, I think I have been more than cordial enough to you since you got here, and I certainly know that Ledru has, so why don't you reign in that prickly ego of yours and make the modest attempt at returning the favor."

"That doesn't answer my question."

"That's what I mean, my dear coffin maker, you keep on vomiting orders up like so much bile."

"I only stated a fact."

"You implied– "

"I implied nothing, it is only you that is making the implication of an implication."

Statletter sat back, tapping his long, pointed chin with the bejeweled end of his cane, immaculately kept; thinking whether it was prudent or useless to continue. After a few brief moments of deliberation on the subject, the blind man eventually decided in favor of the former rather than the latter eventuality.

"If that's how you see it, then I apologize. I am just glad you're on our side."

"As I said before, I'm not on a side. One more thing, Ledru."

"Yes, what is it?"

"You wanted me to make a coffin for a man named Turpin. Is this correct?"

"Oh, I'd forgotten. Yes. Old Danny Turpin. Poor bloke. Religious chap. Dedicated. Kind man. Yeah, really kind."

"What became of him?"

"Well, Michael says it was the wages of sin what kilt him."

"And what actually did?"

"A shotgun."

☼

They sat once more in silence on the drive back into town were Statletter deposited himself at Caldwell's printing shop, leaving with only a flippant wave of his arm to his two companions.

"What business has he with Elis Caldwell?"

Ledru shrugged and made a face that bespoke volumes more of his ignorance than any sentence he could have devised. Eisen studied the ruddy-faced, fat man a moment, then a moment longer; but every muscle moving thereupon was doing so in earnest.

To the coffin maker's perception, his employer wasn't lying but was rather just as much in the dark as he.

"Well, where to now, Mr. Torquiam? My carriage is humbly at your disposal."

"That's very kind of you, Mr. Monteblanc. Have Sievers drive us to the cathedral."

"What? Whatever for?"

"Memory, memory, Ledru; tsk-tsk. An elephant you are not."

"I'm certainly glad of the fact, I haven't the nose for it. So why the cathedral?"

"Kindle, my good man, to pick up Kindle."

"Right ho!"

Ledru slapped his huge beefy hands together and then rubbed them with great energy, a clear expression of his anticipation for action. He fairly leapt from his plush satin seat and flew to the window, which he opened to make room for his head to thrust on through.

"Sievers!"

"Yes?"

"Sir, yes sir! Where is your sense of posterity! Of propriety?"

"Sorry, sir. What is it, sir?"

"Take us to the church, fast as you can, no time to waste, man, no time!"

"Very well, sir."

Ledru then began withdrawing himself back through the trap's little window with great difficulty. Viewing this, Sievers face contorted into – it was not a smile but rather the nearest thing the man could manage. The dour servant lashed the reigns as furiously and as quickly as he could manage, sending the horses catapulting forward with Ledru still half out the window. Were it not for the young, able-bodied coffin maker, the unfortunate Mr. Monteblanc would, in all probability, have had a rather unwanted and abrupt change of scenery.

Gasping with the shock of the event, Ledru lay back upon his plush red seat as the carriage went clattering down the town's main thoroughfare. Eisen released his poor employer and did likewise. Then he smiled and began to laugh.

"What on earth is there to laugh about? Damn it all! That Sievers! He did it on purpose. Why on earth would a man do such a thing? It's abominable, it is. Atrocious and abominable! It's nihilism!"

"Calm yourself, my good man, calm yourself or you're likely to have a stroke."

"I really wish you'd stop laughing at me."

"Remember, remember, Ledru: If you can't laugh at yourself..."

"Oh, I suppose you're right."

Now it was the portly magnate who cracked a smile, throwing off the bad odor of the previous event with the brevity and carelessness of one discarding a ragged shawl.

The unlikely duo's good humor extended all the way to the cathedral drive where Sievers pulled the carriage to a stop in the pale white gravel at Ledru's behest.

So warm had the atmosphere between the garrulous oilman and the rarefied coffin maker grown during that brief interlude that Sievers wasn't even reprimanded for his former insolence in the jostling of his master.

As Eisen got out, Ledru jumped down beside him, feet clouding in the ensuing high rise of dust. They stood staring up at the wild and towering edifice of the grand cathedral, talking, not looking at each other.

"Shall I wait here then?"

"Oh, you're the boss, boss."

"Come, come lad. I know I wanted you to call me "Mister," but really! There's no need to carry the idea of formality to extremes."

"There are a lot of things that should be carried to extremes, but I agree that formality isn't one of them. I wasn't being serious, Mr. Monteblanc."

"Please, call me Ledru."

"All right."

"So?"

"Ah, yes, if you don't mind waiting."

"I mind, but not enough to leave you stranded."

"You're beginning to grow on me, Ledru Monteblanc. I shall be back as directly as is possible."

"Very well."

Eisen looked to his newfound friend, smiled, and then heeled it up the white gravel path, the path where he had seen or imagined that he had seen a man with a white umbrella. He resolved to ask around for such a man when he had the time.

Chapter Sixteen

Serpents Uncoil

A middle-aged woman, plain faced and gray garbed, walked out of the church just as Eisen was opening the door to enter and bumped lightly into him. She staggered back mumbling a hurried string of vehement apologies until she saw his face, whereupon she hissed, "Heathen, murderer!" She departed without a backward glance. Several more people passed by him as he watched her go, all going through the same spiteful routine.

"Heathen, Murderer."

He said nothing to them, merely watched them drain out of the church and disappear into the distance, melding with the gold-orange horizon to become nothing more than walking flames, quickly smothered by the fast-ensuing atmosphere. When they had all gone, he pushed open the huge right side door and passed within the mammoth threshold. Once more he was gripped by the sudden frigidity which lay thick and palpable in the air of the ancient cathedral.

The stained-glass windows filtered the dying sunlight queerly, letting it fall through into the center of the room as an oddly discolored blue, whilst all the four corners of that stony vaulted space lay blacked by shadows thicker than soot.

In the center of the room, between the pews and within the grand seal, scathed into the stone of the floor, stood the Montferiats with Kindle in wayward tow. They appeared oblivious to the intruder, deep in some kind of potent discussion.

Michael was the first to notice Eisen walking toward them.

GRAVE.

"Eisen. What is the meaning of this?"

"How formal. You seem excited by my presence."

"Considering a murderer walks free among us, I don't think it's unusual."

"He didn't murder anyone!"

All three men turned to the little waif, who stood with her fists bunched tightly at her slender sides, furious and fuming.

"He didn't! I was there! He was attacked! They would have killed me otherwise!"

"You're confused, my dear. Why don't you go lay back down. I shall have you moved into a better room tomorrow, as I promised."

"What is this about rooms?"

Michael walked toward the coffin maker, his hands clasped stiffly behind his back, his elegant head uptilted with military stoicism and his eyes growing hard and cold.

"This business is no longer any concern of yours. I suggest you leave before you further upset her."

"You suggest I leave? Why does that suggestion smack of demand?"

"I suggest you leave before I call the sheriff again."

"Go ahead. I've been acquitted of my charges."

"Ah. You have the greedy oil-pig to thank for that corruption, yes?"

"What have I done to you to incur such ire?"

"Nothing."

"Then why?"

"If suggestions will no longer do it, then I'm telling you quite directly to leave our property. Go now. I'll not ask twice."

"Kindle, are you staying here?"

She turned to him with sad eyes and then quickly looked away.

"He offered to find a house for me, a home. Offered to take care of me."

"Those are very choice words, Mr. Torquiam, 'Take care,' not, 'Abuse.'"

"I never– "

"You never what? Never struck her? Will you further burden the already sodden mire of your soul with the sin of deception? No. Don't bother. Now go. I'll not let a ruffian like you harm anyone else, least of all this delicate creature; by God, I'll swing first!"

"Now son, you shouldn't get so worked up, I'm sure that– "

"Leave us, Father."

"My son– "

"I said leave us. You should be attending to Robert anyway. Go, take her with you."

"Very well, but we will talk of this later. Come, my child, come, come."

Kindle departed with her elder reluctantly, looking back only once at Eisen, a look that was equal parts sorrow, shame and accusation.

Michael said nothing further to his father, merely continued to hold the coffin maker's gaze.

Then he smiled faintly and narrowed his eyes.

"When the pillars of your home collapse upon your head I shall, with an airy heart, upon your charnel build a soaring edifice, the talisman of my ascendance– "

Eisen's eyes flashed as he completed the passage. "The brand of mine enemy's bane, a blade terrible, to shatter and rend."

"Very good, Mr. Torquiam." He clapped and chuckled aloud.

"Then I am such an enemy?"

"You have always known that you were, otherwise you wouldn't have come here to confront me."

"I came here for Kindle."

"You came to this town to sully it. Harbinger of godlessness. Kavaria Kallista himself could not have done a better job. But I will see you fall. I will see everything stripped from you, and dispossessed and alone you shall wander the wastes. Perhaps God will show you mercy then in your hour of despair, but I doubt it. I, certainly, shall not."

"I don't need anyone's mercy. I only want Kindle returned to me."

"It was her decision to stay."

"Her mind is clouded with fear; do you know of what that fear is borne?"

"Lies."

"There is a man after her, a jester."

"A jester! I did not realize just how desperately your loins yearned for her."

"It isn't like that."

"Ha. Am I to believe that from a nihilist such as yourself, misguided and fragile with the accumulated filth of his degradations? Do you see this church, that cross? Well, it is not the symbol of any single one amongst our congregation; it is the symbol of us all. That is the power of faith. It is the power of unity, and it is only through unity that man shall survive, not through dissension, no matter how gloriously guised. What has your nihilism and atheism brought mankind? What has it brought you and those you know? Death and violence, hatred and destruction. That is what and that is all. Greed – always greed. Lust – never dissipating. You are ignorant. You are petty. You are beneath the floor upon which you so defiantly stand. Bow to your knees for absolution, for it is the only way to salvation. It is the sole and straight path of your salvation. Bow. For the time of greed and filth, the time of lethargy and negligence, the time of insolence and disbelief is over. The time of the chosen is quick at hand. The time of our kingdom is come. The kingdom of the warrior at long last; The Warriors of God. You would be wise to join that kingdom. But there is in you no wisdom left, is there? Spiritual exhaustion has torn it from you. Pity."

"Well, that was quite a speech. I see you have inherited your father's flair for colorful rhetoric. Yet every successful tyrant rules in much the same fashion. You, I see, are no different. I thought you were lying before, but now I am sure of it. You did spread those rumors about me, about her, about Kavaria being a djinn and a demon. You put on such a convincing show when we met that I really thought you wanted to be my friend. I really thought you were all you pretended to be. And probably, were

I to fathom a guess, you've been augmenting your father's speeches as well, what with all that Warriors of God nonsense. It's been you against me from the very first."

"That's right, Mr. Torquiam. I don't mind telling it to you, since you have already deduced as much yourself. I have been subtly opposing your every move since you showed your true and blackened colors, right here upon this spot. Such vile, grotesque blasphemies I have never in all my life been party to. Never will I again."

"Do you realize what you are doing?"

"Perfectly."

"You're stirring dangerous sentiments better left undisturbed. You're raising a malevolent tide of fanaticism that you invariably won't be able to control. Sooner or later, and probably sooner, it will crush you and very likely everything in this town. The people here are ready to go off like a powder keg, and you are the one lighting the match, heedless of the consequences."

"How dare you! You don't know this town or our ways. You don't know these people. I've spent my entire life amongst them; you're just a judgmental outsider like every other."

"Yes. I am all that you say. But I shall not be ashamed of the truth of it. There is no shame in judgment, only in poor judgment. Even now you judge me to be unfit to inhabit the vile utopia which is your most extreme and violent desire. Do you feel the weight of ignominy? No. Nor should you. Every man should stand unfettered by his convictions, given that those convictions which he holds are in and of themselves liberating."

"There is something about you, Mr. Torquiam, which prefigures your insolence."

"There is something about you, Mr. Montferiat, that prefigures your absurdity."

"Absurdity? God's work? You call this absurdity? You are a lower kind of man than I had at first surmised."

"It is unfortunate that you think of me so, I have the utmost respect for your intellect and compassion. I think you are misguided, but what I think of you or what you think of me is of little enough consequence when compared to the lives you are putting at stake."

"I am not putting anyone's life at stake."

"Daniels still wants Kavaria's head. What do you think all this punish the sinner, an eye for an eye rhetoric is going to incline him to do? You know damn well."

"Daniels is a man of singular tenacity. He will not be dissuaded from his endeavor. As I said before, you don't know these people."

"I know him well enough to know all that. I agree that he'll not be persuaded to stop his foolishness. What concerns me and what should, but clearly does not, concern you, is the men who will go with him who otherwise wouldn't, save for you and your father's preaching. Can't you see the damage this will unleash? Think of their lives, the lives that will be lost."

"I have nothing more to say to you, Mr. Torquiam. You have exhausted my patience. Kindle will not see you, and even if she were to ask for you, I shall make sure that you are never able to get at her again. You'll not harm her while I still draw breath, and may the Lord mark well my words. May you mark them also."

Eisen tilted his head up coolly, defiantly. Then he nodded very slightly, saying only, "Very well. If that is the path you wish to take, so be it."

Their eyes met following the light between them, a corporeal medium to their hardened vision. Then Michael turned swiftly on his heel and stalked militantly out of the gathering room, passing through one of the two wooden doors at the back of the room, and disappearing into the darkness therein. A darkness that held his friend.

Eisen gazed after his foe with wide, wild eyes, his hands clenching and unclenching reflexively, instinctively.

"I will not let this pass."

Then he turned his back to the darkness and walked out of the church.

☼

Outside he was broadsided by the sudden intensity of the sunlight which caused him to tightly shut his eyes. When he opened them he swore he saw the jester of Kindle's darkest plight standing a few paces behind the high iron gates which lead out of the church. But the pain from the blaring sunlight was such that he had to shield his eyes from the terrible, burning rays, losing sight of the masked man in the process. When finally he was able to pull his glasses from his duster's breast pocket and put them on, the masked man had gone, if ever he had been in the first place. Eisen massaged his temples, ruminating and despondent as he approached Ledru's coach, which was still parked outside the church doors upon the wide, white gravel path.

"Eisen, whatever is the matter?"

"A great deal."

"You look dreadfully pale."

"I will tell you of it later, but first there is something I must do. Will you take me to Arlingtons'?"

"The Arlingtons'? Whatever for?"

"For a conversation with Jennifer Arlington about the nature of truth and trust."

"Ah. I don't think that's a very good idea."

"It may not be but you never know until you try, do you? Will you take me, or shall I walk?"

"No. I'll none of that – I'll take you. Climb in. I just need to pick up Percival on the way. He should still be at Caldwell's."

"Sievers, let's be off then!"

"Yes sir."

And then they were clattering out of the churchyard, down the town's main thoroughfare, past the ramshackle hovels and lean-to's of the slums, all the way to the main square and Elis Caldwell's tidy, little print shop; home of the *Town Cryer*, the only magazine about the place. The magazine was called *The Individual*. Several stacks of these papers rose up in squat, but neat, rows all about the front of the compact and newly painted print shop.

Eisen made out figures moving within the building and the vague suggestion of shelves, but the three windows of the place (the largest being the glass pane in the front door and the other two to either side of it) were too covered in grime and wayward dust to clearly reveal much else.

Sievers pulled to a stop and, sighing with his omnipresent melancholy, withdrew a cigarette and a lighter from his coat pocket and set to puffing.

Eisen paused for a moment to stare at the cigarette, about which there was nothing particularly striking, save that it was precisely the same kind of cigarette that Elis Caldwell was smoking when the coffin maker first saw him. This would have been completely ordinary since the town was small, and there was likely two or three brands of tobacco to choose from, were it not also a fact that the particular kind of cigarette was custom made, imported, and expensive. Due that, it was well beyond Sievers' paltry wages.

Eisen filed this away in the back of his mind as he walked into Caldwell's print shop, his expression forcefully blank.

Caldwell sat in an enormous arm chair which was positioned in the far back left corner of the room, in front of which stood a table and two other elegant arm chairs. He was smoking, reading a newspaper and idly talking to an elderly man with spectacles who stood a few feet in front of him upon the Persian carpet which buffered all the main furniture.

The puckered weather-worn man was put out over something, as he was fairly shaking with agitation, brows furrowed deep.

"Print it anyway."

"But sir!"

"Thank you, goodbye."

Caldwell didn't glance up at his protesting second in command. He dismissed the old man with a haughty flick of his wrist and disdainful wave of his hand. Like rats before a flood, the old man swallowed his pride and left, shuffling stiffly through the backroom door. Behind it the sound of sliding papers, clacking of a typewriter and the whirring of a press.

Caldwell exhaled a perfect ring of smoke before he spoke, his eyes never leaving his paper.

"Eisen de Torquiam, I've heard terrible things about you. It's a pleasure to properly meet you. I'm glad that whole Adams debacle went well for you – he was a cunt."

"Well. I couldn't speak for the man generally. I was wondering if you had seen Percival Statletter, Ledru Monteblanc sent me to fetch him."

"Ah, so that's who drove you."

"Yes."

"My, my. And they say that you are supposed to be sharp."

"What do you mean?"

It was only then that Caldwell lowered the newspaper from his face and rather dramatically arched one of his thick, tar-black eyebrows up, high as it would reach. There was no trace of humor upon his face, but rather an expectant and challenging curiosity, as if he were waiting for something from Eisen.

Eisen cocked his head, confused, "Well?"

Caldwell shook his head as Percival Statletter suddenly appeared from the chair closest to Eisen. So large had it been, and so slight was the blind man's frame, that he was completely hidden from view by anyone looking from behind.

"To shame, Mr. Torquiam, to shame. Mr. Statletter tells me you could have made it as a detective. Ha, perhaps in the acquisition of lost lead pencils or stolen floral undergarments."

"Why, Mr. Caldwell, you are quite the trickster," said Statletter.

The printer gestured languidly with his cigarette, slicing the air with a trailing tentacle of smoke.

"Sarcasm quite becomes you, Statletter."

Statletter paused for effect before speaking again, dapper suited and eyeless.

"I presume our mutual friend is out there waiting?"

"Yes."

"Then I had best be off."

With that the blind man left Eisen alone with the icy, cold-eyed printer; a singularly reptilian gentleman.

"You know, word is that your young lady friend from the forest is a witch sent by demons to curse the town, sow the seeds of dissent and all that."

Eisen remained silent, absorbing information, letting his senses consume the seething weave of reality.

"It seemed like it was something you should know."

"Yes, I've heard. Nonsense."

"What are you going to do about the people who don't think it's nonsense? Reason with them?"

"Try," said Eisen.

"Better yet, why don't you send Statletter to the rifle range? Both endeavors would yield about as much fruit as the next."

"You don't like this town, do you, Mr. Caldwell?"

"I've never been in a town I liked. If I found one, I'd very likely move so that I'd have something interesting to talk about every now and again. But I'm curious about you, marginally, I'll admit, but still curious. How do you fancy our fair town so far?"

"Industrious. Superstitious. Like a lot of small towns. Why include marginally?"

"Why? I suppose because I'd like to win your confidence. I heard you respect honesty. I'm not a fan myself, as it's a fairly slippery business. But I can still appreciate one who does and his reasons why; they are invariably the same across the board. So I thought if I were honest with you, you, in turn, might be honest with me."

"And why is it that you wish to gain my confidence?"

"Because we have a common enemy."

"I have an enemy, but I hardly think that he is common."

"On the contrary. Luce and Michael Montferiat and all their ilk are as common as sewer rats, scampering this way and that. Every budding city is infested with them, these rats of the mind."

"I have nothing against Luce Montferiat. He is a kindly man, wise, in a fashion, and passionate; dedicated. It is with his son that I desire a reckoning."

"Yes, a nasty business, him spreading rumors and making up outlandish nonsense about you and that poor little girl. Witches and demons indeed! Laughable. And yet these ignorant peasants gobble it up, as the ignorant do anything that has a catchy ring in its uttering. Sorcery and the supernatural, gods, demons and angels, it's all great theatre. It is a fine production but of little value, and yet these people would stake their lives upon it."

"What have you against the Montferiats?"

"Enough."

"It's personal?"

"More than somewhat."

"That is a disconcertingly ambiguous way to answer."

"Very likely."

"I am at least glad you are still being honest with me."

"I won't lie to you, Mr. Torquiam, but that does not mean I will tell you the whole truth."

"You, like anyone else, have the right to your privacy. I do not mean to impose upon it, that was never my intention."

"What a gentleman!"

"I can but try."

"Hm, well. You need not try very hard, the competition is lousy. Next time the situation arises, just bust an offending man's jaw instead of shooting him in the face, and you shall probably be considered a gentleman around here."

"I don't know about that. Too much pressure and praise is thrown on the title anyhow. Of the many things to which I could aspire, a gentleman would not be among the first, nor even the fiftieth of them."

"Ah, I see it is true! They said you speak like a Greek. Not of course that I know any, or, really, for that matter, how they talk, but the caricature that I have come to know will work all the same."

"A Greek?"

"Dead white men in togas, all that psycho babble. Rich tones and empty phrases."

"Do you really find nothing of interest in philosophy?"

"Plenty of interest – little of value."

"For me one equals the other."

"Ah. Then you are very fortunate, Mr. Torquiam. I am cursed with too utilitarian a mind. If I were to follow my whims, my interests, every glittering stone and colorful bird would gift me with their very presence. I cannot see the point in such diversions. It makes good business an utter impossibility."

"Does it indeed? How curious that you should think so."

It was at this point that upon the conversation an intruder burst, a man whom Eisen had seen well enough before; the Jester, in all his meretricious resplendence.

He was still wearing his mask and was dually flanked by a dwarf upon one side and a tall, wild-haired woman with strange blue spectacles and an equally outlandish purple dress.

The jester stopped just inside the door, looked about for a moment then laughed (for no reason that any other could discern) and took a deep, theatrical bow that was so steeped in affectation as to be sardonic.

"Greetings, ladies and gentlemen, and every variation thereupon."

Eisen looked over briefly at Caldwell and swore that if his eyebrows could arch any higher, they would have levitated straight off his head.

"What is the meaning of this? I don't just see anyone. You have to have an appointment."

"Of course, of course! I just thought you might make an exception if it 'twere in the name of gold."

"Gold?"

"Pure, solid 24 karat."

"What exactly is it that you want to pay me for? No – first I would like to know whom I have the distinct irritation of speaking to."

"I'm no one of particular consequence. I am acting in the name of the carnivale at large and would gladly pay thee a handsome sum of your own naming were it in your capabilities to create for us fliers, number enough to put all round the town, and even at Ledru's mansion."

"Fliers? So you're finally setting up a proper show?"

"We have full permission to do so. Though it is strange, yes, for a town such as this to be without a mayor by elected office."

"We had a mayor."

"And? Now where has he gone? Fishing?"

"Six feet underground."

"Well then, I suppose we shouldn't be expecting him back anytime soon." The jester laughed once more as he said this, causing Caldwell to look to Eisen with pleading exasperation, as if to say, "Please, save me from this fool."

"No. Very likely not. How many fliers, precise numbers now, and what shall they say?"

The jester made a peculiar stabbing motion with his whole body then, bending his torso out and over the rest, parallel to the ground and not looking one jot at anyone in the room. It was evidently a motion for the little man, the dwarf, to approach Caldwell, for that is precisely what he did, his face frightfully austere. Saying nothing, he then reached into his colorful patchwork jerkin and removed a thick piece of paper, quite large and folded over itself several times to save space. It was tied rather officially with a garishly charming piece of red satin.

"All the particulars have been written down to the letter." The tall, imposing woman, whom had accompanied the jester, replied in a high, whispery voice, "If you require anything further, you have but to call on us."

"All right. For this many fliers – mind that my prices are set – it will be fifty dollars, or you could pay with gold, if you prefer."

"We do. We have no dollars."

"I take half up front, the rest upon completion, yes or no?"

The jester laughed his bizarre laugh once more, straightened up and bowed once more saying, "Of course, of course!"

Eisen noticed that the woman with the purple dress seemed hesitant to speak over the jester, as if she were afraid of him. Eisen wondered who this man was and resolved to get to the bottom of it.

"Do you remember me?" The coffin maker cut in sharply, leaning in, a predatory gesture.

"Memory is man's greatest curse, the source of all his sorrow. I resolve every day to make such pain go on and away."

"I didn't ask you for a rhyme about memory. I asked if you remember me."

"True. You did. There you go, succumbing to your curse. That's the point, my lovely!"

Caldwell shook his head, and for the first time since Eisen had seen him, cracked a full-toothed smile, puffing on his cigarette with great amusement.

The dwarf shambled back to his side when the jester clapped his hands furiously and spoke.

"Well, well, we must be off to the far side of Fey, where there are weirder things than a willy tongue. Good day, all!"

And then they were gone.

Eisen and Caldwell watched them go, the former with a firm, inquisitive glare, the other, his head in his hands. Still shaking his head.

"What an extraordinary character; why, he almost makes you seem normal, Mr. Torquiam... almost."

"Indeed. Well, I shouldn't keep my companions waiting overlong. Thank you, and good day."

Elis Caldwell nodded very formally, meeting Eisen's courteous and stately bow full on; more like the departing of two magnates or diplomats than two amiable acquaintances.

On his way out he remembered a most important question which he had forgotten to ask. Turning back to the writer, Eisen discovered that the man had already sunk back into the paper he had previously been perusing.

"Pardon."

"Have you lost your way? I know it's quite expansive, my little shop, but if you can't find your way out, perhaps I should escort you."

Eisen stood with a wry expression tugging at his face, his hand upon the doorknob. Now it was he who shook his head.

"You don't have many friends, do you, Mr. Caldwell?"

"That makes two of us."

"Ha. Well, I was just wondering if James Arlington takes visitors. I mean, does he accept company, or is he a shut-in?"

"Why do you ask?"

"I have business with his daughter."

"Ah, so it has been said."

"Incorrectly and lewdly, I am sure."

"Maybe, maybe not, it's of little consequence. To answer you, no, not usually. He isn't exactly a shut-in, to use your language. But he's not the most amiable of fellows."

"You two have something in common then."

"Ha."

"That's about the worst forced laugh I've ever heard, Elis."

"Stay tuned and I may top it yet."

Eisen waved, walked out, shutting the door quietly behind him, heartily amused.

Chapter Seventeen

Kavaria

It didn't take long to arrive at the Arlington ranch. It was a few miles outside of town, not, Eisen was surprised to learn, very far from his own wood-mired lodgings. The ranch sat in a small, grassy valley that bordered on Kindle's forest. It was the lushest part of the country that he had yet seen, aside from the deep woods where he had nearly lost his mind from a hasty consumption of mysterious flora.

Before he got out, Eisen turned to Ledru and Statletter with his keen, inquiring eyes.

"Tell me, gentlemen, if you are so disposed; what do you know of the jester that travels with the circus folk? You might have seen him about Caldwell's shop when I was there. He came in when we were talking, asking for fliers."

Ledru was first to answer. "Oh, absolutely nothing, I'm afraid, haven't even seen him. A jester you say?"

"Yes. He wears a most peculiar mask – never seems to take it off."

"How extraordinary."

"Quite."

Statletter looked off into the distance out his window, gazing deep into the heart of the desert where it rose up to swallow the dying sun from the sky.

"I can only say that he is very likely insane. I met him once, I had gone down to visit the carnies; a queer enough lot as ever there were, but then again, what circus folk aren't? I couldn't say. But this man, he was stranger still. He hailed me and started shouting off some completely nonsensical poem, assuredly of his own construction, something about frogs singing to the rain and how they had to be set afire or something like that. Gave me quite a stir. I had no idea what he was talking about, but he went on like it was the most important thing anyone had ever said. He kept gesticulating wildly, stabbing the air with his fingers and laughing for no reason that I could discern. He was... like a character from some old story book; queer fellow."

"Interesting."

"Well that's certainly one word to describe him, though I don't think it would be the first one I would chose."

"No, I fancy not. Well, we are here at any rate. Good day, gentlemen, and thank you, for everything."

Ledru smiled broadly and waved a pudgy hand with great, mirthful animation.

"It's no trouble, lad. I'm glad we could be of assistance."

Statletter tipped his top hat slyly to the coffin maker, and then, pushing it back up in proper place with his cane, he sat back languidly into the shadows of the carriage as Sievers touched off the horses and pulled away, heading for the town.

Eisen stood for a moment watching them haul out and then turned and started down the broad sloping hill toward the Arlington ranch. The main house itself was large and sturdy, but consciously devoid of any frivolous ornamentation. It stood three stories tall amidst a small, sparse grouping of ash trees, all of which were shorter than the house. To the left of the house, closest to the forest of all the Arlingtons' property, was a large circular chicken pen where nearly fifty fat and frolicking birds clucked and flapped their brown speckled wings, moving about each other as if performing some intimate ritual dance.

The sun was low slung and bleeding in the sky, mixing with the hazing clouds and wide blue barn to the farmhouse's immediate right to consummate the land in a radiant pall of orange-green light. Ranch hands could be seen strutting in front of their housing, scant wooden shacks built near the outhouse. Five dust-blown and sun-battered specters, trawling heavy work rope or leading obedient, dappled horses to their stables, took no notice of the young coffin maker; too intent upon their current duties to intake their surroundings or the things what moved therein.

Eisen stood before a squat, square tin-roofed tool shed which prefaced the patrician housing by some 150 feet.

Suddenly there was a furious shriek. He spun about in the direction of the fearful sound, the direction of the chicken pen.

A hawk had wheeled down out of the thermals, diving for the scattering birds with talons outstretched.

The beast was a mere dozen yards away from its quarry when a gunshot tore it from the sky, painting its feathers gaudy carmine. The chicken hawk flopped doggedly upon the ground, one wing nothing more than a bloody, rust-plumed stump.

Another shot and the raptor went limp and stirred no more, its shrill cries stilling in the air like an evaporating fog.

Eisen looked toward the shooter, James Gabriel Arlington himself, dressed in a wide-brimmed hat, plaid slacks and an immaculate white dress shirt. He was smoking a pipe and with it gestured commandingly toward his visitor, advancing hastily upon Eisen as he spoke.

"Who are you?"

"Eisen de Torquiam. The coffin maker."

"Well, ain't no one a'dead round ere, boy."

"I fancy not, sir."

"What you want then?"

"Audience with your daughter, if it would not be too much trouble."

"Trouble? Boy, that may as well be your name."

Eisen said nothing, waiting patiently for a question or a threat, something, anything, anything but silence.

The old man was silent a moment, standing but four feet from the coffin maker, sizing him up diligently. He took a long drag from his pipe, crossed his arms then exhaled before speaking.

"You her lover?"

"No sir, but I would consider myself a friend."

He squinted as he peered into the depths of Eisen's open, honest face.

"I kin tell ya not lying, so answer me this: The man you kilt, Adams, did he really attack you?"

"Yes. Unfortunately he did. That is the whole truth of it. Violence turns my stomach."

The older man nodded grimly and gestured to the dead hawk.

"Then I suppose I should apologize for that."

"No. You were protecting your own. Without the chickens, what would you and your men do for meat? Can't go eating up your horses, now can you?"

"Ya'll a queer sorta fella, ain'tcha?"

Eisen didn't bother saying whether he was or wasn't, just stood looking intently into the ranch owner's eyes and squinting against the hard glare of ambered sunlight.

"I tell ya what – have you eaten?" Eisen shook his head. "Well then, your'a gonna ave dinner wit us, if'n that's all right wit you?"

"Perfectly."

"Then you come right this'away and we'll git ya fixed up wit some victuals, finest you ever had, leastways, finest ya'll git round here."

Eisen turned to spy the dead hawk in the chicken pen as he walked toward the house close behind his stern-faced, pipe-smoking host. A few of the chickens had encircled the deceased craniate. Two, the boldest and largest, walked up and began pecking at the corpse. One yanking the wing-stump, the other tugging at a slowly stiffening talon, squawking, leaping aback and then returning. A grotesque piñata amidst a frenzy of feral beaks and savage wings.

Arlington motioned for the closest available worker, a thin, sturdy, sun-baked thirty-something-year-old Italian, with bushy, thickset brows and a long angular nose. The man responded at once, nearly jogging over to his master and cocking an attentive ear. It was clear to Eisen that Arlington ran a very tight ship, though that much he had already induced from his host's stoic, commanding demeanor.

"Yes'sa?"

"Ya'll git that damned fool bird outta here. I don't want my daughter having ta look at that. Now you hurry on. Oh and one more thing, this here is Mr. Torquiam, an we're having him fer supper. So set an extra plate."

"Yes'sa."

"Well, say hello, ya damned fool!"

"H-hello."

Eisen bowed slightly in response to which both men looked at him funnily, saying nothing.

After a pause of what seemed like a minute entire, James nodded and spoke as if to some invisible countenance.

"All right then."

With that Arlington proceeded to his porch and disappeared through a black, near opaque screen door, shutting the inner portal behind him. Eisen lingered behind on the porch, watching the lanky Italian ambling over to the chicken pen. The ranch hand had a funny walk. He watched him open the gate, kicking up dust as he shuffled to the dead bird, scattering the chickens once more. He poked the raptor with the toe of his tattered left work boot. It did not stir, then he nodded as if to confirm it to himself. He picked it up and carried it to the edge of the woods where he flung it carelessly into a wild tangle of briar and vines.

Eisen watched it vanish into the foliage and felt a distant tarriance of sorrow well up and crash against the solid shore of his fortitude.

He passed inside the black screen, the white-washed door and beheld a familiar face looking at him with something like wonder in that brightly gas-lit space.

"Rit? Gerald Fairson, Rit?"

"Mr. Torquiam?"

"Call me Eisen."

"Eisen! What a surprise! What on earth are you doing here?"

"Having supper, apparently."

"Well now, don't that just beat all. How you know Mr. Arlington?"

"I don't, actually. I only know his daughter."

"She's round here somewhere, I think. Here, let me take your coat."

"I've got it."

But Fairson had already scurried round behind Eisen and begun stripping him of his duster, and as he did so, his hands moved too quickly, nearly fumbling the coat altogether. Eisen caught it deftly and handed it to Rit with an amused expression. Fairson blushed and coughed, or pretended to cough. He hung the coat, said he had to get a drink of water and then set off at a brisk jog out of the room.

The anteroom in which Eisen stood was extremely small, consisting of only one long, wall-length coat and hat rack, a washing basin next to a pump, and a pile of work boots thrown rather carelessly in the far left corner. That and the four plain wood-paneled walls that boxed all the rest in were all it consisted of. The anteroom had but one exit which was a short corridor that lead directly out into the aromatic kitchen. A distinctive and strong smell wafted through the stirred and sizzling air.

Something sugary.

Apple.

Cinnamon.

Pie.

One of the ranch hands, another Italian, a middle-aged woman of rugged countenance, with fierce flashing eyes and dark, thick eyebrows, was removing the pie from the oven just as Eisen entered the large, curiously banal room. The floor was tiled, black and white; the walls were bland, tinted beige. There was a stainless steel clock of circular construction hanging above the blackened, antique wood stove and a calendar hanging from the wall directly opposite. The long rectangular dining table was maple and was situated in the very center of the room.

"Take a seat, young man, my daughter will be down shortly. You can talk over some warm apple pie."

"I don't think she would discuss what I wanted to over pie."

"Why not? Unless it's a secret. I thought you said she wasn't ya lov'a?"

"She isn't."

The cook was giggling. She tried briefly and vainly to muffle her chuckling and then placed the pie upon the table.

"Why, Valencia, whatever has got into ya?"

"You're terribly forward." She laughed out loud, no longer attempting to conceal her amusement.

"Am I? I hadn't noticed. Eisen?"

"Yes?"

"Would you like ya food served in the doorway?"

He shook his head and took a seat directly opposite his gruff, sun-baked host.

It was at that moment that both Gerald Fairson and Jennifer Arlington appeared through the door opposite the one by which Eisen had just come.

Their reactions seemed polar opposites.

Fairson smiled and took a seat next to the coffin maker, whilst Jen's eyes widened in apprehensive confusion.

"What is he doing here?"

"You weren't expecting him?"

"No. How did you get out of jail?"

"Help from a friend – several, actually." As he said the latter, he looked her directly in the eye. She quickly averted her gaze.

"I suppose I should thank you."

"No. It was nothing."

"I only wish it were nothing. But my daughter getting drunk and tearing up a jail ain't exactly what I'd call nothing."

"Father..."

"I know – falsely imprisoned – mistaken circumstances, I heard you! I hear you now. Sit down, everyone sit down. Not you, Valencia. Get that other pie outta there! Good heavens, it's gonna go up in flames an takes us all with it!"

"Oh shoo, calm yourself, you grouchy old crab."

"Bah."

Fairson shook his head as Eisen and Jen simultaneously burst into fits of laughter as the old man folded his arms sternly and made a show of glaring them down, which worked rather ineffectually. They continued to laugh as Valencia brought out the second pie and the meal proper, placing it all likewise on the table and then sitting down herself next to her employer.

They ate slowly, conversing pleasantly all the while. The whole time Mr. Arlington looked from his daughter to the coffin maker with a certain degree of curious expectation, though he said nothing, either about the true nature of their relationship or the specific question which Eisen wished to put to his cantankerous offspring.

Gerald Fairson was the most talkative among that cloistered number, gesticulating with great abandon, talking rapidly in a nervous, rambling fashion. His tangents were often confusing, even to himself.

When they had finished their meal, Valencia busied herself cleaning whilst the old man helped her. Rit walked hesitantly away, saying he had things to do, though he didn't seem sure about it.

Jen rose and motioned for Eisen to follow her; he did so briskly.

She passed through the back of the kitchen to the resplendent warmth and color of the living room and from there, up the ornately banistered flight of stairs to her room. She locked the door behind them.

"What is it? What are you doing here, Eisen?"

"You told me your father beats you. That man down there doesn't strike me as the type."

"Looks kin be deceiving."

"They certainly can."

"Why do you talk like that and look at me that way?"

"Because you lied to me, didn't you?"

"No. Why would I lie over something like that?"

"It's a good question, isn't it? I have few clues, but there are many reasons why you might, all of which I can understand but none which I can condone. Now answer my question."

"I didn't– "

"There you go again."

"Eisen, please– "

"Please what, what exactly? Stop your sniveling, it's repulsive."

She was crying now and hid her face in her hands.

"I just, I just wanted you to, to– "

"To what? Pity you?"

"To like me."

His expression did not soften; it grew harder.

"You are an imbecile."

"Eisen."

"I am surrounded by fools. I did not until this moment count you amongst them."

Outside her room there was a creak upon the floorboards and then the sound of boots ascending the steps. They paused to listen. There was nothing.

Eisen was first to break the glassy, unnerving stillness.

"You lied to me about your father to garner my sympathy, so that I would like you? I already liked you!"

"Stop yelling at me."

"Perhaps I would if there was a reason to, yet you haven't given me a single one."

"I'm sorry."

"Yes. I can see that. Hear it in your voice. But why?"

"I didn't think it'd upsetya like this."

"I can't abide deceit, well intentioned or not."

"I'm sorry."

"You already told me as much. I am as well. I lost my temper, forgive me. But, just tell me why."

She approached him and set her hands against his face. She drew him close to her and pressed her lips to his.

Instantly he withdrew and flew from the room as if he had been branded.

He did not pause upon the landing but descended the stairs in rapid succession as she shouted behind him.

"Coward! That's all you are, just a coward!"

James Arlington was not in the kitchen nor the anteroom as Eisen passed through them, and he was thankful to fortune for that.

He walked out unto the porch and exhaled heavily then straightened his collar. He ran a hand through his untidy hair to straighten it and proceeded on his way out of the property.

It was well past midday and the sun was almost swallowed by the mountains rearing up cold and impassable far off in the fog-covered distance. He peered out into that smokey realm of struggle and confusion, of gnashing claws and death and felt a pang of exquisite sadness which he couldn't wholly place.

She wasn't even drunk this time, he whispered to himself as he tersely shook his head, inhaled and squinted against the light.

He turned in the opposite direction, looking off from the way he had come, and beheld dust pillowing up in great rolling coils; horses and riders. They were coming in from the desert, circling out around the town and heading straight for the ranch. But so distant were they that their collective forms were rendered unto nothing more than a dark and patchwork haze of dust and shadow.

Fearing that she would come after him, he left, fully intent on heading to his lodgings as quickly as possible. He was weary of the turbulence which had so suddenly engulfed his life; he wanted only to sleep.

The Italian ranch hand who had disposed of the chicken hawk in the forest sat upon an overturned metal bucket at the far end of the main path which ran from the entrance to the ranch all the way up to the house.

"Howdy."

Eisen paused and nodded to the man and began to turn away, but the ranch hand called him over. He hunched over on his bucket, leaning stoutly on his bony knees.

"Yes?"

"Is it true?"
Eisen waited for him to continue.
"Is it?"
"You're going to have to elaborate."
"What they say. Is it true?"
"And they say what?"
"That that wild girl, that friend of yourn, that she's a witch. Is it true?"
"Nonsense."
"Sense it'll git ya kilt, ya'll mark my words."
"Why is that?"
He continued heedless.
"Sense it'll git ya kilt, round ere, it sholly will."
"Well, I'll remember that."
The man nodded knowingly and then looked away, off into the distant haze, into the long fade of the desert. Eisen followed his gaze out to the horizon. The riders, whoever they were, yet approached, and rather than slow their pace they seemed to have accelerated.
"Friends of yours?"
The ranch hand shook his browned and balding head, flinging sweat.
"Nope."
There was suddenly a loud crack. Then silence. Eisen whirled about, unable to discover the source of the mysterious sound until his gaze flit again to the meditative ranch hand. He was looking down at his chest and the little red hole in it. He upturned his head slowly to Eisen, his features clouding over with confusion and nonacceptance.
"But I – they – they– "
He collapsed as the murderers rode in through the front gate, firing their rifles brazenly into the falling dark. Falling like a curtain as if in homage to the man there sprawled in the dust. Eisen bolted instantly; he could hear a bullet sing over his head, then another. Another.
And another.

The final shot grazed his shoulder, but left him largely unharmed. He ducked behind the tool shed in front of the chicken pen and there waited breathless and wide eyed. His legs ached from the exertion; his chest swelled with tension and air.

He felt fear creep down his spine, reptilian and horribly crass.

Peeking from the corner of the tool shed in the direction of the murderous riders, he beheld them and two rancheros paralyzed and gazing upon the fallen corpse of their former companion. One of them ran and was gunned down by the man who had killed the Italian.

Eisen peered more closely, but could distinguish nothing. The man was wholly obscured by the glare of the sun. A shadow-man enshrouded in a cloak of flame, like some grand and terrible archangel. Some dark, fallen god, newly risen.

He reigned in his horse, a powerful, pure white Clydesdale, and leapt free of his mount. He landed with perfect poise, as if it had cost him nothing and took no effort in its maintenance. A jingling of shells clacking against one another, woven into his thick buckskin pants as he moved.

"Quit hidin – I seeya boyo. I seeya!"

At that moment Eisen knew several things; he knew who the man was, he knew the man knew where he was and he knew what next was coming.

"If ye doint come out, I'll put a bullet in iz brain!"

The remaining ranch hand quivered and fell to his knees, hands clasped imploringly before himself, pleading rapidly in Spanish, eyes tight shut, forehead perspiring.

"I had a feeling you'd say that. It's not very creative you know. Anyway, if I go out there, you'll just shoot both of us."

"I wouldn't dream of it, bha I suspoz yar qui right, not vury creative."

He threw his rifle carelessly over his head to one of the mounted, similarly garbed men behind him. The sun-cloaked man then drew a massive steel machete from a sheath at his belt and walked up to the cowering Spaniard with naked intent. The closer the murderer drew, the more frantic and audible the

Spaniard's cries grew until the sun-cloaked man finally could take no more.

"Cease ya bloody sniveling ye wretched cur, or I swear I'll cut out yar tongue and feed it te ya. Do ya understand?"

He held the blade mere inches from the rancher's mouth. If he had stuck out his tongue, he would have slit it.

"I asked if ya understand."

"Si."

"Then not a bloody WORD. Not a single solitary SOUND. Kin I git nary a piece of peace in this worthless, forsaken dog-spit of land!"

The Spaniard cringed, whimpering. "Who are you?"

"You shouldn't ask."

"Why?"

"Because your ignorance is the only reason you are still alive."

The Spaniard was silent and remained so as the killer turned back to the harbourage of the tool shed and the one resolved and protected behind it.

"Ya voice falls familiarly upon me ears, but I cain't place you with Arlingtons' gang."

"Arlingtons' gang?"

"Aie. His men, his litta group of criminals. Outlaws. Or rather, inlaws, if ye prefer. And what a tone you ave! Why ye sound absolutely petrified. What a pure and delicate flower ya mus bie!"

The man began laughing, convulsing with rapturous, frenzied hilarity.

"You may not remember me, Kavaria, but I remember you well enough. Well enough, Kallista, you hear me! Well enough!"

"Is it... it is. The bloke what 'ad the purple glasses! I thought youdda perished in the desert. Oh, dhis is truly a day of days!"

Thunder cracked like marble splintering in some temple beyond human scope, and the sky fell dark as if heaven's wick had been blown clean. A furious wind howled in across the wide acrid planes, surging and roiling up upon the ranch like the fearsome prelude to a pyroclasm.

Kavaria Kallista, the Demon of the Sever-Sands, Djinn of the Desert, stepped clear of light and shadow overpowering, emerging from a swirling pall of dust that parted as he moved, as if in reverence, and smiled a hunter's smile.

"I neva did get ya name?"

"Eisen. Eisen de Torquiam."

"Vary fancy. It's got a... thing to it, I suppose. Yeah, a real," he raised his free arm and twirled it queerly in the air, "thing. Now ya know I'm hard pressed ta let ye live, situation bein' what it tiz an all."

"We do appear to be at a bit of an impasse."

"You don't sound frightened."

"I'm terrified."

A large, scar-faced grunt pulled up beside the Irishman and snarled out his words in a deep, raspy baritone.

"Feed their bones to the ants."

"Are you givin me an orda, boyo?"

"A suggestion. Only a suggestion."

"Iz dhat what we callin orddas these days?"

The big, scar-faced man merely glared at his master, seething, unwilling to offend, unwilling to back down.

"Do you remember what happened last time you spared witnesses?"

"Yes. We had a jolly time, he played guitar all night long fhor us an tat meh a song just affore'e– "

"Slit three of my best men's throats and escaped. We still don't know where that psychopath is."

"Which iz strange, ain't it? I mean that froo-froo umbrella's gotta stick out like a barn afire."

"That's not the point."

"Sure it tiz, if e wants ta hide any more an not at all, ack, neva mind! I'm wasting time talking."

He strode formidably up to the Spaniard and kicked him viciously in the gut. The poor man doubled over, writhing in agony.

"Where is that shit, Arlington?"

"Right here."

He looked up into the barrel of a shotgun some thirty paces away wielded by a pallid, but resolute, Jennifer Arlington.

"Mistake number one, mah'beauty."

Kavaria delivered his line with flawless swagger, though it was clear to Eisen that the man was shaken and powerfully so. He wasn't scared, but he was irritated and apprehensive.

"Open your mouth again and I'll blow it off."

"Now that'd be a sight!"

"I said shut it."

"Nah yadidint, save fer just now."

The large, scarred man began moving his left hand very subtly toward a pistol strapped at his thigh. Jennifer seemed oblivious to the action.

Eisen shouted to her, pointing at the man. She looked back at the coffin maker just as the man drew his pistol. When she whirled round to face him, he fired, catching her in the gut. She didn't hesitate and returned fire instantly, blowing him clean from the saddle and nearly in half.

Kavaria flung his arms up, not in a gesture of surrender but rather in a motion of exasperation. He turned to his dead confederate then to the grunt's killer. The woman lay on the ground, bleeding heavily, the dust soaking sanguine at her sides.

"Great. I just got that one! He waz a good shot e'waz, a damn fine shot, az ya well know! Do you understand how ard it tiz to find respectable marksmen? Though respectable tizn't quite the word is it, after all, ya still alive."

She tried to raise the gun to fire but he was already upon her, wrenching the firing iron from her feeble grasp.

"Don't even try it, Princess, don't even try!"

Eisen dashed instantly from his hiding place, the horrifying events of the past few seconds all having unfurled far too quickly to have been prevented.

Kavaria turned languidly to him as he shoved the barrel of the gun against the dying woman's skull, forcing her face into the dust.

"Don't!"

Eisen halted instantly some fifteen feet away, his hands up flung in pleading.

"She kilt one of mah men – tis only fair, ain't it?"

"But you killed two of hers first – so no, it wouldn't be fair."

"That's a good point, it tis."

He tilted his head to one side, pouting out his lip and scratching his ruffled shimmering strawberry blond hair with Jen's shotgun.

"Hold on – they weren't ere men, dhey were ere father's men!"

"How do you know?"

"Owhd do I know?" He held the barrels to her head once more. "I know because I have contacts, m'boy. How do you tink I get me information, by carrier pigeon? He waz one of ma contacts, savvy? And now he's gone off and left his daughter to die. Just shameful, ain't it."

He pressed the gun to her skull harder, forcing her face completely flush with the ground, bruising her skin. She was barely conscious now, a beaten and ragged doll of porcelain and blood.

"I guess the rumors are true then."

Kavaria sighed and removed the gun from her head.

"What rumors?"

"That you are insane."

"Insane? Now who would say such a thing?"

"Pretty much everyone."

"You trying ta play at me vanity? Get me riled up and then not shoot her ta prove my sanity?"

"Is it working?"

"If it wasn't, she'd already be dead. It's a good plan, I don't much care for deception, makes me feel... sordid, like I've got grease all ova me body."

"You'll let her go then?"

"No. I'm taking her with me, as insurance. You go find her old man, tell him if he doesn't return ma property ta me, then I shell bloody well do as much for him. You find him. You tell im that.

And don't open your mouth or I may just change me mind bout shooting er. There's a good lad. Go on."

Eisen watched helplessly as the outlaw hefted the young, bloody woman up over his shoulder, saddled up and rode off. His men touched up and followed behind him.

That fell gathering then rode into the desert with only the bodies and the blood any signature of their passing.

Eisen stood and watched them go, breathless and weak, not realizing until that moment that he was shaking.

"Eisen! Oh God, Eisen, I saw it all, oh God!"

The coffin maker turned instantly toward Gerald Fairson who had ran up behind him. Fairson was crying and shaking even worse than Eisen.

He spoke in between sobs.

"I s-should h-have d-done something! Murders! Oh, they kilt them! I s-should have! But I coun't m-move, it was like I just froze. I just froze. Oh God, I was so scared. I've never been so scared!"

"I know this may be too much to ask of you, but do try and calm yourself. You'll work yourself into a fever."

"They took her! Oh, they took her, she's such a sweet girl. They'll kill her or worse, those bastards! They'll kill her just like they kilt... oh, God!"

He was completely hysterical, and Eisen knew well enough it was as good as pointless talking to him, so he lead the poor youth inside and made him lay down upon a sofa in the wide, well-furnished hearth room. Eisen got a rag from the kitchen, wet it with cold water and walked back to Rit and placed it upon his forehead.

"You're not going to leave, are you? What if they come back?"

Fairson was half standing, and Eisen was at some pains to convince him to lay back down and rest.

"But what if they come back!"

"They won't. It would be too risky for them. For him."

"Kallista?"

"Yes."

"So it really was him. People talked about him so much I'd begun to think he didn't exist at all."

"Oh, he's real all right."

"What are you going to do?"

"Find your employer and get him to tell me exactly what's going on here."

"I'll go with you!"

"No. Calm yourself. Rest."

Eisen tended to the ranch hand for a few more minutes before he left through the front door and circled the house.

In his haste, Kallista and his gang had utterly neglected the scarred man's horse, which Eisen had found trotting absently about behind Arlingtons' stables. He saddled up and rode into town.

The journey was hot and long and the day's candle had all but guttered when finally he pulled up at Elis Caldwell's print shop. He tied the silky black mare to an old hitching post outside, and then walked to the door and rapped loudly.

Once.

Twice.

Three times.

Four.

Upon the fourth blow he heard the creaking of a chair and the shuffling of slippered feet over wood. The door opened and Elis Caldwell, appearing in the rent space created, furrowed his high, quizzical brows.

"You show up at this hour looking like that, I fancy something is wrong?"

"A great deal of things. Too many. Can I come in? I know it's a bit of a liberty, but this cannot wait, a woman's life and possibly the lives of many others hang in the balance."

"How portentous. Come in then."

Caldwell walked back to his armchair, sat down, lit up a smoke and kicked his feet up atop a plush, exported Persian foot rest. A bottle of expensive port and two glasses were set like diviner's tools upon the polished wood of the table before him. Eisen sat down opposite him in the other armchair were he had sat on his previous visit.

"Well?"

"Do you know where James Arlington is?"

"Is that all?"

"No, not nearly all."

"Why the dire look?"

"His daughter has been kidnapped. Taken by Kavaria Kallista."

"W-what?"

It was the first time Eisen has seen the man lose his cold veneer of stoicism, his mask of civil disdain gone as if torn away by some invisible hand.

"You knew her then, as I thought."

"Yes. Yes, I knew her. We were quite close. When did this occur? When was she taken?"

"About two and a half hours ago. I couldn't do anything about it. He had a gun to her head. It took some time getting back from Arlingtons' ranch by horse. I rode as fast as I could. We have to do something, and you're the one that runs the papers."

"I can't run that in the papers, it would create a scandal. People would run wild with fear, there'd be chaos. Especially after what happened with Daniels and, and... whatshisname. I don't even want to think what this would make Daniels do."

"Do you know where Arlington is?"

"No. I'm not his assistant, I don't stand by his side every minute of every day. I have my own work to do, so no, I have no idea where he is or could be. Damn! Why did Kavaria take her?"

"So you don't know?"

"Know what?"

"That Arlington is working for Kavaria Kallista. Kavaria must have some kind of hold over him that had waned, and evidently, considerably so. But now that hold has been strengthened, assured."

"I'll go at once to see if I can find him. I'll take some of my men with me. I'll wake them. You should go to the sheriff."

"The sheriff?"

"Don't tell me you hold a grudge, Mr. Torquiam?"

"Grudges are for old women and little boys."

"Good. Then we should hurry."

With that Elis Caldwell rose to his full height from his chair, kicked his slippers from his feet and dashed hurriedly to the backroom where he dressed with similar haste, donning tail coat, cane and riding boots.

"Are you going to the sheriff?"

"Yes, but first I'm going to Ledru. He has more influence in what gets done here, even if the people don't want to admit it."

"A good plan."

Caldwell lurched out the door, carelessly letting it slam closed behind him, which seemed far from keeping with what Eisen had observed of the man beforehand.

Eisen murmured to himself as he watched the reporter dash across the street, striking his cane furiously into the dust as he went along, as if it were some dire and repulsive foe.

The coffin maker exited the press shop, resaddled the horse he had taken from Arlingtons' ranch, and started off toward Ledru Monteblanc's lofty mansion perch when he remembered how everyone (even those who didn't want to) knew Arrgilius.

He rode up to the inn at a furious pace, dismounted and nearly tripped over his own feet in his haste to speak to the loquacious barkeep.

Every head that could turn did so as he surged into the establishment, the flimsy, wood-paneled doors flapping violently behind him.

From the far back right corner a voice arose, saying, "Looks like someone needs a drink real bad." Laughter followed. Eisen paid them no mind. He felt he had little enough at the moment to spare.

"What in blazes?"

Arrgilius started in great befuddlement as Eisen, dust blown, wind battered and direly solemn walked to the counter and leaned over it as far as he could.

GRAVE.

"There's a problem."

"Yeah, I kin see that, what appened to ya? Ya look awfa– "

"Just listen."

"All right."

"Arlingtons' been kidnapped."

"James Arlington?"

"No, you buffoon! Jen Arlington. She's been kidnapped."

"By whom?"

"Kavaria. Kavaria Kallista."

"Lord above."

"He's not going to be of much use, I'm afraid, not in this instance. Spread the word, that shouldn't be too hard now should it? Moving your mouth, flapping your tongue?"

"They say it's what I was born ta do."

"I certainly hope so. Do it."

"Where are you going?"

"To Ledru's. He can get some men together, men other than Daniels and his gang of brutes."

"You're planning on going afta Kallista?"

"Only insofar as it brings me closer to getting Jen back, safe and unharmed, if she isn't already. No, I have to go."

Before Arrgilius could pose another question, Eisen dashed from the inn, resaddled and rode off.

Arrgilius wasted no time doing what he was 'Born ta do.'

Chapter Eighteen

The Man in White

The ride to Ledru's mansion was considerably faster than last time he had traversed that steep and dire slope by carriage in the company of Percival Statletter. He paused suddenly and stiltedly, gazing out at the diminishing industry of the town. A sandstorm was brewing out in the desert, and the sky grew dark again, thunderous and grim.

Thunderheads moved above the barren wastes like the prophets of destruction; that which had already come or that which was still to happen. He wondered where, in that hellish ambit, Kavaria made camp. He wondered, in similar vein, where Jen was and if she was even still alive, thinking that she was; hoping vaguely, uncomfortably.

The horse began quite abruptly to buck and neigh, swinging its head wildly from side-to-side. With every second that passed the beast's frenzied thrashing grew only worse until, with horror and a pounding heart, Eisen realized that if it continued, he'd be thrown clear. Thrown, more than likely, from the high, jagged cliff.

He pictured it all in his mind, a sudden, fearful flash of thought: Falling among the tumulus of the pitted, mossy ravine that washed down the land to the town below. Crack of bones and their breaking mingling with the soft, glassy granulation of the desert, panning smoothly out with the ebb of time until their disparities vanished completely. Only polished bones and that which skittered hungrily within.

As the horse reared, Eisen threw himself to one side, as far from that perilous ledge as possible. He felt ground beneath his skin and something hard collide with his head. His vision blurred. The horse whinnied once more, stomped the ground as if it feared that the sandy, rising trail, rock strewn and serpentine, would surge to engulf it. Then the beast ran off to the manor, snorting and clomping savagely as it went.

The wind picked up, drowning out everything but a low, subdued laugh followed shortly thereafter by the sound of footsteps and something making a muted flapping. It was close.

Very close.

Eisen, straining against the throbbing pain in his skull, lifted his slender, hardy frame from the ground and rose to a kneeling position, one leg bent neath him, the other propping him up firmly against the gravel, grass and sand.

A man stood loosely before him, the stranger's face shaded by the pall of an umbrella. A white umbrella gleaming in the thunder-shine like an acid-etched skull.

"Y-you... who are you?"

"Why question when the question itself makes sense of nothing and makes nothing of sense."

"I don't. I don't understand."

"That is the point."

"W-what point?"

The man looked after the horse and then back to Eisen on the ground as the thunderheads roared in the dark and far away like the boisterous threats of vengeful djinn. Echoing off the high cliff wall on which they stood and the even higher ones above them, lacing the air like a raucous anthem. It was a fearful sound. A hymn. A hymn of fell insurrection.

The man nodded as if the sound and the churning malevolence above the desert, descending, were some satisfying affirmation. He seemed opaquely pleased. Then he continued speaking, walking slowly around Eisen until he stood directly behind him at the edge of the cliff, gazing down upon the gray and wasted fangs of the ravine. A threatening maw. A maw which the man seemed wholly unfazed by. He looked up and still, try as he might, Eisen was unable to see the man's face.

"You're that coffin man, aren't you? Eisen, wasn't it?"

Eisen felt sure the man knew exactly who he was. He wondered at the pretense of ignorance and what possible part it had to play in this shadowed stranger's schemes.

"Yeah. I'm Eisen. Who are you? What are you doing here?"

"The latter question implies that I'm here to do anything at all, and by 'do,' you mean doing something to something else, otherwise why put it all into words? Why not let the silence hang like a corpse? Why am I here? I have to be someplace."

"That's not really an answer at all."

"Course it is. It's just not the one you want. Much as any man may talk of truth, that's rarely what he wants."

Eisen rose as if in defiance of these enigmatic, gently spoken words. They unnerved him deeply, though he did not understand exactly why.

"And what would you know of what I want?"

"You sound offended."

"Oh? So tell me then, what is the sound of offense?"

"That, like anything else, depends on what you mean by it. I fancy you only said that to wound me."

"Yes. You don't sound like you would much care even if you had offended me much or more than any man."

"I wouldn't. And that still furthers your irritation."

"Why have you been following me?"

The man, who had been standing perfectly still and wholly erect, eyes frozen to the abyss beneath him, turned on a well-polished heel and stuck a free, black-gloved hand in his pocket.

"Following you." It was neither a question nor denial nor affirmation, merely a statement of words existent.

"Yes, following me. You've been following me, have you not?"

"Have I."

"That's what I'm asking you. I saw you. I saw you outside the church; you were watching me, staring like you recognized me. I've seen you a few times after that as well."

"Have you."

"Games. Must we?"

"I'm afraid we must."

"Curiously, you don't sound afraid."

"Don't I?"

"I don't have time for nonsense."

"Who does? This town doesn't. Soon its time will run out. Very soon. Perhaps, even sooner than even I'd expected."

"What do you mean? What is that supposed to mean?"

"Oh, I never answered your question, did I? I came here for the view, to see the sights."

He motioned behind him with his free hand over the vast, smoldering vista of sand and stone, dying grass, and the town with its lights burning like the embers of a coal pit beneath him to the unearthly dirge of the storm; flashing lightning in the din.

Eisen looked out and down and across, his vision swooping like a hawk over that pitted cairn. So many lights, tiny undulating fireflies interred in the transience of work and play, in life and love, in house and hovel. There were lights burning at the oil fields, and the coffin maker could smell the oil, thick and pungent and cloying, enmeshed with the acrid, howling air.

With the tar pitch vale, the tiny fires within complemented by the discordant, savage anthem of the storm and the cryptic, darkened figure before him, Eisen felt as if he had, with that blow to the head, been thrust into some other world. A dream world which was all too in-keeping with nightmares and the specters which populated them.

"A view from a grave. Yours and mine. And all of theirs." He motioned once more as Eisen shuddered involuntarily at these words and started moving slowly away from the stranger.

The man with the white umbrella said nothing further as Eisen walked uneasily away, up the steepening slope. He looked back, and as he did, a flash of fey, greenish lightning for the briefest of seconds illuminated the lower half of the stranger's face.

He was smiling.

It was like the gristle grinning of the newly risen dead.

Chapter Nineteen

A Manse of Bravado

Eisen found his horse neighing sharp and ceaseless before the mansion. The coffin maker wondered intently whether it was the storm or the man, who seemed to appreciate it so ardently, which had caused the beast such fright. Both, probably, he thought, shuddering involuntarily once more.

He walked to the horse and threw his arms about the frantic creature's neck, saying, "Hush, it's all right, it's all right. He's gone now, hush." Shortly thereafter he succeeded in calming the beast and led it to the lavish stables where a liveried servant stood quietly and stoically as if in expectation. Eisen had never seen him before. The servant was quite old and was curiously silhouetted by the flashing thunder about which he was bizarrely unconcerned. It was as if he didn't notice the weather at all. Perhaps he did not.

The distance between them, Eisen and the stable worker, was some forty feet, illuminated by the roiling greenish gimcracks in the sky. Odd green figures against a backdrop of thick and solid blackness, like cardboard cutouts from some Martian stage play.

"If you're here to see Mr. Monteblanc, sir, you're not going to be able to do so, I'm afraid."

"Oh?"

"No."

"Why?"

"He's currently engaged."

"Doing what, if I may inquire?"

"You may. He's hosting a party for some investor friends of his, members of a firm interested in oil fields, his oil field, in particular."

"Are they looking to buy him out?"

"I couldn't say. I can say that he's not seeing anyone right now, but I could perhaps make you some coffee while we wait."

"No. I don't have time. The matter which leads me here is of the utmost importance."

"Everyone says that."

"A woman has been kidnapped by bandits."

"What?"

"Jen Arlington."

"I've heard of her. What is it you think Ledru can do about it?"

"Organize a posse."

"You could do that in the town, probably with more ease."

"Probably."

"Look, you can't see him right now."

"I'm going in. Stop me if you can."

"I could."

"Could or will?"

"Could."

"Wise man."

"Practical."

"Exactly."

They exchanged guarded smiles and passed by one another without further conversation, the aged servant leading the horse to an empty stall, Eisen jogging off to the mansion's doors. When Eisen arrived at the doors, he knocked furiously again and again. And again and again there was no answer from the other side, no booming voice calling for dispersion or entrance. He was about to give up when the doors were suddenly opened and a familiar voice greeted him.

"Mr. Torquiam. We were not expecting you. You look terrible, are you ill or has something happened?"

"Something."

"What?"

"Something very bad."

"Well, come in then."

"Where is Ledru? Still at his meeting?"

"Yes, but how did you know?"

"Old man by the stables. We've got to get some people together. Jen Arlington has been kidnapped by Kavaria Kallista."

"I sincerely hope you are joking. Y-you're not, are you?"

"No. Unfortunately, I am not."

"Well, if that's what happened can't wait. Come in, come in. Don't stand there hyperventilating like that. Come in and explain everything to me, then we can do something."

It was the first time Eisen had observed Statletter so at a loss. He seemed utterly befogged by the grim circumstances that had so viciously closed in upon him. Eisen half expected him to know James Arlingtons' connection to Kallista, so omniscient did the blind man often seem; but here, now, his powers utterly failed him. Statletter pursed his lips and slumped his shoulders, hunching over broodingly as he strode beside his guest down the resplendent, trophy-lined hallway.

Eisen was surprised that the little mountain-footed forest in which he lived could possibly have harbored such a wide diversity of species. Upon the walls there were the remnants of elk and bear, deer and boar, mountain lion and coyote, wolf and bison. Eisen figured that he would have noticed at least some indication of all the herds of bison roaming hither-thither through the deserts, and thus deduced that Ledru must have brought these from wherever it was he had come.

"So you think this would supersede Ledru's little tea party?"

"It's not exactly a tea party, though I would say that this venture is only slightly less frivolous."

"At the moment I don't much care about how frivolous Ledru's business ventures tend to be."

"Right. Of course, sorry."

"I think that was the first time I've ever heard you apologize."

"Well, don't make too much of it."

"Where is he?"

"Before we get to that, I'm curious why you didn't just gather up some toughs from the city, they're bound to be for it."
"That's precisely why I wouldn't want them helping me."
"I don't understand."
"Really? I overestimated you. Well, the reason I don't want to gather together any men from the town to go after Kallista is because they would want to, and not because they were overly concerned about either the justice of the thing nor Ms. Arlingtons' safety. I forgot to ask – you don't happen to know where James Arlington is?"
"I can't believe that hadn't entered my head earlier!"
"Well?"
"Yes – damn, yes indeed. I'm a fool."
"Why is that?"
"Because James Arlington is in the library at the meeting."
Eisen didn't hesitate, he instantly shot down the hallway, pausing only momentarily before the huge, ornate double doors of Ledru's library. He burst through the doors. The scene that greeted him was almost surreal in its presentation, for there, sprawled out languidly in Ledru's magnificent throne-like arm chair, was Kavaria Kallista. On the floor, bound and gagged were two servants, one of whom was bleeding nominally from a large blunt wound to the back of his head.
Ledru himself stood anxiously to one side of Kavaria between four toughs with a pistol each. They all glowered at the newcomer and jumped fearfully when Eisen intruded. Kavaria seemed heartily amused by their excitement and quickly waved them away, telling them to "Take care of him." They departed off through the back entrance. James Arlington was nowhere to be seen.
Kavaria reacted as if he was expecting the entrant. He smiled slyly and, drumming his heavily bejeweled fingers against the armrests rhythmically, began to sing.
"Here comes the hero, brandishing vorpal blade. But the rogue's not the rub, no, he's peaceful as a dove, as long as e's getting laid!"

Kavaria leaned even farther back in the chair, laughing wildly and kicking his feet up onto the bound and battered man nearest his reach (who exclaimed pitifully, insofar as his gag permitted him and wriggled futility).

"Kavaria."

"Well, well. Eisen de Torquiam. Come just in time tah join ma party."

"There isn't going to be a party."

"Remains to be seen, though by me it alriddy'haz."

"Where are the Arlingtons?"

"How would I know? Me men's business, ain't'e?"

"Where?"

"Somewhere in one of the hundreds of thousands of places it's possible for them ta be in the desert. Great stroke of luck, me spying him riding on up here, the weaselly little git."

Despite all his fear, Ledru no longer could control his curiosity. The words tore free of his mouth before he was even aware he was uttering them.

"What on earth are you doing here, Eisen?"

"A better question, Ledru, would be why you are untied while two of your servants are not?"

There was then the muffled sound of a cane tapping in tandem with a set of footsteps. A moment later Statletter entered the library. He cocked his head so that his right ear (his best one) was pointed toward the room.

"What's this – Kavaria? Is that scoundrel here?"

"Scoundrel? I'm flattered. The names I'm usually called are quite a bit less... how shall I say, romanticized."

"So you are here! Ledru, what is going on?"

Ledru Monteblanc looked fearfully toward the leering outlaw, silently begging permission to speak. Kavaria shook his head fractionally and then wagged a finger at the portly idler, as if reprimanding a rapscallion. He sneered when Ledru shrunk away from him. The bandit then turned his attentions back to Eisen, whom he seemed whole-heartedly fascinated with.

"You might want te go'on an leave while ya still able."

"I've been told that before, and yet here I stand."

"Me, too."

"I find petty one-up-man-ship distasteful. Don't you?"

"Indeed. My boon, ya a man afta me own art. So I'll just go ahead and fill ya in on everything ya want ta know. Take a seat, boyyo. Take a load off, I don't bite."

"Pardon me if I don't take you at your word."

"Ha!"

Statletter could take no more and, upon hearing Kavaria laugh once again, ran recklessly at where he deduced the "scoundrel" to be, grabbing his cane with both gnarled hands and swinging the stick wildly overhead like a battle ax.

Kavaria smiled a wolfish smile and started laughing with sheer antipathic abandon as he watched the blind man prepare his attack. When he realized that Statletter had correctly determined his position in the middle of the room, his eyes grew wide with amusement and shocked surprise in equal portions. He threw up his left arm a fraction of a second before Statletter's cane would have fragmented his skull. They tussled for a patch, but the moment Kavaria seized the cane, everyone knew the fight was over. Kavaria pulled the stick from the blind man's grasp and with a sudden howl, feral and predatory, the outlaw struck Statletter down with a blow to his forehead.

As the old invalid crumpled to the ground, Eisen rushed forward, grabbing a steel decanter from the posh, wooden lamp table and brought it down upon his foe's head in a powerful, one-handed arc.

Kavaria barely moved; teetering for but a moment, blood trickling from the fast discoloring wound, fluttering his eyelids from the shock and then shaking his head like a water-soaked canine. His composure returned almost instantly. He seemed perversely delighted by this savage turn.

Eisen attempted to bring his knee up into Kallista's gut, but the outlaw merely sidestepped the blow and swept the coffin maker's feet out from underneath him as one might sweep a rug, bringing him hard and low unto the ground.

Ledru attempted to make a run from the room, but Kavaria merely whirled on him, booming, "Don't even think about it, you cheeky fat bastard."

And he didn't.

"Now we're all gonna have ourselves a little chat, understand? Yes or not, doesn't matter, I'm gonna tell ya anyways. I want that oil, I want those fields, and I will have them. I was prepared ta buy, but you just won't sell. Course that doesn't really matter, does it, makes no difference, Ledru, does it – because if you don't, then the people of the town will be just a clamoring to take ya head as reparations for the deaths of little Jen and her poor, poor father. Greedy beast, are you really prepared to let a woman die over a little trickle of black gold? I know I certainly am."

"But the people."

"What about them?"

"This place will turn into a ghost town. Without the oil it'll dry up like the desert, gone, everything! This town is on the cusp of profound expansion, all because of my oil fields!"

"Oh? Listen ta yeself! MY oil fields, YOUR oil fields. Yes, all thanks ta ya! But what do ya mean, I wonder? Or were dhey just so much grease for ya machine, paint fer ya canvas?"

"N-no, I v-value my men – but you can't do this, not to me, not to them. Not to the town!"

"Ledru, Ledru, you think I'm gonna blow up all that black gold, light it up just to watch it glow? Or ferry it all away? I admit it sounds a wee bit enticing, but I've higher aims dan that. Longer aims. Aims what require duration as well as... entertainment value. See, the day before me father kilt hisself he turned ta me an e said, 'M'boy, if you want people to obey you, if you want them ta dance ta what you sing, you don't have ta intimidate, an ye don't have ta charm. You just have ta take all of deir wealth, an once you do dhat, dhen ye will become a god. A god, m'boy, gold is god. I couldn't, m'son, I failed. I kin tell ya won't.' Yah, dhats what e said, that I won't fail, and I don't intend to. Money means nothing to me, but it means everything to most."

Eisen, who had collected himself up from the carpet, chimed in sharply as he calculated his enemies' next moves.

"That's a very childish notion of power."

"I never said it wasn't. Did I? However, if you're trying ta ruffle me feathers, I kin tell ye dat'cha not doing a very good job."

"Oh, I'm not trying to ruffle anything."

As he spoke he began moving toward Statletter, who lay unconscious and bleeding on the ground, his left arm grotesquely twisted behind his back where he had fallen. The scheme he wished to deploy against Kallista would require great precision and even greater speed. And if he failed, well, he didn't want to think about it.

Eisen readied himself; prepared to leap for Statletter's cane, to swing it into Kavaria's left kneecap and, once downed, grab the highwayman's gun from the right of his hip where it loosely hung and...

He crouched. But before he could act, the library doors were thrown open to reveal Henry Collins, Arrgilius Mersan, a motley collection of hard-looking oil workers, and Gerald Fairson, who wore a look of uncharacteristic steel. All of them, save Fairson and Collins, were out of breath and perspiring heavily.

These hasty minute men each carried a weapon unique to his profession and held them with every visible intention of bringing them to bear on Kallista.

Fairson headed the small band of makeshift warriors, wielding Jen's double barrel shotgun like a true huntsman.

Kavaria held up his hands sardonically with perpetually cocked brow and a superciliousness to his countenance that was profound, even for a man of his snide and arrogant dimensions.

"Wild bunch you are. Got a lot a cold-blooded killers on me hands, don't I! Buncha rough-cut soldiers, aye?"

The bandit furnished unto his newest guest a flamboyant, mock salute and began marching back and forth like some over-wound, clockwork trooper.

Fairson tramped forward until he was twenty feet from the sharp-tongued Irishman, shotgun aimed at his heart.

"Shut it or I'll shut it for you."

"Big words from a little man."

"You don't think I'll do it!"

"It ain't something I need ta think much about, I mean, look'atcha. You've never kilt anyone, never felt the warm spray of blood on your face, have you? No. Never seen that look in their eyes, in the eyes of a person what knows they'ir about to die. It's a loss of hope. A complete loss of hope when they know that there isn't going te be any valiant rescue, just like there ain't gonna be now, despite all ya...amateur heroics."

Then Kavaria did something none of them were expecting, he turned his back to the man that balanced his life on a hair trigger.

"Shoot, if you're shooting, I'm a busy man." After no shot was fired, he said, "Weeelp, see ya later. I'll give Jen ya regards, Mr. Torquiam. Ya shill out a litta extra an I might be able ta arrange some flowers."

Then there was no sound but the muted scraping of the outlaw's boots across the carpet, heading for the door opposite the one which the militia had entered through. Eisen swivelled his body slightly to gain a better perspective upon Fairson. His face was contorted with some vague emotion that was steadily unraveling its veil.

It was rage.

Some shouted, "Stop him!"

A thunderclap rang out.

Belatedly, Eisen realized that it wasn't a thunderclap at all, but the discharging barrel of Gerald's shotgun. A spray of buckshot tattooed Kavaria's upper left shoulder, ejecting a thick, undulating coil of misty red upwards and outwards like some fell, eldritch wing. He lost balance, dropping toward his destination, rolling with the force of the blast and gracefully recovering back on his feet, turning round with a slight grimace that was quickly overshadowed by a high, hysterical cackle which grew only louder when he saw the crestfallen expression upon his attacker's innocent, youthful face.

"Better luck next time."

As he disappeared quicksilver fast through the doorway, the majority of the minute men clambered through the confines of the portal, dashing to the middle of the library, to Statletter's unconscious, dark-suited shape. One of them placed two fingers to his neck, directly below his jaw. Looking for a pulse, finding one. As the fact was stated, a wave of relief washed over the small party, which quickly fell away as they realized that, in their collective shock, they had allowed Kavaria to escape. Collins was the first to recover, lumbering savagely forward like a rampaging ox, and just as he was about to reach the back doors, they were slammed shut. The next thing the party heard was the clicking of a latch, the latch of a deadbolt.

Eisen let out a sigh and folded his legs underneath him, dropping down to the floor, and there he sat, meditatively attempting to quell his soaring pulse and eradicate a series of ghastly, unbidden predictions.

As the coffin maker collected himself and his thoughts, Collins called over a few other men, and together they rammed down the door with a shout of, "All together!"

On the other side they found another servant, unconscious like the others and bound tightly and hastily at the wrists with a thin strand of rope. He lay just down to the direct left of the corridor.

One man, whom Eisen didn't recognize, took up the gauntlet with fiery passion, pointing down the corridor and grimacing.

"After him, men. We'll gut the sonnofabitch!"

They took off with Collins' massive form in tow and disappeared down the hallway, only the muted thumping of feet striking carpeted stone.

A shot rang out. Then another.

Someone gave a shout.

A cry of pain.

Eisen unsloped himself swiftly, but measuringly, from his red rug perch and hastened to the doorway, peering cautiously round it. Down the hallway to his left Collins and his crew were exchanging gunplay with three of the four men whom had previously flanked Kavaria in the library. One of them was wounded, having taken a bullet to the upper right thigh. He leaned against the far wall nearest the entrance to the kitchen.

Kavaria was gone, presumably having fled through the kitchen and from there making an easy escape through the lobby, the anteroom, and outside to the stables or wherever he had roped his horse.

The wounded villain raised his pistol with an expression of venomous hatred.

And pointed it directly at Gerald Fairson's heart.

Before Eisen had time to fully evaluate the situation, he rushed forward with such speed that all present were awestruck. He threw himself at Fairson and brought him low just as the bullet tore overhead like a blood-crazed demon whistling away into the night. The next moment one of Collins' crew hurried forth and tackled the man to the ground. He was quickly joined by another, and by swift degrees the villain was subdued. Such was the look of profundity then gilding Fairson's youthful face that Eisen averted his gaze and quickly rose as he did so.

"You'd have done the same. Nothing needs be said."

Fairson was too shocked to speak. To move. To look away. It was as if in that trim and perfectly bloodless figure standing so erect and purposeful before him that he had bore witness to some great truth, to the unveiling of a grand and vexing mystery which had sorely perplexed him, but was now cleaved of its vile power.

Eisen turned smiling to Collins, striding merrily to the big man and clasping him warmly on the shoulders.

"Good show, by God! Good show!"

"We may have got the small fry, but we let the big fish git away."

Fairson shook his head. "If I hadn't of hesitated – it was a second, only a second."

"Don't blame yourself. Everyone does so often for some many things that aren't their fault, it makes my head ache."

"I'm sorry."

GRAVE.

"Are you all all right?" He addressed the men suddenly and powerfully.

They replied that they were and finished binding the three footpads, then left them there in the middle of the floor and took off down the corridor after Kavaria. Eisen didn't bother with it; he knew at this stage that Kallista was gone. Long gone and far away beyond their reach. They wouldn't catch him today.

All the while Eisen helped bandage the men's wounds, picked up the overturned furniture, and headed off for the doctor, he kept thinking of Kavaria's honesty. For so black-hearted a rogue, it had struck Eisen as curious that he was so bald-faced and obvious in his motivations. There was no mystery about it – sheer power lust. No attempt at justification which he seemed to view as an entity entirely foreign to his consciousness. Curious. Of course there was nothing curious about the act; rather, it was the way in which he attempted to acquire his ends that piqued the coffin maker's interest. It was as if the Irishman was more fascinated by the styling of his action than the action itself. And, detestable though Eisen found the outlaw, he couldn't help but sense a certain wisdom in his manner. He thought about that and mused there was a very good reason why in most cultures the snake was as dreaded as it was revered.

Chapter Twenty

Tragedy, then Night

The sky was black as tar and silent as Eisen rode with a vanguard of two armed men at Fairson's desperate, near frantic, urging. "They could still be on the path, waiting, it could be an ambush!"

Collins and a chap named Tanners, a surly, foul-mouthed brawler of forty-some-odd years with a large, fascinating knife scar across his right brow, were the young coffin maker's compatriots. On the way down the cliff, Tanners pointed to his scar and bragged it was where once a Red Indian had tried to scalp him, tried, and failed. He spoke the last words with disturbing relish and a kind of theatrical affectation. Eisen didn't believe a single word of the story, but Collins seemed ready enough to ingest anything, so long as it was suitably entertaining.

"Why would you make up such a story – to impress?"

"Why in holy hell would you need impressing? Shit."

"A question with a question – rather bad form."

Tanners snorted and rubbed his beard.

"Form? Like manners and all that shit?"

"That's the second 'shit' in thirty seconds. You know, I can scarce fathom what your parents must have thought about the bottomless depths of your eloquence."

"What the hell are you talkin bout?"

"It is curious, is it not, Tanners, that we can both be speaking the same language, living in the same society, such as it is, and yet still be wholly unable to communicate. It really is the root of all evil."

"What?"

"Communication. A lack thereof."

Tanners laughed, but Collins nodded solemnly, saying, "There's something in that, Eisen, there sure is something in that."

"Well, at least someone is listening to the words that are coming out of my mouth."

Tanners turned in his saddled mare with one eye asquint, a question and a challenge therein.

"Ya sure are a touchy one, ain'tchee?"

"No. I prefer cagey, sounds more intimidating and respectable."

"You don't need ta worry none bout that."

"How do you figure?"

"You earned the town's respect when ya'll stood up ta the Demon of the Desert."

"Is that sincerity I hear coming out of your mouth? Booze goes in, praise comes out, don't know what to make of that."

"It may just be so. Ya sholl are the queerest man I ever did meet, you know that?"

"Thank you, Tanners. I shall ever wear that rosy-cheeked remark about my bosom, proud as a Vikland scar."

"Don't know what the hell that is suppose ta mean, but it sounds good ta me."

Collins looked to Eisen knowingly.

They laughed as they trotted their horses into town with Tanners looking sour faced and confused, one to the other and then back again.

It was only when they passed beyond the makeshift hovels which housed the grime-encrusted yeomen who toiled wearily out upon those barren fields did they realize the town was in the midst of some furious turmoil.

A din arose then unto the traveler's ears like the buzzing of a hornet's nest.

It was a riot in the streets.

The main square was covered with torn and tattered tents and overturned wagons, formerly so full of color and cheer, now consigned to the wind and the angry swirling dust and the feet trammeling over them with savage, hateful abandon.

It was with supreme horror that Eisen realized what the smashed and shattered flotsam was; the circus caravan, the dismembered remnants thereof.

He could see, over the tops of the houses, in every direction before him, the retreating forms of the remaining performers, clowns and knife throwers, jugglers and announcers, running as fast as their legs would carry them out into the desert with a small gang each, dogging their heels.

Running. And running.

And running.

To their death.

☼

The survivors of the circus caravan, bloodied and exiled, headed out of town into the woods, up toward the mountain pass, toward Old Yellow Eyes and the storm lands where he dwelt. Primeval incarnadine. Liken to the corpses of the unfit and unprepared, victims of the fell specter of hysteria, the fatal scythe of fanaticism. The bodies of the dead lay scattered about town for some hours after the massacre, time enough for the carrion crawlers and winged collectors of that growling, ensanguined expanse to sculpt their own macabre creations.

By the time the townsfolk finally began moving the stinking, swollen cadavers into the wooden horse carts, not a man nor woman among them could recognize such grotesque burdens as their former eventualities.

Eisen watched this all with a lingering sense of horror, a dread so leaden and stifling that he could scarce move due the weight of it. He stood before Arrgilius' inn, watching and waiting.

Near breathless.

Near tears.

Beside him Collins covered his mouth in repulsion as Tanners shook his head.

Collins turned to his two companions with an open mouth, expectant, pleading. Neither of them said anything, the look in their eyes saying, "What was there to do?"

All was already over with, the blood had been drawn and a line crossed, and something was behind the crossing, someone.

Eisen felt he knew just who that someone was, and the force of that knowledge tore at him as no corporeal blade ever could.

"Come," Eisen commanded at length, forcing himself away from the mounting death carts and into the now familiar confines of the quirky little hostel.

"There is nothing we can do."

And they all knew the truth of it and followed him inside.

☼

The three dismayed companions sat round a small wooden table in the corner farthest from the door and closest to the steep, ebony stairs. Shortly thereafter the owner of the establishment took a seat between Eisen and Collins with his back to the door.

"I'll tell it to you just as it happened."

Eisen turned to Arrgilius with the most dire expression the errant innkeeper had ever seen.

"It was Michael, wasn't it?"

"Eisen."

"Wasn't it?"

"Yes. I knew he wasn't too fond of those tramps what were from the circus, but this... it's, it's unconscionable."

"Obviously not."

"Well, Elis, er, Mr. Caldwell, came back and told them to clear out of the square, that they couldn't keep the town's main thoroughfare congested, and he kinda had a point. Sorta. Anyhow, they refused and he just shrugged, Mr. Caldwell that is, being as he is. But those oilmen of Ledru's didn't like it, said they didn't take kind ta outsiders getting large on em. Fancy they were talkin bout you."

"I figured as much. It seems I've become a real celebrity."

"Aye, and not a very popular one at that."

"So I gather."

"Well, like as I said, the oil men didn't like it, but Elis gave em a word or two and they calmed down. They tend to do that when their paychecks are threatened. Like as most."

"Mercenaries, plain and simple," chimed Tanners like an ancient maritime dirge, shaking his head reprovingly.

Collins arched a brow while Eisen didn't seem to react at all.

Arrgilius continued, heedless.

"So Elis waited around until he thought Ledru's men had left. Most of them had, but a few circled back around the square, waiting to do so until Caldwell had left.

"A fight broke out, and Michael Montferiat came down from the church with a couple of his closest followers. Don't know where his father was, busy I guess, he was at the church like as usual.

"Anyhow, he started shouting about blasphemies and abominations (I was in the street, mind, talking to a friend), and that great big blond came on down.

"He said he was a man of God like as Michael, but the preacher just scoffed at that. Laughed right in his face. Called him a Sodomite. A traitor to his faith, if ever he had any at all.

"He said the reason he had come from the church was that he had heard tell that a fortune teller traveled with them. Michael asked the blond if it was true, and the circus master said that it was.

"I swear I've never seen a man as enraged as that young priest became. You would have thought, had you seen the frackle, that someone had slaughtered a child! He screamed then. To his followers, said, 'Get them out of here, get that sorceress gone. I'll not have it. God will not have it.'

"When the ringmaster tried to stop them from throwing his company out, they... they shot him. It was horrible. Blood gushing every which way and him falling to the ground, howling like a wounded wolf.

"Michael bent down to him then and whispered something in his ear which I couldn't make out, and then he nodded to his men and they just, they just..."

Eisen let the silence hang a few moments and then leaned forward and said, "They just fired on him again, didn't they?"

Arrgilius nodded sadly, eyes downcast and shoulders slumped up over the rickety, wooden table round which they had gathered. There was silence then for a minute entire, hanging round one and every man like a discorporate noose.

Then Eisen rose with a clatter and ground his teeth, clenched his fists and set his eyes upon nothing that any of the other men could see. "I need to get some air."

Eisen left the sullen inn as if it were an oven and him afire therein. When he emerged outside, he inhaled deeply and closed his eyes against the light. The sun soaked into his skin like a revitalizing balm, warm and soothing and unfettering the chained and cloistered orbit of his thoughts. But it was a freedom shortly recorded by his seething, hate-ridden mind. He took another breath in an attempt to better calm himself. This time he forced his mind to what he would do, rather than what had already occurred; the sharpening of his senses through the prospect of action.

The sun was now broad and bloated in the midmorning sky, the wind about it, scathing and heady, carrying the scent of oil and wood and horses and the desert beyond. Outside the inn the acrid streets were filled with people still carting the dead away. Some of the townsfolk, men of a particularly staunch disposition, had refused to see the doctor and instead sat on doorways or crates overturned, nursing their wounds and looking about with savage choler.

A cat wandered between the wreckage of the carnival in the town square, mewing and seemingly oblivious to the carnage. Two houses down directly across the street from the inn a woman was weeping with a young babe in her arms, its tiny fists upthrust into the air as if in anticipation of catching her slowly falling tears.

Eisen thought of stepping onto the street and walking up to that sobbing woman, thought of offering comforting words, but knew with sadness greater than her own that it would all be in vain. She would turn away, she would scorn him, she would hate him for the mere presentation of his pity. He would only further her sorrow, not dispense with it, nor his own.

Eisen stuck his hands in his pockets and looked up at the burning atmosphere, like a sea of fire, then, exhaling and slumping his shoulders against the planetary compass surrounding him, headed into the bright. He wanted time. Time to think.

He headed quickly back inside the inn and asked Collins and Tanners if they would go and fetch the medico and take him to Ledru's without him. They replied that they would without asking any questions. Eisen nodded and then walked outside, saddled his horse and rode out of town.

☼

He journeyed the better part of the day out in the wastes closest to the mountains which fenced the city in on three sides. When the light began to fade, he turned the horse around and started in toward his lodge in the forest, arriving there just before sundown and found that he, quite unexpectedly, had company.

Two horses were tied to a thin ash tree inside the clearing of the coffin maker's lodge when Eisen returned and dismounted, patting his heaving horse upon the flanks before tethering it to the tree as well. Then he paused and looked about, but there was nothing. No one. Only silence, trees, the heavy breath of horses and the endless dirge of the softly singing wind.

He advanced to the door with caution and fear in his heart, wondering if Frank Adams sought revenge from beyond the grave, wondering if the dead man's friends had found him out. He passed through the threshold of his house and discovered a young woman, a dwarf and an elderly woman standing tensely within. They leapt when he entered but did not flee the room, nor did they change their positions. The woman and the dwarf he recognized instantly as the masked jester's compatriots, those that had entered upon him at Caldwell's printery. The third member of the party remained a mystery.

"Who are you?"

The dwarf drew a pistol and pointed it awkwardly in Eisen's direction. He was shaking furiously and his eyes were wide with terror and resolve unequally proportioned. The endangered merely looked to the gun, then up to the face of the man that held it as if he were being proffered a glass of orange juice.

"Stay back, stay back or by whatever is holy, I'll shoot! I'll shoot!"

"You are very welcome to kill me after you have told me who you are. As to your purpose, well, that's plain enough."

Eisen began walking forward but paused as the dwarf began shouting hysterically once again.

"He'll be back soon, he'll be back, you'd best clear out – I'll shoot, I swear I'll shoot!"

"Put the gun down, I'm not going to hurt you. This is my lodge, but you are all welcome to it. I remember you two from the print shop. Put that away, I'm not your enemy. My name is Eisen, and yours would be?"

The dwarf relaxed slightly but kept the gun trained on the intruder. The older woman beside him turned to the little man with uncertainty and hope shimmering in her eyes.

"That's enough. I trust him."

"Oh?"

"Yes. Put the gun away. Let him sit, can't you see how tired he is? He looks exhausted."

Eisen brightened fractionally. "I'm not nearly as tired as my horse, we've been out riding all day."

The dwarf furrowed his bushy beetle-black brows and frowned, his tiny, calloused hands clamping down tightly upon the pistol once more.

"Who is 'we'"?

"Me and my horse."

The youngest woman in the corner, who until that time had been completely quiet, suddenly began laughing. The dwarf and the other woman turned to the youth with quizzical expressions while Eisen just stood silently and watched. A few moments later the young woman's laughter subsided into a gentle flow of grief-stricken weeping. She collapsed to her knees and wept quietly and terribly. The elder woman ran to her side and knelt with her, drawing the slender, cloaked youth to her side, saying, "Hush, hush, my dear. There's nothing ya kin do fer yer father. He's gone, baby. He's gone."

The young woman looked up into her elder's face with such despair that Eisen momentarily averted his gaze, so overcome was he with the calamity.

"Soon we'll be gone too," the young woman whispered. "Soon we all'll be gone."

It was only then that Eisen realized the reason she was wearing a cloak.

She was pregnant.

The coffin maker spoke up firmly, taking a forceful step toward the three circus performers.

"No one is going to get you while you stay under my roof. There's a spare bedroom upstairs. Have any of you eaten lately?"

The dwarf shook his head. He looked like he was about to collapse at any minute, and the two women looked worse, if anything.

Eisen nodded and turned to the stove.

"Sit down. I'll fix us something to eat."

☼

After he had fed his guests, he told them to do as they saw fit, to stay or to leave. They stayed and thanked him. He accepted their acknowledgment and headed out alone into the forest, saying he'd be back in an hour or two.

He rubbed his throat as he walked and thought of Kindle and the plight that so fiercely intruded upon his world. Upon her's. He took Kindle's path into the higher forests that led into the mountains and the home of its guardian.

When he arrived at the tell-tale rock, situated in the small, mushroom-clouded clearing where he had earlier collapsed in hallucinogenic stupor, he discovered another man sitting there as if waiting for him. It was the jester from the carnival. He sat upon the strange landmark with his mask in his hands and his back to the coffin maker.

The clown queried, "Are they safe?"

Eisen nodded as he spoke, though he knew the other man couldn't see his gesture. "Yeah, they are all at my lodge. What are you doing out here?"

"Thinking."

"Same as me then. What happened, how did you get away from the riot?"

The jester laughed and looked down at his mask as if in its ghastly, enigmatic smile and cold lifeless eye-holes he would discover some kind of answer or truth. If he did, he didn't speak of it.

The wind soared up to his words as if in appreciation, and the boughs bent and swayed and danced in the dark. From somewhere off in the distance was the cawing of strange birds, and it was as if in warning.

"I got away because I was swift."

"What's this? No more rhymes?"

"Oh, death cannot steal from me my laughing tongue, not of dozens nor of one."

"You don't seem much bothered by the slaughter of your friends."

"And who said the circus men where friends of mine? Not I. Of a certainty, not I."

"Have you ever heard of the Fontaines?"

"Who?"

"The Fontaine family. They owned a large estate some ways off from the town some years ago, before they were murdered. Have you heard of them?"

"No."

"I think you're lying."

"Think what you like. Think and scorn and hate and pray. It makes no difference to what is and isn't not, for that is the way of every one's lot."

"Right. Well, when Kindle first saw you she nearly fainted with shock. Can you explain that?"

"She was afraid of little ole me? Laughable as laughable can be."

"You can cease your japery; I know what you've done."

"And what is that?"

"Murder."

"Indeed?"

"Don't lie to me."

"Why not?"

It was only then that the jester turned round to face the coffin maker, the clown's face obscured in shadow, only a faint glint of flashing eyes in that flat expanse of darkened stillness.

"What do you mean, why not?"

"Give me a reason why I should not lie? As there is no trust betwixt us, no, not but silence falls."

"Speak plain."

"As plain as a wayward fruit fly against a barn wall, new white dried? No, I'll nothing of the sort, and really, try and be more of a sport. More as in my kind."

"You had best answer my questions before I lose my temper."

"He threatens and jeers but wallows in tears. Eisen, how you have changed little these past fifteen years."

"How do you know my name? Who are you?"

"Don't you recognize me? I am insulted, as well I should be."

The jester rose and moved into a leaf-filtered shaft of light, his features finally revealed, familiar and forbidding.

"Daren? Daren Dunshill?"

"The one and only."

Eisen stood perfectly still then. He felt unable to move, as if the world had conspired to constrain him by the agitation of his emotions alone. He began to think the world had some grudge tightly held against him, some dire ax to grind; he felt cursed.

"I had the feeling you were going to attack me. "

The smile vanished from Daren's face. His strangely glinting eyes obtained a far-off solemnity which ill suited his garb.

"Attack you? Yes, I thought of it. I have wanted to kill you, for what you had done, for... many years, too many."

"Do you intend to still?"

"You don't seem concerned."

"That is because I'm not."

"Why?"

"After I killed our mentor... well, let's not mince words, after I murdered him, I fled the state, as well you know. I traveled for many years, trying to outrun my guilt, my shame. I thought of taking my own life many times, such was the weight of it all, but was, early on, too cowardly to carry out the act. Whatever men may say about the cowardice of suicide is a falsity; for its enactment, one must muster the whole of one's manhood, else forfeit the venture entirely. However, I stuck with the notion and I gathered my strength, my courage, my fortitude, slowly and deliberately. And it was with a pistol in my mouth that I realized that such a course of action would prevent me from ever mending my mistakes, those of which still bespoke of mending.

"I was sharing a flat with another young traveler at the same time, a fisherman named Stanley Worsik, bit of a drunk and a gambler, but a kind soul. He entered in and found me like that. With a gun in my hand and its barrel in my mouth, crying. He gasped and ran at me with the firm intention of saving my life and I... I dropped the gun and began laughing. He just looked so hilarious running like that with his legs all askew, you would have mistaken him for a scarecrow. I said, 'Gotcha,' and then, to my very great amazement, he stopped and stared at me and then began to laugh. Louder than me, slapping his knees and twisting about, saying, 'What a ham you are, what a rascal!' And for the very first time in my life since that horrible happening, I felt a weight evaporating from my body. I had been unfettered, briefly, but I had done it.

"So it was from that time forth I have devoted myself to the art of comedy and festival, to bringing some happiness into the world where before there was none. It made me feel alive again, made me feel as if I were finally beginning to absolve my-self, to make a difference, to help, to heal. I joined the circus shortly thereafter as their resident jester and have been working in the same capacity ever since, sacrificing dignity for merriment... until this new tragedy burst upon us all. My actions were monstrous, but this preacher, this Michael, to his villainy I am but a guttered candle and he the sun."

"So you never knew the Fonatines?"

"No."

"Where did you get that mask then? Kindle said that the man who killed her parents wore a mask just like that. She was terrified of it, of you."

"Indeed? It was given me by a stranger, a man I met at the old fort in the desert, the one that marks the border between the plains and the badlands, you may have seen it. This was some weeks ago. I took it and put it on, and he told me it suited me, 'As perfectly as does ones own skin.' Everyone else liked it and said it would add to my act, so I kept it."

"What was this man's name?"

"I don't know. He never gave it and I never asked."

"What did he look like?"

"He wore a dusty traveling suit, very old, and a pair of dark sunglasses. Oh, and he had a parasol. A white parasol."

"A white umbrella?"

"Yes. Always kept it low over his face like he couldn't stand the light. What are you going to do now, Eisen?"

"Nothing."

"Nothing?"

"That's right."

"Don't you remember the old cabinet maker? Don't you remember Will? Don't you still want to avenge our mentor?"

"No. The dead do not seek vengeance. They do not seek anything from those that have wronged them. Neither shall I."

"I thought as much. You are, I think, a better man than me. You know what to do, you always knew what to do. You and William both; did he... live?"

"Will?"

"Yes, Will. Did he survive?"

"Yeah, he lived. I got a letter from him a couple of months ago, he went and got married, has a child on the way. He's fine."

"That's good. Him, you – both will have a testament that will bear repetition, the spectrum of your lives, but I, I have no testament. My life is laughter in the night."

"Only if you want it to be."

"What a man wants is seldom what is, and in the effort to bend the world down to his will, he bends only himself until he breaks like so many reeds neath a maelstrom. All men break. All."

"And all men mend."

The jester shook his head.

"Not I."

Then he smiled and withdrew a pistol. The clown pressed its barrel to the side of his head and pulled the trigger. There was a resounding booming in the forest, then a rustling of wings and boughs disturbed. Several birds rose up in the distance of that fateful clearing and flew off, blending singularly into the horizon.

The clown tottered where he sat and then collapsed, tilting forward and falling to the ground before the feet of the living. As if his death were an act of reverence and his passing a veneration. A red pool gathering in aftermath.

The coffin maker knelt and picked up the pistol and then, with a howl of ferine rage, white hot and consuming, whipped the pistol into the long dark of the forest and began to weep. He sat beside the body of the jester for some time that did not bear the scrutiny of numeration and then rose and walked to the strange rock where the dead man had perched.

The clown's mask still lay upon that curious stone, smiling up at the coffin maker as if in beckoning. He reached through the gloam and lifted the bizarre artifact up to his face, as if he would fasten it about his own head. He didn't and instead just held the mask before his face, looking at it shimmering dully in the pale blue moonlight. With the macabre disguise in hand and a leaden dread coiling in his heart, the coffin maker slowly made his way back through the forest to the lodge and therein collapsed into a deep and dreamless sleep.

Chapter Twenty-One

Rebirth

In the morning the coffin maker, with the cagey dwarf in tow, headed back into the forest to bury the dead man's body. The dwarf had insisted on accompanying him when Eisen had unfurled his plans, saying that he owed it to his friend to give him a proper burial. It was a custom Eisen had never much mulled over, but one that he too felt wholly compelled to enact. Both men carried thin iron shovels slung over their shoulders, and the coffin maker was impressed with the dexterity and strength with which the little man bore it along. When they reached the clearing the body had gone, where to neither knew, but there were speculations aplenty.

"You sure it was here he shot hisself?"

"I'm sure Mr., ah, I fancy I don't even know your name. Any of you."

The dwarf paused and toed the dirt as he spoke, not looking at the coffin maker at all.

"I knew a man who used to say things about names, claimed he knew every name that had ever been. Said that there were ever as many names as any that would be. Said people name things because in their naming one gains a hold over that thing and a hold which no other thing could create. I never did understand it, but he said it, sure enough. My name is When."

"What?"

"No. When."

"Curious name."

"I've never heard of an uncurious name. Not sure what that would sound like. Are you?"

"No. Haven't a clue."

"Don't fancy names get curious?"

"No, I fancy not. What of the women?"

"What of them?"

"Their names, what are they?"

"The older one is Marble, lest she calls herself such so we took after her, and the pregnant one was the boss' daughter. Before... Well anyhow, her name's Emma."

Eisen nodded as if the names and their naming needed some affirmation of their existence outside of those being called upon.

"Think it was wolves that took the body?"

The dwarf tilted his head upward and scratched his chin with his free hand, watching the mist slithering through the trees above him like ethereal serpents searching for prey ever elusive.

"Could'a been."

Eisen nodded and continued his search about the clearing, and then came back to the spot where the jester had fallen and discovered a matting of grass where the body had been. There was a path of pressed green and smears of blood leading higher into the forest, as if something had dragged the corpse away.

"Something big."

Eisen looked to the spot were the dead man had lain, then up into the mountains, covered in mist and snow as if in stark and mischievous defiance of the sparkling heat of the desert below.

Eisen nodded again.

"Wolves."

There was a clamorous disturbance in the distance, a shouting out of pain and surprise, echoing and all too human. It was the sound of a man in pain.

The dwarf looked to his companion, "I don't think that was a wolf, Eisen."

"No. Come on."

They dropped their shovels at the edge of the clearing and dashed through the thick and cloying foliage toward the locus of the waveform agony. They emerged upon a strange scene some half distance between the clearing and the lodge, discovering a peculiarly square hole in the ground near a cluster of ferns and the voice of a frightened man within.

"Somebody get me out, get me out of here!"

The dwarf made for the opening in the ground, but the coffin maker stopped him with a firm hand upon his shoulder and a stern shaking of his head.

He whispered to the little man, "The man in the hole is very likely a bandit. If so, he's sure to be armed. It's best neither of us takes any chances. Don't get too close."

The little man nodded solemnly, scratched his muddy-colored beard and then whispered back, "You laid this trap then?"

"Yes. I was accosted on the road to the lodge some time ago by brigands, one of whom came at me with a knife. I... took care of him, but he had two friends who got away. A quick, thin, shorter man and a bulky, wide fellow with a scar on his forehead. I think this man is one of them."

"How could he not have noticed that hole?"

"I laid a weave of thin wooden planks over the opening, which break at the slightest application of pressure. I've experimented with several different kinds of traps which I've laid all about the outer reaches of the lodge. So, be mindful in future ventures."

"Land's sakes man, what of the women!"

"I already told them. You were sleeping, and you had been so exhausted and stressed from your trials the previous day, I didn't think it prudent to wake you."

"Oh."

"They'll be fine – let's see what we've caught."

And with that plucky phrase Eisen headed to the rim of his trap and then stopped and called down in a cordial tone.

"Greetings down there, you seem to be in somewhat of a jam."

"Oh thank the gods! All of em! Get me out of here; it's some kind of trap!"

"I know. I made it."

"You what?"

"I made it. What is your name?"

"Why the hell would ya do something like that?"

"I don't much care to repeat myself. It is somewhat taxing on my nerves."

"Listen, you little– "

"No. I'm not going to listen to anything you say unless it's what your name happens to be."

"Grady."

"All right, so tell me, Grady, do you know a Frank Adams?"

"It's you. You bastard! It's you – the man on the road! You kilt him, you kilt Frank. Y-you– "

"That's enough of that. You'll work yourself up into a fit. It's unhealthy. Bad strain and all that. Can you stand?"

"I'll kill ya, I swear, you god damned sonnofabitch!"

"I'm not a stiff, but I must say I find your lack of eloquence somewhat depressing. Is that really the best outlet you could think of?"

"Outlet? What the hell ye talkin bout?"

"For your anger. Vulgarity. Violence, whether in word or in deed, has long been an outlet for varying emotions. But when, exactly, did you decide that thievery and murder and rampant profanity were your special forte?"

"My what?"

"Your strong suit."

"Why the hell you even care?"

"Why don't you?"

"Good point."

"I thought so."

"You're not gonna let me out, are ya?"

"That depends."

"What on?"

"On whether or not you have a gun on you. Are you armed, Mr. Grady?"

"Yeah."

"I kindly thought so. You came down here to kill me, didn't you? Revenge for Adams, perhaps?"

"Yeah."

"Where is your other friend, the short one?"

"Not here."

"So I gather. Where?"

"I ain't gonna tell ya."

"Why not?"

"Just cuz I don't talk like no high highfalutin noble like as yarself don't mean I'm stupid."

"No one is calling anyone stupid. Unobservant perhaps, but not stupid, Mr. Grady."

"What you fixin on doing wit me?"

"That also depends on whether or not you are willing to give me your gun."

"Hell no."

"Then I'm just going to leave you here."

Eisen broke off and began walking away when he heard a shuffling of cowhide boots on dirt down below followed by a high, near hysterical shout.

"NO!"

"No what? No thank you, no ice; no ma'am, I'm single; no what, Mr. Grady?"

"Don't leave me down here, fer god's sake."

"Instead of pleading, why don't you just hand me your gun?"

"If I do will ya git me out a here?"

"Yes."

There was a pause, then silence from the mouth of the hole, then a scuffling beneath and the sound of metallic clinking. Something shimmering flew up and out of that blackened maw and landed some distance behind Eisen who motioned for the dwarf to retrieve it. The little man scrambled forth and snatched the weapon up and pocketed it.

"Thank you, Mr. Grady."

"Just Grady."

"Thank you, Just Grady. I'll go fetch a rope. Be back later."

"Hey. Wait up a moment, ya'll just gonna leave me?"

"I can't get you out without a rope."

"No, s'pose not."

"No. I don't either. I'll be back."

"Then what all ya gonna do with me?"

Eisen didn't say what he would or would not do and continued walking away with the dwarf quickly falling in tow.

The little leathery man withdrew the revolver he had procured and handed it to the coffin maker.

"This is what he threw."

"So I see."

"You don't want it?"

"I don't like guns. Loud noises break my concentration. You keep it."

The dwarf nodded in his grave and respectful fashion and tucked the shooting iron away in the folds of his oversized great coat, hiding it away in some warm, inner pocket as if it were a precious gem.

That bizarre pairing, moving through the trees and the ferns and stones, looked to all the world's eye like what flotsam some deviant teller of tales had concocted in a pyrexia of dreams.

They trudged back into the clearing of the previous night's misfortune and then, by Eisen's guidance, wound back down to the cabin, where the two women waited nervously within. Frightened but unharmed.

Eisen walked around the room once and then sat at the dining table with his hands folded before him like a penitent.

"Come, sit down all of you."

They did so, slowly and soberly.

"There is a man on the loose around here who means me harm, so I want you, When, to stay with these two and keep that pistol close to your heart."

Marble spoke up fitfully, wringing her hands about one another as if to wash from them some putrescence.

"Pistol? What pistol, he's never had a pistol as long as I've known him."

Eisen held his hands toward her. "I don't have time to explain, just be ready to defend yourselves, all of you. Understand?"

GRAVE.

They all moved to acknowledgment in their own time and fashion, and then Eisen rose as if from a grave and took with him a length of sturdy rope, form-fitting leather gloves and his heavy, high-collared overcoat.

When he returned to the hole in the ground he didn't say a word, just tied the rope off on a thick oak tree some twenty feet off from the trap and then threw it down. The line went taut, and in a matter of seconds Grady lay heaving in a pile of leaves beside the recess. It was hedging toward fall and the leaves had begun to turn from green to a pale auburn, falling freely now from the skeleton fingers of the trees high above those two opposing forms, silent and dire. The sky was clouding over with a pall of black and smoking tendrils that spun in about the mountain as if in intended embrace repulsed.

Eisen watched the clouds whirling as he spoke to the man he has just rescued, his hands mechanically recoiling the rope and slinging it over his left shoulder like a rancher of old.

"Take me to this friend of yours. This matter needs sorting."

"What do you mean?"

"If you both want to kill me, then have at it, but I'll not allow you to endanger anyone else with your bloodlust. Take me to your friend and we shall speak. If words fail us, then you both may act in whatever manner seems most befitting of the occasion."

Grady rose very slowly and looked at the coffin maker hard and long and cautiously and then nodded and tipped up his hat brim liken to a sealing of agreements.

The bandit adjusted his bracers and then his belt, bent over, re-laced his boots and then exhaled, turning to the hill-lands rising up like the backs of so many whales, interred yet stirring from their graves. The coffin maker followed this dubious guide a full three miles before the thief stopped and furrowed up his thick and heavy brows.

"Where all's my shooter?"

"Your gun is at my cabin, in a friend's safe keeping."

"He likely ain't no friend'a mine."

"Likely."

The highwayman squinted his eyes and then turned away from Eisen and continued on his way.

They went on steadily higher into the mountains, and as they rose, the forest grew thinner and thinner about them and the rocks were more prominent and jagged than before. The air was thick with the scent of green things and strange flowers that neither of the men had ever seen nor smelled before.

"How much farther till we reach wherever it is you're taking me, Grady?"

"Bout another coupla miles, I reckon."

"You reckon?"

"What now, ya'll don't trust me?"

"Not in the slightest."

"Shucks, I'm damn near heart broke."

"Shut up."

"Hey, I'm just playing wit cha."

"No, I mean be silent, I heard something."

"I didn't hear nothing."

"Of course you didn't. You weren't listening."

Eisen stopped dead in his tracks and scanned the thin line of trees that walled on either side of them. Between the border trees was a thick verge of fern and vine and stone and the bones of dead animals scattered as if by the kick of a wayward hermit.

"You ever noticed those bones before, Mr. Grady?"

"Nope. Hell, what is it?"

"It was a deer."

Eisen walked over to the scattering of yellow and wind-polished remains and bent in examination of his find.

"Grady, these bones have scratch marks on them. Deep ones. Do you know what that means?"

"No."

"It means that whatever killed this deer had to tear through the skin and the fat and the muscle. It means whatever did this is very big and very, very dangerous. A bear or a very large wolf, perhaps."

"Ain't no bears round here. And I never have seen a wolf all the while I've been here. Specially not one what would be so big."

"I think we should keep moving."

"Sure."

They left hurriedly and soon the path narrowed to such an extent that both men had to continually duck else be caught up in the low-hanging branches and the vines that hung about them. They traversed the twisting confines of the forest for near twenty minutes in this fashion before they crested the rise of the first of several large, barren hills which rolled up into the peaks. The forest died away and soon only a few scraggly half-living shrubs remained, the only evidence of life in that place at all, save the two weary forms that passed beside them, two legged and pale and awestruck by the sudden desolation of the landscape. It was as if in some ancient time a great and terrible calamity had befallen that stony tumulus, sculpting in its quintessence a wound which could not be healed.

"Did we take a wrong turning somewhere, Grady?"

"No. But you would think it to look at this cursed place. I do. We camp up in those old dwellings yonder."

He pointed to a cliff in the distance in which a network of strange cave-like chambers had been forged in a long-off time. They were so primordial in their construction that they seemed a very part of the mountain, as if they hadn't been built at all but had merely grown that way.

From the tree line all the way to the cliff dwellings there was nothing but a flat expanse of stone and scorched earth, dotted infrequently with boulders and dead shrubbery and the bones of things unaccountable. The clouds grew darker and the mist seeped out of the forest like blood from a wound and found the duo out in their naked position.

Grady withdrew a small metal lighter, enkindled a flame and then held it over his head.

Eisen looked to him and then to the cliff-borne caves where they hung in space in shades of brown and red and gray.

Nothing.

Grady shook his head and backtracked.

"Something ain't right here."

"Are you sure he said he was going to wait here?"

"Yeah. It's what he told me. Told me he'd wait till I had taken care a you, then we'd up and pack it in."

"Are you frightened, Mr. Grady?"

"Ain't nothing ta be fraid of."

"Then why do you think something is wrong?"

"Like as I said."

"All right. I'm going to look. I would appreciate it if you would show me the way; of course if you want to leave, I won't try to stop you."

"Well, seeing as you coulda left me fer dead back in that hole instead of helping me out like ya did, it only seems right that I return the favor."

"I'm glad you feel that way."

Grady shook his head and kicked at the ground vacantly as might an angst-ridden child.

"This is crazy."

"What is, Mr. Grady?"

"All of this. My partner disappearing. Man I was supposed ta be trying ta kill is treating me bettern my own brother and all this fog and mist and what have you – it's crazy. It's like the world is coming to an end and all sense is going with it."

"Would you have liked it better had I shot you in that hole or just left you to die of starvation?"

"No. Kindly not. It's just – hell, I don't know."

Grady was silent a moment and apparently sunk deep in reverie, his face contorted with the force of his exertions.

"Thanks anyhow."

Eisen nodded respectfully and stuck his hands in his pockets. He looked off to where the mist was thickest; the base of the cliff. There was a figure standing in front of the obscured entrance to the caves. A man of moderate height. It was a high portal of rough-hewn stone. The figure before it did not move.

"Is that your friend, Grady?"
"Cain't rightly tell from here."
He lit the lighter once more and held it up and waved it some, but the figure remained immobile, a inscrutable shadow-form watcher; as implacable in that desolate plain as that land was to the world itself.
Eisen and Grady continued their ascent, but the closer they drew the heavier the mist, and the heavier the mist the less they could see of the figure. As they came within speaking distance, the obfuscation was complete and the figure was gone entirely.
"Who's there? Show yourself!"
"Calm down, Grady, it could just be a traveler."
"I doubt it."
"Oh, but I am a traveler, Mr. Grady, much like Mr. Torquiam. Travelers not so much of the terrain without as that within. Is that not so?"
They turned, Eisen calm and discerning, Grady wild eyed and frantic, his breath coming and going now in sharp, grating gasps.
"I said show yourself!"
"They say that seeing is believing, but what of one that believes nothing of sight?"
"What the hell does that mean?"
Eisen remained silent and still. He could see nothing, hearing nothing of the man but his disembodied voice. It was a voice that was strikingly familiar but to which the coffin maker could not put a face.
Grady reached for his hunting knife and it came up in his right hand, sharp and vicious and dull-glinting in the dark-lit sky.
"Where is Vindel?"
"Not where but what."
"Well, what is he then?"
"Dead."
"You bastard."
"He was far more deserving of such a title than I, Mr. Grady."
"I'm gonna kill you. You hear me!"

"With as loud as you are shouting it would be hard not to. But, kill me? Like you killed Mr. Torquiam there? I'm not prone to humor, but you are going to make me laugh."

With a snarl of fury Grady blundered off through the fog before Eisen had a chance to restrain him. All was muted and blurry. Then came swiftly a cry of terror and pain, resounding with such force that it could have been heard for miles around. It continued, ghastly and shrill, for twenty seconds entire. All the while Eisen held his ground, his muscles taut and his mind whirling like a leaf in a riptide.

"Grady? Grady, are you all right?"

There was no reply, nothing but silence, shadows and fog.

"Whoever you are, I would like to know what is going on here. Can you not answer, or will you not? Hello?"

The unknown voice did not reply, neither as Eisen began to nervously move toward where he thought the entrance to the caves was, nor as he passed within that blackened maw, letting it swallow him whole like flotsam passing into the gullet of a whale.

Inside the entrance of the cavern all was subservient to the mastery of the gloom. There was no source of light, save a faint flickering from some point ahead of him, near indistinguishable from the darkness.

"Hello? Is anyone there?"

Again there was no reply.

Eisen turned and began angling left until he hit a wall. Pressing one hand firmly to it he followed the structure's limitations until he found the source of the light. A dying torch lying oddly in the middle of the floor of the next room, this chamber being a floor above the entrance. The torch was very old and made of wood and smeared at the handle with a dark, sticky, odorous conglomeration.

Blood.

Eisen drew back instinctively and looked about; only darkness, only shadows, whispers and fatal imaginings. His mind began to churn frantically.

If the man in the fog had indeed killed this other bandit, this Vindel, then he has... very likely, killed Grady as well. But who is he? What does he want? And if something happens to me, what is to become of the Arlingtons? Of Jen? Or of Kindle? Who will save them, if I'm gone?

He felt a sudden urgency fostered then in his frame, and every newly executed movement was borne out with the strictest economy. He lifted up the torch in his dark-gloved hands and rekindled the flame until it was a soaring pyre and then held it before him and nearly screamed at what the lifted conflagration revealed.

Lying on the floor before him was a man, or what remained of one. A skull stared without eyes, a mouth without tongue. Ears cleaved away and not a single trace of skin anywhere; sinew exposed and nose smashed in. Hands and feet lobbed off and positioned around the corpse as if in preparation of some dread ritual. The horror's chest cavity had been ripped apart, revealing an empty vaulting of blood and rheum. And all around this macabre figure was arranged a strange circle of animal bones. Birds and lizards and cats were all pointing toward the lifeless thing which had once been a man, as if even in death they had gathered in observance of this singular atrocity.

"Isn't it beautiful?"

Eisen turned very slowly to behold the speaker from the fog. His breath caught in his throat and suddenly he realized who the man was.

The one from the church courtyard and the manor road.

The man with the white umbrella.

He stood in the doorway with the stark parasol held loosely in hand and his hands at his sides. The stranger's teeth shone in the light of Eisen's torch like sea-washed stones, and his eyes glinted ferine and deep in the flickering darkness. He waited awhile, expectant and very, very still, before he spoke again.

"Have you nothing to say?"

"I'm not fond of conversing with murderers."

"Oh."

"Do you think this is funny?"

"Marginally."

"You're disgusting."

"Of what consequence is your opinion to me?"

Eisen had no idea, so he didn't reply.

"You've no understanding of what a marvelous shield one can make of apathy – or perhaps, worse still, you understand perfectly and yet are afraid of the implications of such a notion."

"Do you intend on killing me as well?"

"Why would I?"

"Why wouldn't you?"

For the first time since Eisen had met him, the man with the white umbrella began to laugh. Throwing his head back he expelled such sounds of cruel and godlike hilarity as never before were heard upon such a plane nor any other; fey, unnatural sounds. As the man's laughter subsided, he thrust the umbrella out at the skinned and bloodied cadaver within the circle of bones as might a teacher gesturing toward a chalkboard.

"Man has always been a creature of ritual. Of habit. To imbue a deed with significance beyond the mere action itself and to such a degree, he is alone in this amongst all the denizens of the earth. But to stagnate in the edifice of past ceremony is to kill the creative spirit – is to kill one's self. One must create new ritual, else only hollow men will remain in place of the creators; only ghosts will wander in the shadows of gods."

"And is Grady wandering?"

"In a fashion."

"Where is he?"

"Outside."

"Alive?"

"What does it mean, to live? I've seen men breathing the same air as you or I, but they were as lifeless as the stones upon which they daily tread."

"Don't play at semantics."

"And if I do, will you do for me as I have done for Vindel?"

Eisen remained silent. The man watched him, and his eyes were wide and dire and strangely colored. His skin the bone-pale beige of the moon.

"Why do you not answer?"

The man walked forward through the portal and into the room, his eyes fixed on Eisen all the while. As he moved, Eisen backed away slowly, holding out the torch defensively, but the man didn't seem to care, for he grabbed hold of the burning shaft and ripped it effortlessly free of the coffin maker's grasp and threw it aside. The stranger never took his eyes off the coffin maker all the while, even as his hand smouldered and bled.

He did not flinch, but rather smiled.

In the air. Smell of flesh.

Burning.

Close and far.

Eisen recoiled farther until his back was to the stone wall. There was no exit, no escape. Only the stranger and his glinting eyes and burning hand.

"You should thank me."

"And why is that?"

"If it were not for me, this man would have killed you."

"You don't know that to a certainty."

"How do you know what I know? You could have thrust that torch into my eye, but you let me take it from you. Very foolish. Yet you question my sagacity? Of such matters I am peerless on earth above of all men and things. I am suzerain of a domain, singular and entire."

"The only thing you are is insane."

"Generalizations of such stark banality are better kept in waste bins than on tongues. Save perhaps for Vindel's. Do you detest me for what I have done?"

"What do you want of me?"

"An answer."

"What do think?"

"The same as you think I do. So tell me then, why do you draw away?"

The man withdrew a dagger, one which Eisen recognized as belonging to Grady, from some inner pocket and proffered it to the coffin maker without discernible expression.

"If you've a notion of import, then act upon it the moment of its conception, do not shy from impulse or desire, whether quaint or malign. If you want to kill me, then do the deed with weightless heart and steady hand. Morality is the shield of the weak."

Eisen hesitantly took the blade, his eyes darting quickly back and forth between the stranger and the shimmering steel. He inhaled deeply and tightened his grasp upon Grady's blade, his eyes now fixed upon the stranger as if there was nothing else in all the world. There was only the man and the blade and the darkness and the will to act stretching the whole fabric of existence and curving back upon itself like a mirror within another and the seeing thereof picture to an eye.

Eisen readied himself and smiled fractionally. "If I am a fool then, for this, what are you?" He raised the dagger and brought it down over his head at the man who thrust up his unscathed appendage, dropping the umbrella, catching the blade with a naked hand and wrenching it from the coffin maker's hold. Blood fell to the floor and slid down the cool steel of the knife, speckling stone and shoe alike.

The eyes of the two opposing figures met like the collision of planets in their forming, and they held the other's gaze and did not look away.

"You hesitated, but your heart was in it. You'll do fine."

Then the man pressed his bloody hand to Eisen's face as if in adoration of a lover. He imparted the dagger to the coffin maker once more and then bent and retrieved his parasol and departed soundlessly as a chill wind began to blow. And it was a dirge which rattled the bones upon their red stone sepulcher. The coffin maker shook, but it was not due the cold.

Eisen's head spun and his vision began to fade, fluttering black in the blackness that was darker still. He looked to the bones and the thing upon the floor that had once been Vindel and then to the space where the stranger had been and passed from the waking world into the void of unconsciousness as the wind swept about him as if in reverence.

☼

When he woke it was to the sound of padding feet across current-worn stone; a wolf was staring at him. A wolf larger than any Eisen had ever seen, its great yellow eyes opaque and filled with a wisdom that did not bespeak of a telling nor of a receiving. It stood just beyond the doorway that lead down to the entrance of the network of caves, staring at him and sniffing the air and looking off to the bones and the body of Vindel. Rooted to its shadow as if from there it had grown, there was no fear in its stillness. In its eyes or the misting of its breath.

Eisen rose slowly, his hands held out before him; a plea and a hope. The wolf watched indifferently as he rose and then turned and padded away, stopped and looked back, as if watching to see if the human would follow. He did, and it was with the manner of a noctambulist.

Out of the room of horrors and down the small incline to the entrance and then out and into the dark and moonlit night. Rain fell in great torrents, but the wolf continued on heedless and serene. Eisen followed at a distance, mesmerized by such an implacable creature.

Suddenly paranoid, the coffin maker scanned the horizon, but the man with the white umbrella was nowhere to be seen or heard or smelled or felt in the shifting of the world. He heaved a sign of relief and then, realizing that he was following a wolf, berated himself wordlessly and thought that he must be going mad. It struck him powerfully that he didn't much care.

The wolf stopped suddenly and made a muted noise and gestured with its head toward a figure laying face down in the mud before the cliff face.

Grady.

Eisen ran to his former companion and turned him over, recoiling instantly in terror – the thief's face and been sliced off completely. He stood and inhaled and exhaled the sweet scented air and opened his mouth to taste the rain. Passing a hand over his soaked face, as if to wash the nightmare images from his mind, he closed his eyes and then sought after the wolf; seeking as one might their elder brother to act as both friend and pathfinder, mentor and mentored.

It had stalked to the very edge of the forest and stood there, archaic and illusive, as if in waiting. When Eisen approached this time, it bounded off and was gone. He wondered at the creature and its motivations, and whether or not such beings were possessed of such things. He didn't know and thought that no one else did either. Then he entered the forest and started the long trek back to his verdant-bound domicile.

Chapter Twenty-Two

Posse Comitatus

It was nearly daybreak when he finally stumbled out of the forest into the clearing wherein lay his lodge. He felt sick, and his whole body ached with both the strain of the journey and the dark impressions of his travails. Wanting only to sleep once again, he walked up to the door and laid a hand against it, but instead of supporting his weakened chassis, it gave way instantly and swung open to reveal the dwarf, When, and the two women, Marble and Emma.

All dead.

Bullet holes through their heads; executed.

Eisen fell to his knees and just stared and stared. Then he wailed and began to cry, his whole body trembling with the pain of such experience and the sorrow that permeated his entirety. The house echoed with the furious hammering of his fists upon the wooden planks of the floor.

He knew most would ask, "Why, why?" thinking it would lessen the pain, thinking that understanding would ease one's suffering, would provide some measure of comfort. But he knew the truth, knew that knowing only granted the sufferer further torment. Still, he knew also that he had to uncover the reason for such heartless slaughter, regardless of whatever distress had to be endured.

He crawled to the little man who vainly clutched Grady's pistol in his fist. In death he had struggled; an effigy of resistance. His eyes were closed and upon his lips was an ironic smile. He had seen the end coming, had seen and accepted. The older woman, Marble, was sprawled out with a look of utter horror frozen upon her pale and lifeless features, her limbs contorted grotesquely. One of her eyes had filled with blood, clouding over red and the redness seeping down her face like tears of sacrifice. Emma had tried to run and lay crumpled up over the stairwell, a sanguine mural of life excised dripping down the wall, and her hands cradling her unborn child, never to be named.

The place had been turned over, but nothing had been taken. It appeared as if whoever had come had done so solely for the sake of killing.

Eisen rose and looked off at the rising light in the spacing of the world and then to his newly fallen guests and walked outside to the toolshed and retrieved a shovel.

He buried them at dawn behind the lodge without ceremony or indication, and then ate a handful of black berries he had picked from the surrounding wilderness and looked for the horse he had borrowed.

It was gone.

As were all the others.

Stuffing an ancient leather satchel, which he had discovered in Kindle's junk room, full of several days' worth of provisions, he trekked into town and then headed straight to the sheriff's office. Before he could reach his destination, however, he was accosted by a gang of workers, headed by none other than James Daniels and Johnson, the foreman.

"Pretty brave."

Eisen stopped as the men surrounded him, Johnson at the forefront, mere feet from the coffin maker's face.

"What is it, Johnson?"

"Showing yer dirty face round here after what ye done to this town. Blaspheming, sex, drugs, killing our peaceable citizens."

"Frank Adams was neither a resident of this town, nor remotely peaceable. As for the rest of it, I can only wish I had done as much." Eisen sighed and shook his head slightly, his eyes on Johnson.

"I don't suppose that there is any way of talking this out in a civil, level-headed fashion?"

Johnson walked forward menacingly but was quickly shunted aside by Daniels who, having pushed past the foreman, head-butted the coffin maker and brought him to one knee. Eisen rose and held up a hand and with the other wiped at the blood now pouring from his carmine-speckled nose.

Daniels raised a fist and sneered, "Haven't got your little whore to protect you this time, have ya? If you're planning on begging, now would be the time."

"The only thing I plan on doing at the moment is try and convince you that you're wasting your energy. Kavaria has got the Arlingtons, and you busy yourself with misdirected anger."

"Misdirected?"

He kicked Eisen square in the face and then again in the gut; savage and unrestrained.

"Is that direct enough for ya, Eisen?"

Through spittle, blood, a fast-hazing consciousness and a badly chipped tooth, Eisen was still able to manage a reply.

"No – fraid you're just not getting through."

Daniels hit him again. And again. Each blow more furious than the last and the crowd rising to the spectacle with glee. With cheers. With excitement such as they had never known. In the deep and secret places of their hearts, it was acknowledged that such a happening had long been awaited; had long been dreamed of and hoped for.

Johnson and several of his workers began to grow weary of their savage enterprise. One shouted, "That's enough, James, he's finished." To which Daniels furiously replied, "I ain't."

So badly wrought was the coffin maker that he could barely raise his head. His breathing was coming quick and sharp, and his face was covered in dust and blood. Despite this, he continued clinging to consciousness and with such tenacity that even Daniels was given pause.

In that moment of quiet Eisen took a deep breath and rose very slowly and unsteadily to his feet. He looked about solemnly.

A large menagerie of onlookers had gathered round the bloodletting on either side of the street; some cringing, others amused, others crying. No one spoke and no one moved.

One of the toughs exclaimed, "He's plum crazy." Several others nodded their agreement. Eisen took no heed of any of them. He produced Grady's knife, much to Daniels' excitement.

"Finally! Now we're getting down to it. I was beginning to lose faith in you, Eisen."

Eisen extended his arm, proffering the dagger to his adversary with an expression that was both unmitigated and far away.

"If you want to kill me, then do it properly."

"What in hell's wrong wit you?"

Johnson shook his head and put a hand on his friend's shoulder, whispering into his ear like a Roman senator conversing with his emperor.

"He's mad, James. Plum insane."

"I'm no more insane than you, Johnson. Take it, Daniels. Go on, take it. Isn't that what you desire? One clean thrust between my rib cage is all that you would require."

James Daniels rocked back and forth in grimmest indecision, his face a vortex of emotion that was equal parts fear, confusion and rage. He stopped and then surged forward and snatched the dagger from Eisen's hand as if it had been stolen from him. Instantly, he pulled away, unable to take his eyes from Eisen's face. The former, shaking with a rising sense of fault, whilst the latter remained impassive and immobile.

Finally, Daniels let loose a cry of supreme fury, shouting, "Damn you, Eisen, damn you!"

He dropped the blade to the ground and collapsed to his knees, his eyes brimming over with tears, his face flush and his breathing erratic. To everyone's surprise, Eisen, saying nothing at all, knelt with him and enfolded the weeping man in his arms as any might a brother in need, or some broken child.

When they had rested in that position for some time, Eisen whispered into the broken man's ear, a hand firm and demanding upon a shoulder.

"I will help you, James, if you allow me."

Daniels nodded solemnly and then, with Eisen's support, rose and looked about at the aggregate that rung them round. There was no more shouting or leering, no jeers and cursing. There was no sound at all, save the whistling wind and the distant braying of horses. The show was over and every member of the throng knew it. And in their knowing felt the depths of their shame; none more completely than Daniels himself, who could no longer look his former adversary in the eye.

To Eisen's immediate right the crowd was parting, and a large, muscular, black-bearded man was striding forth, his expression worrisome and his brows tight-knitted in concentration.

"Eisen? What happened to you – who did this?"

"It's all right, Henry. It's all right now."

The coffin maker bent to the ground and collected from it Grady's knife and then sheathed it and turned to Collins.

"Where is the sheriff?"

"Cain't say as I know."

"What of his deputies?"

Collins shook his head.

"Did the doctor see to all the men who were hurt yesterday?"

"Yeah. Fixed um up better than new, I reckon. This ain't right – what all happened to them circus folk."

"What happened? When you say it like that, Henry, you make it seem like some natural accident, like a twister or a hurricane. Something ineluctable. What happened was no accident, whatever else it may have been."

"No."

Eisen whirled upon Johnson and Daniels with flashing eyes.

"Will you assist me, or will we squabble petty differences? Will you allow this town to fall even farther into chaos? Allow even more people to die – like those circus performers, like Braze?"

"Well, what do you intend on doing bout it? Ain't none a Michael's folk going to listen to you."

"No, Johnson, very likely not, but they might listen to you. Or to Daniels. Or to Collins. There are still members of the carnival out there, in the desert, those that weren't slain but only driven out of town."

Johnson intruded, fuming, "We didn't have nothing to do with that madness. It was Michael and his following."

"What did you do to stop it? What have you and your lot done about it since? Has anyone been apprehended? Has anyone been made to answer for this?"

Johnson fell silent and looked to his shoes and then stepped back with his friends, dissolving into the crowd.

Eisen nodded and continued, his voice rising to meet his passion. "When I returned to my lodgings in the forest, I discovered that three of the carnival workers had fled there to escape the riot. I told them they were welcome to stay for as long as they wanted. I left them to attend a matter of great importance, and when I returned they had been murdered in cold blood. Shot in the head. One of whom was no more than two and twenty years old and some four months pregnant with child."

Several horrified gasps rose from the crowd. Others only nodded as if that was the natural way of things and not a way to be feared or despised or altered by the hand of mortal man. Certainly not their own. It was just the way things were.

"I'm going to sort this with Michael, and when I have done so, I'm going after Kallista, with or without help, yours or another. It may not yet be too late to save the Arlingtons. I must, at the very least, try."

"Then I'll try it, like as you."

"Thank you, Henry. I appreciate that. Well then, if you have indeed made up your mind, we should get going, time is wasting."

As Eisen began walking away from the crowd, his head swam and his legs gave way. He collapsed to the dirt as Henry Collins and James Daniels ran to the floundering form. They grabbed him under an arm and dragged him to the shade of a tobacco store porch where he thanked them weakly and sat for some time, breathing heavily.

"I'm sorry, Eisen, I'm so sorry."

The coffin maker held up a hand feebly and gestured dismissively.

"Don't trouble yourself, what's done is done."

Collins whirled upon Daniels and grabbed him about the collar, whipping him about like a rag doll.

"You did this to him?"

"Y-yes."

Collins would have then throttled the man to death had Eisen not intervened.

"Leave him, Henry. Leave him be."

"Why?"

"Because you're doing the same thing he did to me."

Instantly Henry Collins released the poor man and looked away sorrowfully, his visage grimmer than the coffin maker had ever seen it before. More grim than ever he thought it could grow.

"What is happening to this town? I've lived here my whole damned life, ain't never seen this kind of crazy in all that time. Maybe you were possessed like Michael thinks, maybe we all are."

"You shouldn't think like that."

"Why not?"

"It isn't going to help."

He nodded.

"No. Don't s'pose it will. Feels that way though, feels that way."

They sat for a little longer, all in silence, neither looking at another, and then passed from their shade into the purview of the grand and gilded star and made for the church like some wayward funeral procession, mordant and steady and unspeaking. When they arrived at the looming stone monolith, they found their passage barred, sealed by a fore-thinking hand. The great double doors had been shut and locked upon them; their hammering fists availed them nothing.

Only Eisen refrained from action, standing a slight distance away from the entrance to the cathedral, looking up at the grand

and towering spires, paying no attention whatever to his companions' clamor, as if in comparison to whatever was there revealed to him they, and their endeavors, paled markedly.

Some five minutes passed before he spoke, and when he did it was quietly and without direct attention.

"We're wasting time. Come."

With that and nothing more he walked away down the little gravel lane and passed beyond the high iron gates of the church, disappearing utterly from the view of his familiars. Belatedly, they followed some distance behind, talking of frivolous things to one another to pass the time in the manner of the nervous and uncertain.

"Where to now then?"

"To Ledru Monteblanc."

"What for?" queried Collins hastily.

"For help."

"Will he?"

"Help, you mean?"

"Yeah."

"I don't know. We shall see. We must try every resource available to us. We three, even with the addition of some of your friends and your map, James, will be a paltry force to Kavaria and his rabble. To say nothing of the desert and the innumerable dangers it contains. The sun. The heat. Scorpions. Snakes. Coyotes. Dehydration and sheer fatigue."

Daniels walked up behind the coffin maker.

"You survived it. The badlands."

"Yes. But I knew, to a vague degree, where the town was and that I wasn't far from it. The map you possess may be inaccurate. Regardless, every provision of forethought should be mustered. Some of us will die, of that I am nearly certain, and I would like that number to be as small as possible."

Neither Daniels nor James said anything more until they reached Ledru's manor. They took the cliff path, riding up its stone-speckled length on the strong curving backs of three borrowed horses. Old breeds. Powerful and steady as the wind which curled round them, screaming unintelligibly into their ringing ears like some banshee of lore and them the brave knights set against it.

They stabled the beasts at midday and hailed a servant at the water trough near the entrance. He admitted them without qualm. Inside and down the trophied hallway, that strange necropolis of unfortunate beasts, there was a great collection of gentlemen in expensive garb situated upon the garish, red satin divans that lined either side of the passageway before the library. Eisen recognized some of the faces; they were the same businessmen who had gathered with Chester Chesney the day the coffin maker had first visited the mansion and its sanguine host. Chesney himself was nowhere to be seen.

"Who are you lot? Have you an appointment? If not, you're wasting your time as well as ours. Mr. Monteblanc is consulting with the members of the Union Oil Board, namely the chairman, Chester Chesney, you might have heard of him. Are you listening? Hey!"

As the man had been speaking, Eisen had kept walking, past the businessman and his acquaintances and into the library itself. Throwing wide the doors, striding to the middle of the room and ejaculating in a derisive tone at the top of his lungs.

"We stand amidst a crisis and you chirp at coinage!"

Ledru, situated in his usual position, lounging in the chair that Kavaria had previously commandeered for his throne, jumped to his feet, startled by the sudden intrusion.

The other members of the Board all stayed seated, save for the chairman who leapt from his rest and practically snarled at the intruder with a bestial ferocity.

"What in damnation do you think you are doing?"

"I'm interrupting an important meeting for one of even greater importance."

"That remains to be seen."

"Indeed."

Ledru approached with great confusion shrouding his small dewy eyes and thin, brownish lips.

"What is this about, Eisen? You can't burst in here whilst I'm–"

"I fully understand this is a liberty but it is one that, were the positions reversed, I would implore any and all of you to take."

"What situation, damn you?"

"I shall explain presently, Mr. Chesney. Pray take a seat and compose yourself."

"I shall do nothing of the kind!"

"As you will. You are all aware that the carnival that had been camping in town has been attacked and driven off into the desert?"

Ledru nodded grimly, as did a few of the other businessmen behind him. Chesney merely raised a char-black brow and scoffed.

"And what has that to do with us? With you, for that matter? Are you a carney?"

Several of the businessmen gave up obnoxious snorts of laughter. Ledru looked from the chairman to Eisen and back whilst the latter merely held the speaker's gaze, impassive and unfazed.

"One of them – one of the 'carneys' you so disgracefully deride – was pregnant with child. She had been shot though the head with a rifle, along with two of her friends. I found them at my cabin when I last returned, after that mess in the town."

"Oh, now I see. Predictable. Predictable and ridiculous."

"Excuse me? What is ridiculous, Mr. Chesney?"

"Money. You want money, isn't that right?"

"I don't follow your digression."

"Obviously not. If you were smart enough to do that, then you wouldn't be flopping in on respectable persons, such as ourselves, pining for our strongboxes like as you are."

"Are you drunk or something?"

"Drunk? Drunk! Who is this clown, Ledru? He looks distressingly familiar."

"That's because you've met him before, Mr. Chesney, this is Eisen de Torquiam, the coffin maker. Remember? The one from the city..."

"Oh. Yes. Now I do remember. You interrupted us before, now again. It's fast becoming something of a habit for you, isn't it?"

"No. Not really."

"So, let me guess, you were so distressed that you feel you need some goodly compensation for your ills?"

"Now really, sir, you go too far!"

"Not nearly far enough!"

Ledru ran up between them, his hands working over themselves in motions of nervous excitement.

"C-come now, we're all f-friends here."

"This man is no friend of mine, Ledru. Nor, I hope, of your own. Have him removed, will you; his presence is beginning to wear upon me."

Eisen looked from one to the other despairingly. "Have you heard nothing of what I have said? People are being murdered!"

Chesney was practically screaming, "And what would you have us do? Tell us! See into the future? What, exactly?"

The dark-suited aggregate quickly took up the sentence as a shield against their conscience, following after their leader.

"That's right, coffin boy, what?"

"Yes, what can we do about it?"

"It doesn't have anything to do with us."

"People die every day."

"Why concern yourself?"

Last of all his fellows, Ledru spoke, hesitantly and with great animation, his breath heavy in his throat and his eyes shimmering like one in a fever.

"Yes, Eisen, I fail to see what we can do about it, it's their own affair after all."

"Their own affair? Who is 'they'? Do you even understand what you are saying? Michael Montferiat is working up his followers into a fit that threatens to destroy the entire town as it has already destroyed those innocent wayfarers, and you would dare say that it is their 'own affair'? Do you think it cannot possibly affect you?"

Ledru was silent a moment and then looked up gravely.

"I would like you to leave, Mr. Torquiam."

"I'll leave; just let me state my case. Hear me out, that is all I ask."

"We've heard you well enough."

"I don't believe I was addressing you, Mr. Chesney. This is Mr. Monteblanc's house, if he should wish to toss me out then let him do so, but let him say that he is doing so."

Eisen turned to Ledru searchingly. The latter averted his gaze, a motion childlike and ill fitting so prestigious a personage.

"You should really leave, Eisen."

"These people need your help, I need your help. You haven't even heard what I–"

"That's enough, just go and we'll say nothing more about it."

"I had thought I could rely on you, had thought you a friend."

"Eisen please, forget these schoolyard heroics and abandon this foolishness. Now kindly leave, we are in the middle of something."

"Very well."

Glaring disdainfully at the portly redhead, Eisen spun sharply on his heels and exited the room; the slamming of wooden doors the final proclamation of his ireful departure. Outside in the hall, some distance from the library, his two companions waited with reserved aspects of doubt and uncertainty.

"Well?" James Daniels prompted shortly.

Eisen shook his head tersely, faintly, and disgustedly.

"We shall receive no help here. Come."

"Didn't think so. Ledru wouldn't help his own mother were it ta cost him a buck."

"You mustn't consolidate blame so unduly."

"All right. Who is to blame then?"

"A one Mr. C. Chesney, in particular, but, truthfully, all of them. There is great cowardice in greed. Cowardice and fear."

"Why do you think that Kavaria took Jen?"

"We'll speak of that later if it's all the same to you. We should eat and begin preparing for our journey. Once we sit down to sup, then I shall lay all the facts before you."

"All right, meet me at my house tonight and we'll do that."

Daniels was silent a moment, and then he looked away into the distance but spoke to Eisen as an adoring child might speak to an understanding father.

"You're being uncommonly kind to me and this town. I don't aim to forget it."

"My dear man, I never for a moment thought that you would."

They rode back to the outskirts of town in silence and there parted ways; Daniels heading off to round up his men, Collins to tell his worrisome, surrogate mother, Ms. Whitum, and a few of his friends why he would soon be vanishing from the town; and Eisen, to collect necessary provisions and equipment from his lodgings. On his way out of town he encountered Peter Logan, the sheriff's right-hand man walking back from some wilderness-bound adventure.

"Logan."

"Mr. Torquiam."

"Very formal for you."

"Well, I should be downright insulted."

"Should you?"

"What brings you hereabouts?"

"I didn't know you were interested."

"I kin tell you were about to ask something, something important, I would guess. That's interesting, if it's a thing."

"Well, your guess is true. Where is the sheriff?"

"Cain't say."

"As you know?"

"That's right. What you need him fer, anyhow? After what he... and me, put ya'll through... well, I didn't expect ya ta be askin after us."

"Normally I wouldn't have, though not for the reasons you likely think. It's about the Arlingtons. You've doubtless heard."

"Kidnapped."

"By Kallista."

"If that's what has you seeking out the sheriff, I kin tell ya right now you're wasting your time. He ain't for shit going ta do nothing bout it, he'd sooner shave his head, not that there's much to shave. He'll just shake his head and shrug and say what a pity it is, what a shame. And that'll be the long and short, you mark my words if nothing else."

"I'll do that. What of you, Logan, or are you as apathetic as your boss?"

"Hell, that's twice in two minutes ya'll up and insulted me, I was planning on offering my help, but shoot, I mightn't reconsider. What do ya aim ta do?"

"I'm surprised you didn't tell me there wasn't anything I could do."

"Course there is. A man always has a choice of doing or not doing, sometimes it's a harder one than usual. You aim ta go after him? Kavaria?"

"No. I only plan on going after the Arlingtons. Aside from that, I've no business with Kavaria."

"No business? Heard he damn near kilt ya."

"Not quite. However, he did nearly break my jaw. But kill me? I think not, I don't die so easily. If the desert can't kill me, certainly no cantankerous Irishman is going to."

Peter erupted into a wild cascade of laughter. His horse threw its head about and stomped the ground furiously, as if disturbed by the outburst. He steadied his mount, still smiling broadly, and pushed his hat up and wiped his brow with the back of his hand and spoke, looking at the coffin maker peculiarly.

"I like your style, Mr. Torquiam."

"I'm glad, Mr. Logan."

"I hear Daniels has a map. An old map of near the whole desert. Any truth in that?"

"Much. I've seen it. He showed me. I'm the only man in town that can translate it, save perhaps for the Monferiats."

"Translate?"

"It's in Latin."

"Ah. So when you leavin?"

"As soon as possible, a day or two. Probably in two. Certainly no more."

"My house is near the old, run-down part of town, closest to Ledru's manor. You still need help come leavin time, you just waltz on over and knock on my door and I'm your man."

"I appreciate that more than I can describe."

"Is this the part where we hug?"

"No need for sarcasm, Mr. Logan."

"There's, fer that, always a need. I'll see ya soon."

"Good day, Peter."

"Eisen."

Logan reigned up and rode into the haze rolling off and up from the desert, blurring like a mirage and disappearing over the small hill that crested into town. Eisen watched him go then switched up the horse he had borrowed from Daniels' stable and rode on with his hat pulled low against the sun.

At the lodge he packed hurriedly, locked his doors, shuttered the windows and returned to town with a heavy satchel, backpack and overcoat the very same day. On his way to Daniels' house to dine and fully explain the situation, as they had planned, Eisen was met by a quartet of solemn-faced women, two of whom he vaguely recognized as belonging to the church. They transfixed him with a disapproving glare but said nothing until he was no more than five feet away.

"We don't want you round here, stranger."

"You hear? You hear us, stranger?"

He stopped and looked at them a little while, squinting against the harsh golden rays and the fierce growling wind which blew in from the dark heart of the desert like the intransigent breath of calamity. They stood closely together at the side of the street, near the general goods store, some few buildings away from Arrgilius' inn. All wore visages of displeasure and pain and fear.

Mostly fear.

The longer he looked at them, the more fearful they grew until at last, when he was near prepared to speak, they turned and went away. One, the youngest among that gathering, looked back, the look a question. A question unanswered. He watched them vanish around the dry goods store and then furrowed his brows, frowned slightly and rode on. Passing several similar troupes, all grim and forbidding in the presentation of their attitudes. A surly glare. A snarling mouth. Teeth showing, gums exposed. Hatred breeding in that dire collective like mosquitoes in a fetid pond. He passed by a group of children near the outside of the town square. A rock was thrown; missed. Another. It too, missed its mark and sailed up and over Eisen's head, careening into Elis Caldwell's shop window.

The children scattered at the sound of shattering glass, some laughing, others too frightened at this sudden, criminal turn, to utter a sound. Caldwell emerged moments later holding the offending projectile loosely in his right hand as if it were a poisonous reptile. He tossed it aside, under the porch of the store adjacent his own and walked into the street.

"What was that all about?"

"Just some kids having fun."

"They could have killed someone. They could have fractured my skull."

"How do you know?"

"Because they were aiming for me. That was the second one they threw."

"I see. I hear you have a notion that the Arlingtons' plight merits action."

"That's right."

"You're going off to die if you are going where I think you are. You do realize that, don't you?"

"It's likely. Yes."

"Don't you care?"

"Yes."

"Then why?"

"Because if you were in the same position as Jen and her father, I'd be doing the same thing for you."

"If I were in such a position, I'd advise you against it."

"Very likely. Everyone has their principles, and for better or worse it's a finer thing to stick to them, even if they are poor, than to have none at all."

Elis nodded faintly and looked up at the reddish sky and then back to the coffin maker.

"Eisen?"

"Yes."

"You're a fool."

Eisen smiled and tipped his hat cordially, leaning forth in his saddle like some knight errant of old addressing his liege.

"At your service."

Elis withdrew a cigarette from the inner breast pocket of his well-tailored suit jacket, then his immaculate lighter, and, with the small, bone-white cylinder smoldering between his lips, he offered the pack to Eisen, who held up his free hand.

"I don't smoke."

"Course not. You know, well... you probably don't, but I want you to know that it was a pleasure to have known you. I doubt, once you leave, that you or anyone that is fool enough to follow you, will ever return, that's why I'm saying what I'm saying."

"If it were true it shouldn't matter when you say it, only how."

"Yes, you're right. An irritating habit of yours."

"You can't please everyone all the time."

"You'd know that better than most, I'd wager."

Eisen nodded and tipped his hat. This time the gesture was solemn and respectful. Caldwell returned the gesture with his cigarette. Their eyes met deeply, and then the coffin maker turned his horse and sounded away down the road with the dust whirling behind him, the diluted after-trace of his passing.

☼

He arrived at Daniels' house at nightfall. He stabled his beast and trudged inside through a thick and sudden onslaught of rain; hat pulled low, shoulders slumped against the biting chill.

The stables had been bare, aside from a lone stallion which Eisen recognized as James' own and so gave no indication of the plethora of individuals who awaited the rain-soaked traveler.

Daniels' wife opened the door, admitting Eisen with a strained smile. The remnants of a bruise, slowly fading from her right cheek and beneath it a cheap dress, fraying and thin-worn.

"Goodness, you must be drenched to the bone."

"Well, ma'am, I certainly feel like it."

"Come on, we'll rustle you up some dry vesture. The men are waiting fer ya in the dining room. I swear I've never had so many guests in all my life, not even on Christmas."

Eisen nodded vacantly, following his host up a flight of wooden steps and emerging up into a wide hallway lined with two doors on each side and one door at the very end of the enclosure's length. There were no windows. A lone and battered portrait hung upon the far wall to the left of the final door; a picture of the Daniels' family. James, his sad-eyed wife (whose name Eisen had never been told) forcing a smile, a rosy-cheeked babe and a very young girl of no more than six or seven years of age, looking away into the distance.

Eisen gazed into the frame a moment and then followed Daniels' wife into the room at the far end of the hallway where she searched through a wooden dresser standing in the corner. From the dresser she laid out a smart patchwork suit, a white cotton, long sleeved shirt, dark serge pants, light cotton socks and a cracked pair of leather riding boots with long blue laces. She left with another strained smile, shutting the door gently behind her and moving so quietly that he could barely hear her depart down the stairway. When she had gone he dressed quickly and gazed at himself in the looking glass which was positioned directly across the room from the dresser. A good fit, he thought, with a swelling sense of pride. He set his wet clothes upon a rocking chair made of dark and well-polished wood which had been slid into the far right corner near the looking glass, then he strode quietly downstairs with the rain sheeting off the roof like heavy, metal stones.

☼

Daniels sat at the head of the fully seated dining table. Collins was beside him, as well as Tanners and Gerald Fairson and a few others who the coffin maker recognized by appearance alone. Fairson averted his gaze when Eisen looked to him, hunching over the table, pretending to study the chinaware before him. There were five rough-looking men that Eisen had never laid eyes on before looking at him with muted expressions of distrust and fear. Everyone sat, save for Tanners who lounged in a corner, a pipe in his mouth and a faded leather pouch of tobacco in hand. There was no room at the table, so Eisen stood until the wife brought him a stool, setting it down next to Collins with a thoughtful nod of her head. The coffin maker nodded back and took his seat.

"Eisen, you took your time."

"I'm here now, James. So let's get to it."

"Coffee?"

"Please."

Daniels poured his guest a steaming cup full of the dark, aromatic brew from a large, black carafe situated before him on the table. As Eisen drank Daniels leaned forward, his palms flat against the table like a military commander before a speech.

"Every single one of you gathered here tonight because you want to be. If that ain't the case, then I want to know it. If someone is forcing you here against your will, you say and then you leave – I won't have it. I won't force a man to follow another if that ain't his aim. My aim is to see Kavaria and his gang brought to justice, to ensure the safety of this town and... put Braze's soul to rest." Some of the roughs nodded solemnly. Tanners shook his head and puffed at his pipe. "This is my aim, and if it's your own then you tell me; and if it ain't, you say all the same."

The leader of the toughs, a pug-nosed, barrel-chested man of no more than five feet in height, raised an ill-fittingly high voice; arms crossed, brow furrowed.

"How is it that you think you can possibly find Kallista?"

"With my map."

Eisen turned to the barrel-chested man. "It's an old, but thorough, map of the desert, all in Latin."

"Latin? Hell, then how we gonna–"

"I can read it. Latin, that is. I'll translate it and act as the guide."

"James?"

"Donners."

"Kin we all trust this'en here?"

"You kin trust him same as me."

"All right."

The barrel-chested man named Donners turned from Daniels to Eisen and looked him in the eye long and hard and searchingly and then nodded; an affirmation. An agreement.

Eisen nodded back and then began to clear a space upon the table before him, sliding the cups and the carafe away. Daniels plucked the map from the cupboard and returned, laying it down and smoothing it out. Everyone gathered round, bending to the map as if it bestowed upon them some magnetic property.

"See this mass of rocks here? An outlying formation of the mountain range, and directly behind this is a little drawing of a wide, hexagonal building – this is Kallista's compound."

Donners leaned down, hand cupping his chin meditatively. "How you know that?"

"I don't know it, not to a certainty. But given the rapidity with which Kallista and his men seem able to rush into town and then away, this spot would be ideal. Plus, it is the only large building for fifty miles around. I would wager a great sum of money that it is here that Kallista calls home."

"All right," Tanners swaggered up to the table. "I take that bet."

"I wasn't making a–"

"Too late. Already been called, Eisen."

"Fine. Twenty?"

"Twenty-five."

Daniels struck the table with his fist, a grimace of disdain writ large upon his craggy features.

"This is no time for games, damn it all!"

Donners turned to his friend and put a steadying hand upon his right shoulder, a sadness in his eyes.

"Take it easy ole son, take it easy. We need you in good spirits for the trip."

GRAVE.

"Yes, sorry, yes, you're right."

"Passion can be a prison, ole son."

Eisen scanned the room and then turned to Daniels. "Have you any pens?"

"Sure."

"I'd like one to work out the best routes. Are there any geographers or surveyors among you?"

Donners nodded and replied that he had once worked for many hard and toilsome years as a surveyor for Union Oil before he went freelance and was, ironically, hired out by Ledru, a primary shareholder in that same company.

"Good, then you can help me."

Donners nodded.

They bent to work, and their slowly melding thoughts were the balm which drove from that sphere the whirling cluster of madness, gathering in the desert so far and deep away; a storm to birth a god.

Part Two

Rex Tremendae

We must be greater than God,
for we have to undo his injustice.
- Jules Renard.

Chapter Twenty-Three

The Ocean of Sand

It was half a day entire before the map had been appropriately marked out and the journey fully primed. That day, early and cold as it was, doors aplenty were rapped and savaged and opened to reveal the tearful eyes of loved ones, pleading in vain. Don't go. Don't go, were the words echoed all about the town, from every frowning, curling mouth, suggested with the motion of every pair of wringing hands and shaking head.

No member of Eisen's party heeded the pleading suggestions. They all met at the northern-most end of town where the main thoroughfare ran from the square, out through the ancient iron fencing that had been erected adjacent to Ms. Whitum's little shack and off into the great, howling flat of the desert.

Eisen had sent word to Logan's abode, and as he finished packing, the man himself appeared half an hour later, the last member of the newly forged company.

Logan nodded to Eisen but said nothing, as nothing needed to be said. They saddled their horses, steadied their packs and rode off at daybreak without further delay. Eisen and Daniels rode as vanguard of that dire-eyed assemblage, side by side, whispering solemnly to one another like generals in darkest conference.

The star above them was red and swollen and filled the land with its roiling tendrils, distorting the whole of that barren plain and all those that trespassed therein as if seen through boiling glass. There were no birds nor clouds in the sky, just a vast swath of purple and blue and the strange colorings in between.

The sky bled out and down and drew the land in its own selfsame coloring, and the men of that wayward company looked about fearfully as if in abhorrence of the eldritch hues.

Only Eisen and Tanners remained impassive to the phantasmagorical radiance which glowed before them like a dreamscape hewn free of the mind of some delirious virtuoso. The latter smoking his pipe vacantly, his eyes straight ahead and unconcerned, the former the solitary picture of serenity, everything else within his being interred in the magnitude of the land; opaque and illusory and magnificent. They traveled in this fashion until dark, then bivouacked in a large outcropping of rocks that, at the top of their blunted spires, curved inwards, seeking the center of their forms. This variance of stone formed an arena, benchless and floored by sand and several scraggly tufts of greenery. Eisen unrolled his pack and prepared to sleep, but sleep never came for him, never carted him away unto that world of aberration and horror and sublime beauty. He looked at the sky and the toothless, icy hole of the moon, like a puncture in the fabric of the firmament. The latter itself speckled with tiny dots of fire that sparkled like crystals in a frozen whirlwind painted black and unfurled for all to see. He watched the sky for the better part of an hour and then rose to a crouch and scanned his following. Then he rose entirely and walked the perimeter of the camp.

Once.

Twice.

Three times, now four.

Upon the fifth time he paused in place near the entrance into the wide stone enclosure and listened to the strange voice spilling in from the darkness on the wind. A voice that was as familiar as it was ghastly.

"Look at you now. I told you."

"Told me what?"

"That you would do well."

The man with the white umbrella stepped into the light of Eisen's torch, and there faintly illuminated, he leaned against a massive boulder of smooth red stone that rested directly between the encampment and the road that let out into the north into the darkness.

The man did not raise his parasol and showed no sign of his former injuries. He wore the same ragged patchwork suit he had worn previously with dark leather gloves upon his hands and a wide-brimmed traveling hat pulled low over his face. He appeared to be amused by the coffin maker and watched him closely, barely moving, more statue than man.

"Why are you following me?"

"Would it change anything if you knew? People like you, rare as they are, cage themselves in their questioning. If I could fear for you, that would be what I should fear. What do you fear, Eisen de Torquiam?"

"Dying."

"Not death itself?"

"It is an action. It has no self. The word, in such a context, loses all meaning."

"True. But that makes no difference, should you choose to perceive it through a different lense."

"But I don't. Nor will I."

"Of course not. It is not in the nature of your becoming to do so. I just thought you should know."

"I'll tell you something I know, since you seem so keen on speaking with me, I know Kavaria is looking for you. That you stayed at his camp. That you murdered his men."

"Did I?"

"Yes. I also know that you gave this mask to the jester. Why give it to him?"

Eisen stood in the starlight, torch held loosely at his side and the strange, smiling, bone-white mask held in his left hand, extended forth into the dancing shadows and the man standing therein.

"I didn't give anything to anyone. You did."

"What do you mean? I did?"

"You don't remember?"

"You try my patience again."

"Rage, again? Violence, again? Yes. Wonderful. You should wear that mask; you are more deserving of it than I. Wear it as a reminder of all the terrible emotions and thoughts that you suppress with that icy veneer in the name of nobility. In the name of good form and showmanship. In the name of 'Humanity,' whatever that means to you. When one meets a man of such distinct reserve, it is ever prudent to ask, 'Why is it that he is as he thinks he ought to be?' Do you, yourself, even know?"

"You have a passionate love of questions. From the onset I knew you were no fool from the very fact."

"No, just like you. No fool. But a truthsayer."

"The truth of what?"

"Oneself. You. That of which you are ignorant."

"You may not be a fool, but you certainly are arrogant if you think you know me better than I do."

"Why is that?"

"Because–"

"Because?"

"Because I know myself!"

At that moment there was a call from behind, from the camp; the voice of Henry Collins, concerned and uncertain.

"Who you talking to out there, Eisen?"

Eisen turned to Collins then back to the man with the white parasol, but he was nowhere to be seen.

"No one, apparently."

"Apparently?"

"Yeah."

"Y'all start scaring the men, you keep on like that."

"Then I shan't keep on. What did you want, anyway?"

"Nothing – just heard voices. I swear you were talkin to someone."

"I'm not to be keeping on, remember."

"All right."

"Go to sleep, Henry, you'll need your strength tomorrow."

"Yeah? And what of you? Won't you need your strength too?"

"No. Go to sleep."

"All right."

He walked off, leaving Eisen alone once more, staring out into the lightless void that swallowed all the world before him; he the lone source of luminescence therein. Suddenly there came a howling from off in the dunes, then another.

Coyotes.

A shriek of pain.

Silence descending.

Then nothing.

☼

In the morning they awoke to find one of their number dead from snakebite. In a delirious stupor he had stripped to the waist, left his things and run off in the direction of the dunes. He, however, was felled by the venom before he could reach his destination, if, in such a time and situation, he even had one. The body was discovered by Tanners and one of Donners' men who identified the dead man as Eric Salvis, a forty-something contractor and former shoemaker; citizen of the town for nearly his entire life. Now lifeless and stiff and bluish and pale. His hands positioned strangely in the air as if he was trying desperately to reach something in front of his face. Donners' men wrapped him in a sheet and buried him at sunrise beneath the ashes of their fire pit. They then mounted and rode as vanguard to their quest whilst Eisen, Tanners, Collins, Fairson and Daniels stayed behind, staring blankly at the grave.

At great length Daniels spoke, looking to each and every face and then to the nameless entombment, unmarked and ashen.

"Shouldn't we say something?"

Eisen looked him in the eye.

"If you had something to say to the man, you have happened upon the words too late. Funerals are for the living, not the dead."

Daniels began to cry. He turned away from the sepulcher, a hand covering his face, and then hurried toward his horse.

Collins, still looking at the resting place of the dead man, spoke to his three companions, not to one more than another.

"I knew him well. He lived a good life. He always told me that when he died, he hoped dearly that it was in an interesting way. S'pose e got his wish."

"He sounds like a man who was happy with his life."

"He was, Tanners, he really was."

"Then dry your eyes, man! Tell his tale, tell it well. It's only his story what's ended, not your own."

At last, Fairson spoke, his voice a hushed and heavy whisper, like one speaking quietly underwater.

"That could have been anyone of us, anyone."

Eisen walked over to him and gripped his shoulders firmly.

"Could have, but it wasn't. You mustn't live in a world of 'if's.' If's can kill. As surely as a snakebite."

"I don't understand."

"It's all right."

"It's not all right! Nothing is all right! It's all wrong, horribly wrong!"

"That's enough of that."

"It ain't enough, it ain't at all!"

Eisen released his grip on the young man's shoulders and turned to Collins and Tanners.

"Why don't you two go ahead, we'll catch up in a few minutes."

Both nodded and departed without another word. When they had gone Eisen walked back to Fairson.

"You must fight your despair."

"I cain't do it, I just... it's like a, like a... damn it all!"

"You don't have the words?"

"No."

"I know what ails you, what gnaws away inside you with an endless hunger."

"The man is dead! And Jen..."

"Is kidnapped, is held up, very likely in some dank, and filthy cell, beaten, violated–"

"Don't say this to me!"

"Why? It is the truth. It is a burden you must carry if you want to help her. Would you prefer me to tell you that the man in the ground was only pretending he was dead, that it was a ruse?"

"No."

"No, of course not. So then why should Jen's situation be any different?"

"We shouldn't speak of it."

"Why not?"

"We just shouldn't!"

"Wrong. You are so, very, horribly, utterly WRONG!"

"Don't say this to me, don't you say this to me, Eisen! I thought you were my friend, that I could confide in you. You saved my life, and I liked you before, but I cain't hardly say as to how I feel now – and you're, you're..."

"Being honest."

"But Eric, he'll be watching out fer us, won't e?"

Eisen said nothing.

"Won't he?"

The coffin maker said nothing and watched the younger man; pain on both faces, pain in the silence as much as the sounding.

"You tell me he'll be watching out fer us, damn you! You say it! You say it now!"

"He won't be watching anything, Gerald, you know it as well as I. There is no Eric Salvis, he's gone–"

"He was my friend!"

"And he's gone, nothing in him that was his own self, he's just a bunch of rotting meat."

Fairson drew back his left arm and struck Eisen upon his right jaw, staggering the coffin maker, drawing blood. Fairson, his eyes clouding over with tears and his mouth contorted with the force of his anguish, took a step backward and then shook his head and started walking away.

Eisen wiped his face with the back of his left hand and then trudged on after the weeping man and stopped him with a steady hand.

Fairson whirled furiously, breaking free of his grip and then glared at the man, harshly and purely and weakly. Then he shook his head again and ran a feebly shivering hand through his dense curly locks.

"I'm so sorry, Eisen, I–"

The coffin maker walked forward and eased his arms around the sorrowful figure and held him tightly.

"It's all right... if you strive to make it so. Let that be your solace. Let that be your peace of mind."

And then, quite suddenly, Fairson drew up and kissed the coffin maker upon the lips, their eyes meeting, fulminate and tender. Breath suddenly sharp and sucked away. And then, just as quickly as it happened, Fairson drew back from his companion and hurried off with his head down like a man shamed and defiled. He ran through the large opening in the rock formation that led to the main road, a shadow moving against the sun.

"Fairson! Fairson?"

Eisen thought of giving chase, but didn't want to cause a scene in the middle of the venture and thought it best to wait until they had reached the end of their quest before he dealt with the matter. So he walked out of the stone arena with a heavy heart, his mind a fog of blank confusion and sadness. But then there was that kiss, and whatever else he thought about it or the day, it made him smile.

☼

The next day they reached the quarter mark in their journey, the place the locals called The High Dunes. An apt title, for there was nothing before them but small bundles of cacti and the high rolling tumulus of the sandhills. The wind blew in from behind them to the south and stripped thin sheets of sands from the tops of the dunes, spun them up in great dancing circles and then scattered them like so many ashes. There was little to indicate direction, and, despite that errant company's compasses, they were often lost. In an hour's time the wind had developed in ferocity to such a degree that one could barely see three feet in front of one's face.

They had to stop in the shelter of a large, viciously sundered boulder that was split down the middle but only fully at the bottom, such that it created a short, high-roofed cave. The entrance to this odd and wondrous place faced in the direction from whence they had come, the south, and within it they discovered the remnants of another party. The remains of a small fire and discarded clothing, finely soaked in blood, laid within. It was a tight fit, but all of the men were able to gather inside the hollow boulder without too much jostling. The dimensions of the corridor-like cave were such that every man could lie to his full length or stand to his summit without agitating another. There encamped they spent the night; a night sightless and cold and filled with black dreams.

Donners and his men had prepared a fire and it burned low and smokeless, flickering with the force of the wind which whistled in through the wide and jagged fissure that had long ago rent and made vasiform that towering monolith. Most of the men slept with their pistols at the ready, hearts pounding with terror from their excursion even in their dreams. Eisen remained awake once again and sat before the fire, examining the bloodstained clothing before him. He held a once white, now brownish cotton shirt up to the light and nodded as the light shone through a small hole in the fabric, illuminating his eye a peculiar shade of gold.

"Bullet hole?"

Eisen turned to the speaker who had come upon him unannounced. It was Logan.

"Yes. I believe so. Here, take a look."

Peter Logan nodded and then lowered himself beside the coffin maker and took the stained piece of fabric in his hands, turning it over and over and back and forth and squinting. "Scorch marks around the edge of the hole; it's the right size too, definitely a small-caliber round, definitely a bullet."

"So the question is," Eisen began pouring himself a cup of tea from his carafe, offering one to Logan which he gladly accepted, "was the blood on that shirt there before or after the gunshot?"

"Why then would it matter?"

"Because if you wanted someone to think you were dead, you would do that, wouldn't you?"

Logan cupped his chin and nodded slowly and thoughtfully, his eyes fixed on the tattered shirt before him.

"I see what you're getting at."

"Yes. If you wanted someone to think you were dead, then you'd pour some blood on a piece of clothing you had, shoot a hole through it and then leave it for the desired party to find."

"See here? The blood is completely brown and dry, the fabric is stiff with it, but the burn marks from the shot itself are much newer. Look at how dark the marks are – you see?"

Logan nodded and turned to the coffin maker with admiration.

"Very clever."

"Thank you, Mr. Logan."

"But what's it all mean?"

"Someone else was hiding from Kallista and his gang. We should try to find him."

"How do you know it's a him?"

"Does this look like a woman's shirt to you, Peter?"

"No, it kindly does not."

"Then we need to find this man."

A look of supreme realization leapt to the fore of Peter Logan's craggy visage; a furtive rabbit scurrying about a cliff face.

"Because he likely knows the fort!"

"Exactly."

The two men exchanged prideful smiles and cups of tea as they talked long into the night, of their childhoods and their victories and the great sorrows that had beset them. And by the end of their words had come to a solemn, half-shaded understanding of the other. Both knew now that their words to each other could no longer be casual, could no longer be superfluous, could no longer be derisive and mocking. And they were glad at heart for it, happier than either had been since the journey had begun. They said nothing of their feelings, feeling that nothing needed to be said.

At sunrise Eisen rose from a light sleep to discover Fairson watching him from across the fire pit.

Quickly, Fairson turned away from the waking man.

"Do you need something, Fairson?"

"Everyone needs something."

"No."

"What?"

"That's not true."

"What do you mean?"

"Everyone wants something. There is no need without want. When wants are strong enough, then they become needs."

"That's probably true."

"Why did you do it?"

Fairson looked away from the coffin maker, out into the blinding brightness of the wasteland, and the coffin maker followed his gaze. He was staring at the jagged cluster of rocks that lay several days away from the cave; that blocked their passage to Kavaria's castle-keep, or rather, where the map said it should be.

"Fairson?"

"I don't want to talk about it."

"Yes, you do."

Fairson folded his legs up underneath his lithe, youthful body and returned the coffin maker's gaze steadily; the gesture a challenge.

"So maybe I do."

"Why did you do it?"

"You know why I did it. Don't pretend–"

"Yes, I know why. What I don't know is, why you didn't say something sooner?"

"That's pretty obvious, ain't it?"

"You were what? Scared? Scared to say something?"

"If anyone knew, what do you think they would do? Say, 'Oh, ain't it sweet.' No, we both know... we both know that ain't what would'a happened."

"Probably we do."

"Sorry. I ain't angry at you."

"No. But you are angry. You shouldn't let that sway you."

"How kin I not?"

"That I cannot say."

Between them suddenly emerged Tanners, still smoldering on his bizarrely oversized pipe, his small, coffee-black eyes twinkling proudly. There was something else in his expression; something suggesting fear, but of what or whom, Eisen couldn't say.

"We found something, your Excellency."

Eisen looked at the man with an expression that was half curious, half amused by the unexpectedly nominal form of address.

"Your Excellency?"

"Well, I know who is really running the show, despite what Mr. Daniels seems to think. I like to call um as I see um."

"Indeed. Well, let me inform you that this is a joint venture and will only resort to leadership when the occasion calls for it."

"Ah, and so who is to decide when one is to call for it, then?"

"You make a good point, Tanners, but what of this thing you have found; what is it?"

"Come and see. Though, to be honest, it was really a joint venture, like as you said, tween me and Mr. Logan. Don't kindly know how it is that you convinced him to come along with us, but I'm sure glad you did. A hard man, that one."

"Not nearly as hard as he appears."

"Oh? You two shacking up, come twinkle time?"

"Do shut up, Mr. Tanners."

"Very well, your Excellency, very well."

Tanners started toward the back of the cave where the fissure grew, by pronounced degrees, ever smaller until a man could barely fit through the passage. It was all they could do to follow Tanners, willowy as he was, as he slipped easily through the breach in the stone. Finally they had to turn sideway to pass between the high black walls which seemed to press in upon them as if with some malicious intent.

"How much farther, Tanners?"

"Not much. It lets out just up here."

"Lets out?"

Right as he spoke, Eisen heard the muted voice of Logan echoing before them in the darkness of the narrow passage; the murmuring din of the rest of the company rattling away behind them in the cavern proper, along with the brightness and dimness alike. A few more feet and they were in total darkness. Again Eisen heard the rumbling bass of Peter Logan.

"Is that you, Tanners?"

"In the flesh."

"You brought them?"

"Yes."

"Well, I'll light it then."

"Not yet. We aren't out of the pass."

Tanners turned suddenly, stopping in his tracks and faced them in the blackness, the muffled scrapping of boot upon stone and the cool dampness of the cave the singularity of sensation in that strange and ancient place.

"Maybe the kid shouldn't see..."

"I'm not a kid, Tanners."

"Calm down, Fairson. He's right, Tanners, if he wants to come, it's his choice. What is it we are meant to see?"

"Light it, Logan."

Suddenly, a flicker in the darkness.

Tanners passed before them in the dark. They followed and found that the fissure now opened up into another cavern, this one larger than the first. Peter Logan, lantern in hand, stood some distance away in what appeared to be the center of the enclosure. Tanners walked up to him apprehensively and looked back at his followers, his expression grim and haunted.

"The walls."

Logan walked to his left and brandished the torch aloft, shearing a swath of bright through the darkness, absenting the blanket of shadow from the high, stony edifice.

Everywhere there were bones; skulls and bodies entire stashed and stored in the cool recesses which lined the otherwise barren partitions of rock and what lay between. The in-curvatures looked hewn of stone in some olden time, some time beyond reckoning, obscured entirely to the imaginations of those who happened upon them. In those myriad niches lay the bodies of the long dead, skeletons with leering grins.

Eisen strode hurriedly to inspect them, his mind a flurry of questions unanswered.

Fairson followed at a distance, cautious and ill at ease.

"It's a tomb. This place is a tomb. How wonderful."

"Wonderful?"

"Yes, Tanners, this place is old. Very old. Ancient. Emeritus from the world. Locked away, sealed mostly. No one with sense would venture this far into the desert without a potent reason, and such people would be rare. Thus it has been largely undisturbed. Shame about the condition of the bodies, bacteria and the elements have wiped them clean. Yes, a shame."

"Were you an archeologist as well as coffin maker before you came to our quaint little town?"

"No, Logan, but such things stir something within me. Do they nothing for you?"

"Not really. Though I must say, it was some work cutting out all those little chambers in the wall. The manpower it must have took... s'pose that's something, if it's a thing."

Eisen turned back to the wall of the massive sepulcher, his eyes wide with the dancing light of wonder. He laid his hands up against it, feeling the cool stone beneath his outstretched palms.

"Can you hear it, gentlemen?"

Fairson scratched his head and finally spoke, "Hear what?"

"The whisper of history's weave."

Logan smiled in amusement whilst Tanners shook his head as one might gesture to a foolish, if good natured, child. Fairson said nothing but watched the coffin maker intently, as if the lines of his body and their curvatures would reveal some virile secret unto the lad.

Tanners scoffed at last, shattering the silence with all the integrity of a tree falling upon an immobilized leap frog.

"Is history still whispering?"

"Always. More so now than presently."

"You're batty. Anyone ever mention it to ya?"

"No one worth regarding."

Logan gave a start, laughing heartily whilst Tanners shot him a vile scowl, crossed his arms and continued to shake his head in a manner that was attempting disapproval, but only managed mocking playfulness. The sentiment was so potent and infectious that even Fairson smiled.

"Still scared of the tomb, Fairson?"

"What? What you talking about, Eisen. I wasn't scared, still ain't."

"Oh, my mistake. Come, we need to get moving and find this gentleman who once called these caverns home – agreed?"

All replied that it was so, and they left hurriedly back whence they had come, departing so briefly that they failed to notice the strange eyes that watched them from the back of the hollow. Eyes that looked out from beneath a taintless white umbrella.

Chapter Twenty-Four

Old Man of the Desert

They departed from the cave at midday and traveled toward the jagged stone cluster in the far off and away; in the distance between the tomb and the toothed peaks, was nothing but flat and long and death.

There was no longer a road to speak of, only the sand and the heat and the din of winged things wheeling high and silent above. Churning darkness on the softly spinning ground; a pirouette of shadows, fell and fair.

Watching.

Waiting.

Hungering.

Three hours into their travel and one of the men noticed a shape stirring in the distance, through the haze of the heat, walking toward them through the remnants of an old lake, now nothing more than a cracked, empty plain.

Daniels rode forth and looked toward the shape with a pair of binoculars.

"Most definitely a man. We can reach him before dark if we hurry."

Donners spoke up suddenly, "Kin e see us?"

Daniels nodded hesitantly.

"It's likely, us kicking up as much dust as we are."

"So there's no point in hiding."

"No, likely not."

"All right."

They whipped up their frothing mounts and turned in the whirling sands toward the lone man, fickle form and dream-like in that blistering atmosphere.

Logan rode up beside Eisen, his brow furrowed, obviously deep in some grim reverie.

"You think it's the man we been looking fer? The one what was in that cave back yonder?"

"Why speculate when you can find out directly?"

Eisen kicked up his horse, riding faster than all the rest, his company quickly diminishing behind him. He reached the man in an hour's time, pulling up slowly in front of him and dismounting languidly, as if it had all been done before.

The man at first looked terrified but slowly relaxed as Eisen smiled at him and tipped his wide-brimmed hat.

"Good day."

The man said nothing, only nodded. Beads of sweat dripped from both faces, both faces star-burnt and weary, yet resilient.

"Who are you?"

The old man looked up at Eisen firmly, opaquely, the way one might look upon the face of an old friend who has gone away, seen the world and returned bearing the colors of the map; the hue of his experiences. Eisen returned the firmness of the gaze and realized that the man had a strange bundle upon his shoulders, a large red basket, thin and of a material that the coffin maker could not place. From within the container a little white shape emerged and swiveled about, sniffing the air, tasting it.

An ermine, nearly pure white and very restless. A long, thin string ran about its neck, loosely tied, down to the old man's left wrist where he had been tied off on his leather vambrace.

The old, dark-skinned man watched the coffin maker observing the little weasel and then smiled gently.

"He gets very tired traveling in the heat. He was not built for it, were he built at all, so I carry him."

"That's very generous of you."

"As it is of you to say as much."

The rest of the company arrived, encircling the man so as to ensure his immobility. The old traveler and his furry friend looked about placidly, as if it were a flock of hawks they were seeing rather than a gathering of dire-eyed hunters. The men glowered at this archaic figure who seemed to have grown up from the earth itself. Born of sand and heat and danger; the agglomerate wisdom thereof shining brilliantly in his dark, ruby-colored eyes.

"Are you oilmen? You don't look like oilmen. No, you are not oilmen, this... yes, this I can see now. You do not seek oil, but you are seeking something, scouring this place with such aggression – I can feel it like the warm breath of a dying sow."

Tanners produced his pipe and lit it, shaking his head and turning in his saddle to Eisen.

"Is e mad, eh?"

"No more mad than a man what would willing inhale that which chokes him. You find this strange, no?"

"He is mad and you with him."

"Enough, Tanners."

"Oh, shut it, Logan. You don't frighten me."

"Maybe I should."

"Maybe."

"Maybe I will."

Eisen ignored their bickering and approached the old man farther, striding forth until they were merely two feet from the other, face to face. As he approached a sudden wind whipped up about them, as if to protect this frail and wizened wayfarer. So powerful was this sudden gust that Eisen was nearly thrown to the ground by its barreling howl. He spread his legs a pace and braced himself against the gale, his eyes squinting into the wind with his hat pulled low over his face. He raised his voice against the wailing of the sky and addressed the old traveler solemnly.

"Me and my men discovered a cave about a day's travel to the north, carved by time out of an enormous boulder. Have you ever camped there?"

"Yes."

"Recently?"
"Yes."
"I did not think you would be so forthcoming."
"You shouldn't be so suspicious."
"It's strange you should say that."
"Why?"
"Because I was saying that same thing some time before. You are evading Kavaria Kallista?"
"Quite skillfully, if I may so observe. I forgot something... you found my shirt?"
"Yes."
"I thought so. Careless of me; age may blunt precision, but not determination, at least not yet. It was to that cave that I was headed, to retrieve it and to shelter from the sun, not for me but for my friend. He is very susceptible to the heat."

The old man reached over and ran his tanned and wrinkled hands along the weasel's head, smiling as it purred.

"About this man you seek, this bandit," the old man began again, "what is it he has done to you? Stolen from you? Kidnapped a friend? Killed someone undeserving?"

Eisen nodded gravely. "All of the above."

"Then you should turn back."

"Kavaria does not frighten me."

"Perhaps he should, but it is not him whom you should fear."

"Who then?"

The man gestured around at the gathering of men and horses, an urgency to every movement, to every gesture.

"These are good men. I've no reason to fear them."

The old man walked to Eisen, so close that their noses nearly met, his eyes wide with concern and something else, something powerful and placeless.

"No, you have no reason to fear them... no, not yet."

"What do you mean?"

"You do not understand the gravity of the situation."

"So tell me and then I'll know."

"You will see."

The old man struck out from the coffin maker, heading in the direction of the ancient tomb when several of Donners' men reigned out their horses and blockaded the way.

"Could you move please?"

Donners spoke up, amidst a mouthful of chew.

"Cain't do that."

"Yes, you can."

"We can, but we ain't gonna."

"Yes. I already know that."

"Well aintcha a smarten! That's good. So then why don't ya'll tell us where we kin find Kallista. We know you know him, our clever friend over there figured that out. So why don't you just make this easy fer everyone and cooperate?"

"No."

"No? What on earth ya mean, 'No'?"

"Precisely what I say."

"That ain't vury promisin. No sir, it ain't."

"I reckon not. For me, and for you. All of you."

Daniels rode up with a hand extended toward Donners, whose face was slowly contorting with a hideous anger borne of the old man's words.

"Just calm it, Donners, now ain't the time to be losing our heads. I done enough of that my own damn self, so don't you start on me as well."

The old man smiled faintly and gestured to Daniels while fixedly gazing at Donners.

"Your friend is a wiser man than he at first appears. To him you would do well to listen."

"Shut your goddamned mouth."

"I said calm it, Donners."

One of Donners' men, a craggy-faced chap with slicked-back hair and a ragged leather vest, spoke up, glaring hatefully toward the old traveler.

"You'll tell us where he is, and you'll tell us now."

The old man paused, as if lost in thought, then he looked to the man with the leather vest, and then all around that errant company with his sad, mournful face, the lines thereof like rivers of sorrow hewn of flesh as a monument and a warning. The wind died away and fell clouds covered the rumbling sky as his voice boomed out of his throat like a thunderbolt.

"Listen well, you raiders of the earth, I shall help you in any way I can, save that way which you desire of me. I know well enough and more why you seek this man, what black impulses drive you. Of it I shall have no portion. I will not be party to murder, not of the righteous, not of the baneful, not of the strong nor of the weak. Every life that is lived is of a singular occupation in space and time and therefore should, of its own accord, be worshiped, above and beyond all other things. Life is all there is, all we have, you, me, one man and every; this furry beast upon my back; all. Doubt this not, lest you should incur the ire of the harbinger, and he of your own destruction."

Collins nodded toward the old man warmly. "Boyd, Burke, Cruler, Donners, go ahead and let him through."

Fairson voiced his stalwart agreement. "Yeah. This ain't right. We got no right to detain him."

"Bullshit. We have every right, you little whoreson."

"I said calm it, Donners, and leave the kid alone."

"Sorry Dan, but we cain't let him go."

"We have to."

The old man tilted his head up and watched the sky as they argued amongst themselves. Their voices, myriad and dissenting, a chorus of chaos, a chant of insurrection brooding unseen and unchecked in their hateful hearts like flames in oil-tainted streams. Rivers of poison; poison burning the rivers dry. A sonorous thunderclap; subtle rain began to fall.

Eisen lunged forth, moving in front of the old traveler and raising his voice above the din; above the men, above the elements.

"Cease your yammering!"

Almost instantly the shrill bickering gave way to an uneasy silence. The men looked on, expectant and wary. Looking to the old man, then to Eisen, then back again.

"This man here, this benevolent mind, has extended his heart to you, has bared the truth, and the way you repay him is with veiled threats. Threatening him, you squabble before each other about the appropriate way to do so. This is unacceptable. I will help you bring in Kavaria – kill him, if necessary, along with all of his men. I will do this because they are dangerous and unreasonable, they are a threat to the community which I have seen striving so hard to emerge from the pit into which it has sunk – the stagnation, the poverty, the anger, the rage, the hatred. All of this is the bane upon which Kavaria and his men feed like bloated leeches. They are beasts of chaos, will you then join them? Become one yourselves? I, for one, will not, now or ever."

To Eisen's surprise it was Daniels who replied first to his pertinacious challenge, riding over to the coffin maker's side guardedly, as if in preparation of defense.

"Nor will I. I suggest the same for the rest of you."

All of the party then gave agreement to the notion, save for Donners and his friend with the ragged leather vest, Cruler.

Daniels looked them over warily, flicking his eyes from their dour faces to their gun belts and back again.

"Come on, Donners, it ain't worth it."

Donners looked to the man with the ragged vest and nodded sadly but firmly.

"He's right, Cruler. So you just calm it, all right, think if that old man were you."

"I'm done thinking. Do you and Daniels think that you two were Braze's only friends? Well, do ya? I'm making damn sure that none of that don't never happen again. You hear that, old man? You hear me?"

The old traveler nodded placidly, the whole of his posture relaxed and likewise; his expression difficult and arcane and piercing.

Some of Daniels' men had already begun to ride on ahead as Cruler bellowed at the wayfarer. He now shouted to them with a scornful fury.

"You'll just ride away when he kin show us the way? Cowards! Come back here – Donners! Donners, don't you shake your head at me, we... Donners, don't you dare ride away. Daniels? Daniels..."

Now only Eisen, the wayfarer and Cruler were left, staring at one another.

After a heavy spell of silence the old man spoke.

"You should ride. A storm is coming."

"Come on, Cruler, don't do anything rash, anything you'll regret."

Cruler looked up to the sky and then let his hand fall from the polished pommel of his shooting iron and then rode off after Donners without another word or glance at either of the two men.

Eisen smiled at the traveler and turned to leave but the old man stopped him, pulling the younger man back toward him with a strength that belied his eld. He whistled sharply, a peculiar tune, high and charming, at which point the ermine reemerged with a small leather flask in its mouth. The old man took it from the little beast and pressed it into the coffin maker's palm.

"A gift. For snakebite."

"Thank you."

"It was nice to have met you."

The man departed, still heading toward the cave, as a great swelling gale crashed down from the burning vault of the sky, sending up a vast wall of swirling sand, like the dancing cloak of an ethereal vaudevillian, consuming the diminishing figure by subtle degrees until he was obscured completely. When the sand cleared he was gone. There was no trace of him left, not even his footprints in the sand, only the parting gift in the coffin maker's hand.

Eisen turned, mounted up his marbled horse and tucked the flask away in one of his greatcoat's inner breast pockets. Then he rode on.

Chapter Twenty-Five

Mockery from a Jagged Spire

By midday the wind's savage increase had rendered travel impossible. The sand storms stirred so thick that the errant company could barely see ten feet before them.

At nightfall they holed up in a small arroyo which provided a slight shelter against the vicious incursion, huddling in their tents like frightened children after the telling of a ghost story; eyes wide and hearts quickening in their collective chests.

Eisen lay upon his back, sprawling, his hands cupped cradling his weary head. He hadn't bothered to undress. The temperature was low and getting lower with every passing hour. The tent was not his own and had been borrowed from Daniels. It was small, a two person fit, but only just, a brownish-green and of a heavy canvas cloth. It was fully proofed against the elements, and not a trace of sand speckled the interior of the abode.

Once again, he could not sleep; only this time he could not stray, too dangerous with the storm. If I get lost, he pondered flatly, if I get lost, they will only find my bones... my bones, nothing more.

There was a muted sound emanating from somewhere close by, somewhere outside. It was a voice, the voice of a familiar. Gerald Fairson.

Eisen got up and unzipped the tent carefully, such that a minimum of sand would blow inside. However, the only sand he saw was on the ground below Fairson's feet. The latter stood hunched over, eyes hopeful and bright, his features composed.

"Can I come in? Oh, you don't have ta worry none, the wind's all died down now, we're lucky."

"Come in."

He did so, without looking at Eisen, taking a seat at the far end of the tent, sitting cross legged and very still. Eisen moved back from the entrance flap and sprawled out as he had done before, hands behind his head, eyes to the gently rippling ceiling, like the skin of a strange and gelatinous beast.

"I wanted to talk to you about before."

"About a kiss."

"Yes."

"You have feelings for me."

"Yes."

"You feel guilty about it, that's why you aren't looking at me."

Only then did Fairson raise his head and look to the coffin maker. Eisen sat up like his guest, legs crossed and back straight.

"Yes, it's a sin."

"What is?"

"For a man to want another man."

"Says who?"

"God."

"Too bad for him, I suppose."

"I'm being serious, Eisen."

"So am I."

And with that the coffin maker drew Fairson forcefully to his lips and then to the floor of the tent.

☼

The morning heat rushed upon them, silent and insidious, killing two of the horses and leaving their riders grief stricken.

Tanners rapped upon Eisen's tent flap, whereupon it was opened very provisionally, a pale sliver of skin and dark questioning eyes staring out from the gloom.

"What is it, Tanners?"

"It's the heat, this damnable heat!"

"What of it?"

"It's kilt two of our best horses, Donners' and Daniels' prized steed. He cried, he's still crying. It was the dehydration and the hard riding, well, it was just too much for them. Far too much."

"That is unfortunate. I'll be right out, and I suppose I'll talk with him, try and do something for the poor man."

"Thanks. If anyone kin pull him out of his reverie it'd be you, I wager – you've a way."

"A way?"

"With words. Hold on, something moved in there, is someone in there wit ye?"

"Yes."

"Is that – Fairson, what are you doing in there?"

"We were just talking."

"Some of the men were looking fer ya."

"What for?"

"Ya'll weren't in your own tent."

"Oh. Tell them I'm with Mr. Torquiam."

"Will do. I'm off ta bury the damned animals. Some of them have got it in their thick an empty heads that the one thing a dead horse needs above all else is a proper burial. They're digging a pit now. Bloody ceremony. Waste of time."

Tanners shook his head and then very reverently produced his pipe and brought it to his mouth, lit it and began puffing meditatively as he walked slowly away, trailing dust and squinting up against the sun, raising a hand to visor off the harshness of the omnipresent rays.

Fairson sucked in a shuddering breath, panic permeating his every furtive movement.

"Do you think he knows, Eisen?"

"Probably."

"Oh God."

"Don't distress yourself. Not now, we can't afford it, not you, not me, not the rest of them."

"But, Eisen, Tanners will–"

"What?"

"He'll say something."

"Not now he won't, he's got bigger concerns than idle gossip; we all have. Besides, I doubt Tanners would care either way. I certainly don't."

"Yeah, that could be true."

"Have there ever been any before in the town?"

"Any what? Men that have slept with other men?"

"Yes."

"No. Course there ain't been. They'd have been run out of town soon as it was known."

"Because they think it's a sin?"

"Because it is a sin."

"Sin is affectation; berating oneself to inflate the sense of purpose, of importance, of grandeur in one's workings. It's nothing but vanity."

"Your words sting me."

"Because you think they are true, or because you think, like the preacher, that I've gone astray of morality?"

"Both, I guess. I just don't know. Too much has happened, too much needs reconciled; faith and reason and this what we've done, too much... far too much."

"You're still tired, rest. I need to attend to this horse business, then I'll suggest we take an extended break before we depart this place, all right?"

"All right. And Eisen?"

"I'm still listening."

"Was it good?"

"Very good."

"You don't despise me?"

"Don't be thick in front of me, it's annoying."

☼

Donners and Daniels buried their horses side by side upon a wide hill of clay and dry, black earth which rose 300-odd feet from the campsite. They marked the graves with two small stacks of stones, the work of their grief-stricken sentiment.

Eisen watched them with the detachment of a scientist for a long while and then turned his face to the burning atmosphere, squinting against the light. The sun, high and fat and red-orange, effulgent; the clouds, few and far between and those that were shown orange and sanguine as well, like they had sucked of the warmth its color, like wild-blown slivers of cloth absorbing a mixture of pigments from a paint spill.

A flock of birds, or the afterimage of birds, moved within the coffin maker's ambit, indistinguishable against the sky, save for the flapping of their wings. They moved away into the soundless distance, over the clustered mound of rocks to the south, oracular and perilous, and he watched them, all the while smiling.

Something, at least, now and in this moment, was beyond conflict, above it; something elegant, something beautiful. After they descended, who could say what became of them, but for that single, short space of consciousness, they existed without strife. They existed perfectly free.

Daniels moved away with Donners at his side, commiserating. Upon seeing this, Eisen began moving toward him but was blocked by Cruler, who shook his head slowly.

"Give him some time."

"He must have been very close to his horse."

"He was. I've never seen a man what cared so much about animals, especially those that were down and out, or least ways, nearly out. Did you know that his horse, Flanks, was sposed to ave died? No, course you didn't know it, why would you? But it's the truth, back then it belonged to his father. His name was Patrick Daniels, real mean sumbuck, but a just man. Just, not kind. Anyhow, he all up and gits fer his gun and walks out one day into the barn at his ranch. Me, Daniels and Donners were looking at the horse, I was teasing one of them and Daniels – James, that is – he tells me to stop it. Told me I was asking fer trouble, askin ta git bit – or kicked. He tells me I'll git kicked cross-eyed fer sure. Well, then his father comes in with a strange mood on him, he's all faraway and misty eyed and vacant. He walks to the farthest stall were they kept the horse - he hadn't been named at the time – and the horse being just a youngster, just a little creamello colt. And he goes fer the little gate that boxes the horse in and James asks him what he fixes on doing with that gun and he says, 'Fixing on doing what guns were made fer,' then he grabs the horse and leads him out. Well, James didn't take kindly to that. He throws up a fit. Says that he loves that horse, that it's a good horse, kind. One what didn't cause nobody no trouble. His father just looks at him awhile and then says, 'Boy, he's sick, real sick. He'll just die soon, ain't no point in keeping him around, he cain't do nothing fer us, better just ta put it out of its misery.' James said, 'He's only sick, not dead.' His father shook his head, said it was all the same, so James ran up in front of him, right up in front of the gun and folded his arms. He was only eight, and me nine and Donners twelve; not moving, not speaking. Just standing there, looking up at his father and his father looking back at him. Finally, Ole Pat up and nods, like he was waiting fer it, and says, 'All right, he's yours til he dies.' Then he walked out."

"But he didn't die. James nursed it back to health, didn't he?"

"That's right. Named it Flanks cuz everyone said, 'That horse is skinny as a bone; ain't got no flanks to him.' He thought it was fittingly... what's the word? Ironic. See, people get the wrong impression of him, being as quick to pick a fight as he is, but I'll tell you what, James Daniels is the best man I've ever known. You remember that, Mr. Torquiam. You remember that, if nothing else about him."

"I will. Thank you, Mr. Cruler."

Cruler squinted up one eye against the quickening bright of the sun and then nodded, stuck his hands in his pant pockets and left for his friend's side.

☼

Two hours later the party was once again on the move with doubled-up riders, a quickened pace and a renewed sense of purpose. Before dark they reached the jagged cluster of stones where, according to the map, Kavaria's keep lay. However, there was nothing but flat, dark red stone, shimmering with quartz deposits and crawling with snakes, lizards and all matter of that which skittered and snarled. The men were uneasy and the horses fearful and wide eyed. One of them bucked up suddenly, knocking its rider free, and tried to run off but was effectively routed by Eisen, Collins, Cruler and Daniels. Logan and Tanners laughing raucously in their saddles all the while.

"Weren't really a laughing matter. Man coulda been kilt!"

The voice intruded so suddenly and so potently, echoing as it did off the high stone walls which encircled the posse, that the men froze. Even the horses quieted; doing nothing more than pricking their ears and snorting.

Eisen was the first to see him. Next nearly all the rest of the men, their guns drawn and aimed at the leering figure so high and yet so low before them.

Kavaria Kallista, his powerful, deeply tanned arms crossed and his buckskin-covered legs spread firm, leaned arrogantly against the fore of a room-sized niche in the highest of the dark, volcanic stones. The peak from which he surveyed them lay directly to the south of the errant company, merging by steady degrees into the high and towering mountain behind it. There was no readily visible way up or down. Eisen wondered at that and fancied that there was likely a cave to the back of the hollow in which the bandit stood.

"How did you get up there?"

"That's fer me ta know an you te never find out, ain't it?"

"Where is she?"

"Only concerned wit the lass? Tisk, tisk, really, you disappoint, not even a fair mention of her dear ole daddy. It's shameful!"

"You answer the question, ya goddamned sumbitch, or I swear I'll shoot!"

"Yes, I'm sure ya would, Mr. Daniels, but you'd miss and I'd laugh and that wouldn't really be any good fer anyone, now would it? Cept fer me, of course."

"You goddamned sumbitch."

Eisen turned to Daniels and waved a commanding hand in entreaty.

"James, don't let him rile you, that's just what he wants."

Daniels looked to Eisen uncertainly and then back to the sneering outlaw so high above them.

Logan spoke up, and it was in a tone without anger or resentment; a tone curiously affable and removed from the situation.

"So you are Kavaria Kallista then?"

"The one and only."

"Are they still alive?"

"You don't much sound as if ye care."

"Maybe I do, maybe I don't, what's that have to do with you?"

"A strong point, duly noted. If'n ya must know, and I spose ya must, the girl is safe and sound. I've not allowed a hair on ere pretty head ta be touched. She's fine, in quite good spirits. She told me that you were coming for her, told me that it was Eisen de Torquiam I should fear. Oh how I laughed, spose I shouldn't ave, seems she was right. At the time I hadn't fer a moment thought that you would actually show up! And with a posse, a proper posse, like in a dime novel. All fer me. I'm so pleased I kin scarcely begin ta thank e!"

Eisen looked up and adjusted the brim of his hat to better view his opponent as he spoke, "Don't thank us yet."

"Why not? You've gone and killed yourselves already whilst simultaneously inflating my ego. A better use of one's time could not be contemplated."

"What of Jen's father?"

"That dickless sod. He's not... how shall I say, ambulatory."

"What did you do to him?"

"Now, now Eisen, didn't your mother never tell ye ta mind your own? Oh, and by the way, did you lot happen across an old shine in the desert? A black man with a ferret or somesuch ridiculous creature?"

"Why do you ask?"

"I'll tell you, Mr. Torquiam, I ask because he is the only one within your reach who knows the way into my house, tucked away deep in this mountain. You'll like as not die before you find it without him, scorpions are epidemic in these parts. Course he kin be quite tight lipped, might have your work cut out fer ya loosening it. Happy hunting."

"Hold on, let's talk about this."

Kavaria turned and with his back to the posse walked into the darkness at the back of the high stone hollow and disappeared from sight.

"Kavaria!"

The muted sound of laughter hurled down at them, more painful in that moment than any conceivable physical blow. Painful because it was the consummation of their powerlessness, their helplessness. The slow burn of their hope draining away with the fading of Kavaria's manic laughter.

Fading.

Fading into the dark.

Chapter Twenty-Six

Blood have Blood

Darkness fell, swift and ineluctable, over that disheartened company, bivouacked once again, in the wide arroyo before the jagged stones of Kavaria's mysterious mountain keep. This time they posted a continual guard of four men in rotating eight-hour shifts at the outskirts of the camp, in case Kavaria or one of his men decided to take a starlit stroll. One to the east, one to the west, one to the north, and one to the south.

Eisen had volunteered and, working in separated concert with Henry Collins, James Daniels and Peter Logan, scanned the berth of the flowering dark. Nothing to be seen, not even the glistening of a solitary star. Nothing to be heard, not even the whistling of the wind. Nothing to be felt, except the shifting sand beneath one's boots. No one came as the hours passed away.

Eisen was replaced by Fairson, who nodded shyly to him as they exchanged places. Eisen nodded sleepily back and then trekked down the slight incline to where his tent lay staked firmly into the hard, clay-packed ground. The men all about him were still mostly sleeping, but a small trio of Donners' men sat about the fire, cooking sausage and beans and laughing gaily.

He opened his tent flap, climbed in and took off his shirt, then he spread his bedroll and laid down upon his left side. In his sleep he dreamed of Kavaria and the old man in the desert.

There was an enormous cavern before him with a great chasm at its center, which ran the length of that stony, vaulted space such that the only way from one side of the room to the other would be to go straight across. To jump; a jump that was utterly impossible. Upon the far side of the room, across the chasm, stood the old man from the desert, his ermine nowhere to be found. The old man waved and smiled and then suddenly froze as a terrible clamor resounded in that ancient expanse. He fell slowly to his knees, staring up at the coffin maker as Kavaria emerged from the shadows behind him, laughing through the darkness and raising his pistol to the man's head.

"No!"

"You can't stop me from the other side of the room, kin ye!"

"Stop. Please."

"Your desires are not my own."

He fired and blew the man's head apart, chuckling as he hurled the corpse into the void before him. Turning he vanished back into the shadows. Eisen fell to his knees wailing, consumed in sorrow, as lost as the dead man in the darkness. He began to cry and realized with horror that they were tears of blood – his eyes burst.

☼

He awoke to a rapping at his tent door.

"Eisen, are you all right in there?"

"Yes, Fairson, I think I am."

"You were moaning. Was it a nightmare?"

"Y-yes. Don't suppose telling you emasculates me anymore than whining like a coward."

"You've made some of the men rather nervous."

"Well, I shall be out momentarily to quell their fretful nerves."

Fairson laughed and then walked away. Eisen dressed hurriedly, thinking of his dream and of Kavaria and the old traveler. If the old man really was the only one who knew the way, then they had already failed. The traveler would not give them a lead, would not be part of what he perceived as fuel to an all-consuming fire.

Eisen knew it was futile to return to the tomb and question the man, but he knew also that the men would press him at every turn to do just that; knew that they wouldn't believe that they had failed so utterly, so completely. An idea struck the sleepy-eyed man in that wind-battered tent. If they split their forces in half, one group to the old man, the other to search the mountains for an entrance, then perhaps...

Perhaps...

Eisen leapt off the ground, dashed out of his tent and walked straight to the fire pit, round which they had ringed their tents.

The pit itself was five feet wide and circular. It smouldered languidly. All the men sat or stood about it, most on squarish stones they had found, a couple on thin folding chairs they had packed with them. Daniels stood closest to the fire, talking to Henry Collins and Peter Logan about what they were to do about their dilemma.

"We have to – do you understand! We have to go after him!"

Collins shook his head, crossing his massive arms firmly, his lips a tight line. "We need to stay here and look fer an entrance. You already know he ain't gonna help."

"You're right."

The speakers turned to the entrant, both wearing expressions of mild confusion. Logan only nodded.

"Just what I was thinking, Mr. Torquiam. Split up?"

Eisen replied that it was so.

Daniels and Collins thought it over carefully and decided that it was their best bet but asked who should go where.

Eisen spoke up instantly, decisively.

"I'll go after the old man we met yesterday. He took a liking to me, and I to him. If he is going to talk to anyone it would be me, though to be honest, I still think our chances are slim."

Donners and his men, with the exception of Emmanuel Cruler, offered to search up in the mountains, mark out a map of the region as they went along. The discussion carried along these lines for ten minutes, laying out plans and forming their respective groups, before the men buried their fire, erased all trace of their habitation and departed camp.

Eisen, Collins, Tanners, Logan, Fairson, Cruler and James Daniels headed off toward the old man's cave, whilst Donners and the rest of them rode up into the treacherous reaches of those dark and solemn mountains.

☼

On the way back to the tomb, Eisen and his followers passed a wagon, broken and half covered in sand, laying in the shadow of a massive dune. Beside it lay the skull of a young man, a bullet hole clean through it, and a small travel satchel, open and filled with scorpions seeking shelter from the sun. They looked at the macabre sight for a time and then kicked up and rode on.

A mile down the flat stretch of sand they found another skeleton, or most of one, some of the clothing still clinging to its clean-picked frame.

Eisen pulled up short and took off his hat and wiped his forehead with the back of his sleeve.

"If it's only a tomb we are after, we need look no further."

Fairson looked to his friend and shivered.

"I don't much like it when ya talk like that, Eisen."

"Neither do I."

They rode on.

When they finally arrived at the cave, there was no sign of the old man nor his furry, four-legged pet, not even a fire. The previous one had been covered with dirt and sand. Eisen began to wonder if the old man's presence hadn't just been some heat-induced delusion, some collective mirage. Had it all been an illusion of the desert? Nothing more? Eisen shook his head and dismounted, walking his horse into the shade of the cavern and looking about. Suddenly, he remembered the back passage and gave a loud cry of recognition, startling everyone but Tanners, who merely raised a brow, muttering, "I knew e was mad," under his breath between long drags of his pipe. The rest followed Tanners' more tentative approach, waiting silently for Eisen to reemerge; he didn't.

Inside the darkened pass Eisen moved as quickly as he could, often scraping his shoulders painfully against some jagged edge which protruded from the high, near invisible walls. And the deeper in he went, the more invisible they became.

When he emerged into the burial chamber, there was a small fire pit dug into the dank earth, one which had not been there previously. At this fire sat two men. One, the old traveler from the desert, his dark skin glistening in the dancing light. The other, the man with the white umbrella. The man who had followed him from town, the man who had slaughtered two men in that ancient monolith of horror. He thought of the wolf and the similarity of their eyes, this enigmatic man and that primal beast.

The old man had his back to the coffin maker, and he spoke without turning as the third member of that gathering leaned back expressionless and masked in layers of ever-revealing shadow, flickering away with each rising of the flames, returning almost as quickly as it had departed.

"You arrived far quicker than I would have thought possible. This means you traveled all night at great speed. You must be tired, to say nothing of your mounts. Sit. Here, all are welcome."

"I am... very tired, but you know why I'm here. You must help me."

The coffin maker waited for the old man to speak, uneasy in his mind and cautious in his stance. Cautious not of the wizened traveler but of his mysterious companion.

"What I must do is not betray my ideals. That is what I must do. Why don't you understand this?"

"I do understand, but it isn't vengeance that drives me."

"No. Only your men."

"Some of them."

"Most."

"Perhaps, but Kavaria has taken a young woman and her father from our town. We need to save them, they're suffering surely. Saving two lives must fit into your ideals somewhere."

"Yes. This I did not know. Kidnaping. This changes things. But please, sit, whatever happens, you will need your strength."

Eisen walked to the old man, eying up the stranger who sat across from the aged wayfarer as he did so, completely inert. It seemed as if he wasn't even breathing.

"You are right. I need my strength. Who is this with you?"

"I met him last night at the rise of the moon. I do not know his name."

"He did not give it?"

"I did not ask."

Eisen took a seat beside the dark-skinned traveler, extending his hands tentatively over the fire and looking to the man in shadow, the man with the white umbrella that lay before his feet; an albescent line drawn against the realms of normalcy and discernment.

Eisen was careful not to extend his hands too far over the fire, not for fear of the flames but of the man who lurked behind them.

"Who are you?"

The man with the white umbrella looked up deliberately to meet the coffin maker's gaze, half in shadow, half in flame. The light of the fire caught and reflected in his eyes strangely, gilding them fiercely. His skin, too, pale as a dead man's, shimmered oddly with the primal illumination, granting him an otherworldly aspect, a ghastly sheen.

He smiled faintly and replied with the same deliberation with which he had moved.

"I'm just a traveler. Like him. Like you."

"You have followed me from town. Perhaps a great distance more."

"What does it matter?"

"It matters a great deal."

"You are angry because you cannot find an answer to my existence. Isn't that so? You needn't answer, I know it is."

The old man looked from one to the other, his expression placid and relaxed. It was the face of one who had resigned himself from conflict, save when it was absolutely necessary. Not so was it now. Resigned, perhaps, from conflict, but not from curiosity.

"I had, at first, just thought you a mirage; a heat-stricken imagining, something I had just... conjured up."

"Oh, I'm quite real, I assure you. Much or little as anything."

"What do you want?"

"Right now I just want to warm myself by the light of this splendid fire and wait."

"Wait for what?"

"The show to begin."

"What show?"

The sound of heavy footfalls threw Eisen from the pall under which he had been laboring amidst the man's words. Moments later Cruler and Daniels appeared, next Fairson, Collins and Logan. All held lanterns, save Fairson, who brandished a tarnished metal lighter before him. Tanners was nowhere to be seen, likely lounging with his pipe near the horses in the front of the cave. They tramped down the slight incline of the stone until they hit moist dirt and then stopped as if before some unseen barrier.

"Eisen? Is that you?"

"Yes, Henry, it's me. Come sit."

The old man nodded without looking at his newest batch of guests. All of them, save for Daniels and Cruler, began arranging themselves about the fire in a tight living circle, sitting on the dry, cool stones that the old man or some other had positioned about the pit in the absence of chairs.

Fairson looked over his shoulder, his expression quizzical, even in the gloom.

"Aren't you two coming to sit?"

"No. We didn't come here to pow-wow. We came here for information."

The old man rose to his feet rather suddenly and turned to Daniels. "And what will you do with that information?"

"You already know that, just like you already know what we want."

"Yes."

"Well?"

"I will not help you."

Now it was Eisen's turn to rise. "But you said–"

"I said that it changes things. I did not say how."

A sonorous wind swept in through the hollow. The man with the umbrella laughed. Somewhere in the tomb there came a rustling of wings, and instantly dozens of bats were turning wild circles over the men's heads, dancing on the intrusive current like haunted leaves.

"This ain't nothing to laugh about."

The man with the white umbrella cocked his head strangely at Cruler, still smiling, and then squinted up one dire, golden eye.

"Everything is worthy of a laugh. A man can't live on fortitude and courage alone."

In the middle of the room Daniels was trying to convince the old man, ignoring Cruler and all the rest.

"A friend of mine, a very good friend, has been abducted. Can you understand that? She could be dying right now! I need to find her, and I need to find Kavaria!"

"It sounds like that would be just what such a man wants you to do. It will only lead to further tragedy."

"Further? To further tragedy? Well, let me tell you, you kin git right the hell off'a that high horse of yours. My horse, that I nursed as a colt, is dead, one of my friends is dead in this desert, another kilt by the man I been trying ta find. I'm losing the confidence of my friends and the confidence I used to have in myself, and I'm losing a woman who is like a sister to me. Her and her father, like as mine own, are being held hostage by a madman and could be slaughtered at any minute. How could it possibly get more tragic, old man? Tell me that! Tell me!"

By the end of his tirade Daniels had the old man by the collar, whipping him wildly about. The wizened traveler attempted to steady himself against the hard stone floor but was overpowered by the sheer force of the other man's assault. The old man uttered a muted cry and fell. Before anyone could reach him, he struck his head against a rough projection of stone and lay bleeding and silent. Unmoving.

Daniels looked on in shocked disbelief, shaking his head fractionally, his fists tight, bloodless knots, his mouth a quivering line. He trembled on the precipice of nervous collapse. Cruler was first to reach the old man, running with all of his speed to the unfortunate party's side. He bent to the dark-skinned journeyman and felt for a pulse. He withdrew as if bitten and then tried for a pulse again, then he rose and hung his head.

"Wha...what is it? Tell me Cruler, he's fine, isn't he? He's fine? Right? Fine?"

"He's dead."

"No. You're wrong Cruler, he can't be dead. He can't be, do you hear me; do you hear!"

Cruler said nothing, he just stood there immobilized by the horror of the thing. Eisen rose and went to him, followed hesitantly by Fairson and Collins.

Collins looked to Daniels as if he were something less than human and shook his head, tears in his eyes. The water held there the culmination of their internal fears and desires finally manifested for the judgment of those who held firm to the ageless foundations of the reasoner.

Collins, his hands grasped firm against the sides of his legs, contorted his visage into the mask of the betrayed, wailing.

"What have you done?"

Daniels looked to the dead, then to Cruler, next to Collins, his expression one of utter despair. Daniels' mouth was open and his teeth were showing his face horribly contorted with the knowledge of his deed. He said nothing.

Collins flew at him in a rage, throwing his massive, muscular hands about the smaller man's throat.

Fairson extended his hands toward them, as if he could pull them apart by sheer force of will.

"Collins! No!"

Henry Collins squeezed and squeezed until Daniels dropped to one knee, gasping and moaning in terror, his eyes wide and bulging from his skull, his face flush and perspiring. He let loose a distorted howl and produced a long, vicious hunting knife from his left boot and drove it deep into Henry's leg. The big man wailed and fell back, clutching the blade as Daniels rose and moved away, gasping wide mouthfuls of air and holding his purple-bruised throat.

Cruler quickened to the big man's side and told him to lie still. He did so and the knife was quickly removed. The scream that permeated the cavern sent the bats spiraling back into their holes. Cutting through the howl was the frothy laughter of the man with the white umbrella who still sat cross-legged before the fire, watching the unfolding drama with a languid, half-interested expression, vaguely amused.

Logan, who stood ten feet from the cackling man, whirled on him with a pistol directed at his head.

"That'll be about enough of that."

"Oh, go on and shoot then. What's the point of living if a man is prohibited his mirth? It's the smiles what keeps us going, bit of laughter and good cheer."

"Put that away, Logan, put it away now!"

Logan looked to Eisen and then back to the enigmatic man and then nodded very disdainfully, holstering his pistol.

"All right Eisen, all right."

Eisen then moved hastily across the room, picking his way around the jagged stones and snake holes, to the spot where Daniels leaned against the wall opposite the sepulcher. He was gazing at the skeletons in their wall niches with wide, uncomprehending eyes.

"Give me your gun, Daniels."

"Who?"

"Your gun. Let me have it, you aren't yourself."

"No, no you stay back. It was you who got us into this mess, with your clever words, your Latin!"

"What are you talking about?"

Daniels was still a moment, looking up into the high-vaulted dark, listening to the whispering wind and the muffled cacophony of the bats. Then he drew his gun and aimed it at Eisen.

"It wasn't you... no, it wasn't. It was me, a murderer."

"It was an accident, give me the damn gun!"

GRAVE.

"No."

Daniels looked away from the coffin maker to Cruler. He smiled, a humorless gesture, and pressed the barrel to his heart.

Daniels opened his mouth to scream.

He pulled the trigger.

Chapter Twenty-Seven

The Stranger Joins the Fold

They buried Daniels and the old man in the front of the cave, their graves marked only by stones. Cruler and Fairson prayed over the burial. Eisen and Logan stood askance of it and said nothing. Collins, his leg wrapped with some of Eisen's medical gauze, limped with the aid of his long-barreled rifle, using it like a crutch, weeping silently as they finished their benediction.

The man with the white umbrella stood in the sunlight several yards away from the mouth of the cave, as if in waiting. Eisen walked out of the shadowed gloom to meet him, a lump forming in his throat before he thought of what to say. The enigmatic man made him uneasy in more ways than he could describe.

"You and that other man, you had both been captured by Kallista, isn't that so?"

The man with the white umbrella looked out from under the shade of his parasol.

"I was traveling along the road, the only road, into town when he and near all of his men jumped me. They heard me playing. I've a certain proficiency with guitars, and they said they wanted some music for their feast, amusement which I gladly provided. Amusing boys, the lot of them."

"Boys?"

"Men in body only. At any rate, you want my help now that our poor pacifistic is gone?"

"Yes. Much as it pains me to ask," Eisen said.

"You don't like me, do you?"

"I don't have to like you. What does it matter?"
"It doesn't matter to me, Eisen."
"You laughed."
"Hmm?"
"You laughed as they died. Is that funny to you?"
"It certainly isn't sad. Everyone has to die sometime, would you prefer everyone to weep at your own passing or to laugh?"
Eisen squinted up his eyes and looked away, then adjusted his purple-tinted glasses on the bridge of his nose and lowered the brim of his hat against the rays, at a loss for words. "Will you help us or not?"
"Yes. I'll lead you there. I would very much like my guitar back."
Eisen waited for him to say more and when he didn't, decided that it was time to press a certain point.
"What do we call you? I never got your name. "
"I'm not fond of names."
He began walking to where they had stabled the horses, to a high thick, leafless shrub which grew between the wide cracks in the stone in the front of the cave. The rest of Eisen's party eyed the stranger with a potent mixture of fear and loathing.
Fairson moved slowly behind his horse, pretending to look through his equipment, evading the stranger's presence instead.
When the stranger grabbed the reins of the horse Daniels had borrowed from one of Donners' men who was riding doubled up and prepared to swing up and mount it, Cruler viciously intervened.
"What the hell you think you're doing!"
"Mounting a horse. Eisen, is this one slow?"
"Now, I don't often wish violence against my fellow man, but you are tempting me."
"Of course I am. So is everyone in your temper's relation."
"What the hell does that mean?"
Eisen quickened to the horse he had borrowed from Daniels, the horse that was never to be returned, and laid a restraining hand upon Cruler's shoulder.

"It's all right; he knows the way."

"He... what? No – no, I'm not having this, I won't have him riding with us, I won't."

"If this is too much for you–"

"Ain't nothing too much fer me, damn it, but I ain't riding wit him!"

"I understand, but he's our last shot. We have no choice. Do you want Daniels' death to be in vain?"

"Don't you even dare..."

"Do you?"

"Don't."

"No, I didn't think so. If I think correctly, and I do, we ride and we ride with him. Understand?"

"Damn you, and damn me as well."

They saddled up and rode on.

☼

The next day they arrived back at the spired base of the mountain where Kavaria had taunted them from the cave at the mount's highest peak. There was no sign of Donners nor any of his men.

The nameless man, his umbrella shading his face, pointed carelessly to the southeast, their direct left, saying that a pass lay through that way which branched off into two more.

They followed the rocky pass high into the mountains, winding round scraggly shrubs and piles of bones and an errant rattlesnake that seemed not to notice them at all. When finally they came to the fork in the path, the sun had reached its apex and the land shone white-hot, an endless jewel before them.

The path to the left rose higher into the mountains whilst the path to the right led down into a shrouding, shrunken forest that rolled away with the hills into dust and death.

The nameless man kicked his horse and rode to the left, the rest following, discovering that the trail leveled out two miles on. With every mile the land grew steadily greener and more luscious about them, until they walked amidst a small, deciduous forest. Most of the trees were only as high as the top of the riders' hats, others shorter still; none taller. A moist and curling mist hung heavy in the air, so thick one could feel its presence like an invisible wall.

Quite abruptly the horses stopped and pawed the ground, swinging their heads side to side, wide-eyed and in terror.

Eisen slid off to the right and walked a ways up the path before him, and his foot struck something as he went, nearly tripping him. Pausing to regain his balance, he backtracked slightly, looking down. He gasped and leapt back.

Lifeless eyes stared back into his own.

Donners' eyes.

"Come here! All of you, I've found... I've found... Donners."

Donners had been shot through the abdomen, clean through. He'd bled out. All of his men were spread around him upon the ground in varying grotesque positions behind him. All of them shot. All of them dead.

Fairson ran to the man and knelt, feeling for a pulse. Eisen told him not to bother. Fairson began to cry. He wiped away his tears angrily and rose, his movements stiff, his fists knotted and jaw tense.

The man with the white umbrella leaned slightly toward Eisen, looking at Fairson.

"Does he always cry this much? Don't get me wrong, I'm all for a good melodramatic weep myself every now and then, but this is just shameful."

"Why don't you just be still?"

"Are you angry with me, Eisen?"

"Yes. Shut up."

"You are so much more amusing when you are furious. Are you aware of that?"

Eisen said nothing more to the man. He remounted and asked Fairson to do the same.

Fairson protested in the strongest of terms. "We cain't just leave um like as is, kin we?"

"Yes."

"But Eisen..."

"Get on your horse, we're wasting time. There isn't anything we can do for them. Nothing, understand?"

"But what about a proper burial?"

"What exactly is proper about a burial? it's just shoving someone away so that you can't see the worms eating them, as they will one way or another. It's a ritual for the living, not for the dead. This you already know."

"Of course he does, " the man with the white umbrella chimed in opaquely. "That is why he is suggesting it."

"I told you to be quiet."

"You should show me more respect. Haven't I done enough for all of you to earn some? Not least you, coffin maker."

Eisen ignored him and motioned to Fairson's horse. "Come on."

Fairson said nothing and slowly, as if in pain, climbed aback his horse, reigned up and then sallied out, looking back one last time at the fog-covered figures of his fallen friends.

They rode on.

Chapter Twenty-Eight

The Keep

The path gave out to gravel and rough blasted pits of blackened stone. What caused them, no one knew. All about them was a vista of such supreme beauty that they could scarcely believe what they were seeing. The sky curved blue onto gray, meeting with the mountains and them lying upon the orange-red sands which warped around to meet the travelers at the base of the mountain. The immediate landscape was walled on three sides by sharp, black cliffs, snowless and impossibly high. It was a canyon, one way in, one way out.

Crows turned lazy circles in the air above them. Their cawing was like the trumpet call of lords long departed returning to their own domain; a return unwelcome. There was no plant there save lichen, and even it grew sparsely.

The man with the white umbrella extended his hand directly in front of the party. There was a massive hole in the stone, a portal to some antediluvian time. The travelers looked down the twisting path behind them and then rode through the darkness.

This portal led through a long and curiously straight passageway which had been hewn from the stone by old and intelligent hands. Some ancient civilization; certainly not by dynamite. After two hours of their dark passing they emerged into blinding sunlight on the top of a wide crescent-shaped plateau which extended 300 flat feet from the mountainside and then dropped off into a vast abyss, the bottom they could not see. To their direct right, fifty feet of stone and then a ledge; to the direct left, a grand fortress carved into the mountain itself, vast and terrible to behold.

"Good Lord."

Eisen smiled faintly and replied to Collins without turning.

"No, good architecture."

The fortress itself was made of stone and mortar, like the castles of old, and seemed to have only one point of entry, a front gate, facing the party where they stood before the mouth of the mountain pass.

"How on earth are we going to get inside of that?"

Eisen turned to the man with the white umbrella.

"It shouldn't be too hard, we are prisoners, after all."

The man with the white umbrella raised his eyes to the coffin maker and they flashed like the coming of a storm.

☼

Amidst the cawing of crows and the wailing of the wind there came a sudden knocking upon the high, double doors of the fortress.

A scuzzy figure emerged from the wind-worn parapets, leaning out over the edge slightly, squinting his eyes at the small, dusty band of travelers beneath him. They were all bound and gagged, save for one, a slim man wearing a battered, patchwork coat and snowy parasol. He alone seemed pristine in that dust-blown expanse.

The bandit produced a rifle and aimed it at the unbound man's head.

"Hold it right thar. Who the hell are you?"

"You don't recognize me, Barret? I'm insulted."

Barret leaned further over the high stone wall, squinting further, something emerging unto his face, recognition and something else, something deeper.

Dread.

"You recognize me now, Barret Jane Sullivan?"

"Yes. I know you. We all do."

Barret was silent a moment and then gestured with his rifle to the subdued men below him.

"What is all that?"

"Gifts. If Kavaria will accept them."

"Hell, he's mighty cross with you."

"I imagine so."

"You kilt Old Lawson and Wilkes and Dimitri and Kible. I liked Kible, nice lad."

"You will open."

Barret wavered, uncertain if this sentence was a question or a command or some other variation unknowable. The dread that this uncertainty instilled in the outlaw was such that he had turned quite pale, his eyes going slightly wider, his breath coming fast, going faster. Not knowing; not knowing was horror. He fumbled for words, his brigandine brain consumed with the fever of the nameless man's presence, with the presence of those words; fumbled and flailed in vain. He nodded vacantly and then turned with hesitancy, uncomfortable with turning his back on this strange, heat-conjured visage. At length the lookout turned and went away, the effects of his meeting writ large upon his stride and the afterimage thereof and of even the sound of his passing, apprehension clearly drawn in the sharp clacking of every step.

Eisen could hear Logan chuckling through his gag. He shook his head and waited. The gates swung open for them shortly thereafter, opened by Barret and a man whom the coffin maker did not know. A fat, middle-aged man with a greasy beard that seemed to have swallowed his mouth, sucking it clean from the eyes of the world into a blackened tangle. Everything about the man bespoke of venal foulness and disrepair; his marked limp, his red nose, his bloated gut, his puffy, bloodshot eyes, milky and yellowed.

Barret, by contrast, was quite fresh and athletic though, perhaps, of similar age. His hair was prematurely gray, and he dressed in a manner which he believed would complement this singular characteristic.

Eisen wondered at their lives and the tangled skein thereof that had led them to this; to the employ of a madman, dwelling inside a castle in the clouds. He couldn't fathom the motivation, all he knew was that it was direly desperate in construction, but he knew not the architect. This distilled in him great unease. He shifted in his saddle as he allowed the nameless man to lead him, alongside his surviving companions, into the looming depths of Kavaria's mountain keep.

Fear in every fiber.

☼

Kavaria Kallista laughed. Such was his humor that the throne room reverberated with his mirth. His gifts kneeled before him, bound and gagged.

"You want to trade what fer what? I can't exactly believe I'm hearing this. So you want to trade these pestering imbeciles fer your mangy guitar, is that right?"

"Yes."

"Fer a guitar?"

"Yes."

"Ha ha! When opportunity comes a knocking... well, it's a deal, shall we shake on it? No, didn't tink so. All right. It's all the same ta me. Barret? Barret! Barret, damn your eyes, where are you?"

"Sir?"

"Bring Mr. what's-his-name his precious guitar, and be careful wit it."

The man with the white umbrella said nothing as he gazed steadily into the bandit-king's eyes. Kavaria sat upon an ornate throne at the far back of the high, vaulted room on a raised dais which looked to have been looted from a grand and exotic cathedral from times long since cleaved of history's weave. He shifted uncomfortably, disdaining the silence his guest bore upon him.

"Aren't you going ta say anything?"

He did not.

"Still the talkative type, I see."

Again the nameless man said nothing. He stared strangely, unflinchingly. Kallista shifted again and then slammed his palms against the arm rests and leapt from the chair as if the thing had suddenly caught fire. A rattle of seashells, the clinking of spurs and the clacking of boots on stone were the only sounds fracturing the oppressive silence aside from the collective breath of the captives. Pale sunlight warmed the lull and all the variations therein.

Shortly, Kavaria swooped in upon the bound and helplessness forms, kneeling before him as if in sublime subjugation to their seignior, like vassals in waiting.

"Is that you, Eisen? My lucky stars, it tis! Eisen de Torquiam, short time, long see."

Eisen de Torquiam looked up from under his brows, from under his matted hair and his battered and sun-faded wide-brimmed hat. Even then his anger was still clear and poignant.

Kavaria was unaffected and continued to sneer with a rising intensity of tone.

"I was going ta say, 'The mighty... brought low,' but then that wouldn't exactly fit you, now would it? No, I'd say rather not. Oh ho, what have we here! The little fag what ran me off! You shot me. Remember? Course ya do. Fucking hurt."

Kavaria knelt before Fairson's face.

"You shot me."

Fairson, too frightened to speak, averted his eyes to the floor, his head hanging limply; he was straining against the tears but they came anyway, faint and splashing to the floor. Cold stone warmed with his sorrow.

Henry Collins attempted to speak up in protest, to defend the young man, but his gag converted his cries of outrage into vain and muffled nonsense.

Kavaria laughed in Henry's face and kicked him in the chest, beating his own in a pantomime of the infliction as the captive thudded to the floor. There was a muted thumping, the sound of Henry's skull bouncing upon hard floor. He moaned, his eyes rolling about in his head and then lay still, barely breathing, barely conscious.

"All right, enough fun for the hour, Hanson. take them off to... I don't care exactly where, somewhere secure, and lock um in, proper, mind. I don't want them running off soon as we've picked them up."

The fat man named Hanson walked behind the captives for whom he had held a door, his expression bleeding puzzlement.

"Why?"

"What do ye mean, why? Why what?"

"Why keep um? Why don't we just be done wit um? That one thar nurly blowed yar whole shoulder clean off."

"Yes – good aim fer a little pissant what has never used a gun before. Still, we keep them."

"Why?"

"Because more hostages means more leverage to barter fer whatever we want, you blithering buffoon! Shut your mouth and do as I say!"

The man flinched, averted his eyes and obeyed instantly, drawing his six-shooter and gesturing threateningly with it at the prisoners.

Eisen's heart began to quicken. He wondered if the nameless man really intended on trading them for an old string instrument, or whether he would stick to the plan.

The coffin maker looked to the man with the white umbrella, pleading, his eyes a story of entreaty. The stranger looked down and their eyes met. Neither attempted to speak. Everything that needed to be said had already been discovered, affirmed or denied. Whether the former or the latter, Eisen didn't know. He stood hesitantly as their bulbous, venal warden motioned for him to move. He stood his ground firmly even as all the others moved away, Tanners foremost among them.

In the background Kavaria resumed his regal seat and with that simple, seemingly innocuous motion, cut himself off from further interest in the matter. He seemed to be daydreaming, a languid, childlike smile playing about his red lips. He hummed then rose into song and carried on as if for a vast adorning public, his tone joyful and bright. To have heard him then one would not have thought he was a man to whom fear was the greatest homage, to whom wanton violence was a form of sport.

Barret returned brandishing an old, ornate wooden guitar before him, some of the strings rusty, the E string broken. He walked through the vaulted steel door with the instrument held in his arms like a dying babe and looked inquiringly to Kavaria, who merely rolled his eyes and gestured offhandedly toward the stranger.

The stranger looked at the guitar a long while and then took it and ran his hand jarringly along the strings whereupon they shrieked bizarrely, sounding for all the world like music from some other.

"The E string is broken."

Barret said that this was so, but that he didn't know how.

"The humidity. It plays havoc with such an instrument. You really are an unrefined fellow."

Raising a brow and crossing his strong, youthful arms, the bandit tilted his head jauntily, arrogance interred in the gesture.

"Look, pig shit, I don't give a damn about your bloody guitar, much less your opinions. You've got it, we made the trade, so fuck off."

All the members of Eisen's band had been herded from the room by Hanson, save for Eisen himself, who stood at the threshold to the room, his back to the scene unfolding, his ears pricked as a woodland hare's.

The stranger looked blankly to the guitar, the broken E string, back to the man whom had fetched it, then back to the severed steel twine. He knelt and unfastened the slender string with the ease of an artist and then rose and flung it about Barret's neck. He swung behind the choking man and pulled the wire taut as Kavaria rose with befuddlement playing louder than any guitar over his every movement. Hanson raised his pistol and ran back through the open doorway as Eisen extended his foot, his muscles pulled tautly against his skin. Hanson, blinded by the fulminant enormity of events, collided into Eisen's outstretched leg and careened heavily to the floor, loudly fumbling his six-gun. Quickly the fat warden was overtaken by Eisen, Fairson and Logan, who kicked him until he lost consciousness. At this point

Barret was spitting blood, the wire having slit deeply through his throat, and shortly thereafter collapsed with a loathsome gurgling. His face and the contortions thereof the mask of some depraved and quondam ritual, like the visage of blood sacrifice; the sacrifice unwilling. His body floundered for a few moments, and then he moved no more and lay still and soundless, eyes unseeing.

From behind the bloody calamity came the sound of applause, monstrously misplaced in the aftermath of those charnel events. The stranger turned in place over the body of his victim very slowly, to the clapping maniac upon his garland throne.

"Wonderful! Just wonderful! You are a beauty. A true beauty. You've misplaced your loyalties. You should set up wit me, ay? I could well use a man like as you."

"Use is an indicative word."

Kavaria sat down on his throne, sprawling lazily, indifferently.

"So this was all just a ploy, ey? Te rescue the lady?"

"No. I just wanted my guitar."

"Well, it was a good plan, regardless."

Eisen snatched up Hanson's fumbled shooting iron with bound hands tightly clasped, dashing to the stranger's side.

The stranger, with nary a second of deliberation, withdrew a familiar hunting knife and severed Eisen's bonds. The coffin maker walked slowly to the front of the dais, standing before the throne and the man upon it with a mixture of fear and rage and curiosity; the latter strongest of all.

"It is of note to me that you don't seem concerned, Kavaria."

"Why should I be? You'll never git out of this place alive. My men outnumber ya three te one, you've already lost. Ya lost as soon as ya came here."

"This isn't a game to me."

"Everything is a game."

"That how you see it?"

"If you aren't going to use that pistol, I'd appreciate it if you lowered it from my face. Not very original."

"You're right, of course. First throw your pistol on the floor."

He did so without much inflection.

Eisen stuck the brigand's pistol in the front of his belt, then his own and arched over the first of the platform steps, now only a man's length from Kavaria.

"Why do this, Kallista? Why?"

"This? What tis, 'This'?"

"Damage. All the damage you've done to the town, to those people. Have you ever thought for a solitary moment about the people whose lives you've destroyed?"

"Life is short and ever so distracting - no time fer trifles."

"Trifles?"

Kavaria rose, adjusted the high, fur-lined collar of his overcoat, his blades jingling in melodic tandem with his rattling spurs.

"This conversation has been held before."

"Not by us."

"Nevertheless, it's been done. The answer is always the same. You don't really care about anyone I've hurt, save those that you know, and then, even then, it's unlikely. Ain't it? Course it tis, all this moaning and wailing about morality and injustice, it's all just conceitedness and gaudy sounds. Ye don't really care about all the people I've robbed or killed, cuz ya don't know them. How kin yeh care about people ye ain't never met? Ye can't, ye kin only pretend. An actor of the first degree."

"Are you aware how you sound? What you sound like?"

"And what do I sound like, Mr. Torquiam?"

"A psychopath."

"Psychiatric terminology? But like I said, it's been done before. So has Daniels' death and Donners,' the deaths of so many good men – my friends, my enemies, those to which I was indifferent – I did not wish this upon them, I never would. Daniels? Daniels was a firecracker, loud and alarming, but not very dangerous. Daniels was nothing, he could never ave killed me. It was you that interested me since we first met, seems like so long ago."

"Daniels was a good man."

"Good, bad, fat, old, what's the difference? You stand before me, privy to a great indifference; the indifference that is party to the re-imagining of humanity itself. Everything is a game. Not a game where the rule is survival of the richest, nor survival of the strongest. It's survival of he who can most amiably withstand horror. Who kin laugh at death and all his apparitions. I am such a man. Like as you."

"You are partially right. We are very much alike. But what sets you apart from me is not something you have, but rather something which you lack."

Eisen paused and then hardened his gaze. "Where is Jen Arlington?"

"Come, I'll show ya."

He swaggered down from his dais, pausing next to Eisen and smiling challengingly, and then continuing the rest of the way, making sure to step on top of Barret's corpse and gesticulating in great irritation out to the men gathered before him, freed from their bondage by the stranger's blade.

"Lower those blasted boomsticks - no need fer threats. Right this way. Right this way."

"You hold it right there!"

"Mr. Collins, there's no need ta raise your tone."

Henry Collins lumbered toward the outlaw, drew back his left arm and dashed it into the man's face. Kavaria spun to the floor like a top and slid several feet, lying there, unmoving, apparently insensible.

Logan frowned mildly and spoke to the big man.

"He was going to show us were she was."

"You trust him?"

"No, he's clearly mad; he ain't got no idea bout what e's doing. He probably thinks it's funny. Tanners, help me pick him up."

"No need, me darlings, fit as a fiddle." Kavaria rose to his knees and then, leaning against the wall for support, unsloped himself from the ground. He seemed thoroughly amused. Running two heavily bejeweled fingers against his bleeding lower lip, his hand came away wet with blood. He smiled and rubbed it between his fingers and then raised his hand to his left eye and drew a circle with his red. Then sauntered up to Collins and spread wide his arms, as if he were about to embrace his assailant.

"A target fer yer better aim!"

Collins kicked him in the stomach, folding him back to the floor. Tanners, Cruler and Logan moved to block the big man as he attempted to rush the outlaw once again.

"You let go of me, Logan, or I'll drop you just the same. Let me through!"

Tanners shook his head. "That's just what he wants, he wants you to hurt him. He wants you to be just like him. Think of Daniels, think of him."

Cruler winced at the mention of his friend.

Logan nodded and then slapped the big man's back and smiled.

"But you're not and we got him now. We got the bastard."

"Got... me? The only thing you've gotten into is your own grave."

With those words Kavaria produced a small whistle made of polished bone and blew upon it furiously. From the courtyard came the vicious baying of hounds followed swiftly by raised voices, curses, shouted commands.

Logan surged toward the outlaw to seize the whistle, but was repulsed by an expert kick to his shin, dropping him to a knee, howling in pain. Kavaria leapt upon the opportunity and drove his elbow into Logan's face. The man fell back, bleeding and near unconscious. The brigand then fled the room with such speed that none of his opponents had time to stop him.

"What do we do? What do we do?"

Logan looked to Fairson and shrugged.

"Storm the castle."

Logan produced his gun, loaded it, set his teeth, inhaled deep and heavy and then barreled the air out through the doorway, followed closely by the rest of Eisen's party, save the stranger.

He had vanished, insensate to the world. Eisen took one last look in the throne room at the bodies lying on the cold stone, one living, the other dead. He steeled his nerves and pressed on.

Outside the room of Kavaria's emblem of authority the barking of dogs, loud, recalcitrant, drawing inexorably closer with every passing second and with the passing a sadistic humming in the air.

The area that stretched wide ahead of the runners was covered in stone; a stairwell descending with furious rapture into the barren courtyard where a small, flimsy-looking shack had been thrown together to shelter the thieves' equines. The horses stomped about, wild eyed and braying, saliva dripping from their mouths, nostrils flaring. Three avenues of departure afforded themselves to the escaping cluster of travelers; two were blocked by the bandits', the third, the portal directly before the dashing adventurers, was curiously unguarded.

A slashing howl cut the air, an omnipresent and terrifying reality. Eisen's party barreled on faster as a black and quick-form shape rushed them in that plugged and stone-bound yard; a feral hound, trained only insofar as it would kill upon command. Nothing further. Nothing less. Barring its fangs, it leapt upon Henry Collins, felling the big man. Tearing into his right arm; a bloody fusion. The big man thrashed back, striking the beast repetitively upon its huge, squarish skull. No longer separate entities, fused by their struggle they merged into one, a blurred phantasm of violence. Blood sport. Primal and relentless.

A crack broke through the sunderous wailing coming from the huge man and the vicious rasping of the canine. The dog whimpered and fell from its target, wriggling strangely through the dust-covered ground, like a hairy, beached fish. Tanners planted another round in the beast's brain and then, with Cruler's aid, hauled Collins up from the ground.

Another crack. Sound shattered as its barrier and bone with it. Cruler whirled, screaming; shot through the left leg. He grit his teeth and aimed at the dark man who had shot him, landing a bullet in the man's gut as the dying thief responded likewise.

Cruler slid to the ground coughing blood. Fairson stopped and verged toward his fallen comrade, but Eisen jerked him back, ignoring his lover's tearful protest. Tanners, Collins, and Logan had already made it through the door which lead back to the great hall and from there to the castle's entrance. Fairson turned on the stone threshold, half in light, half in shadow, a hand extended to Cruler as Kavaria Kallista strode out to the bleeding man and produced a knife, the bandit-king's eyes fixed upon Fairson.

"Gerald, don't look."

But he did.

He looked as Kavaria pulled back Cruler's hair and drew his grin of red all about the heaving man's throat. Kavaria watched with supreme elation as the man bled out upon his boots, then he slid his hands free of the corpse's hair and began stalking toward his prey. His stare reached beyond the fragile pane of human bondage, taboo and decency as utter irrelevancies. Kavaria raised the bloody knife, a macabre salute, as Eisen pulled Fairson free of the horror and drew him back into the shadows of the castle keep.

Logan, Tanners and Collins waited for them up ahead. Stunned, disgusted and terrified. Fairson couldn't stop crying, subtle tears of a loathsome heart, and very soon Collins, too, began to weep for their fallen member.

The passage through which they moved was unlived in, cold, barren and devoid of ornamentation. Only the bare essentials prevailed in that Spartan expanse. They passed few doors and all of them locked. Torches lining the damp, stone walls provided the sole source of illumination. The smooth and vaulted ceiling, the enduring creation of a masterful hand, warped the sounds of their pursuers, distorting them beyond human recognition, transforming them into something aeriform and more consummately insidious.

As Eisen drew up before the doors he noticed that there was something behind them, something dark laying in a pool of something darker still. It was a man. Inanimate.

Shot through the head.

Suddenly from the hounds of the courtyard roared the unmistakable sound of Kavaria's uninhibited, nihilistic glee. Then gun shots. The killers outside were firing their guns into the air, some sort of wartime ritual for the fortification of their collective constitutions.

"What happened to that man over there?"

Logan looked to the dead man and spat. Disgusted.

"Tried to kill me – backfired on him."

"We have to find her. And her father."

They all agreed that this was so, that they had come too far and sacrificed too much to give up now; to give in. To madness. To evil. To Kavaria and his desolate host.

Before them lay the entrance, their exit. They didn't move, even as the sound of footfalls shuddered through the darkness behind them.

Eisen looked around at the sea of doors that stretched behind and before them. He nodded to no one in particular and then set his jaw firmly.

"Split up. Pick a door. Ambush Kavaria's men if you have to, but focus on finding the Arlingtons. Yes?"

They replied in affirmation and bolted like ants spilling through a subterranean compound. Eisen took to the door closest the entrance, it alone was unlocked. He dashed inside and shut it silently, bolting the latch. He found himself inside a makeshift kitchen and storage room, small and square and overflowing with victals. Some were laid out upon a long wooden table at the far left of the room, others shoved carelessly in a towering stack of barrels to the immediate right of the door, pressed against the wall and layered to the ceiling.

Cabbages, carrots, corn and tomatoes; clearly stolen due the vast quantity. The livelihood and, very likely, life itself, stolen with those items passing from rightful hands to that palace of destruction. He exited the room through a door exactly like all the others at the far right of the room and passed into a bland and musty stairwell. Spiraling up. Spiraling down. He chose up.

Running. His heart thumping with such force that he clutched his chest in pain; fear and exertion mingling to a venomous singularity.

Up the spiral stair he emerged unto an ornate landing, replete with silken divans and oil portraits of people who looked very much like they did not want to be in them. The landing was braced with high columns in neat rows of two, between which stood a burly guard with his back to the intruder.

Eisen crept behind the first column, his foot scraping a fallible stone as he moved into place. Its muted scraping catching the watchman's ear, he paused and cocked his head uncertainly, hand on his pistol. He drew it from its holster and thumbed the hammer as he turned slowly in Eisen's direction.

The coffin maker held his breath; made no sound. He was invisible, dormouse quiet, an assassin steeled. The man moved slowly to the pillar behind which Eisen stood. The man went to the right, Eisen moved to the left. The bandit reversed his game, consequently, the coffin maker did likewise.

Then Eisen stopped and waited until the thug stuck his head round the bend, behind the pillar and then clubbed the criminal over the head with the tail end of his gun. The tough went down, crumpling into unconsciousness.

Eisen snatched the felled man's weapons; two heavy-caliber pistols and a hunting knife. Then dashed off to the first door upon his right.

Directly across from this door on the other side of the room was its mirror image. His furious motor clocked away as his shaking hand clasped full round the cool-dry copper of the door handle and turned it to a clicking. He inhaled deeply and pushed the door inward. The space between the full ambit of its swing revealed a young woman, unbound and sitting on the edge of a wool-lined mattress which had been thrown carelessly into the spacious, barren room.

"Jen?"

"Am I dreaming this?"

"We have to leave, Jen."

She just stood in her thin-worn dress looking on with parted lips, dry and soundless, her eyes uncomprehending.

"Jen!"

She bolted instantly to his side and together they fled back to the main hall and from there disappeared into the descending night.

Chapter Twenty-Nine

Exodus

Night rose to eminence amidst the moon-call of coyotes off in the dust-plain. Beyond the mountain and the cracked and stoneless tract of land upon which dual pairs of weary feet staggered, their muted crunching the sound of man's abject desolation.

Eisen looked to Jen, her skin pregnant with moonlight and her eyes glimmering like fey spheres of scrying. He stopped quite suddenly to better study her. She took two steps forward, looked back and then stopped as well; her face contorted indecisively, tumultuously.

She rushed into his arms, sagging against him as if he were all that could sustain her, he and he alone. She was crying and sobbing and laughing all at the same time; the aggregate outpouring of her tortured mind.

"He killed my father. K-kavaria."

Eisen said nothing; he wrapped his arms slowly about her, pressing the young woman tenderly to his body.

"Oh God, they killed my father... they killed Henry... Braze... they could have killed you..."

"But they didn't. He didn't. I'm still here. I'm not going anywhere. Can you walk a little farther?"

"Yes. Those overhanging rocks by the withered trees. Let's rest there."

Eisen nodded.

☼

They were winding down the pass through the mountain to which the stranger had led them earlier, as they talked and a mist hung like a spectral noose about the mountain's throat. They entered the sparse and withered forest that Eisen had passed earlier that day, far from any path, man-made or otherwise, and settled rather uneasily under a large, jutting cliff of shale halfway down the mount; halfway between Kavaria's keep and the old man's cave. Grass grew thinly on the ground, and here and there bits of pallid green lichen teased up the rock face. A large bush of a kind which neither of them had seen before grew directly adjacent them such that anyone not viewing them from an extreme left or right angle would miss them entirely behind the thick and tangled shrub.

Eisen leaned against the cooling stone, closing his eyes and exhaling like the last breath of a dying man. To have seen that unmoving, alabaster form, one may well have thought him nothing more than grave fodder, strangely preserved, but this dead man stirred. Beside him Jen pressed her sweating body against the rock, heaving breaths and eyes dancing with starlight. Her hair ablaze as a gas lamp, a flame that did not warm, could not warm the bone, the skin. She shivered and drew her arms about her breasts. Teeth catching like colliding cubes of ice in a jostled shot glass. Eisen pushed slightly off the rock and looked to her, looked away, removed his heavy greatcoat and handed it to her; she refused.

"You'll die of cold, all you have is that rat-thin dress and a pair of dress shoes. The temperature is dropping. You're worrying me, so take it."

"All right."

"If a maiden in distress won't accept one's chivalry, then how on earth is one supposed to be a gentleman anymore?"

"Quit fussin."

She leaned against him and wrapped them both in the long coat, her head lolling softly against his own, and as it did he thought of Fairson and his kiss and hoped he was still alive.

"Yes, ma'am."

They lay like that until each fell asleep in turn and the moon fell into gray cloud and the whole night moved with the sounds of its teeming multitude. A dark-borne symphony. It lasted until breaking light, whereupon the wanderers stirred to a sudden sounding.

A rattle in the distance; something moving toward them, scrapping at sand and kicking up stone. Eisen shook the young woman to wakefulness with as gentle and hasty a hand as possible.

"Someone is coming. Get ready to run."

She nodded and he could tell she was steeling herself, coalescing her despair and uncertainty into rage, into hatred, into the will to destruction. It frightened him, the look in her eyes, the feral posture of her body, like the charred mirror image of Kindle. Kindle... his thoughts wandered, but were drawn back to the concrete, the actionable, as a human figure trussed through the trees directly before them. Eisen peered through the bush at where the man stood looking about.

It was Gerald Fairson Rit.

Eisen rose instantly and hailed him.

Rit just looked on for a spell without speaking, without moving, his nostrils flaring and his eyes going all blank and undiscerning. His hands spread wide at his side and his back stooped as if he were just about to pick up something. Then he ran, ran toward them and clasped them in embrace, Eisen, then Jen, and them embracing back just as truly.

"Oh, Fairson. I thought you were dead."

"I'm not so pitiful as you think."

"I don't think that."

"Jen, are you all right, you're not hurt?"

"No. No, Rit, I'm fine. I mean, I'm not hurt."

"Tanners?"

Rit paused and then stepped away from them, shaking his head, eyes downcast. "Didn't make it."

"Who was it?"

"Kavaria."

"Damn it. Damn it! What of Logan?"

"I don't know. All I know is he sure as hell wouldn't go down without a fight. He'd kilt four of them afore I lost him."

"Tanners... how did he–"

"Knife."

Eisen ran a hand through his hair and then readied himself to take charge, knowing that either of the others were too shocked and weary to lead, to think straight in such a dangerous position.

"We need to get out of here as quickly as possible, Kavaria and his men might–"

But even as he said it a plume of dust in the distance of the desert plain before the town cut through the words like fins through water. They all squinted out against the sun, straining to see what or who it was. They were riders, of that all three were certain, they were close and getting closer. Now they were nearly at the old man's cave, then they disappeared behind the rolling land, the rise of the mountain shrouding them, its ancient magic trick.

"Someone has been tracking us."

Rit spoke to Eisen without turning, the ambit of his gaze still cast over the desert plain like a fisherman's net.

"Why would someone be following us out here?"

"I don't know, but they have and they're about a day's ride from us."

Rit walked up beside his lover with his eyes to the distant horsemen; twenty in number.

"Looks that way. What do you think?"

"I think we should get close to them and see who they are. They're likely from the town, but that doesn't necessarily mean that they're friendly."

"No, it certainly don't."

They walked all day and half of the night, and when they awoke they were surrounded by the riders, cold-eyed men with dark-gloved hands and long twisting cloaks about their backs like regimented cavalry. All heavily armed. Eisen had never seen them before. He asked what it was they were doing in such a place.

One man amongst them, a middle-aged man with a large saber scar upon his right brow, tilted up his head and waved his hand toward the coffin maker.

"I could well ask you the same question, Mr. Torquiam."

"You know my name... how?"

"By way of a mutual friend, Ledru Monteblanc. He had occasion, some months before, to hire me and my associates for a little cattle rustling problem he had promised James Arlington he would deal with. Turns out these rustlers, well, they was all just part of some larger outfit, Kavaria's outfit. So we've been hired again to bring him in, or kill him, failing more gentile methods. Ya'll found him?"

"You've been following us?"

"No. Tracking you. During the war I was a scout, so tracking your lot was, well, not to boast, but was pretty damn easy. Out here a body should be more... cautious."

Eisen unsloped himself from the warm stone of the old man's tomb and leaned against the left wall of the enclosure, sizing up the company in the light.

"And what's your name, scout?"

The tracker removed his black, flat-brimmed hat and unsaddled, throwing his hat over the pommel and adjusting his belt as if it were the center of gravity and all that held him to his feet.

"Strade. Karlin Strade."

"Well, you already know me, so this is Mr. Fairson and this is Jennifer Arlington."

"How do you do?"

Neither Fairson nor Jen said a word, crouching where they had woken, cautious and ill at ease over these windblown riders, these spectral pursuers. Uncertainty of purpose; the quickest vessel of death and the fear thereof.

"Charming company ya'll got, Mr. Torquiam."

"What is it you want, Mr. Strade, exactly?"

"No man kin say exactly what he wants, can e?"

"I can."

"And what is that?"

"To have you answer my question."

"Cagey. I like that. Well, we all was hired, like as I said, by Ledru Monteblanc, and he wanted us to come here bouts an bring ole Kavaria in. He thinks he kin win over the townsfolk with that; win um over from the preacher, or rather the preacher's son, Michael. He's been giving speeches recently, Michael that is, lots of them. Pretty powerful stuff. Dangerous, one might be tempted to say."

"Dangerous?"

"Look, I don't mean to be uncouth, but we're wasting time talking, and I'm sure you kin understand."

"I can."

"Well, here's what, you tell me where Kavaria is, and I'll have three of my men take you back into town, two to a saddle, safe and sound. Tit for tat. Deal?"

Eisen thought a moment, decided that they had little enough choice if they didn't want to die of dehydration. He didn't know if the man was lying or telling the truth, but there was something earnest in the man's face. Something plain and unhidden. Unscreened from the world. A hardness as well, scars of experiences, cruel and tenebrous, expressed in the hard draw of his words and the firm line of his mouth, the scan of his eyes and the restless forethought of his feet. But it was blunt honor that was his singular aspect, and Eisen wagered on it; wagered all. All and more.

"Well I'll tell you where Kallista is, and I'll ride with one of your men. But I can't make my friends do the same, they'll go if they want and not if they don't. But I'll tell you all the same."

"I like the way you talk, friend. A straight shooter, they used to say. It's a deal - so?"

"You see those jagged rocks over there? It's a pass that leads into the mountains. There's a faint trail that ends quickly, follow it, you'll come to a withered forest, then some shrubs. Past those and up about seven miles is a cave, a tunnel, through it is an arroyo and Kavaria Kallista, his keep and his men."

"Thank you kindly. Hey, Flats, ya'll lettin thisin here ride back into town, understand? And Richard, Fleck, ya'll help these here others."

Eisen saddled up with the man called Flats and then looked to Jen and Fairson, the latter already riding with the man whom had been addressed as Fleck. Jen stood alone, feral and cornered in that space. Afraid.

"Jen, it's all right – come on."

Hesitantly, she did so, and the three riders and their collective passengers turned their mounts to the north, to the town, indifferent to the plight of these others, these wayward creatures.

Eisen called back over his shoulder.

"Mr. Strade."

"Yes?"

"Take care with Kavaria, his manner belies his cruelty, his cunning. Don't underestimate him."

"Words of wisdom, friend, words of wisdom."

Karlin Strade lifted his hat from the pommel of his saddle, placed it on his head, tipped it cordially to the coffin maker, to Jen, to Fairson, then saddled up and rode into the dawn, his men following, following and gone.

They kicked up and headed for town.

Chapter Thirty

Aftermath

Eisen, Fairson and Jennifer Arlington stood before Ledru's manor two weeks after Strade's return and Kallista's subsequent capture. Eisen rapped shotgun fast upon the polished wood, slowly soaking with the newly fallen rain, his mind in tumult on distant plains. The sky was dark and thumping, aswirl with mindless malignancy; thunderheads building, building to break. The ground going to black like the shirt cloth of a dying man and the grass dancing about its hinges amidst the southern wind's roiling symphony. Instead of the usual wait, the doors were thrown open almost instantly after the percussion. It was Elis Caldwell who opened it.

"So glad you could come to the party. Come in, be quick about it or you'll miss the music. The pianist is divine. And I think there's a fiddler somewhere..."

Caldwell turned and stalked back down the lobby, saying something in a murmur over his shoulder, clearly unconcerned with whether or not they heard it. They didn't. The trio's guide led them into the library, which had been converted into a party room, and there left them, disappearing into the crowd with a final mumble of, "Glad you're not dead." Then he was gone. Jennifer watched him go and shook her head, arms crossed and her hair cut newly short and wild.

"I don't trust that man."

Fairson looked to her, clearly amused and raised his chin. "I don't either but I like him, he's got a style about him."

Eisen smiled and set off for drinks as his companions set into a discussion, something about styles and personality. He wasn't listening. Instead, he was wondering why it was he had come to Ledru's party to begin with. Kavaria's capture was notable, but not something which he wanted to dwell on, and by extension not something he wanted to celebrate. There would a trial, hardly that, then a hanging, or worse, soon; he didn't want to think about that either.

He moved through people and their after-sounds like a ghost or some remnant of one. In front of nearly all the bookshelves along all four walls long wooden tables had been set up, covered in elegant satin covers of white and gold. The silverware repeated this garish motif; white and gold. He moved to the left of the doorway, the left back of the room where a man sat with a fiddle, looking to the ground as if he had lost something upon it. His rosined bow held gingerly in his right hand and his legs curled up underneath him like a native. The sound of piano strings being struck reverberated through the ballroom, rising up and dancing over the heads of the guests.

Eisen reached for a tray of fluted wine glasses, listening to the piano and then stopped, noticing the cornered man afresh.

"You look sad."

The fiddler looked up, his lids heavy with some unseen weight and his hair lank and greasy and falling over his face like half-cleaved vines from some aberrant cliff.

"I suppose I am."

"Why?"

The fiddler gestured out over the crowd with his broad, pointed chin; motioning toward the air, nothing to be seen, something to be heard.

"What is it?"

"The music."

"The piano player?"

The fiddler nodded slowly, as if such movement cost him great reserves of strength.

"Why does the piano depress you? It's rather a happy tune."

"It's a tale that takes some time in the telling, friend."

Eisen squinted up one eye and tilted his head, picking a shrimp off a silver platter and scanning its plump, headless body curiously.

"Is there something hasty in my manner, or do I just strike you as an impatient man, fiddler?"

The fiddler shook his head, suddenly vigorous.

"No – not how you strike me at all, sir, not at all you don't. It's just people want a spectacle, that's why they want music at such functions. Why they hire people like me, like Ms. Voantsrig--"

"Who?"

"Pardon me, the pianist, that's her name."

"Ah. What were you saying?"

"That it is due a want of spectacle that music is desired. What else is music but the audible outpouring of internal profundities? Yes, it's melody and beat, rhythm and tempo, but that's not the entirety of the thing, not the quintessence of it. It's experiences unable to be put to words. It's caged revelation unfettered, and I'm not sure I can deliver that with my story.

"In Africa I once heard a chant – no beat, no tempo, no discernible ordering of notes, no sustained pitch, just this feral wailing tearing out across the plains; and I swear it was one of the most beautiful things I've ever heard. Music is art in sound. It's only a difference in medium that separates it from other art forms. It was difference that I sought in my youth – seems like so very, very long ago, lifetimes – in piano, with the piano.

"I wanted to play it. But not just play it, play it with a verve and fresh light, such as never had been heard before and would never be heard again. I wanted to make a new sound, like the sounds I heard coming from my grandmother's study – extraordinary woman. A pianist herself, as you might well have guessed, inherited a big old terribly drafty manor house from her father, some great tycoon of bygone times.

"There was talk of him gambling, fixed horse races, smuggling, but no one believed it. At any rate, she learned from the servant, an old, amiable hand named Carpenter Merridin, and he said it was fitting that a house that came from music should have a musician in it, one for future times and future sounds. For he said his time was upon him, that his god was calling and that his heart was weak. Weak and failing. Getting weaker.

"He taught her every damn day and every damn night – times when he should have been resting, taking his medicine and sleeping. My grandmother, you see, was a spirited woman, vigorous and unrelenting when she set her eye on something, believed in principles and in sticking to them. Everything was a matter of principle with her, she always had a reason. And usually it was a damn fine one.

"All his doctors, since they couldn't argue with her, told old Merridin that she was no good for his health, and he knew it; didn't care. What good, he asked, was the life of the terminally infirmed? To him the answer was plain; not much. Every plan would be made in fear of its incompletion. Every action fettered by inaction, by a bed, by restive sense and mind swells; night terrors and worse, streams of undue pity. He wouldn't have it; didn't want that... to die alone, sick and pitiful and useless, even to himself.

"I didn't blame him and secretly I was cheering him on, even as I seen the signs of swift-approaching death; the shaking of his once powerful, lightning hands, the wan pallor of his skin and the way his thin, arrow straight body started, more and more, to stoop in on itself. Even still, I was happy for him. It got to such a point that the doctors started coming round and scolding him, scolding my grandmother. Well they tried, but she always sent them off with a flea in their ear. Er, more than a flea, really. 'We're making music, you cunts!' She'd yell this all about the streets at the top of her lungs. Always made me laugh and flinch at the same time, the woman had the most colorful vocabulary I'd ever heard. He taught her straight for a month and a half, ole Merridin did, everything he had ever wanted to pass to another he did in that month, just a normal month. And then one day, at breakfast, he was making us some tea – tea just like any other – when he up and collapsed. And that was it.

"He died, right there. No final words. No moaning, wailing or cursing the gods and crying; none of that.

"I went to him and looked at his face. I tell you sir, he was smiling, like a little child, smiling. Though he couldn't see it or her any longer, I knew what he was smiling at: it was at my grandmother and her piano, the happiness she would create with it; with her fingers moving and her heart awhirl in her ancient breast and gathering ears and lingering imaginations.

"This I knew and then, in that time and that place, even through my tears, I smiled and was glad. Yes sir, glad. Happy. Happy all the more to have seen his death, for to know that the end of a man's life could be so peaceful, so... beautiful, why, it filled me with wonder and with a renewed sense of joy.

"We called the doctors, there wasn't anything for them to do, and then we stood there in that sparkling kitchen, in the silence, looking to each other. Me and my grandmother, and I knew we thought the same, felt the same tearful joy, the same sadness and had the same desire.

"There was no guarantee of an afterlife in my grandmother's philosophy. Her a pragmatic soul, right down to her bones, she wouldn't wait around for a miracle to make things better. She knew as well as I did that in this life the man we had known as Carpenter Merridin was gone only so long as he was forgotten. For us he would never be.

"And so in the following months my grandmother and I would sit down every day, and she would teach me as she had been taught before, and we would play to the rising of the sun, like we were welcoming it home. We would play for the flying of the moon and its pale blue light as in homage to its tender illumination, and we held parties and dances and I played and played; my hands the greatest dancers amidst the jocund whirl of bodies.

"But then came the accident; I don't relish its retelling. I was a machinist you see, working long hours in a local factory, very rank and file, good honest labor for good honest pay, as they like to say. Well, I was on a sheet press one unremarkable night when one of the operators slips up and it all goes wrong. He shouts, screams, but it's too late and my hand is crushed. Crushed to the bone. Mangled."

The fiddler set his bow upon the floor and held up his hand, mangled and terribly scarred, his little finger missing entirely.

"And that was that, all my plans of a career in music with the piano, gone. What was worse was knowing that my link, the last link to a man what had been like as a father to me, was gone, I thought forever. But then I met a man at work who slapped a fiddle in my hands and said, 'You only need one good one for it.' He was right in a fashion, and I kept on with it. With the pay I had received as compensation for my injuries, I started traveling and playing on the road. A true minstrel. A bard. Wayfarer. Troubadour. And so here I sit crying like an unsuckled babe listening to Merridin's echo, still there, even after all these years. Silly, I know."

Eisen looked on awhile then knelt and helped the man to his feet, bending and picking up the bard's fine horse hair bow and placing it back in its owner's ruined hand.

"If Merridin was still here, I fancy he'd want you to play, whether it was on the piano or not, wouldn't he? Like you said, in music, with instruments, it's only the medium that changes, not the essence of the thing."

The man took the coffin maker's hand and bent to it, brushing it tenderly with his lips; a kiss that was a benediction. Then he rose and there were tears in his eyes, joyful drops. He took his bow and his fiddle and spun out unto the dance floor whirling and smiling and plucking at the strings. In that moment Eisen felt a potent, indefinable bond with that tumultuous figure, so stark and gesticular within that humming sea of force and sweat and bodies. Music his solace and his weapon, his house and his path, shelter from the sun. And in watching the dancing bard, Eisen suddenly took the guests into account. Before they had merely been props, vague background shapes, shadows and so much mist. Now he saw them for what they truly were, a conglomeration of fulminant intimacy. They danced and turned, drunkenly, limbs askew and awkward, laughing, smiling, kissing and shouting. Some even sang, making up a tune to the fiddler and pianist's fiery volleys. In that ballroom was every style of man and woman, from every walk of life, joined by drink and laughter, by song and dance, bound in a mad quest for mirth.

Eisen smiled as he watched them bounding ceaseless and wild and then turned to the table, snatched up three fluted glasses of wine and returned to his companions where they stood, bunglesome and shy near the doorway.

When he approached them they were speaking in muted tones, their eyes cast over the heads of the dancers to no certain spot upon the adjacent wall.

"Well, well, he finally returns."

"Yes, and I've brought some liquid courage for your consideration."

Fairson screwed up his features, huffing loudly.

"What makes you think that we need courage?"

"The fact that you both look as if someone has a gun held on you."

Fairson took the flute from his lover with a suggestive smile and then downed half of it as soon as it was firmly in hand.

"It's just that I'm not used to these kinds of things."

"To these kinds of things? It's a dance, Gerald, not an orgy," said Jen.

Fairson turned to his female companion and flicked her in the forehead whereupon she jabbed him in the gut, nearly causing him to spill what was left of his drink.

"If you're done beating our mutual friend, perhaps you would care for some refreshment yourself, Ms. Arlington."

"Certainly, Mr. Torquiam."

Fairson rolled his eyes and tipped back the rest of his wine, then looked across the sea of smiling faces and gestured with the empty glass.

"How long do ya think it'll be afore anyone notices us?"

Eisen turned to the man, sipping at his own drink as Jen took hers.

"Just because you notice someone doesn't mean that you must speak to them, Gerald. Anyhow, you're allowed to do what you like, no one is stopping you from having a good time."

"Yeah, I know, but..."

"But?"

"I'm a chicken shit, all right? You were right. Happy?"

"Well, I'm not unhappy. Why are you so shaky? Are you afraid of parties? Having a good time never... well, actually I'm certain it's killed lots of people, but none that I can think of off the top of my head. Live it up a little is all I'm saying, maybe go and find a pretty girl to dance with."

Fairson was in the middle of arching a brow to accentuate the look he was hurling at Eisen as Jen cut in, a mischievous smirk playing across her face like the harbinger of disruption.

"I doubt Gerald will be doing much of anything if it's to do with girls."

Eisen feigned profound interest.

"Oh, and why is that?"

Gerald hissed. "Shut up, Jen."

"Why is that, you ask? Well, first there was the time I tried to dance with him, he nearly ran from the room. And when I kissed him – a little peck on lips was all – he went pale as a ghost, eyes got wide as saucers. One time I kin remember seeing him looking at one of the local stable boys, handsome fella, looking at him real funny like, as if he–"

"Yes, I know – he fancies men."

Fairson looked from the coffin maker to the redhead as if they had suddenly transformed into creatures from some other planet.

"It's all right, Fairson, she may as well know. You know I don't like pretensions."

"Yeah, damn your eyes, I know you don't."

Eisen looked to Jen long and hard and appraising, searching for a sign. Very slowly, he found one; her face, at first blank and uncomprehending, suddenly forming the complex contortions of one undergoing a trek through astonishment. Suddenly she drew her hand to her mouth, covering it, as if she were about to spit out her drink.

"No. Ya'll didn't?"

"We did."

"But you ain't a–"

"Not exactly. I like new things. Don't you, Ms. Arlington?"

"Well, no wonder you ran out on me when..."

Fairson turned instantly to her, anger and confusion stark on the notes of his whirling breath.

"When? When, what? What?"

Eisen smiled faintly as he noticed her cheeks go from pink to red.

He smiled wider.

"Go on, tell him. Friends should be honest with each other – tell him."

"Oh, all right. I tried to – I was drunk, now you remember that Gerald, drunk, ya mind. I tried to get him... to sleep with me. He ran out."

Gerald Fairson's face went suddenly and ominously blank. Then, quite abruptly, he burst into a high, shrill volley of raucous laughter.

"It ain't funny, Gerald."

"The hell it ain't. That's hilarious."

"You're an ass, Fairson. A royal ass."

"He ran out on you, not on me – guess I'm a privileged ass."

He began laughing again as Jen Arlington proceeded to turn several shades of red, clenching her fists and furrowing her dark, crimson brows.

Eisen took another sip and wagged a finger, faux-sternly.

"Make nice, you two."

Jen folded her arms in the manner of the disconsolate.

"Fat chance of that. But still I cain't believe it, how long have you two been, you know, a couple."

Eisen and Fairson spoke up at nearly the same time; first the former, then the latter.

"We're not a couple."

Jen unfolded her arms, the scowl melting from her pale, freckled face as she watched them gazing so hesitantly into each other's eyes.

"You two are painfully awkward. Anyone eva told ya that?"

Eisen laughed.

"Yes. I suppose we are. A dance to alleviate it, perhaps. Fairson? A dance?"

"You crazy? No, no way, I'm just fine where I am."

"Milady?"

Jen paused dramatically before answering, even though they all knew exactly what she was going to say.

"All right – but just one dance."

"Of course. You're not going to be jealous, are you Fairson?"

He waved them on wearily.

"Git if yor gittin."

Hand in hand, Eisen and Jennifer Arlington walked to the outskirts of the dance floor, giddy and elegant in their shabby attire. Eisen was in his one and only suit, a patchwork affair of serge and tweed and something else which he wasn't sure about, and his shoes were brown leather and bootlike; strange in that space of dandified sandals and exquisite leather loafers and tap dancing shoes. She wore a creamy satin dress that fell only to her knees, a risqué choice of attire, attracting quite a few errant eyes; lewd stares, repulsed stares. She was a very shapely woman but it was only now, as Eisen twined his arm through her own, pressing it delicately to the small of her back, that he realized this.

"You look very beautiful, Jen."

"No Ms. Arlington?"

"No. Just Jen."

She smiled and kissed him on the cheek in the manner of a princess rewarding a noble knight for loyal service to her kingdom. He looked slightly abashed but said nothing, just gazed at her, her face and the light in her eyes and the shine of its outpouring gilding over her newly cut hair. Then she placed her arms about him and swung him gently in a circle, tracing the after-lines of the dancers before them. He worked off of her momentum, and soon they were nothing more than a melding of sinewy limbs and arcing motion.

The faster they spun and twirled, the less the world around them held its shape, no longer maintained in the glow of the cheerful amber lights. There was only their entwined body and knowing eyes and the sonorous piano, the shrill and delightful fiddle, and the fiddler stomping on a found wooden plank somewhere in the distance of the din; a rousing percussion. The song was nearing its crescendo when the music abruptly stopped, the fiddler falling out of beat and then silencing his instruments.

Ledru Monteblanc's voice boomed brightly out over the ballroom floor.

"Forgive my absence, my dearest ladies and gentlemen! I'm glad you've carried on without me. I told Mr. Caldwell to keep up the dancing and the booze and you won't miss me at all! At any rate I'm very glad you could all come to my little party. This is a time for comradeship, for celebration, and most importantly, for drinking!"

This received a fair amount of laughter from the crowd and even Eisen cracked a smile, such was the atmosphere of gaiety and joviality. But there was an uncertainty about the laughter which Eisen discerned, a faint wavering in the mass of bodies, the pillar of voices, as if they didn't know when to quit; thinking that perhaps they had been expected to laugh louder and more boisterously or shorter and more quietly.

Standing at the doorway with Ledru was Mr. Chesney, Percival Statletter, the sheriff (who looked dreadfully out of place with his six-shooters and snakeskin boots) and a crisp assortment of businessmen in dark suits; all of them wearing dire expressions, looking as if it were a funeral rather than a garish party. A few servants shuffled about behind them, looking apprehensive and unhappy. Ledru continued.

"Food will be served shortly. Until then, pray, continue! Ha, ha!"

Some of the attendants bowed to Ledru and his company, while others turned nonchalantly back to their conversations, their dancing and their drinks.

Ledru spotted Eisen, and instantly a bright white-toothed smile broke out over his puffy, reddened face.

"Eisen, my dear man, I didn't think you were the party type. How good of you to come. And my dear Ms. Arlington, I am ever so sorry for your loss."

A quivering flashed across Jennifer Arlingtons' face as if struck by a live wire under the skin. She broke away from Eisen, turned to face her fat, ingratiating host, her manner cold and her expression forcefully blank.

"Why should you be sorry, it was that pig Kallista that did him in. More is the better, he was a wicked man what never cared for anyone other than himself. It's a pity Kavaria didn't get on with it sooner."

Ledru and his company, save for Statletter, who merely seemed amused, were so taken aback by this bloodless comment that they fell into a shocked and awkward silence, staring in utter wonderment of this fiery-haired creature.

One of the businessmen to Ledru's right spoke up in a manner that was clearly affected to console.

"Surely you don't mean that, ma'am."

"And how would you know, three piece?"

Eisen spoke in a tone that was both slightly louder and more imposing than usual; his question not merely a question, but a demand.

"Where is Karlin?"

"Oh, Mr. Strade?" Ledru grabbed a flute of wine from a passing waiter as he spoke, and gulped half of it. "He's still at the jail."

The sheriff intervened, gravely shaking his red and doughy head.

"We've had more lynching attempts than we kin count, more than I ever even heard of. They all had enough of this thieving and killing, and I don't blame them. Frankly, if I wasn't a lawman I'd be inclined to help um."

"Would you indeed?"

"Yes, Mr. Torqham, I would."

"It's Torquiam."

"That's what I said."

"How would you help them?"

"Well, it ain't really important."

"Surely, it's a matter of principles, yes?"

"Well, I suppose."

"Then you're saying that principles aren't important?"

"No. That ain't what I'm saying."

"Then what are you saying?"

"Now ya'll trying ta run some kinda game down on me, and I don't take vury kindly to it. No, sir, not at all."

"No game, just a question you haven't answered. Since you are a resident-elected official and I'm a resident, I think I'm entitled to know about your principles, in as far as you have any."

Chester Chesney fairly exploded.

"You're a mockery, Torquiam! A sham!"

"Oh, how's that?"

"You're intolerable!"

"And you're shouting. I have sensitive ears, you know."

"I've heard enough of this; I'm going to find some civilized company."

Before anyone could stop him, Chester Chesney spun on a well-polished heel and struck out into the seething mass of bodies, two of the dark-suited businessmen trailing him.

Ledru was furious.

"Eisen, that man is the chairman of my company!"

"I am aware of that. Don't you remember that it was at one of your company's precious meetings that I asked you to help me save the life of this young woman here, her and her father – remember what you said?"

"I thought you said you weren't a man to hold grudges?"

"I'm not. But neither will I curb my tongue or don a mask for that man just because he is your superior, and neither will I do the same for our misanthropic sheriff."

The sheriff squinted up his eyes and scratched the side of his bulbous, balding head.

"Mis-a-what?"

"Never mind. I appreciate you bringing us out here in such style, Mr. Monteblanc, just as I appreciate all you have done for me, furnishing lodgings and pay as you've done, but this is different. You're not just asking me to help you, you are asking me to betray my principles without reason. That I will not do, for you or anyone else. Not ever. Understand?"

Statletter laughed.

"And the master is commanded."

"Oh, put a cork in it, Percy. And I'm sorry if I or Mr. Chesny have upset you, but you really must take other people into the equation, you know."

"No, frankly, I don't."

"Oh, goodness, you really are the most inscrutable fellow. I... I must entertain my other guests..."

"And you have already thoroughly entertained me so, I bid you a goodnight, Mr. Monteblanc – and of course, you too, Mr. Statletter. A pleasure, as always."

The blind man bowed slightly in the direction of the coffin maker and then departed with Ledru, who looked to all the world like a man who had just endured some unspeakable, yet terribly enlightening, torture. The sheriff nodded uncertainly toward them and then followed dutifully in tow. Jennifer giggled once they had gone.

"You really gave that fat-headed toad a talking to."

"Hey, now, he's not all bad. He's a good man, really, he's just mired in a tradition that values greed and politesse above honesty. I can't abide such a stricture. But he was brought up in it."

"And you weren't?"

"Well, I suppose I was."

"Didn't stop you from making up your own mind about how you'd act."

"Oh, Mr. Monteblanc is no robot; he's just... easily cowed."

She giggled again and then paused, realizing that her dancing partner's face had fallen quite meditatively.

"What is it, Eisen?"

"Did you really mean it, what you said to the sheriff, about your father?"

She thought a moment, herself unsure.

"Yes. I meant it."

"Every word?"

"Every word."

"He was really that bad?"

"Yes."

"And you think he really deserved to die?"

"Yes."

"Even though he was your own flesh and blood?"

"What does that matter?"

"It wouldn't matter to me, but it matters to most people."

"Well, not to me."

"I hope I haven't upset you..."

"No. No, Eisen, it's just, all of this that's happened, it's all... it's just–"

"So sudden?"

"Yeah. So sudden. When we three were out in the desert with those riders, I just didn't know how to feel, didn't think I wanted to find out, and when I did, I realized I was right. How kin I be glad my father is dead? It ain't human. Oh, Eisen, I don't want to think bout this any more. I just want to dance, can we do that, just dance, you and I and tell the world off fer a while. Kin we just do that?"

"Nothing would give me more pleasure."

And she leaned in toward him, catlike and heaving with breath, whispering, "I doubt that."

Then she kissed him wet and full upon the lips and he, holding her tightly, rekindled the gesture. And in that space of pounding hearts they were a completion of some unsolved and unseen puzzle; everything falling perfectly into place, a superlative ordering. Into warmth, into heat, into desires and thoughts there born, which were whispered on the still air of night, stirring in secret places, secret things.

When he withdrew from the fondness of her lips he looked into her eyes, and for the first time, allowed himself to fall into those dazzling green pools, endless and shimmering.

Drowning in them.

One minute a lifetime.

There was suddenly a clacking far behind Jennifer's head. He drew away from her slightly, craning his thin neck over the left side of her shoulder to afford a better view of the commotion, and to his utter surprise he spied Peter Logan, his left arm in a sling and a long strip of gauze girding his skull. The injured man was standing very near to where the fiddler had been before, in the corner to the extreme left of the doorway. He was collecting a drink and had apparently fumbled it. Broken glass lay scattered at his feet and a dark, sanguine liquid was slowly soaking his ruffled and weather-worn riding boots, as well as the carpet beneath them. He cursed under his breath and bent to pick up his shattered glass.

"Excuse me a moment, Jen."

"What is it?"

"Logan."

"Who?"

"Peter Logan – he's over there, I'm just going to go talk to him. I'll be right back."

"You better be."

"As you wish, ma'am."

"And don't you forget it."

Smiling like a fool, Eisen ambled easily over to the wounded man, carried on with confidence and strength in every movement, the thought of Jennifer's lips a cooling balm to the heated frenzy of the crowd, of the dizzying din, the shrill cackles and shrieks of laughter. Sound of feet scrambling and the brush of bodies cocooned in cloth. Glare of the lights and the fiddler's rekindled sense of urgency, now he was alone on the stage at the far end of the room, directly opposite the doorway through which the coffin maker had come. The fiddler was turning round and round and the pianist was watching him with great interest, the idle beginnings of admiration.

Eisen was now no more than thirty feet from Logan and was preparing to call out to him when a voice spiked out from his right, a voice that seemed to protrude from the bookshelves, some character unburied from a musty tome.

"I didn't think I would be seeing you again."

"Mr. Montferiat."

Luce Montferiat inclined his head respectfully toward the coffin maker, exerting tremendous pressure upon the flatness of his features, his face kept purposefully blank, though every couple of moments there was a flickering of something just under the facade. Something genuine. Something real.

"I seen you were going to talk to Mr. Logan. I'm sorry to inconvenience you, but I need to have a word. Several words, actually – you don't mind?"

"No. What is it?"

"I know we haven't always been amiable with each other, but I want you to know that I have always respected you, your talents and your intelligence, your confidence and reserve and... your purity. You are a good man, Eisen, whatever my son or the members of my congregation may think."

"Thank you, Luce. If it matters at all, I feel likewise about you."

"That's very kind of you to say, but... but there is something else."

"Yes?"

"What my son... did, to those poor people, that was not the will of God, that was his own will, and in good time he will be punished for it, him and all who helped him."

"And until such a 'good time,' he is still at liberty, here, in the town, basically running it. If you have any say still left with the people of your church, then use it to help them bring your son in. I know it's not what you want, how could it be–"

"It is."

"What?"

"It is what I want. Killing. Murder. This is not the way of our faith, lest not my own. I should never have allowed him to talk me into changing my speeches. I should be brought in too, for crimes against these poor souls as well... the people of this town, those traveling performers, you, Kindle."

"How is she?"

"Fine, but she misses you. When we told her that you had gone off with Daniels, she was determined to go after you, to make sure you were all right. She said that you had protected her and that she would rather die than fail to do the same for you."

"She's forgiven me then?"

"Forgiven you? For the incident, yes, y-yes, I imagine so. She is the most perfect creature. She hasn't taken well to the faith, though."

"Oh?"

"She is very inquisitive. I keep trying to tell her that inquiry isn't the point of it, but then she asks me why it isn't, and I've nothing to say!"

Both men laughed and a liveried servant came dashing by, stopping at Eisen's command. The coffin maker scooped up two wine glasses, handed one to the preacher and then sent the waiter on his way.

Eisen turned back to Luce, still smiling.

"That does indeed seem to be a problem. But I fear amidst all this gaiety we are neglecting a serious point of concern."

"My son."

"Yes. Nothing is to be done? He incited a riot. He very likely broke into my lodge and murdered three people, leastways some number of his followers, not to mention all the others who died in town or in the wastes."

"Your lodge? Oh, yes, the sheriff said something about it."

"He 'said something'?"

"Yes."

"What was the something he said?"

Luce looked away, clearly ashamed.

"Luce?"

"He said, 'Everyone should be thankful that it wasn't their own houses what was broken into, only a two-bit leech and his dandied whores what died, after all.'"

"Two-bit leech?"

"Yes, I'm afraid that the stronger my son's influence grows, the harder life around here is going to become for you."

"It hasn't exactly been easy so far."

"No. That's why I wanted – all I've really wanted to tell you tonight is that I will do everything I can to help you. You and Kindle and Jen, the poor girl. It's my duty, even if you don't believe it is."

"Well, thank you."

The preacher nodded as a vassal might to a noble king and then departed hesitantly, as if there were still some words lingering, demanding release. When he was gone, Eisen turned to find Logan, but he was gone. He looked back to where Jen had been, and there she still stood, watching him intensely. Behind her the crowd parted, and there was someone standing in the void left by the passing bodies. Someone else was watching the coffin maker.

Michael Montferiat.

Eisen was shocked that they had even let him in to the party. Did no one care, he thought in a whirl of anger and misery, that this man had caused the deaths of an entire carnival?

Eisen had hardly time to think of it since his return, knew that it was a fruitless project and yet still could not push it from his skull. There the problem vexed him, thumping away like a madman's jackhammer. Did no one care enough to say that this must stop, that he must be punished for his transgressions and all whom followed him on his bloody errands?

Then he realized, if they had let the sheriff and Chester Chesney in – no, not "let," invited, and very likely with high honors – well then they would invite pretty much anyone, no matter how barbarous and retrograde they happened to be.

Even still, he could scarcely believe that the man, due to his following and local popularity, hadn't been arrested; it was inconceivable. Not just inconceivable, but wretched, perverse. It occurred to him then that there was no justice in the hearts of men, but only in their well-reasoned minds.

Michael watched him coldly from his distance until the crowd once more subsumed him, and when they had twice parted, he was gone. Eisen heaved a sigh of relief and realized that he had balled both hands tightly into fists. They were sweating, and with a grunt of irritation he wiped his palms on his pants and walked back to Jen where she waited with a perfect smile, and for the briefest of moments his heart once more was still.

☼

After the dance, dinner was served in the same room since Ledru's kitchen was far too small to accommodate so many guests. Long steel-frame tables were brought in, then squat, steel-frame chairs, then towering sets of brightly colored tallow candles. Ledru sat at the table in the middle, the longest, at the left end, and Chesney sat opposite him at the far right (a predictable affair, though none of the guests seemed to mind).

For a long space of time there was only a shuffling of planted feet, the clinking of silverware, the rasping of fork tongs dragging against ceramic plates, fine china and other oddments. Tea and coffee gurgling in samovars and carafes, and wine in tall, leering pitchers pushed and pulled about by greedy, Dionysian hands. Conversation was consigned to small groups of individuals; the oil workers talked to the oil workers, the churchgoers to the churchgoers, the ranchers to the ranchers, and the businessmen to the businessmen. Eisen, Fairson and Jen sat next to the fiddler and the pianist, Ms. Voanstrig (whose first name remained a mystery to them all). Speeches were made, garish and seemingly unending, between dramatic pauses and faux-sincerity. Jen and Fairson looked to Eisen, his face an utter blank, wondering what he was thinking.

The coffin maker said nothing until the final speech had ended, whereupon he rose and clinked his glass gently. It rose before him, and when no one took note, began fairly slamming his spoon against the vessel cupped in hand. Silence descended like a dark god. Eisen's face a stoic mask, his eyes opaque and far away.

No one spoke; all watched with building anticipation.

"I would like to make a toast."

A few of the more severely inebriated partygoers eagerly raised their glasses, with cheerful expectations. Others wriggled up their brows with concentration, cocking an ear, raising a brow, tapping a foot.

"A toast to–"

He surveyed the faces around him and then smiled, a hollow splitting of the skin.

"Injustice."

A wave of puzzlement washed over the crowd like cold sunlight in August. He barreled on, heedless.

"You may ask why I would do that, toast such a thing as injustice. I shall tell you; because injustice is, here, the mark of normalcy. I have tried – how I have tried – to see all the arguments, from every side, every angle, every slant and perspective, but I cannot ignore the summations of my own mind. There was in this town a horrible calamity, the death of a man you knew as Braze. As you know, he was killed by the man who now sits in your jail awaiting his execution. This terrible affair was close cropped on its heels by the wanton slaughter of dozens of innocents; circus performers, actors and showmen, and singers and dancers. Clowns and oddities and strange talents wiped clean from the face of this desert for no reason other than that they were outsiders, deviants. I, myself, maligned by this man here," he pointed firmly to Michael Montferiat, who looked on, both halfheartedly amused and irritated, "and all his following. Nothing has been done about this, nothing. Here we all sit, drinking and dancing – later some fucking – but no justice."

The assemblage blossomed into furious uproar, a hissing, clangorous mash of rage and confusion; of truth and its headsackers and blindfolders. Eisen's voice rose, combating the din, consuming it.

"A young woman and two of her friends fled to my cottage after the riot that either killed or sent flying all their company. I left them, telling them that they could stay for as long as they wanted, and when I returned... they...they had all been killed. Shot through the head – executed. The young woman was pregnant with child. Killed by some number among you. Do you call that justice? Someone here did."

"He's lying," someone shouted angrily from the back of the room.

"Must be drunk," an old woman decided out loud to her company the next table over to the left from the speaker's.

Ledru rose with his mouth agape, but no sounds escaped it. Opposite him Chesney fumed, bellowing and slamming the table with his manicured fists. "Someone get this clown out of here now!" No one did.

Peter Logan raised his glass with a hearty Scottish cry of, "Here, here! Moral bankruptcy or death!" Then he laughed.

At the eye of this storm of angry voices and nervous gesticulation stood Eisen de Torquiam and Michael Montferiat. Neither saying a word, neither moving, both locked to the form of the other, their eyes meeting with the force of clashing rapiers. The most powerful words between them, the words left unspoken. The words that hung in the air like sheets of venomous muslin, encompassing the ballroom entire and every life within it; some protean miasma of unmaking.

The narrative of the crowd was an old one, older than the stones upon which they stood, older than the forest girding their resplendent domicile. It was a story of broken bones and bleeding faces, of screams and cries from the darkest of nights, sounds of agony and despair to rattle the skies. It was a narrative Eisen knew all too well, one he often wished to forget. But he well knew the folly of such a notion, knew and acted upon his knowing, sundering his cowardice wherever he found it like so much rotten wood.

Something was thrown and struck Jen in the head. She fell off her chair and collapsed to the floor, rising slowly, blood trickling from her temples. Someone had thrown a bottle.

Eisen helped her to her feet with the aid of the fiddler and then turned to Fairson.

"Get her out of here – both of you should go."

Fairson nodded dutifully and half-carried her out.

The fiddler leaned in as the sheriff and several of his friends came careening about the table from Chesney's side, dire expressions bellowing their intent.

"You should leave yourself, if it ain't too bold a me to say."

"Good idea."

Eisen pushed his chair away with a swift, backward kick, and then struck out from the table as a flash of movement collided with him and brought him to the floor. A man with a dark suit, terribly drunk and wholly enraged by the coffin maker's indelicate comments, held him down and pulled back his arm to strike.

Eisen, furrowing his brows, shucked the man aside like a sack of wheat and rose, dusting himself off as a full blown brawl erupted behind him. Someone had thrown a punch at Logan and he hadn't much cared for it, leaving the bloke lay bleeding on the floor. But the attacker had friends, and almost immediately they jumped on Logan. Very soon the sheriff, now ignoring the prospect of throwing Eisen out entirely, attempted to intervene. He was promptly kicked in the shin, releasing a horse wail up into the arching ceiling boards. Elis Caldwell watched from the far right corner of the room, lurking behind the well-polished grand piano with an expression of mild disdain. Chester Chesney roared for silence, for order; no one listened. He left with a gaggle of the dark-suited businessmen and ran out through the back doors, which had remained shut the entirety of the party. Now Ledru was shouting, his face completely red, as Statletter, tugging at his arm, tried to get the man to leave. There was a crash. A plate broken over someone's head. More shouting. Thrown chairs. Thrown bodies. Yelling.

Eisen looked out over the chaos ensuing behind him, watching for a few, brief moments, then he turned and passed through the enormous double doors of the ballroom and vanished into the trophy-lined hallway beyond. The fiddler followed at a distance, his case under his arm, the pianist, hesitantly, in tow.

☼

Outside, Fairson waited with Jen under the pale moonlight. They waved the coffin maker over and went for their horses. Eisen stopped them.

"Jen, are you sure you're fit to ride? That was quite a blow you took to the head."

"Nah - it looks worse than it is. I'm fine. Very gentlemanly of you to ask, though."

He nodded, unable to stop himself from cracking a sly grin, and followed them to the rectangular, flat-roofed, dirt-floored stables that ran nearly the entire length of the left side of Ledru's manor. Both men helped her along.

The wind struck up a ghastly keening. No clouds mired the faintly glowing sky. As the muffled sound of horses grew, so to did the muted sounds of footsteps behind the exiting trio. Eisen whirled, ready to defend his friends, but it was only the fiddler and the pianist from the party.

The fiddler was the first to raise his voice above the howling wind.

"That was quite a scene. I get the feeling that you kindly wanted that to happen."

"Maybe I did."

"Was it true what you said? About all that... killing, the pregnant girl and the carnival?"

"Why would I lie about something like that?"

"I didn't mean to offend ya."

"No. Of course not. Please accept my apologies, it's just, I was there, it's hard to keep a level head when I'm thinking about – but no, I wasn't lying. That was the truth."

"That's what me and Ms. Voanstrig thought, there was some kind of earnestness to you, in your voice, in your eyes. And we decided that we didn't much want to be a part of such a gathering, if it contain such as you described, Ledru among um."

"It wasn't our mutual employer with whom the majority of blame lies, but with Michael Montferiat."

"The preacher's son?"

"Yes. Come, let's leave before someone comes out after us. I imagine the sheriff and his men are rounding up as many as they can. We should leave."

Voanstrig nodded reservedly, the fiddler at her side, her elegant hairpin sparkling like a diamond in the moonlight.

"Good idea."

They, all five of them, mounted and rode off, Jen riding double with Fairson and the fiddler with Voanstrig. They rode off, down into the dark.

☼

When they arrived back at town, Eisen inquired where the musicians were staying. They replied that they were going to stay at Ledru's but had since decided against it. He offered them lodgings at his home, which they readily and respectfully accepted. He told Jen to lead them there, since she knew the way, and said that he would be back sometime before midnight. Then he rode out of the square toward the jailhouse, disappearing into the black.

Upon arriving at the jail he found it horribly transcribed with paint and knife marks. Writ large upon the door of the jail in red paint was the phrase, God will have justice. Beside it, written smaller but more precisely was, The Wicked Shall Perish. Vengeance is mine. This was followed by an assortment of carvings and paint flingings, Scum, death is coming, murderer, heathen, blasphemer, defiler... and so on and on they went. Nearly the whole of the little wooden prison's facade was covered by incensed scrawling.

He walked up the rickety wooden porch, hardly three feet off the ground, and tried the door, jimmying it back and forth; locked. A light flashed inside. Then the sound of shuffling feet, clumsy movements. The door opened.

Jimmy, the deputy, stared back at the moonlit coffin maker, dumbfounded.

"Uh, Mr. Torquiam, what you doing here?"

"Hello Jimmy. How's the arm?"

"It's fine, thanks, listen, I'm, sorry about everything, sorry bout hitting you like as I did. I was out a line."

"That's all right, I don't hold grudges. So how is he?"

"Who?"

"You know who."

"Kallista?"

"That's right."

A voice cut through from the darkness near the cells.

"Who is it, Jimmy?"

"Mr. Torquiam, the man ya'll met in the desert."

"Let him in."

"All right, ifn you say."

"I do. Hello, Mr. Torquiam."

"Hello, Mr. Strade."

Karlin Strade sat on a stool next to the cell where, only days before, Eisen himself had occupied. It had a new tenant, Kavaria Kallista.

The outlaw smiled from his shadowed corner like a caged lion smelling its next meal.

"What have we ere - Mr. Torquiam come fera nighttime visit. I'm flattered."

Scattered all about the small, square interior of the stockade was a motley assortment of Karlin's men, every single one armed as if they were preparing for war, and by the look on their faces, one would have thought that perhaps they were.

As the coffin maker entered, they looked at him as one might a deer when passing through a field, then they returned to their various activities; playing cards at the sheriff's neatly kept desk, polishing a shotgun in the corner as if preparing it for a gun show; one man just standing with his back to the wall opposite Karlin and the cells, near the door, sipping a steaming cup of coffee, looking suspicious and concerned. The dark, frothless liquid in his mug rippled with his unconscious shivering, residue of his fear.

Karlin looked to the coffin maker, an unspoken question in his eyes.

"I just wanted to see him. That's all."

Kavaria arched up a brow, furrowing his well-tanned forehead. He rose from his cot and walked to the bars which he leaned against with a strange kind of ease, as if prisons were no mystery or danger to him, nor the consequence inherent in such a position; such a place.

"You just wanted to see me. Lies, well become you though they may, do no fly so easily past my ears."

"It's not a lie, Kallista, it's just not the whole truth. Kallista – strange name for an Irishman, isn't it?"

"So I've been told."

"I reckon there's a story in it."

"A long and boring one."

"I'm never bored. Tell me, Kallista, because I want to know, are you afraid of death?"

"Were you afraid when you were as yet unborn?"

"That's interesting. I had never thought of that."

Kavaria smiled slyly, clearly pleased that he was culling admiration from even his most stalwart opponent.

"Why would a man such as you, so clearly brilliant, ever stoop so low, to such base and ignoble action?"

"Base and ignoble. Someone is utterly fascinated by anachronisms, aren't they? Haven't ye noticed, Eisen, there is no longer such a thing as 'The ignoble,' for there is no longer such a thing as 'Nobility.' Twas a false premise from the start. Having its birth in aristocracy, in elitism, in greed and disdain for all those whom don't carry about them the sniff of pompous obscenity. The obscenity of cultural tradition."

"Something happened to you, didn't it? To make you this way."

"HA! No, you fool, nothing happened to make me this way. I LIKE acting in this way. Tell me, Mr. Torquiam, are you a happy man?"

"What?"

"I do hate it when folk what don't know what te say answer a question with one of their own. ARE YOU A HAPPY MAN?"

"Why do you ask?"

"Of course ye ain'te a happy man! When I first met you, out there, in the badlands, in the wastes, it was as if the land were telling us both something, wasn't it? Like a reflection. Of you. No, you are filled with suffering. I kin see it in your eyes. But it's not the per usual inflictions – there's no guilt. You are a guiltless man. A shameless man. Like me. Like I said. We're brothers in arts, you and I, disciples of the same school of thought."

"No, you're a psychopath."

"I know that you don't believe that anymore than I do."

"You could be right."

"They tell me that you were in ere not too long ago – is that right?"

"Yes."

Kavaria slapped the bars suddenly and with vicious force. The man with the mug was so taken by the fulminate outburst that he fumbled his cup to the floor where it shattered.

Strade shook his head, commanding to the man, "Pick it up and get out of here. Go an git some sleep or don't. I don't much care, just git."

The man did as he was told. All the while Kavaria watched with predatory glee molding every gesture of his face, every flinch and flicker, every grin and snort.

"What were you in for, Torqy? Rape with probable cause?"

"I'm not the rapist here."

Kavaria paused strangely, screwing up his face as if someone had offered him a carton of rotten eggs. He wagged his finger at the coffin maker disapprovingly, his voice curiously serious.

"I resent that, Mr. Torquiam. I've never raped anyone. What an appalling thing ta say. I'm offended! Truly. What an utterly distasteful act, downright disrespectful. I would love to meet whoever spread that damnable rumor about, for them I might make an exception."

"I did not know this. My apologies."

Kavaria laughed with wild abandon as Strade jabbed the coffin maker in the shoulder with great animation.

"Don't you be apologizing ta that piece of shit in my jail."

"Well, it's the sheriff's jail–"

"Not anymore."

"You're the new sheriff?"

"Until all this," he waved toward Kallista, "is taken care of, yes. Why did you think he was at that fancy party of Monteblanc's?"

"Well, anyhow, just because this man has done something barbarous doesn't mean we should return the favor. I fancy that's just what you want, isn't it, Kallista?"

Kavaria smiled, his eyes dancing in the fickle lamplight.

"It's not just me what's the only one that wants it, cuz it's like I said, birds of a feather, Torqy, birds of a feather..."

Eisen thanked Strade for his time and then set out for home, all the way Kavaria's words ringing in his ears like cannon fire. Ringing. And him wondering whether or not they rang true.

He just didn't know.

☼

There was a long line of shelves, pure white and filled with enormous black boxes, pure black, blacker than dark. Eisen stood simply before them. There were hundreds of people walking through the towering shelves, walking and walking, never stopping, never speaking, but their faces were blurred, as if some god hand reached down into their collective and smeared out all semblance of visage with some ethereal eraser, leaving only a murky pall.

Eisen looked about and realized rather belatedly that he seemed to be inside of an enormous warehouse, but it was unlike any warehouse he had ever seen. The floor was checkered, black and white, and continually was it rearranging its pattern, as if it were alive. The little squares sliding about lazily as if of their own languid volition. He looked up, and up, and up farther still, a height beyond comprehension. The ceiling, impossibly high and vaulted, braced by some kind of enormous black entity which seemed to be moving as well. What it was he could not say. Something like hissing steam sounded from above. Cocking an ear, the coffin maker listened intently. Again came that strange and ceaseless sound but it was not steam, nor did he know exactly what it was, but to all his sense it seemed to be a cacophony of voices, all yammering incessantly in uneven concert.

Reaching.

Calling.

To him.

A sudden feeling of panic slithered into his spine, and his vision began to fade. Screaming, he ran for an exit.

There was none.

There were walls that seemed to spring out of the very air at every turn, as if something or someone was boxing him in. Losing all sense of place and all sight and sound, he collapsed in a heap, and when he awoke he was in a lift. Standing. A man was standing next to him wearing a dark gray suit, his face expressionless, save for a faint quivering of his lower lip, as if he were, at every moment, about to say something important, yet perpetually decided against it.

"Where are we going?"

The man did not look at him, did not even seem to know he was there, that anything was there.

"Sir?"

Quite suddenly the man's eyes shut tight and his hands moved in an instinctive gesture toward his stomach.

"Where are we going?"

A series of spasms overtook the man's body yet he remained standing stoutly, his eyes still shut and his arms over his chest like the figure of a sarcophagus. There came then from that otherwordly icon the hissing sound which Eisen had heard coming from the roof of the shelved construct. Sibilation in the dense dead of air and Eisen withdrew slightly from the man, as unsure of him as he was of the lift and the very world into which he seemed to have fallen.

The man's lip quivered another time and as it did, his eyes flew open, pupiless and vacant; something was coming out of his mouth. Tiny little claws, blades of black and squirming, like the legs of some tar-born centipede.

The creature, floating easily as any gustblown kite, drifted free of the man's mouth and then oscillated toward Eisen. A thousand whiplash antennae seeking out the man, seeking out a mouth. A new vessel. Some other transient boiling pot, a cauldron-copy of its birth.

Eisen backed away from the thing, his eyes going wide, his hands outstretched defensively, feet scrambling to push himself through the wood-paneled walls of the lift. Now he could feel its spindly legs caressing his face, so gentle, so seductive. He opened his mouth. After the creature had slithered inside, he could feel a gravity in his stomach, something pulling him; he looked down and beheld a darkness. A darkness in his stomach, like a black hole contained there and it some kind of door to the opening of another. Reaching inside he could feel a flat surface, something on it – a key. He retrieved it and then waited for the elevator to stop. When it had, the doors having been flung open by obfuscated mechanisms, he walked out, stopped and looked back for the man. He had melted, nothing more than a puddle of organic afterbirth. Afterdeath.

Eisen walked on and came to a door set into a wall of seashells all shaped like human hearts; human ears. The door itself a perfect oval, gilt with a spiral that never seemed to end. There was no handle, only a key hole. And as the coffin maker reached forth to place within it his key, there came again a fell and unreckonable hissing. He placed the key in its slot, fitting perfectly, then he turned it. Nothing happened, or rather, nothing seemed to happened, but then he realized that the door itself was gone, vanished, and so had the building around him.

He was standing on a large, circular platform, a platform he had seen from his view down upon the construct's shelf-lined floor. Before him the strange black aberration loomed, and he was now close enough to realize what it was.

A massive insectoid creature. Similar to the centipede-thing which in the coffin maker's belly still resided, only it was more skeletal and expressive and infinitely larger. It seemed happy, yet the coffin maker didn't know why that should be the first thing to occur to him upon seeing this augustly grotesque being. The thing, million legged and black carapaced before him, was the source of the unearthy keening; the noise escapint from 100,000 little holes all over its vaulting spine that ran the whole length of the building and back again.

Eisen looked down over the floor of shelves and the black things upon them, realizing now what those curious containers housed – more of the creatures, a breeding ground for the beasts, seeping in their color, some bodily emission thus changing.

All the people amongst the shelves had stopped walking. They stood completely oblivious, like the man upon the lift, arms straight at their sides and eyes pupiless and vacant. Their mouths quivering, as if something was fighting to escape. Emerging from their host's hollowed and lightless cavities.

"For what do you hunger?"

Eisen turned on the towering platform, now audience to the great, coiling monstrosity which spoke in a rasping concert of countless voices, young and old, dead and alive, voices of the past and of the future.

"Hunger?"

The lusus naturae drew closer, its upper body and head floating slowly through the air as if held by invisible strings.

"Yes. For it is in the nature of man to seethe with want until it has become a need, forcing desire into action. And for that there is always a toll..."

"You speak in riddles."

"Were that true, one such as yourself should find no purchase to complain. You are a clever man, a clever man would understand my words."

"Yes, I think I do understand them. I hunger for power and a will noble enough to use it with delicacy."

"What a refined answer. There is, as they say, ever a time for firsts."

"What are you?"

"It is not in the nature of man to ask questions he thinks will be answered. They will or not, but they do not question."

"Why not?"

"For fear of getting an answer."

"What are you?"

"What I am is of no consequence to what you would like to be – what you nearly are. Why waste what little time you have left within your mortal coil scrambling up trees which you know you cannot climb?"

"I don't know whether I will climb or whether I will fall, I just want to try."

"No, you wanted, and you have wanted for so long that it has become addiction, a need. This is your hunger."

"And what is your own?"

"To consume all other hungers and make of them examples – examples to their desecrate hosts."

"That is monstrous."

"That is necessary."

"Why?"

"Because I want it to be and, like you, have corrupted my own intent with its longevity. Now there is no other option. You... shall be... consumed."

Eisen backed away to the edge of the platform farthest from the aberration which produced its shrill hissing and reared up magisterial in all its grotesque geometry.

"It is pointless to run."

"I know."

"You are not afraid. Why?"

"Because when you consume me I will fail, but my failure will not be due a lack of exertion on my part. It shall not be for nothing that I fall."

"Good! My domain could use more like you – more wills of note. There are fretfully few. I attribute it to a lack of creativity."

"I thought you said you would consume me?"

"I already have."

"What?"

"I consumed you ten minutes ago."

With horror Eisen reached for his stomach, feeling only a hardened carapace instead.

He tried to scream, but a dozen squirming black legs skittered from his throat and only hissing remained.

☼

The silent secret of sunlight slid smooth and smothering over the coffin maker's skin as he rolled over upon his back, his back upon his blankets and them upon the floor. He still had no bed. There was birdsong and a merry, dancing wind rustling through the open window near his head, the heady scents carried there rousing him back to life. He unfurled like a length of rope and fussed his hair, then moved to the window and looked out to the blinding brightness and the long stretch of green that vanished in the pooling shadows of the forest.

A sudden creaking of footsteps on the wood-paneled floor. Eisen flashed about from the window and beheld there Gerald Fairson, in boxers and a tight fitting, short sleeved work shirt.

"What's the matter, Fairson? You look depressed."

"I, well, I mean, nothing. Nothing. Never mind."

"All right."

"All right?"

"Look Rit, if you don't want to tell, I'm not going to press you for information."

"All right."

"Where is Jen? By the way, I hope you two found a comfortable place to sleep. I know not having beds is somewhat inconvenient, but I figured if you can manage as well as you did with nothing but a tent and the sand it's on, I figured you would do all right with only a bedroll and a pillow and a nice comfy stretch of wood paneling."

"Yeah. It was fine. Thanks for letting us stay, and well, everything else. You don't know how much it meant to those two musicians, they were so happy, so grateful that you let them stay here. Apparently Southern hospitality ain't all it's cracked up to be."

"Apparently not."

The sound of additional footsteps swept into the room along with Jen Arlingtons' brash, red hair and pale alabaster skin.

"That is some very interesting hair you are wearing, Ms. Arlington."

"Don't even–"

"Looks like a bird has been living in it. Eh, you need help with the eggshells?"

"Oh, shut up. I just woke up from hardly any sleep on the floor – I don't think I need ta remind ya."

"You needn't, and yet you do."

"Just shut up and make some breakfast, I'm damn near starving."

"Now I'm being ordered around in my own home. Why, I've never heard of such a thing."

"Oh, don't even tell me you aren't hungry too."

"Starved. I'll whip something up."

As he said this he noticed a peculiar look flash between Jen and Fairson, some secret, wordless message. Shame in the man's eyes, irritation in the woman's. Eisen turned away from them like a dervish, half-tranced and busy with it, and began pushing in the chairs and setting the table.

He made pancakes with blueberry jam and sausages with herbs he had gathered from the woods, serving it all with orange juice, green tea and coffee that was dark and strong. They ate for a space in near utter silence.

Eisen looked up once, twice, both times catching Fairson's gaze, a worried one if ever he could recognize such. Finally, the coffin maker looked up again, hunched over his plate, and caught Fairson's eye once more. This time it seemed as if the latter could no longer bear whatever strain had been laid upon him and burst forth a frothing mudslide of words and gesticulations.

"I didn't really mean for – please, you musn't hate me none. I mean it was her and it was me, but it weren't one more an the other. I'm sorry Eisen, I'm so sorry."

Eisen straightened up, lowered his fork and held a hand forth commendingly, fingers spread, palm flat and forward.

"Slow down a space."

Jen was irate – so irate, in fact, that she bashed the table with her fists, glaring down the man beside her.

"You idiot, ain't none of his business who I sleep with. Damn it all and you as well."

Eisen looked from Jen to Fairson and back with great composure. He leaned against his chair, awaiting the story.

Fairson looked down at his plate, though he saw it not.

Jen, still glaring, turned to Eisen with a petulant toss of her head, a gesture of defiance; a challenge. A challenge the collected man met head on with a sly grin.

"Seems you two were having fun without me. But you know what they say... the more the merrier."

"Damn it, Eisen, this is serious to me."

"Fairson, you're a fine fellow, but we've made no commitments to each other, no promises. This may sound callous, but who you choose to sleep with is of as little consequence to me as what kind of cigarette you might decide to buy."

Jen gave a jerky laugh.

"Oh, it wasn't him that chose to sleep with me, more like the other way around, isn't that right, Gerald?"

"Why are you acting like this, Jen?"

"You're such a twat, Gerald, sometimes ya really are."

Eisen interrupted firmly.

"She is acting like this because, and perhaps this is just my egotism speaking, I think she thinks this will somehow make me jealous and then I'll just have to cede myself to your oh, so comely advances. Is that it?"

Jen smiled despite herself, shaking her head and leaning forwards in her seat, a finger pointed mock-disapprovingly at the man across from her.

"You're about as subtle as a warthog in the underbrush."

"Perhaps, but despite their lack of eloquence, one must admit that they have never received a lie from one."

Fairson rose, his face red, hands balled into fists, breathing fast and uneven, and his eyes roving back and forth in disbelief and mounting fury.

"I caint believe this. Ya'll treating me like I'm somekinda...toy. I aint a god-damned plaything!"

Jen's face fell whilst Eisen continued to look on without revelation.

"So the only reason you had sex with me was to make him jealous? All those things you said bout liking me fer being honest, fer being who I was, all of that was just a lie. Weren't it? Weren't it!"

Jen rose, face flush and muscle shaking her frame like a rag doll in a mischievous gust.

"No, Gerald, it wasn't a lie. Quit being so... childish."

"Childish!"

"Yes!"

"Both of you shut up and sit down. We have company. Remember? Or have you forgotten?"

The bickering youths' eyes went suddenly wide as they realized that the company their host was referring to happened to be standing at the base of the stairs, looking on uncomfortably.

The fiddler was the first of the musicians to speak.

"Is everything all right?"

Jen nodded, returning to her seat and shoveling a pancake into her mouth, speaking through the mesh of food as if it were some kind of safeguard. Smoke screen to her shame.

"Yes, everything is fine. Sit down, Fairson."

"I'll stand, thanks. I think I've lost my appetite."

Without further comment Gerald Fairson left in as calmly a fashion as his raging consciousness would allow, ever the consummate gentleman, in every sense of the word.

"I fancy that whatever that was ain't my business, so you needn't be bothered – I won't ask," said the fiddler.

Eisen turned congenially to the fiddler and smiled faintly, motioning warmly to Fairson's empty seat.

"I'm not bothered. You may ask if you want, there's no need for secrets among us. Sit, I made more than enough for everyone. You like pancakes?"

For the first time since they had met, the pianist addressed the coffin maker directly, somehow stately even in her ragged traveling gown and patchwork tights.

"Your stress upon honesty seems almost pathological, if you don't mind my saying so."

Eisen rose and pulled out a chair for her, like reenacting some scene from a stagey melodrama.

She thanked him and sat down.

"Well, I don't mind. If one is to be pathological of mind about anything, one could do far worse than continual honesty."

"Yes, there is a soundness to what you say. But I would think it better to avoid pathology altogether, wouldn't you?"

"Well, to be honest, ma'am, it's a rather gloppy term."

"Gloppy?"

"Amorphous. Protean. Blob-like. No distinct shape. Sorry, does this not make any sense to you?"

"It makes sense to me. Go on."

"Right, well, it's like when people say their 'Heritage,' it sounds concise, and that's the way that people most typically use it; however, it is anything but concise, it's a sprawling labyrinth."

"That's an interesting point."

"Really?"

"Are you so starved of attentive ears, Mr. Torquiam?"

"I guess I am. Your last name was Voanstrig, yes?"

"Indeed it is, and you must excuse us both for failing to introduce ourselves to you more promptly."

"I don't stand, or for that matter, sit, on ceremony here."

"So I gathered from what the townsfolk told me when I arrived four days ago. But enough, it is perhaps not fitting to introduce oneself to one's host at the breakfast table, but I feel I no longer have a choice. My name is Severine Salelis Voanstrig."

The fiddler picked up a thick slice of bread slathered over with blueberry jam. He raised it to his mouth and opened his jaws as the pianist jabbed him in the ribs with a near cartoonish scowl.

"Manners!"

"Ah right. Ah course." The fiddler flushed a peculiar shade and then set his toast carefully back upon his plate as if it were a sacred idol. "Me name's Arron, Arron Arkin."

Eisen smiled at both of them and raised his glass into the air before them.

"A pleasure. Let us drink to our new guests and make a ceremony all our own."

They did just that, and for an hour full there was nothing but laughter, good cheer and the sparkling collision of glass.

☼

After breakfast, Eisen found Fairson out by the toolshed looking at the coffin his host had been working on, caressing the wood hesitantly and with great meditation, as if he feared some physical harm would befall him if he tarried too long upon the grim and motionless construct.

"You'll end up in one of those one day. The very notion should make everything which troubles you seem utterly frivolous, save for the striving over it."

Fairson turned with a pained expression, his back to the wall at the left of the door.

"But it doesn't. I'm not like you, Eisen. I cain't just will away my troubles, wish them off like so much sand in the wind. I just cain't."

"Of course you can, you just don't want to. You like being troubled, most people do, a little bit of drama goes a long way. Makes one feel more alive."

"No. That ain't it at all."

"Are you sure about that?"

"Well, hell, I ain't sure bout nothing no more, everything is whirling and my head feels like it's been put in a pressure cooker, like everything has gone senseless. I kin scare tell whether or not I'm in a dream anymore."

Eisen walked up to the right side of the casket such that it separated them by equal degrees, the door facing the unplaced feet of the vacant occupant. A gas lamp burned low in the right corner on a work table. A moth sadisticly danced to the light, unending, unyielding and predictable as it ever was. Faint wind and the smell of wood and steel, iron and leather, rain building far and away swept into the shack. Damp earth resounding with its selfsame shifting and the clutter of noise upon it, boots and human feet and things many legged and less fore-thinking.

"You think that there are only two outcomes: the first being me furious at you for sleeping with someone other than me – very quaint, isn't it? The second is that I won't care what you do or with whom, and you think that means that I don't really care for you – isn't that right?"

"In a register of it."

"I thought you would know me better by now," said Eisen.

"I hardly know myself, how kin I know anyone else?"

"You know me."

"Yes."

"Then look at me and tell me what you see."

"What do you mean?"

Eisen spread his arms at his sides, as if unfurling some ethereal cape.

"Do you see anger?"

"No."

"Do you see jealousy?"

"No."

"Then what do you see?"

"A friend who I guess I've mighty slandered."

"Not at all. It's like I said, we haven't made any commitments, and Jennifer is a fine woman, your polar opposite, perhaps, but a fine woman. Though people often say that opposites attract, I suppose you two are a testament to this."

"Oh, and what, you and me are peas in a pod?"

"I suppose that is a good point. Do you... love her?"

"Jen, you mean?"

"Who else?"

"Of course I do, we've been best friends from childhood, she's like a... sister to me."

"You make a habit of sleeping with all your siblings, or just your sisters?"

"You know what I mean, don't be an ass."

"Yes, I know what you mean. That's a good thing, really, don't let that slip through your hand."

"And what about me?"

"Oh, I won't let you slip through my hand either."

Fairson smiled.

☼

Later in the day Eisen decided it was well past time he spoke to Kindle, who, as far as he knew, still resided in the gaudy folds of Montferiat's cathedral. He wondered with great deliberation what Michael's next move would be and how he could counter it; there occurring to him the folly inherent in attempting to confront the future. His mind aflame with a single phrase and it recurring like the light of the moon: one cannot avoid that which has yet to transpire.

He shook his head, looking up at the toffee-colored clouds that wafted serene and playful in the misty blue ambit of his gaze. Another storm building, rumbling, out in the desert, and it swirling with more than just the heat. He was, however, whole heartedly dissuaded from the venture by Jen, who pleaded to him as if he had just said he wished to walk into the mouth of an active volcano. Shortly after hearing her plea, Jen was joined in her crusade by Gerald, who ran with her flag at an equal pace, his expression one of consummate dread. Eisen, though he well understood their motivation, could not allow himself to be so easily deterred, and he made this fact well known.

The three stood outside the front of the house where the porch would have been were there to have been one. The coffin maker in his usual garb, a dark, crisp suit, white dress shirt, small purple glasses, serge pants and thick, leather riding boots. Jen wore only a thin white blouse, like some fairy out of Fey.

Fairson repeated the pattern in his garb, the same as Arlington, only a tight sleeveless shirt and a pair of baggy purple striped sleeping pants.

"You cain't go down there, Eisen, after what you said at the party, they'll lynch you like as they'd talk to ya."

"I appreciate your concern, and it's partially justified. I mean, there is some danger going down there, especially now that Michael is effectively running the church, not to mention Kavaria's current residence in the jail and Chester Chesney's ire at my... well basically, at my everything. No, I'm not a popular man here, but I haven't been since I got here. Since I stepped foot inside that church and spoke honestly. I'm not going to hide like a snail in a shell just because of it, nor because of your fear, much as I appreciate it. Nor should you. Either of you."

"Well, then I'm coming with you."

Jen nodded in agreement. "So am I."

"No, one of you should stay here and keep the musicians company – not to mention that this place could use as many sets of eyes at all times as anyone can manage. Like I said, dangerous times."

Jen nodded again, more slight this time.

"I kin agree with that. I don't want to, but I cain. You know what your problem is, Eisen?"

"No, but I'm sure you're going to tell me."

"You make too much damned sense."

They all laughed, Eisen heartily, the rest nervously, especially Fairson who seemed consumed with a sudden and enigmatic compunction. It was a trait which Eisen noticed with growing frequency and prominence in the days following their ill-fated wasteland escapade.

"Anyhow, I can't linger, it's getting dark and quicker than I thought. This place is a breeding ground of storms of the most fitful sort, coming and going like screams in the night. One of you stay here and the other can come, I wouldn't mind the company, to be honest."

"You go, Fairson, and... I am sorry for–"

Fairson held up his hand and then drew her to him and kissed her upon the cheek, smiling like a child.

"Apologies have had their day, wit me most of all. I've grown weary of their company. You go, I know you haven't really got anytime to talk to him one on one like as you wish, I'm always the, what's it called? The gooseberry. Third wheel and what have you. Ain't fitting. Anyhow, I love music."

Jen nodded, clearly pleased but subduing her pleasure such that it did not prick what she perceived as the shallow skin of Fairson's sensitivity. She hugged her friend and then walked up to Eisen.

"All right."

"Ms. Arlington."

"Yes?"

"Are you going like that? Mind you, I haven't any mind to oppose it... it fits you."

She looked down and realized she was still wearing her nightgown. She cursed and fled back into the house to change just as a slight, misting rain began to fall. Like the curtain to some otherworldly stage, its setting and functions unknown and unreckonable.

"What kind of music do you like?" asked Eisen.

Gerald Fairson retreated under the overhanging shingles at the front of the house before answering, flimsy shelter against the steadily increasing downpour.

"Why do you ask?"

"Because you said you loved music."

"Cain't rightly say as I know a music in particular, we haven't got anything to play records on round here, as you've probably noticed."

"Ledru has a record player."

"Course he has. What about you?"

"Prokofiev."

"Who?"

"Sergie Prokofiev. The Russian composer."

"Ain't it something."

"What?"

"Even on the other side of the world they still have music, fancy that don't sound like much ta most, but it's really something to me."

"It's the closest thing there is to a universal language – music."

"That's a fine way of putting it."

"So what are you going to do now, Fairson?"

"Well, now that Kavaria has been caught... I don't know, I was going ta join the oilmen. What else could I have done? There ain't nothing else to do in this town cept work a rig or shake a Bible. I don't have the contacts or funds ta open a store, and I don't suppose that would matter much anyhow."

"Why?"

"Cuz as soon as someone finds out about what you and I did, we'll be run out of town."

"We're already out of town."

"It ain't a laughing matter."

"I'm not laughing. I understand. If that's so, I know of a place we could go, you and me, without the expectations and the businessmen of shame or any of it. Just you and me and Jen, if she wants to go. I've lived in cities big and small my entire life, and there is wonder there, but I've seen it now, lived it. I want something different, not merely on a whim, but on principle."

"What principle is that?"

"The principle of freedom. Everyone will go on for hours about this freedom and that freedom and how you should be so glad you have it, them; but they never say what everyone knows, that the freedoms which they expose are held hostage, held at the end of a gun."

"'The end of a gun'; what do you mean?"

"I mean that in every town, in every city, in every village there are codes spoken and not. Trespass against either of them to the fullest extent which you can, and we will see how many threaten violence and expulsion. There is always a line which one draws around oneself, against which no trespass is allowed, no dialogue, no conversation; so too is it for groups of people, states and countries. To cross it means a cut, in mind or body or both – usually both. That is what you fear, here, in this place, that is what most people fear most of the time, and that fear is the arbiter of their lives."

"And what is the arbiter of your life?"

Eisen paused a moment before speaking. "Love."

Then he drew Fairson to his lips and held him as thunderclaps resounded off the high cliffs of the mountains, echoing far into the duneland and from there farther still. Upon their melding stumbled the stately pianist, her mouth parted slightly in anticipation of some asking. Seeing them there entwined, the musician's hand flew instinctively from side to mouth, and there muttering something under her breath before leaving hastily back through the door.

Eisen withdrew slightly, watching her go, half in worry, half in amusement. "Oops."

Fairson returned a steady hand to his friend's shoulder. "Come here."

Chapter Thirty-One

Riot and Rain

The sun was midway through its cyclical orbit and the rain fell in steady gray sheets shrouding the town in a muting pall, but even through this cloying color, the excitement of the crowd roared forth into the world like the carnival fanfare of some psychotic fun house, seeping, untrammeled unto the travelers' unstraining ears.

Jen Arlington and Eisen de Torquiam stood before the jail in the rutted, sucking mud of the road, their hooded cloaks spattered nearly as much with the weeping soil as with the draining sky. A ring of armed men in dark, somber attire stood about the front of the compound, rifles and shotguns pointed and precarious, half in the air, half at the heads of whoever screamed loudest, nearest. And their screams were dreadful and unending.

"Let us at him. You're going to defend him, a killer? He kilt ma boy, e kilt him and I'll do the same fer im. Don't you point that at me, you gutless bastard! Let us have him, let us have the whoreson. Yes, give Kavaria to us. What does he mean to you, weren't your boys he kilt?"

And on it went as Eisen and Jen watched wordless and uneasy, some mirror image of Arrgilius and the tenets of his tavern across the street, looking on through the rain and the feral shapes within it. After several minutes the din began to waver and then dissipated almost completely; someone had arrived. Someone of import. Eisen craned his neck out and thrust himself unto the tips of his toes to see who it was, and when he had, wished he hadn't.

It was Michael Montferiat, surrounded by a entourage of ten, all men and grim faced, imposing ones at that; their attire nearly identical, all dark suits with dark shirts and long, high-collared overcoats of deep gray. No color to them.

Eisen noticed rather belatedly that the foreman, Johnson, Daniels' friend, was counted among their number. This baronial gathering proceeded from the road that let out into the town square, likely coming from the church. As they made their way into the crowd, a path was shorn of its own volition, and the gray coats continued unimpeded until they stood before the porch of the jail, Michael foremost among them and unafraid.

The preacher turned to the crowd and spread his arms wide, some waterborne puppet master and them a willing audience, rapt with the show.

"This is the face of degradation, my brothers and sisters, that mercenaries," he flung his hand to the men behind him as if gesturing toward fetid refuse, "have now become our arbiters, the mediators of justice! Will you let this stand? In your town?"

He began pointing to people in the crowd, randomly and with great animation, his voice rising to a harsh and rending outcry.

"You? Or you, ma'am? I will not! I stand for true justice, that which is ordained by our master, not something that can be bought and sold like a cheap whore!"

An Englishman, who appeared to be Karlin's placeholder, stepped down from the porch to greet the gray-garbed orator.

"Just calm down, Mr. Montferiat."

He moved closer and spoke in hushed tones.

Eisen watched his lips, reading his words therefrom.

"These people are in a bad way, and if ya keep on like as ya are, then, by God, my friend, we'll have a riot on our hands."

Michael cocked his head, his profile catching the light of the cloud-shrouded sun, and it coming down on him pale and distorted through the deluge.

"Riot? Very likely so. You shouldn't be milling about."

Eisen came forward, at first at a slow, trance-like walk, then at a run, the mud flying about him and him tripping with its accumulation, falling then rising, determination his sole support.

Jen called him, her voice rising shrill against the rain.

"What are you doing?"

"I don't know yet – something."

"Eisen!"

But he did not heed her, did not heed the curious eyes about him. He had a wide hood pulled low over his face, such that very little of his visage could be seen. That, combined with the rain, left him faceless at a glance.

The people began to whisper among themselves as he walked into their midst, past them and up to their orator.

"Michael!"

"Mr. Torquiam."

The gray-garbed priest turned to his challenger like a knight in preparation for a duel, his stance and manner exuding confidence and power.

"Your speech at Monteblanc's party was quite impressive."

"Don't do this."

"What? Congratulate you? Why ever not?"

"You know precisely what I mean. These people are set to attack the jail. This whole place is going to go off like a powder keg, and you're happily positioning yourself as the match!"

"You know, instead of grasping at the mantle of past heroes of myth, you might have better situated yourself as a poet."

"Do not condescend to me."

"Threaten all you like, Eisen, it isn't going to make any difference in the end, save that now I shall do what I must with the pleasurable knowledge that you failed to stop it – to stop me."

"A man as intelligent as you knows that there is another way to resolve this."

"Of course there is! Just none that I want!"

"Oh, you, is it? I thought this was for your master? You do not speak as a slave."

"If the very existence of Kavaria Kallista could not shake my faith, how can one such as you?"

"Because to you, I am far worse than he could ever be."

"I've tried with all my might to despise you, for what you are, for what you have done and said. But I cannot bring myself to hate you, not completely, because you are better than the corruption which you expound. Far better. It is therefore saddening to me that I must still see you crushed and broken, a maimed and soul-stricken sufferer."

"That remains for the witnessing."

Eisen began to walk away, but the priest stopped him.

"Oh, by the way, Kindle sends you her regards. She is ever so... open minded to our doctrines. Isn't that wonderful?"

The coffin maker did not say whether he thought it was or wasn't. He walked up to the Englishman, the guard whom had previously spoken to Michael, hailing the man.

"You can't let him keep provoking them."

"Who are you to be giving out orders?"

"I'm not giving orders, just suggestions. My name is Eisen de Torquiam."

"Oh, I've heard of you; you're not a very popular man at the moment."

"No, and neither shall you be if that mob storms the jail. You don't have enough men to stop them. They'll take Kavaria out and execute him in the streets."

"That would mean very little to me."

"I don't think you understand–"

"Oh I understand. It'd be a bit unsightly, but it's only a paycheck to me. I've made a good wage, but I'm not being paid for mob control. If Chesney and Monteblanc want that, then they kin pay double or choke on their ingratitude."

"You'd just let them take the man out to be lynched?"

"Seems ta me, from what I erd, that e deserves it. Like unto like. Blood will have blood. He's a killer, after all."

"Well, perhaps one day they will find you out as well. As you said, blood will have blood."

With that Eisen turned in the mud and trudged back to Jen where she stood thirty feet off to the right of the crowd near an overturned cart, abandoned in the downpour, wringing her hands and gritting her teeth.

"What were you thinking, Eisen?"

"I was trying to prevent a lynching. I still am. I just need to think..."

"Prevent a lynching? For him? For Kavaria?"

"Yes. Either one has justice or one does not, there is no middle ground. These people don't want justice, they want blood. They want sport, they want spectacle. I shall not let them have it. They can game well enough with their own lives, but not with others', whether they be outlaws or circus performers."

"Eisen, it's sweet, all these notions, but there ain't nothing you kin do. Anyhow, you were going to visit Kindle, aren't ya still? Don't you want to see her?"

"Not anymore."

"Oh, no, don't even start with all your highfalutin nonsense!"

"Nonsense?"

She lowered her voice and drew in close to the rain-soaked man.

"I don't want to see you killed, Eisen."

"Well, if that is the case, then I would appreciate your help – much less of a chance of dying when you have a lookout, isn't there?"

"You are impossible; an impossible man."

"I hope it is clear that that isn't true. Are you going to help me or not?"

"What can you – we – possibly do?"

"There are really only three options that I can think of, only one of which is likely to do any good. Come on!"

He took off suddenly toward the town square, the crowd following him with a hawkish gaze, or as hawkish a gaze as it was possible to maintain in such a gray and bleary atmosphere. Jen, with an utterance of exasperation, quickly took up after him and shortly thereafter caught up beside her errant friend where he slogged through the mud down the middle of the road with the wind at his back. Their cloaks were twining in the turbulent air, vestigial sails from a strange and water-bound time of fins and darkness.

When they were completely out of view of the jail behind Elis Caldwell's lifeless print shop, Eisen scanned the road before them, then backtracked his gaze, making sure that they were well and clear; indeed, they were. He turned upon Jen with haste, his hands gripping her shoulders tightly, tighter than he intended. The wind increased.

"We need to get Kavaria out of there."

Jen was silent, deliberating, making sure the words she heard and the words she thought that she heard were one and the same. She shook her head, backing away from him slightly like a lamp that grows hot to the touch.

"Did you hear me, Jen? We have to get him out."

"That's..."

"No, it isn't."

"Yes, it damn well is. Insane. Mad. It's mad, Eisen, are you actually listening to yourself, to the words you're saying?"

"Jen..."

"He killed our friends, damn it, he killed Daniels and Cruler, Tanners... Henry Collins, so many good people. My father..."

"I know. And if we were in that jail, and there was a mob after us, he would let us hang in the streets; he'd let that mob rip us to pieces, but we aren't him. That's the point."

"I know that, there's nothing to prove. We aren't like him."

"We are, if we let this happen, if we let them kill him."

"Eisen..."

She drew close again, as if pleading with the whole of her body, its movements some secret language, primal and potent; Eisen flinched.

"If you don't want to help me, as you clearly don't, then be on your way."

Anger shone bright as boiling lead in her eyes at his words and their dismissive quality. Her voice rose up, not just above the wind, but by steady degrees above the ceiling of the sky. Notes of fury. Notes of wrath.

"How dare you? Everything, everyone ain't good enough fer ya, are they? No, no one is idealistic enough, they ain't got the conviction to do what is necessary, what is right, what is just or reasonable – but you do, cuz you're a fucking god!"

"Why are you so angry? I'm only trying to do the best that I can, should not everyone, every man, every woman? I'm not begrudging you – but quick with an answer, time is in short supply and the demand is quickening."

She said nothing, shaking her head, tears in her eyes and them torn away by the wind, tiny streams of sadness snaking down to the mud and the filth. She ran off, back toward the tavern, to Arrgilius, to familiar and warm surroundings, to comfort and the unchallenging; herald of the unchallenged.

Eisen watched her go without protest and then turned to Caldwell's shop. No lights were on and the blinds were drawn; he figured he would receive no help there. He walked on like a ghost in a waking nightmare, feeling utterly powerless and tortured with the burden of his perceptions.

In the ancient world, he thought blackly to himself, men threw one another into pits, wild beasts therein, with cheers and gaudy showmanship. And watching the death they had incurred they were glad, bright at heart, for such was the nature of their self-construction and it the architect of their history's weave, and so all others stemming from it. The loom must be broken. Sundered. Rent. For ever and a day. The action beyond any one man – beyond man at all. Were I a god...

So hideous had the weather become that the coffin maker was nearly blown free of his boggy anchorage, his cloak flying up as if to strangle him, as his heart had already begun to strangle itself; choking with the venomous residue of his inaction. He paused abruptly in the middle of the road, in a deep, coffee-colored rut, his heart and mind steeled with the brunt of his duty; unyielding. There he resolved himself and, with great passion, ran through the town square, fast as his legs would carry him, to the back of the jail where he rapped furiously upon the door until an answer greeted his tilted ears in that waterlogged waste.

"No one is budging, so you may as well go back inside. We ain't giving him to ya, much as we'd like to."

"I don't want you to give him to them."

There was a brief intermission, in it only the arrhythmic patter of the rain and its clatter upon the roof of the shabby jail. Eisen watched the water trickle down the worn and peeling paint, stucco and fragmentary, as if it would revel to him some pertinent intention, some willing unclouded. The door opened at length to reveal Karlin Strade wearing a visage of great curiosity.

"What do you think you are doing out here in this?"

The wind was, at this point, so overwhelming that the very words were torn from his mouth and sent spiraling away into mist and rain-marked darkness.

Eisen cocked an ear. "What?"

"I said what are you doing out in this kind of weather, Mr. Torquiam? What do you want?"

"To help."

"Come in."

He did with great pleasure, shivering with the icy damp that had soured his frame. He felt peculiarly vestigial to himself, there in that sheltered space of frenzy and hatred and warmth, as if looking in on his own person through a magnifying lens from some space other than his body. The jail itself and the men within it were almost entirely unchanged from his earlier visit. The only difference was that the door had been barricaded from both sides by, in the front, the sheriff's desk, and in the back, a folding chair placed against the knob at such an angle that it prevented immediate entry.

Before Eisen or Karlin could address each other, one of his men came bounding up from the windows, a little bald man with a strange, croaky voice.

"They're comin in round ta the back. Bastards. What should we do?"

"Nothing. Keep the door barricaded and wait them out. They're probably all bluff to begin with."

Strade stroked his thin, well-kept mustache and reached for a bottle of brandy upon the floor near where the sheriff's desk used to be. He tipped it back and gulped the liquid down like sweet tea, finished with a well satisfied, "Ahhhh."

"The one thing, Mr. Strade, these people are not is bluffing. They will storm this jail."

"Then why the hell are you here?"

Kavaria Kallista burst into a fit of his uncanny, manic laughter, rolling about in his cot like a bitch in heat.

"I kin tell ye – would you like to hear, Mr. Strade? Course ya would. He came ere ta save me, tinks it'll ease his mind, tinks it will, at long last, separate him... from me. But it's all wrong from the start, if he had a brain in his head, which e does, e should let them hang me from the highest tree."

"And I might just give them the green light if ya keep at it like as ya are."

Strade turned to his guest. "Is it true, what he said?"

Eisen looked from face to face to face; the dour, cynical mercenaries, unconcerned with his presence, nervous of the mob, eager for a whiskey, a paycheck. Karlin Strade, consummate professional, disenchanted with his lot, his life, his work, precise but coldly so, vain contempt mingling with the broken blade of justice, reforging ever slowly somewhere in the hot amber of his eyes. Kavaria, still cackling like a madman, his brow caked with sweat and his cell a mess, blankets thrown about and his food tray thrust furiously through the bars, now laying prone upon the floor, and a bloody gash about his skull, a reprimand, a warning, one obviously unheeded. His electric blue eyes leered out from the darkness with singular relish; his teeth shone in the dim light as did his hair, some ordering of the dead wings of crows.

"What are ye gonna do? Usher me out under your arm, put me up in your home? And they call me mad! What silly pictures we paint."

"I'm trying to save your life."

"Why?"

"I thought you knew me – you tell me."

Eisen stood before the bandit's cell, his hands about the cold iron, tightening and growing more taut with every passing moment. His eyes lingered curiously on the man in the darkened cot. It was only now that he realized just how terribly young the outlaw was.

"How old are you, Kavaria?"

"Old enough."

"How old?"

"Why do you care how old I am, it's not like I'll live te see me next birthday, is it? So what's the point?"

"The point is, I want to know. If you are so convinced of your own impending death, then why not tell me?"

"I'm convinced, not concerned. There's a difference."

"There is indeed. Either way it should be all the same to you."

"I'm twenty-seven and a half years old."

"You are younger than me."

"Only in body."

"What do you mean by that?"

"Nothing."

"You meant something."

"It no longer matters. Since I will be dead shortly, I might as well tell you that I am tremendously fond of you, Mr. Torquiam, tremendously fond. And that, though I took great pleasure in slaughtering your friends, one must admit that it was their own fault and not mine – they were trying to kill me. They come into my house, in wonderful style. That little trick was your idea, wasn't it?"

"It was."

"I thought so! Anyhow, they came in under false pretenses, with the firmly set intention of sending me to the dark-cold and silent."

"Only because of your past crimes against them, against their home, their friends."

"Crimes? What crime? There is no moral law, that is why wild animals devour their own children, why floods sweep infants and the infirmed away without compunction, that is why I steal and kill. It is necessary to my condition, to the very ordering of the world."

"Are you saying you don't have a choice?"

"Ha! Everyone has a choice. I have a choice, many, ever-changing menus present themselves to me everyday at every turn, I just ignore them. Just because one kin do something doesn't mean that they should. To live as these people do... it were better I was dead. Far better."

"If that is your wish, then I will leave you."

"Go on then – weren't me who invited you."

"I don't hate you."

"Oh, you don't have ta prove anything ta me."

"Even still."

Strade stepped urgently between them with plain and utter disgust.

"If you are both done holding each other's hands, then kin, one; you shut up; and two; leave?"

Kavaria rose once again, leaning against the bars like a sloppy drunkard and arching a brow disapprovingly, humorously.

"Oh, my dear, Mr. Strade, you have absolutely no thematic sense. This is the end of the first act, my dear man! The curtain is about to fall. You should have a more profound sense of showmanship with these matters, lest you act the cate come your own turn to swing."

"Mr. Torquiam, kin ya please leave us to our work?"

"Yes, I was... just leaving."

He walked out the back door, whence he had come, into the cold wet of the rain and the frenzied outcry of the crowd before him. Someone ran forward and threw a punch. It collided with his brow; everything spun, feeling warm. He collapsed into the soaking dirt with the rain pouring over him like a transparent coffin. Someone else ran behind the man who had struck the coffin maker and kicked at the downed man viciously, then ran up to the half-open door at the back of the jail, screaming. Enraged.

Eisen's pain came secondary to his wonderment; did they even know why they lashed out, or was it now purely instinctual, primal and unending?

A hand reached down to him where he lay in the mud and filth, in the blood and darkened ruts of misshapen earth. The hand of a friend. He grasped the appendage, apparitional in the newly risen moonlight, and allowed himself to be tugged to his feet. He stared into the face of Elis Caldwell for the faintest fraction of a second and then dashed sideways as the mob surged into the jail, a seething mass of hatred and violence erupting to the barking of the priest.

"Today is a day of reckoning! A day of justice – you are its harbingers! You alone! You."

A sudden howl of death-terror.

All faded to black.

Chapter Thirty-Two

Harborage

When Eisen woke it was to the sound of music, flighty and fair; a piano. Keys manipulated in quick, masterful succession and the feeling of warm cotton, wool and bed springs beneath his twisting spine.

He sat upright, ram-rod straight and sweat soaked as if from fever, his eyes wide and searching, his mind fuddled and uncomprehending.

"Where am I?"

"Take your rest – question later."

"I know that voice."

"Of course you do. It's me."

"Tavis?"

"Yes. You made my father's coffin, remember?"

"Of course, forgive my confusion, it's just... my head..."

"Your head won't improve from jostling it around."

"Caldwell?"

"Yes."

"What happened? Where am I?"

Jen Arlington appeared quietly in the doorway, her expression both dour and sympathetic to the wounded coffin maker.

"You're in my father's house... well, my house now, I suppose. It isn't safe in town, especially not for you. Not that it's all that much safer here."

"Kavaria? What happened to him?"

Caldwell looked across the bed to Tavis, then behind him to the doorway and to Jen, as if wondering whether or not such information should be disclosed. At some length the printer spoke, his voice flat but tinged with a subtle degree of sadness. A stillness to the air.

"Dead. Hanged."

"Michael's mob?"

"Of course."

"And what has Ledru done about it?"

Caldwell shook his head.

"What is that supposed to mean?"

"He's dead as well."

"What?"

"Hanged, hung in his own library, right from the chandelier, I saw it all with my own eyes. There was nothing I could have done, there were so many of them."

"Statletter?"

"Hanged beside his friend. This town belongs to Michael now."

Eisen was dead-still a moment. Time seemed to slow, his breath came and went unnoticed like the lives of the men he had failed to save.

"What has happened, has everyone lost their minds? I feel as if I am losing my own. If only I had let Kavaria kill me in the desert, none of this would have happened."

Tavis shook his head, laying a comforting hand upon Eisen's aching shoulder and speaking quietly to the bedridden man.

"Of course it would have... would only have been a matter of time. I knew how it was in the town, all the animosity, the frenzy, the hatred – it was inevitable. There wasn't anything you could have done, there wasn't anything any of us could have done. The people that didn't want it done were too scared of everyone that did, same thing what happens in war, everyone fights for fear of fleeing – ones that flee git shot. Like dogs. Like creatures diseased. Plagued things."

"Is that what you feared?"

"No – I've been away, didn't you know?"

"I had no idea. It isn't in my nature to keep tabs on people I trust."

Caldwell broke in sternly, and his voice was strangely emotional.

"Leave the man to his rest, Tavis, we can bring him up to date when he wakes once more."

"No, I can't sleep now, not even if I wanted to. Thanks for the concern, though."

Caldwell inclined his head suavely.

"Of course. It's been twice now you have willingly gone out to die, and I find myself wondering if you are harboring some kind of death wish; it would certainly seem that way."

"Well," the coffin maker propped himself up to a sitting position, "I can assure you that my only wish at the moment is to get a hearty meal and drink something cold and very strong."

Caldwell smiled faintly. "I'll see what I kin do."

The printer walked out the door, giving Jen a look which Eisen couldn't quite make out, then he was gone.

Jen swiftly moved to her injured guest's bedside, her fiery locks catching the sunlight filtering in through the solitary window and then trailing out behind her like lengths of molten lead. She turned to Tavis suddenly, a weight to her voice as to her movements, some kind of newly discovered mastery.

"Go and see if you cain't find our guest here some vestments."

"What am I, a serf?"

"Just do it."

"All right, all right, jeez, calm down, I'm going, I didn't mean to... I'm going."

He left in a hurry with his collar all cockeyed and his hair all mussed, the patter-clack of his boots fading away, and then nothing for sound but the faint creaking of the house in the weather and somewhere the disarranged calling of a bird.

"I thought he was the man in the relationship?"

"Shut it. You need to rest, not bound all over the place, I know how you git."

"Do you? We hardly know each other."

"I know enough. More than."

"And what do you know, Jen Arlington?"

"That you're the best man I've ever known. Smartest too."

"You're going to make me blush."

"I know it."

She leaned in and kissed him, this time without the prying eyes of the public, more freely, more deeply and more passionately than before.

Holding the young woman to his aching body, Eisen parted from her lips and looked at her, drawing her breath into his own, some soundless placeholder for conversation, all words passing on muted wings, unhindered in their flight. A delightful voyage, one that both of them wished to lose themselves to. So potent and seductive was this energy, so opium-sweet that neither could speak a word.

At length the sound of footfalls in the hallway ended the matter, and both, quite unconsciously, broke away from the other.

Tavis returned with an armful of men's clothing.

"A gift for Your Majesty."

"Thanks, Tavis. You are the sweet song bird of my restoration."

"What?"

"Never mind, thanks for the clothes."

He dressed hurriedly, seeming not to care that two others watched him, pale and unprotected til his new shell had been mounted.

Tavis broke the silence, eyes to the ceiling and arms crossed in embarrassment. "What will you do now?"

"What do you mean?"

"I mean you can't exactly stay around here. I'm sorry if that's too blunt, but–"

"No, I appreciate your honesty. You know this. Don't force shame upon yourself for no good reason or apologize when no one has been wronged. And to be honest in return, I don't know what I shall do now. I don't know what I can."

He paused for a long moment as a long, dark thought began roiling out from the depths of his sleep-stalled mind.

"Gerald?"

Jen laid a hand on his shoulder, looking him in the eye, attempting reassurance, failing utterly.

"Fairson is fine, he'll be fine. He didn't come, remember?"

"Of course I do, that's why I'm concerned. It's just him and those two musicians, all alone... they'll be coming for me, they'll find him there."

"Now, come on Eisen, why would Michael come after you? I know these past few weeks have been, well, awful don't even begin to describe it. But that, what you're saying, sounds to me like paranoia."

"I know it does, but he told me... I don't have time to explain all of this, you have to trust me... or not. I have to go, I need to leave immediately."

"Whoa, take it easy."

"I can't, Tavis. I need to go. I have to get to Fairson before Michael's cronies can."

He leapt from the bed, his whole body trembling with emotion, unconstrained and erratic. He was breathing quite quickly, heavily, and his hands clenched and unclenched furiously as if he were crushing something in them.

"Where is my coat?"

Jen drew up to his side, whispering in muted, urgent tones.

"Eisen, I need to speak to you."

"I have to – where is my coat?"

Tavis rushed off again.

"Eisen, do you forgive me, for leaving you like I did?"

"I will if you will forgive me for being so reckless."

She smiled, finally a gesture of genuine happiness in a realm, that to the coffin maker's mind, had become so steeped in tragic darkness that there could be no glimmer of light, no ray of hope. His heart swelled like a riptide in some far-off sea as he cupped his hand about her chin and tilted her head to one side, kissing her on the cheek.

"Take care. I will return as soon as I can."

"You take care yourself."

He nodded. Nearly at the same moment Tavis returned with his coat and glasses and various oddments.

He finished dressing, the coat no ordinary one, but a vestment of power; battle mail from a long gone time of bloodshed and madness, it the only protection from the violence of the world short of the will inside it.

Then he exited the house, saddled James Daniels' horse and rode off.

☼

When Eisen returned to his lodgings he found Fairson and the two musicians waiting for him, wholly ignorant of the various tragedies which had so recently transpired. Fairson himself sat upon one of the dinner chairs in the green before the front door, his chin cupped in his hands and the whole of his being evidently in deep concentration. The musicians sat on the right-most edge of the porch. The fiddler plucked at his strings with his bow lying silent upon the planks by his side, and the pianist listened with a wide, beautiful smile; a simple, uncomplicated gesture, like the gesture of some concentrated happiness of youth preserved against the ravages of time.

The coffin maker spoke before they had taken notice of him.

"Fairson."

"Eisen. Where on earth have you been? We've had no word from you for nearly two days."

"I know it. There are... things have happened, it isn't safe here, pack your things and I'll explain on the way."

"What? What way? What's going on?"

"Do you trust me?"

"Completely."

"Then continue to do so. Go pack your things and tell the musicians to do the same, we'll leave in... half an hour?"

"All right."

Eisen nodded and rode to his workshop. Dismounting, he rummaged through his toolkits which he kept stacked neatly to the right of the door on a set of thin, wooden shelves which he had built himself. His hunting knife, sheathed and sharp as the tooth of a lion; he tucked it away in his greatcoat's inner breast pocket and then turned.

The snapping of a twig.

Someone approaching.

Footfall after footfall; more than one traveler in the underbrush, in the cool dark of the trees.

The musicians stood, still waiting for their host to address them, confused with his dire, frenzied state and concerned with the sudden noise emanating from the forest. The coffin maker turned to the minstrels with fear in his eyes, command in his voice.

"Get inside and lock the doors, now!"

As they rose to do as he asked, a voice like a thunderclap sung forth from the branches of the nearest tree, sonorous as birdsong and deep as a desert canyon.

"There will be no need for that, my dear brothers and sisters, I am no enemy of yours."

Luce Montferiat stood before the lodge with Kindle at his side, the former dressed in faded hunting attire and the latter all in black, frock and skirt and knee-high dress shoes, as if she had just come from a funeral procession.

"Kindle?"

"Hello, Eisen."

The coffin maker ran forth to embrace her, but she flinched away as if scalded by his very presence, her now luxuriantly combed locks swinging in the hard sunlight and her eyes going suddenly wide and faraway.

"What is it, Kindle?"

"Nothing... it's nothing."

The coffin maker, squinting against the sun, pulled the brim of his hat low over his searching eyes and turned them to the preacher, who stood still and solemn with his pale, spidery hands folded before him as if in mourning.

"What are you doing here?"

"My reasons are several fold. I wanted to let you know, firstly, that it isn't the entire town that is against you. You have many friends, many like minds. But they fear my son. Oh, my dear boy, he does not know how he has sinned."

"Come inside, it's safer that way."

"Thank you. You needn't worry about retribution from Michael for what you said at Ledru's dinner party. Ledru, how my hatred burned for the man, for him, and now, now that he is with the Lord, it is too late to ask for his forgiveness. Oh, what have I done, I can scarce begin to comprehend."

"What did you mean, about me not having to worry? Why?"

"Because," the preacher looked from the coffin maker to the feral girl, her countenance utterly expressionless, and there was profound sadness in his face, "he thinks that there is no greater punishment unto man than the feeling of powerlessness. He has often told me so, often spoke with me of his own feelings of powerlessness and the despair it caused him. He thinks that this is the most severe punishment he can bequeath unto you. The most severe."

When Eisen spoke next it was with great difficulty, for there were tears in his eyes, and his words came with much stammering and hesitation.

"Then h-he... would be r-right."

Neither Luce nor Kindle said a word as the musicians came up behind their host with looks of worry, concern and confusion. The fiddler spoke first. "Is everything all right, Mr. Torquiam?"

"Everything all right? What kind of ridiculous question is that? Everything all right, ha!"

Everyone turned to the latter speaker who stood at the edge of the forest to the right of Luce Montferiat, suckling at a bottle of whiskey as if it were some elixir of life; knocking it back as if it were nothing more than a glass of orange juice.

Eisen was first to address the newcomer.

"Logan? Peter Logan?"

"The one and only, in the flesh and so on and so forth. Fuckin bottle's almost empty... fuckin bottle's..."

Luce queried next. "Is everything secure, Logan?"

"Yeah. No one's trailing anybody, you're good. You're all good. It's fine... all just fine and... fucking dandy."

"I have advised you to stop drinking. Why don't you listen, my son?"

"Perhaps, Mr. Montferiat, becuz I aint ya son; secondly, perhaps cuz I like my whiskey like I like my women, cheap and readily available."

The preacher assumed a horrified visage and looked back to the musicians and their host and the softly drifting clouds overhead.

Eisen broke in with a long, regal gesture toward his lodgings.

"Why doesn't everyone come inside, we can all talk inside."

The fiddler broke in, his brow as furrowed as a newly sown field. "What's going on?"

Eisen spoke without turning to face the man, his voice low and heavy with what curled like a venomous snake in the great hollow of his chest.

"I'll explain everything later, Mr. Arkin. I'm going inside."

Without another word he walked up the slight incline of the green and soft to the house, leaving the door open behind him. His heart was racing, and he reached up to his brow, realizing that he was sweating profusely. He went to the kitchen and poured himself a glass of water from the pump, then drank it all at once and bent down, searching for a towel to dry his gleaming brow. He heard the footsteps of his friends upon the lawn, trampling grass as easily as Michael had tread upon his life.

Maliciously.

Irrevocably.

Utterly.

Standing with all his force he slammed his fist down upon the kitchen sink with a furious bellow. "Where are all the damn towels!"

A pile of freshly washed dishes was stacked in a neat, trim row along the edge of the counter. He gave a grunt and dashed them to the floor and then spun to the doorway where all eyes gazed on apprehensively.

Eisen watched them watching him a moment and then bent, as if to pick up the shattered pieces. But at the last moment, he decided against it and kicked them aside instead, trudging into the living room and sitting down heavily in one of the spindly wooden dining chairs.

Outside the watchers began, very slowly, to file into the living room, the last, Logan, shutting the door quietly behind him, bottle in hand.

Eisen looked up at them, each face and form before him, then nodded as if in response to some well-posed question.

"Make yourselves at home, it's getting dark and it's a long walk back. You can stay the night if you like, preacher, you and Kindle. We don't have any beds, though, I hope you won't mind."

Luce shook his head faintly.

"No. I don't mind. I appreciate your hospitality. The reason I came was to tell you that Chester Chesney was able to get away when the riot was going on at Ledru's manor. Some of the oilmen fought Michael's men, but most joined in. Anyhow, Chesney, Karlin Strade and a few of Strade's men were able to escape. Strade rode back and found me, told me that Chesney and him were going for a magistrate to sort the matter, and I told him that he had my full cooperation. But I said that truth be told, there was nothing much I could do, and he said that this was so. There was nothing I could do. And there is nothing you can do either, Eisen. Leave. Leave this place. When Chesney returns, he will not return alone; and when he does, I fear there will be yet another bloodbath to soak sanguine the stones of this town. You, none of you, should be around for that."

"He is a good man, you don't think he is, but he is a good man."

They all turned their attention to Kindle who had wandered to the opposite end of the room, leaning against the kitchen doorjamb, looking off at a spider scurrying about the rafters.

Logan scoffed and set his empty bottle down on the floor adjacent the doorway as Eisen queried from the table.

"You don't mean Michael, do you?"

"Yes. Michael. He's a good man. Like you."

"Kavaria was like me, but I am nothing like Michael. Neither of them have proven themselves particularly just."

Luce, with furrowed brow and uneven steps, walked forward and bent to the coffin maker, incredulous.

"Like Kavaria? What on earth do you mean?"

"Precisely what I say. It is of no consequence to you. You ask me to leave – will you?"

The preacher nodded, "That's why I brought Kindle."

Kindle looked to the preacher with a harshness that ill suited her pale and innocent face, then spoke to Eisen, addressing both.

"I'm not leaving Michael. I'm not leaving you."

"Then why did you come?"

"To see you."

"Does Michael know you've left?"

"Yes. Luce told him we were taking an evening stroll in the forest together. And we did, but I only went because I wanted to see you. I missed you. I know it hasn't been that long, only a couple of weeks, but I've missed you anyways. Strange how a couple of weeks can feel like months. "

Luce turned to her sharply, his voice reprimanding and harsh.

"You little fool, think what you're saying? You must leave, you must! Michael thinks you are some kind of miracle, you will only... fuel his delusions! He's going mad, can't you see! You stupid little fool!"

Kindle pushed off the doorjamb, furious, her eyes wild as any woodland beast and her voice suddenly spiking up, shrill and hysterical.

"He protected me! He protected me from your flock; a fitting word, that's all they were, sheep, empty vessels! Nothings! They said I was cursed and cursed me likewise for it, it was only him that protected me, only him, not you! All you did was talk!"

"I tried!"

"And you failed!"

Eisen rose, knocking his chair out from underneath him and sending it clattering to the floor, his voice erupting out of his throat and slamming about the balks.

"Enough! Both of you. Calm down."

Belatedly they obeyed this command. Luce began heading for the doorway, stopping once and looking back to Kindle.

"Your mind is your own. So is your choice, but if you don't come with me, he will find you. If he does, if he discovers that you are staying here, with Eisen, I don't know what he will do to you, and by God I promise you'll not want to find out."

With that the preacher left and vanished into the forest. All the party remaining watched him as he went, save for Logan, who had taken to the floor at the base of the staircase, his legs crossed under him and a new bottle glued to his lips. His throat swelled with the thick golden liquid; chug-chug and the gasp of refreshment. He threw his free arm limply in the direction the preacher had departed, scowling childishly and flapping his lips about like an angry infant.

"Pah, let him go, wasn't no fun anyhow. He's mister higher than thou, better than thee, you're all shit in a shotgun shack to him, me most of all. So let him go. Pah!"

"You're terribly drunk, Logan."

Logan turned to the coffin maker with a wily grin, a flash of large, white teeth.

"Terribly drunk or wonderfully drunk?"

"I'm inclined to think that you're inclined to think the latter."

"Right'ho!"

At that moment Eisen rose and Fairson, fully packed and ready to depart, descended the stairs, determination writ large upon his visage. He paused to observed a rummy Peter Logan waving with obscene relish in his direction up the short flight, smiling like a fool and humming to himself some nonsense tune.

"Fairson, we have company–"

"What about leaving?"

"We'll delay our departure for the time being, if that's all right with you."

"You're beginning to worry me but... if you're sure?"

"I'm sure."

"All right."

"Would you help me lead our dear, inebriated friend, Mr. Logan, upstairs."

"Onto one of the bedrolls?"

"No, I was thinking you could sling him in the closet."

"You and your sarcasm. I just don't know sometimes."

The fiddler leapt forward, offering his assistance. Logan gladly took hold of his shoulder and allowed himself to be half carried up the stairs, leaning heavily against the impressively resilient little musician the entire way, protesting that he, "Didn't need no damned help," and that he was, "Fit as a fucking fiddle."

As Fairson and Logan reached the landing, Eisen walked to his kitchen where the dining table had been moved, dragging his chair along behind him. He set it down, leaning with his head in hands, thinking, and his every waking thought a torment, needle sharp and white-metal hot.

The pianist stretched up to the cabinet drawer above the sink and produced something that clinked and sloshed and shimmered, then she sat down beside her host, fastidious and courtly. She took two glasses from the sink, two of five which Eisen had failed to destroy with his rage, and set the glasses down upon the table nonchalantly, as if it were any other day, any other time and him an old friend. She poured his glass first, then her own. Finally he looked up and realized what the sloshing thing was. A bottle of vodka.

"Will you be joining me, Mr. Torquiam, or will I be drinking alone tonight?"

"I had better not."

"Why not?"

"There's so much to do–"

"No, there is so much to worry about, very little for you to do, aside from relax. I've seen men that had the same problem as you many times before, course they weren't anything like you, save for their problem."

"Which would be?"

"You're incapable of letting go, of yourself, of a situation, regardless of what it is; what it will do, to you, or to others. You can't always win."

"I was almost about to say that it wasn't a game... but that's something he taught me, something true. Everything is a game, there is always a winner, always a loser, rarely, very rarely, there is a draw, but only for a short time. Truce never lasts."

Kindle drew near to the table, something wary still in her face, her movements. But to the coffin maker's perceptions she seemed to have mellowed somewhat, perhaps remembering when first she arrived at the ramshackle place in a time that seemed ancestral to her loose and faulted reckoning.

"Who is he?"

She asked the question so quietly that Eisen had to ask her to repeat the question.

"Kavaria. Kavaria Kallista."

"He was an evil man."

"But great."

The pianist looked on with confusion.

"Are you talking about the bandit, Mr. Torquiam, the one from the desert?"

"Yes."

"And you consider a rank and file desperado to be, what? A great man? That's ridiculous."

Eisen leaned forward upon the table, inhaling, as the sonorous scraping of cloth patches and sanded wood rose up to the listening ears. Smell of alcohol. Scent of women. Perfume. Expensive. He picked up the little glass and raised it to his lips, now slightly parted and spoke.

"Good men and great men, are seldom one and the same."

He downed the shot in one fluid motion and then sat, looking in folds of deepening awareness across the pianist's pleasantly rounded face. There was the faint line of a scar than ran from the base of her right ear to the middle of her neck and two others, fainter still, duosecting it, like some macabre hieroglyph. Some after-trace of blood ritual and sacrament; narrative placenta. In a flickering motion, the pianist's free hand flew to her neck, guarding the pain incarnate vestige of her past.

"It's all right. I won't ask."

"Thank you."

"Don't trouble yourself."

"Yes, you've made it your job to be troubled for all those that don't do it themselves. Can scarcely imagine I'm lightening your burden acting so defensively."

He shook his head and slid the bottle toward Kindle where she slouched in the close, right corner, near the sink, the counter, the table. He kicked out the empty chair at the head of the table as if it were a mooching cur and then poured himself another glass.

"Will you be joining us, Kindle?"

She was silent for a moment that seemed dreadfully long, then, with expansive deliberation, nodded slowly and took a seat; averting her eyes to the pitted and water-stained table. Some sense of shame in her form, the drowning of her eyes in the depths of the wood grain tabletop; something that was frighteningly familiar to all present. A muted horror. Urban and ingratiating, more befitting a bleak and windswept moor, full with meretricious moonlight, than some hasty assemblage of wood and glue and force.

They all ignored this aberration and instead turned to conversation once again.

"How has it been, with Michael, with Luce? Staying in the church and with the people there. You said they cursed you."

"Yes. They hated me. They told me I was possessed by demons. First they asked me to leave, then they demanded it, then they came at me, all of a sudden one day, seven of them. It was Michael who stepped in to defend me. Luce was just standing in the corner, watching like it was nothing but a sunset. Oh he was concerned, but that was all. Well, Michael, he took me up to his quarters and told me he'd fix everything. He went downstairs for about two hours, and when he came back he was smiling; said everything was fixed. And it was. So you see, he's a good man."

"One kind act doesn't make a person what he or she is."

"It's part."

"I think Kindle's right, Mr. Torquiam, I think it matters."

"Of course it matters. But Michael is... this killing... it has to stop."

"Another glass?"

"Yes. Thank you, Severine."

"At your service. I'd better be since it's only because of you that I have any place to go at all. I mean, I could always stay with Ledru, since I know he'd let me back–"

"He's dead."

"Wha–"

"Hanged. In his house from the library chandelier. Michael's handiwork."

"No, that's impossible."

"Oh, it's quite possible, Kindle. Where were you when all this madness was going on?"

"In the church. He told me to stay there, to be quiet, to have faith in him. I did."

"You had faith in a man who said he was going off to kill?"

"I didn't know what he was going to do! How could I? He told me nothing about it! Sometimes things just happen!"

"All right, I'm sorry, Kindle. I'm not thinking straight. With each passing day, every passing cataclysm, I find it harder and harder to do so. This town, this situation..."

The pianist leaned forward, pouring herself another drink, then the coffin maker and Kindle in equal measures.

"What we need, Kindle, Mr. Torquiam, is a little bit of revelry."

"At such a time, Ms. Voanstrig?"

"At what point could it be more fitting? I have to use the outhouse, you both better be here and not off gloaming together when I get back. Promise?"

Eisen shook his head, chuckling to himself.

"As you wish."

"Promise."

"Fine. I promise."

Ms. Voanstrig smiled and hurried out the back door behind the kitchen, dissipating into the long, breezy dark; forest bird calls lauding her departure.

As soon as the pianist had gone Kindle placed both her hands across the table, upon Eisen's, looking him pleadingly in the eye.

"I'm sorry."

"Don't start that."

"I'm sorry, I shouldn't have drawn away from you."

"I shouldn't..."

"Yes, you should have."

"Don't talk like that."

"If I didn't talk like that, I'd still think it."

"So don't think like it. It's Michael that should be asking for forgiveness."

"And would you give it to him?"

"I don't know," he moved toward her slightly over the top of the table, grasping her hands as she had his, warmly, lovingly, "but what I do know is that I give it to you."

She seemed so stunned with this revelation that she nearly cried. Her eyes glistening in the dim light looked to the coffin maker like a kind of blue that had never before been, perhaps never again to be. She bent and kissed the back of his left hand and then released his digits, untangling them from her own. There was a sudden conviction in her movements, as if his presence had somehow fortified her.

"You haven't touched your drink, Kindle."

"No."

"You once told me you weren't afraid of anything. You weren't lying were you?"

"You challenging me?"

"Maybe, pest."

"Scaredy cat."

By the time Voanstrig returned to the table, Eisen and Kindle were drunk as sailors on shore leave, laughing wildly and dancing about the living room arm in arm.

The fiddler sat upon the steps and rustled up a jolly, scatterbrained tune with his rosined bow; his brows pulled tight like as the corners of his mouth in equal measures mirth and meditation.

Fairson sat two steps above the fiddler, clapping along and smiling broadly, apparently quite drunk as well.

Moments later Logan shambled down from the landing. He was scowling, looking deadly serious.

The fiddler stopped and all faces turned.

"What is this?"

"J-just a bit of music and dance."

Logan loomed above the fiddler, still scowling.

"And no one invited me?"

Slowly the fiddler smiled like as every other face.

Eisen called out from the dance floor.

"Consider yourself a last-minute reservation!"

With a laugh Logan swirled down the steps like a dancer and took up the fiddle and bow himself, strumming a mighty jig.

Arkin cheered on and Fairson moved out to the dance floor, taking the pianist by her delicate hands and twirling her about.

Long into the night was the sound of their merrymaking, the stamping of feet upon the shuddering floor and their shrill, slurring voices flying up, spirited about the baulk and shadow; some song half remembered and half birthed from their bottles.

Everyone was embraced and laughed with the others, all voices turning in a tumult of loose direction, the direction of exemption from their pain.

They danced until they fell exhausted and sweating to the floor, still laughing, holding their friendship to their hearts like shimmering anthems of that happiness which they had lost upon the soil of their own lands, alone and disenfranchised.

More bottles were broken out and poured, all glasses filled. And after some interval upon the floor, stories shared and newly created, they rose and again Logan took up the bow for their flighty feet. He cried as he played, saliently and with profound emotion, tears for what or who none knew. When asked, he would only reply, "For all that I've never had, I see it."

The fiddler vanished into the kitchen and returned with an empty coffee can, the duo's newest instrument, a primal drum; and how he played it. It was passed back and forth between the fiddler, the pianist. Kindle even took her own turn and was hailed as the best among them in its sonorous manipulation.

They danced and played and sang all through the night and long into the morning until they fell, one by one, to the sneaking specter of sleep. There they stretched upon the floor, folded over each other like some tatterdemalion family of the road.

Chapter Thirty-Three

Undeath of the Djinn

In the morning Eisen and Voanstrig cooked breakfast and all ate with relish. Afterward Eisen invited Kindle and Fairson on a walk, saying only that he wished to speak with them in private. They both agreed and left into the cold morning light, heading north into the forest, into the mountains, where the soft soil gave way to clay and stone and strange minerals. They paused in a clearing five miles up the hill-land wood. The sun was fat and warm, and soft light careened like spectral spears between the puzzle pieces of the sky under that verdant canopy.

Eisen explained the whole situation to them, some of which each already knew, the other half the completion of their aggregate worry. He told of how Michael had sworn to destroy him, how he had took insult to the coffin maker's ideas, his lack of faith, his very nature. He told of Kavaria and their myriad conversations and of Chesney and his ire, of Monteblanc and Statletter and his friendship and contention with them. And he told of all that weighed heavily upon his heart, and his friends listened with kind solemnity, offering no words, only attentions.

Afterward they talked amongst themselves, offering opinions, suggestions, telling stories of brighter times. They walked leisurely and arrived back at the outskirts of the coffin maker's lodge.

There occurred then a stillness; the wind died down, the birds ceased to call, and the only sounds which remained were the creaking pillars of the pine and oak, old and weathered and looming. Dark shadows all about, pitted and bleeding with luminance. Footsteps clacking, and the crush of leaves under the plodding of soles.

Then a great explosion of noise, so sudden and startling that the trio could, at first, hardly comprehend its nature. Eisen was the first to discern its quality.

Gunshot.

They ran back down the slight incline of pine-covered ground which lead down to the flat expanse of green upon which the lodge rested. They moved cautiously, careful to make as little noise as possible. They emerged from the thick forest upon the northern-most side of the cabin, facing a corner of the building. Nearly at the opposite end of the clearing, that closest to the town, a small group of dire-eyed men stood, as if in terrible wait. All carried double shotguns or hunting rifles.

Eisen motioned for his companions to get behind the nearest tree as quickly as possible. He moved silently to the back of the house, neath the large rear windows. Looking in, he discovered that the musicians and Logan had risen from the dining room table, and the fiddler had ran to the windows and then back to tell of the intruders. Logan seemed amused and otherwise unconcerned. The musicians shared looks of fright and deep apprehension, speaking quickly and apparently in raised tones, for Eisen could hear a muffed murmur behind the glass. He rapped upon the pane, hurriedly, deadly urgency in every carefully restrained knock. Logan was the first to notice and instantly leapt for the window, speaking under his rum-laden breath.

"Where do you keep your guns?"

"I haven't any guns. We just got back, why are they shooting?"

"They want you, you and Kindle. I know most of them, a few are oilmen, came in only a month or so ago off the continent. But the other two, they're good men, mostly, I doubt their bite is worse than their bark."

"I do hope you are right."

"What do you mean? You get out of here, it's not safe."

"I'm not running. This is my home."

"I don't think they give a rat's ass whose house it is. They could get rough, there ain't much point in taking chances."

"Of course there is. Call through the window for Kindle and Fairson to come in, they're over there behind that cluster of trees. If Kindle wants to leave, let her."

Logan nodded gravely. Eisen then inhaled deeply and adjusted his greatcoat and set forth from the window, walking close to the walls of the house, around the back, turning the corner and following it till he emerged around the front doorway. The hunters spied him instantly.

"Eisen de Torquiam."

The man at the fore of the group was Stockholme Johnson, friend of the late James Daniels. He alone seemed without anger amongst those predatory faces. The hunters were five in number, three were oil workers whom Eisen had seen briefly in his sojourns to Arrgilius' tavern, the other two were Johnson and a man he had seen with him once or twice.

"Firing shotguns into the air in front of my house is about the least hospitable way to garner my attentions, Johnson."

"But we've got it, ain't we? Now, where is the girl?"

"What do you think this is? A dime novel? I'm not going to allow you to burst upon my home and strong arm me into telling you this and that and the other thing."

"Where is Kindle?"

"She's a grown woman, she can be where she likes. Frankly, I'm not very fond of that tone you're taking with me, Mr. Johnson. Are you aware of that?"

One of the oilmen spoke up viciously, spittle hurling in wide white arcs from his crinkled, bluish mouth.

"We don't give one flying fuck what you think of our god damned tone, outsider. Now you tell us where Kindle is, or we'll be putting you in one of them caskets ya'll so fond of making."

"As far as threats go, it's a little lengthy, isn't it? A bit... taxing."

Johnson addressed him again, taking a pleading tone and stepping forward with his gun lowered and his muscles relaxed.

"Look, I know this isn't easy for you, hasn't been since ye arrived. I was part of the reason why. But you've done me no harm, don't make us do you any. We know you've got the girl."

"She's a woman, not a little girl."

"Beg pardon, but this is about the least important of the details, I think ye'd agree wit me on it. Just turn her over ta us and we'll be off."

"Did Michael send you, or have you taken this upon yourself, so as to garner the new king's good graces?"

"You don't know what you're taking about."

"I know enough. I know Daniels would be ashamed."

"Don't you even–"

"What? Speak honestly? I got to know the man, better I think, than you ever knew him."

"You're trying to wind me up, boy – I'll tell ya that ain't wise."

"I'm fed up with being threatened."

The furious oilman who had spoken earlier raised his shotgun to the coffin maker's head, his brows raised challengingly. He had broken into a sweat and his hands trembled upon the shooting iron.

"Well that's all well and good, cuz I'm damn well tired of threatening! Now you bring the bitch out or I swear to god..."

"Just put it down and walk away. Johnson, keep your dog on its leash before he hurts himself."

"You little shit, you fucking little shit."

Rather abruptly there was another gunshot, and the oilman's head exploded in a gush of blood and gore, bits of brain and fragments of bone scattering to the wind. His eyes rolled up like pool-cued eight balls, white and lifeless and unseeing; body falling and dead before it hit the ground.

The party jumped back from this horror, sucking the sweet fall air into their fast flexing lungs and going pale with the serpent of fear, there coiling its endless bulk about their frantic-numb and heat-soaked minds.

Directly to the Johnson party's left, at the edge of the clearing, stood an utter impossibility, the face of laughing into death and rising from its fathomless depths.

There stood Kavaria Kallista, discernible to the coffin maker's keen perceptions despite a ragged checked scarf covering the lower half of his face. The dreadful apparition wore a long duster of pure, untainted white, tipped at the collar with black fur, no shirt underneath. His pants were of pale gray serge and bore all the hallmarks of long and arduous travel, like as his heavy black cavalry boots.

Almost before the other men could discern his figure, the shadow-phantasm aimed and re-opened fire, a bullet in every chosen skull.

Gunshot howls and the screams of the dying the harbingers of little rose petals of red and hot-wet spurting from skin and cloth and showering the green like spilled paint. Bodies falling, heavy-hard, then motionless.

After the smoke cleared only Johnson stood unscathed, the last vestige of that grievous party, his free hand raised slowly and trembling with terror; his eyes wide and wild and his chest heaving with the strain of his situation.

Eisen looked on with uncomprehending perplexity, mouth agape and his frame frozen as if by some slithering length of ethereal chain.

The apparition of Kallista turned to the coffin maker with grotesque glee shining about his eyes as the infernal lamps of some demonic king.

"What say ye, Eisen? Shall I kill him, or shall I not? Ye kin decide. Cain't ye?"

Johnson met the coffin maker's gaze, their movements of such profound unity that the whole of it seemed orchestrated by some unseen hand. So pathetically imploring was the look in Johnson's eyes that Eisen averted his regard, lest he should be tempted to act upon his sudden, abominable impulse.

"No."

The coffin maker outstretched his arm to the undead outlaw.

"Don't shoot."

Kavaria nodded and began walking toward the trembling foreman as the latter stuttered out a pathetic query, practically folding and falling within himself with every uttered syllable.

"W-h-ho are y-you?"

Kavaria walked up the man, now within arm's length, and sized him up with flighty humor. Then he removed his scarf and tilted his head upward with an unspeakable grin. Upon his neck was a great and ragged scar, raw and unhealed, red with congealing blood and purple-blue with strain, the remnants of dread and deathly ritual.

"K-ka-v-varia?"

"Oh splendid! You recognize me! Isn't that wonderful, Eisen? He recognizes me. I'm flattered."

"No... don't–"

"Don't what? Shoot you? Why should I shoot? Twas you what tied the rope, you what slid the noose round me neck. Most importantly twas you what checked that I was dead. Not your best hour, mate, t'must say. Sides, he told me not ta shoot."

Kavaria, with a showy flourish, holstered his dueling pistols and patted the man upon the shoulder warmly.

"T'was you what checked that I twere dead. Thanks for that."

Then the outlaw drew a dagger from his belt and drove it into the man's chest, piercing flesh, bone and heart and twisting it home.

There was a ghastly spurt of blood as the man gasped and flailed backward, tripping upon the corpse of one of his fallen friends, arms wind-milling wildly at his sides, grasping at something, anything, nothing. Screaming. He shuddered twice, coughed blood and then lay still. Evermore. The whole of the world dying in the flickering reflection of his dull and glassy eyes.

Kavaria turned with theatrical hilarity, hands up-risen and shoulders shrugging, a smile on his face.

"Opposite day."

Then he laughed, clutching at his belly and throwing his head backward.

Eisen howled and let off at the bandit where he stood in his gory longcoat, hair dancing in the wind. Their bodies connected with savage velocity and went spinning down to the hard, green ground in a whirl of fists and blood and primal grunting.

Kavaria, through a massive exertion of power, was able to throw the lighter man off of him. Both rose to crouching positions, bent to attack, ferine.

Kavaria held up his hands, still grinning.

"Whoah there, boyo, easy now. I just saved your life. Downright ungrateful."

He rose and primly dusted himself off, then looked down at the blood upon his coat as if it were some sneaky kitchen stain and grimaced.

"I just stole this coat, too. What a shame. Just when you get something new..."

"You didn't have to kill him!"

"Course I didn't. He didn't have to threaten you, but he did. Could have, would have, should have – you're living in the past, boyo. Sides, I didn't shoot him. Should count fer som'tin."

"Get out of here. Now."

"And go where? I'm a very wanted man, ya know. Least I used to be."

"Exactly. Now that everyone thinks you're dead, no one will be looking for you."

"Yeah, but those dead men are gonna attract some eyes, unfriendly ones I'd wager. No, no, now you need me, so here's how it's going to work. I'm your man, if you put me up for lodgings. Come hell or high water."

"No."

"Come on. Ya haven't really got a choice."

"Yes, I have. I can tell them it wasn't me, or I can bury them myself."

"And how do you suppose Michael is going to react to that? Dead or disappeared, they're still his men. I heard the talk, in the jail, from rumors before that meddler Strade caught me. I know what the young little vicar thinks of you, not a flower in his rose garden! So when you say, "It wasn't me," he's going to do fer you like as he did for me. Perhaps more."

The outlaw rubbed his horribly mangled throat obsessively.

"So what's your answer?"

"You had better be gone when I get back."

"Oh?"

Eisen whirled about and discovered that Peter Logan, pistol in hand, stood indecisively at the doorway, some sort of powerful meditation in his face, in the stillness of his pose.

Logan took Eisen by the arm before he could pass.

"He's right. Once Michael realizes that his men have disappeared, he'll blame it on you. It's the perfect excuse for him to bring half of the town down on you with rifles and hunting knives."

"That may be so, but I'll not have him here."

"We can't stay here."

"Of course we can't. But I can."

"That's suicide and you know it."

"You could be right. But this is my home. I'll not let them take that from me."

"That kind of stubbornness is what gets people killed."

"I'll not argue over it. Now, you know the Arlington ranch?"

"Everyone does."

"Jen is there, waiting for me, tell her–"

"You tell her whatever it is yourself. I ain't helping you ta kill yourself."

"Damn you then."

Eisen went into the house where the musicians, Kindle and Fairson stood warily, relaxing fractionally as they realized who it was that had come in upon them.

"Fairson, are you still packed?"

He nodded.

"Then take Kindle and get out of here."

The fiddler interrupted with much stuttering and gesticulation.

"W-who w-were those m-men... w-h-ha... w-what is g-going on-n?"

"You have no time to hear it. You all need to get out of here and as far away from the town as possible. Now go. I said GO!"

Fairson nodded again and ran up the stairs as the fiddler and Ms. Voanstrig followed with forced determination, their frames shaking with fright. There was no conversation between the three, no discussion. They moved and acted as most often the fearful do – without question.

Kindle moved to stand before Eisen with forceful resolution; a mirror of his own fire.

"I heard."

"And?"

"I'm staying with you."

"That's your choice then."

"You're not going to tell me to go?"

"I could see in the eyes of everyone the fear of staying, everyone but you, so, no. Do what you will. Just know that things will become very dangerous, and I worry they will become so very soon."

"Michael won't hurt you while I am here."

"He's already hurt me more than he knows. Perhaps that is fitting, I've done likewise."

"What about the djinn?"

"Djinn? Do you mean Kavaria?"

"Yes. The people in the town, that's what they call him, a djinn, whatever that is."

"He wants to stay here. I have an inkling he wants me to... no, there's no point in talking about it."

"He wants you to help him kill Michael, doesn't he?"

"Why do you think that?"

"I just do. Does he?"

"I think so."

"But you won't help him."

Eisen did not answer. He looked away from her.

"You won't, right? Eisen! Answer me!"

"If it comes to it."

"What is that supposed to mean?"

"I mean, if it comes to it. You should go with the rest of them. Leave. Be free of this."

"No."

"You could be killed. I don't want to see you in such a situation. You are... precious to me."

"And would I be more precious if I were a coward?"

Eisen gave a humorless laugh. "No, I suppose not. Nor do I suppose I can argue with you about it."

"No."

"You're a remarkable woman, Kindle."

The trio returned, fully primed for the journey ahead and left quickly at Eisen's urging. Fairson embraced his lover tightly and kissed him upon the cheek before he departed.

Eisen watched them go, turning a wide, wary circle around the corpses and their creator and vanishing into the dark, green dance of the forest. The coffin maker returned to the lawn and addressed Logan, who stood staring down Kavaria, who seemed wholesomely amused by such an overt display of mistrust.

"Aren't you leaving, Logan?"

"I don't know or much care what you consider me to be, but I want you to know that I hold you as a friend. I don't turn my back on my friends, even if they want me to."

"Then I don't suppose there is more to say."

"No, I don't suppose."

Kavaria turned to the forest and then to the men.

"This is good, very...ha...thematic. Shall ye help me with the bodies?"

They carried out the deed efficiently, without ceremony, and buried the cadavers in the deep woods far to the north of the lodge.

When the corpses had all been interred and the sun had antiqued its selfsame apex, the men looked at the teeming, shadow-colored dirt and the uprooted mushrooms and grass and the little beasts within. There was, upon that multitudinous mound, no marker nor signage of any sort, the final place of those men's unavailing absolution. There was no resting place, for there was no rest for the dead, no peace and no justice; there never was, nor ever to be.

After it was done Eisen turned to the outlaw coldly and curiously. "How did you survive?"

"Dogma, it's a funny thing."

"What do you mean?"

"When I t'was dangling, nearly unconscious wit it all and assumed dead, d'hey wanted te put a bullet in me brain, just ta make sure, as it were. But Michael, standing in front of um, all commanding like, strikes up a righteous cord and starts booming, saying, 'There will be no desecration here, save that which The Lord hath ordained. He has given you no sanction, disperse and go about your affairs, for I shall not suffer the desecration of the dead!' And dhey fuckin did! Bloody hilarious. Anyhow, the rope was a flimsy ole thing, and it gave way shortly after they left, and me, well, dropped straight down like a sack 'o feed. Bunch a amateurs... who hangs a man what sees dhat his neck ain't broke and then just leave. Anyhow, that's more or less the tale, so here I be."

"And the clothes, the guns?"

"Some faggy fop I found wandering about the woods, friend of Chesney's separated from him during the riot."

"Did you kill him as well?"

"Course not. No, I just broke his arm was all. Say – that mask, the one ye'er wearing about ye'r hip, where didja git it from? Seems familiar somehow."

"From a late friend," said Eisen.

"I absolutely covet it. Tell ya what, you give me the mask and I'm your man."

"Meaning, what exactly?"

"I'll do like as you please from here til safety. Anything you say – good as done."

"So, if I tell you to stop, you'll stop."

"I would, but you won't."

"But you would?"

"Yes."

"And you promise?"

Logan snorted in disgust, drunk once again from a flask of whiskey he brought with him upon their grim sojourn.

"What do promises mean to men like him?"

"I suppose we shall see. Do you swear by all that you have said, Kallista?"

"Cross me heart – I promise."

"Then take it. Weight it in your hands as I weight your convictions."

He unstrapped the macabre, bone-colored mask from his belt and handed it off to the bandit.

Kallista snatched it up eagerly, grinning from ear to ear, a slight faltering as he discerned the gift-giver's intensity, but then the taker straightened up, and all was well.

Eisen walked off into the gloom as Kavaria raised the mask to his face, looking out to the innumerable bark-walled corridors, something appearing in the far haze of his surrounded eyes. He pulled back, thrusting the mask clean off his face and looking again.

Logan turned to him bemused, but still cautiously perceptive.

"What was it?"

"I thought I saw a wolf."

☼

Once and only once did Logan again beseech the coffin maker to reconsider his stubbornness. Eisen replied only that he "Had to see it through." Neither of them said anything further on the matter, progressing in utter silence.

The three men sat around the dining table, which they had dragged back into the sparse living room, playing cards and drinking. When Logan had first proposed the idea, the coffin maker had been irate and disgusted. Games! And at such a time, he had snarled, but then he remembered his own words concerning games, his own words and Kallista's. He thought on them and then decided that so long as the three of them were to be cooped up, awaiting their judgment by minds unfit to deal it, they might as well have some fun.

That fun, however, was not to be had.

For on every game would Kavaria emerge the victor, and by some great length, this continued so consistently that finally Logan decided that the bandit was cheating and leapt from his chair red faced, clumsy and shouting.

"You litta whoreson! We ain't even playing for money and yet, and yet you still hav'ta cheat!"

"I'm not cheating and you're drunk. Hardly the ideal state to be making such outlandish statements."

"That's as may be, but it don't change the facts, do it?"

"I already told you I'm not cheating."

"The hell ya ain't! On your feet, let's have it from ya."

With that Logan threw up his fists in the most ridiculous of fashions, looking to all the world like an old-timing fisticuffs pastiche; some melodramatic, mustached ecthing from long-yellowed magazines.

"All right, but ye asked fer it, remember that, boyo."

Eisen leaned across the table sternly.

"Sit down, Kavaria."

"What?"

"I said sit. Down."

"Oh, you are getting large, ain't ye! I made a promise – weight my convictions then, like as ya said."

The outlaw resumed his seat, crossing his arms and looking from a still-seething Logan to Eisen, where he sat composedly.

Eisen motioned to the chair across from him imploringly.

With great hesitance and pride-swallowing, Logan sat down, looking to no one, falling only further into his bottle and his grim meditations.

Around an hour later Logan lay face down on the table in a little pool of spittle and booze, snoring loudly.

It was Eisen's turn; he dealt a winning hand at which Kavaria gave a start and then furious applause.

Around midnight, after they had woken Logan and him going up the stairs to sleep, they discerned a shambling figure through the front windows, moving toward them from the woods.

Luce Montferiat.

His dark blue suit had one of the sleeves torn off and the collar horribly mangled. He was wide eyed, huffing and sweating profusely, his figure moving awkwardly, clumsily and vacantly, like a somnambulist. The puffy, frightful man practically fell against the door, slumping his wide, withering hands against the frame rather than knocking.

Eisen opened the door almost instantly, bracing the large man to keep him from collapsing to the floor, with fear or exhaustion, or both.

"Luce, what are you doing here? What has happened?"

"It was Michael. He tried to kill me!"

"Why?"

But before the preacher could answer, he saw Kavaria lounging on the corner of the dining table in the middle of the room, one foot resting upon Logan's former chair and the other dangling childishly to and fro.

"You! N-no... this can't be – you're dead! I saw you die! You're dead!"

"Not anymore."

"No, the dead should stay dead – begone, vile shade, you corrupt spirit, begone!"

Kavaria erupted into a hearty laugh as Eisen attempted to move the older man to a chair, but he would go nowhere near the table.

He began twisting with terror and finally broke free from the coffin maker with a shrill yelp and left through the door, running wildly into the dark of the woods.

At this uproar Kindle came running down the stairs, stopping at the bottom and looking about fitfully.

"What was that?"

Eisen turned first to Kindle then to the outlaw and pointed at them firmly.

"Stay here. Both of you."

"Sure."

Then the coffin maker bolted out the door.

The preacher wasn't hard to find again, so loudly did he howl and flap about that even in the near total darkness his shape rose starkly.

Eisen chased the frantic man down a small, rock-studded decline that petered out into a little stream, nearly dry. Halfway down, the preacher gave another hideous cry and fell, tumbling uncontrollably down the hill and dashing his skull about the bottom.

As Eisen drew to his side at the bottom of the bantam vale, he turned the man over hurriedly, shouting his name again and again.

A large and usurious gash was branded across the fallen man's pale, prominent brow, and his breathing was shallow, his eyes fluttering like moths in somber moonlight. He grasped at the coffin maker feebly, muttering strained, guttural cries, and then fell back and lay still.

Eisen rose even as the world seemed to fall about him. He looked around aimlessly; the trees swayed strangely with the night-song wind, as if bending to listen, to watch, commanded perhaps to do so, their skeletal boughs, hangman's appendages and portents of that which was still to come, rattling like the demon shaker of some brain-sick Merry Andrew.

Then he turned back to the dead preacher and looked on awhile before turning soundlessly to the hill and walking away.

When he returned to the lodge Kavaria was standing in the doorway, whistling oddly into an empty rum bottle and watching the night horde skim the dark flange of visible sky.

"So?" The bandit inquired without much interest.

"Dead. He fell; there was nothing I could. What does it matter telling you how I feel, you don't care."

"I'm hurt, really I am. 'I don't care?' How you wound me!"

"I'm in no mood for your games."

"What man ever is?"

"I said I'm in no mood, damn you!"

Eisen shoved past the man, nearly throwing him to the floor, and stormed into the living room, and then up the stairs to the junk room where he sat upon the floor cradling his head in his hands.

Trying not to think.

Failing.

He didn't know why he chose that room as opposed to any of the others, it just struck him as right at the time. The cloistered mess, the brilliant colors, the shimmer of metal and glass; a room of petty distractions, but distractions all the same.

Shortly, Kavaria appeared in the doorway, leaning heavily against the doorjamb.

"You're right, fer the most of it. I don't much care bout one thing or another, but you've given me... an amusing time. That counts for something, so I'll give you something in return, if you've the ear for it."

Eisen said nothing.

"The people here, in the town – heh, in every damn town I've ever been'ta – they all think I'm mad, crazy... but fearless. Dauntless. Scared of nothing, and... it ain't nothing but a damnable lie. I feel shameful of it sometimes. Well, rarely, but still... And what am I supposed to do, stop in the middle of a robbery and raise me hands up an say, actually I'm just as scared as you. Course not, I mean that usually isn't true, robbery ain't frightening – child's play. No, but... you remember that friend of yours, the man with the umbrella?"

"He's no friend of mine."

"Good. He terrifies me."

"What?"

"See, you believed it too, didn't you, that I wasn't afraid of anything. I should ave been an actor."

"I suppose."

"When he strangled that man, I mean, my man – what was his name, I can't remember – when e kilt him, I was... horrified. I've never seen a man move like that. And afterward, that look in his eyes. It was like breathing to him, like nothing, like life and that man's were just so much breath being blown away. Like... nothing could touch him. I've never seen his like before, never hope to either. Me an dha boys, well, when we first seen him coming down the road, toward the town, we thought he was just some rich traveling musician, what with that fancy guitar and all. So we held him up, didn't have a damn penny to his name. One a me boys stuck a pistol right in his face – didn't even flinch. We took him to our fort and thought bout ransoming him off. He was wearing this fancy suit and all, so it weren't that far off of a thought. Well, we held him there the entire night and e rarely spoke, but when e did, it t'never made any sense, but it got all de men in a letter-perfect fright. And he played that guitar, the strangest melodies I ever did hear, long into the night. And when we woke e was gone, and three of me men were dead. I never did know his name."

"Why are you telling me this?"

"Cuz – hell, I don't really know. What kin I say, I follow me heart. Maybe I'm feeling sympathetic te yeh."

"Because I'm like you?"

"Because we're in the same horrible mess."

"So is everyman."

"That's the spirit!"

Chapter Thirty-Four

Straw Dogs

The next day an icy rain fell about the land. Eisen watched it from the kitchen window, a steaming cup of coffee in his hands, sole source of warmth. Of comfort.

He had yet to tell Kindle and Logan of Luce's demise; he didn't know how. No longer could he search within, so barren was his every thought, his every emotion. So he set his eyes to searching instead, reaching far beyond the pane of glass, beyond the tree line and its shadow, beyond the sky and the cold arc of its vasiform emptiness. He had not slept at all the previous night and could do nothing to rake his thoughts away from Luce and his death. He could now easily understand the superstitions of native peoples, or modern peoples; for he, too, felt as if the whole of the universe had hatched some grievous plan against him. As if Fate itself willed to ride roughshod over his waking life for some unscreened transgression.

Kavaria washed his face in the sink and then turned from the draining water, grabbed up a towel and addressed his host with uncharacteristic solemnity.

"You're not going out there to get him, are you?"

"Yes."

"In this?"

"Yes."

"He's dead."

"I know it."

"Then what's the point?"

"It isn't up for discussion."

"Your whole profession revolves around a rite in which you don't believe."

"Yes."

"So what's the point?"

"I don't know! I don't – I have to do something. I must."

"There isn't t'anything you cain do. In the house you're protected, out there... out there you're a sitting duck."

"I realize that."

"So don't be a fool."

"You could run for the mountain pass and disappear, steal a coach and horse and vanish. Why do you stay?"

"Are we being honest with each other?"

"Yes."

"It's more fun this way."

Eisen rose from the table and pushed his chair in, set down his glass and walked to the front door, peering through the windows, two at each side, left and right. Outside, nothing but the rain and its misty aftermath. The charged smell of the deluge seeped into the very pores of the house, and the whole thing breathed with it.

"I saw a wolf, a giant wolf, pure white, yellow eyes like sulfuric fire. In these very woods. Kindle says she saw it too, once, long ago. Maybe it was... just a dream."

Kavaria moved to the doorway with Eisen's discarded glass in his hand, now filled to the brim with rum, and it thoroughly tasted.

"What in blazes are ye talking about?"

"Nothing, never mind. Look. Someone is coming."

Three figures moved from the forest's pall, through heavy sheets of rain, and behind these indistinguishable phantoms moved an indeterminate number more. The coffin maker was astounded to discover that the three figures were headed by none other than Ms. Whitum, a long hood pulled low about her face and her plump, little body eschewed from the cold by a thick fur cloak. It was she who knocked upon the door; a steady, protracted, rhythmic hammering, urgent but restrained by an even temper.

Eisen whirled to Kavaria and hissed, waving his hand, shooing away.

"Get upstairs. If Kindle and Logan wake, tell them to stay where they are and be quiet. Go! Hurry!"

Opening the door, Eisen stepped out under the awning of the roof and cast his eyes into the crowd before him. They were eighteen in number, and all looked to him expectantly with shame. Shame and something else which he could not place.

"Ms. Whitum, you must be freezing. Come in. Come inside, all of you."

The travelers entered gladly, shrugging off their coats and drawing close round his roaring hearth. Before turning to them, the coffin maker threw another log on the blaze and then dragged the kitchen chairs to his guests. There were only four chairs, the first he gave to Whitum. The rest were divided up by seemingly equal consent.

None of the travelers seemed happy, and all moved under the weight of some squirming sorrow.

"I hope this doesn't sound too curt, Ms. Whitum, but what is this all about?"

She took off her thick, leather gloves and gripped them tightly in her hands before she spoke, rarely looking at Eisen.

"Two things, just two. Ya'll knew Henry well, right?"

"Yes. He was a friend. A good man."

"How did... how did he... die?"

"He was stabbed to death."

"Oh God. Oh God, lawd above..."

She writhed in her chair, mashing the gloves under her blue-veined hands, grasping and turning them in her lap as she wept, her control falling clean away under the sudden strain of the coffin maker's words.

A tall, thin man approached from behind and laid his hands upon the weeping woman's shoulders, profound sympathy shining in his eyes.

She reached up and cupped at his hands with one of her own, pressing her face to the back of the chair as if the sight of the world were too grotesque any longer to endure.

Eisen opened his mouth to offer words of kind consolation. None came, so he said nothing and instead just stood quietly, looking on.

When Ms. Whitum had retained some self-control, she turned back to the coffin maker and sniffed her running, reddened nose and then shoveled on.

"Second, second thing is, Michael. He's looking for Ms. Kindle. Cain't find her or his father anywhere. They were seen going in this direction, so he thought you might know."

However, she relapsed once more into fitful sobbing and could speak no more, so the tall man whom stood behind her spoke in her place.

"We came to warn you, Mr. Torquiam. It ain't right, what all has happened, and that so many want the same to happen to you. It's unconscionable. Especially after what ya'll and Daniels did fer this town. He gave his life to protect it, and if it weren't, from what I hear, for that fella Strade, youdda lost yourn as well. Yes sir, that's the way I hear it. Now, I know you don't want to hear it, but it might be better ifn ya just left."

"You are right, of course. I don't want to hear that. This is my home. All I want is to be left in peace."

"Don't we all."

Eisen nodded and then furrowed up his brow with confusion.

"I thank you for coming all the way out to warn me, but why have so many of you come when you could have just sent one man out to meet me?"

The tall man who stood behind Whitum gestured toward the town with his head disgustedly.

"We're all leaving, it ain't safe for anyone here anymore. Rioting in the streets, killing strangers, robbing and talk of judgment and days of reckoning. Killing Ledru and Statletter like that, lynch mobs... doesn't sit well with me. No sir, don't sit well with any of the other peace-abiding folk you see here neither.

We're going over the mountains, leaving today for it gets any worse. Well, like as I said, I suggest you do the same. Goodday, Mr. Torquiam, and you take real good care."

Ms. Whitum rose and walked up to the coffin maker and took his hands in her own, smiling warmly. She said nothing, then they all left, and it was as if they had never been there at all; no sign of their passing. They walked out to the tree line to the back of the lodge and mounted their horses, then passed through onto the forest trail that led to Kindle's woods and from there to the mountain's ascent.

"Think they'll make it?"

Eisen spoke without regarding the outlaw.

"I don't know."

☼

When the next batch of townsfolk rode up to the lodge, Eisen and Kindle were tending to the dying hearth, and Kavaria lounged near him upon a pile of pillows he had found upstairs like some errant Persian king. Logan was drinking in the kitchen, doing his best to ignore the brilliant fall sunlight, sliding cold and glistening over the dead leaves like serpents of light, red, gold and brown, dancing about the grass to the witherwills of the wind.

"Here they come," the bandit sneered curtly.

"You don't know that."

Kavaria ran a hand through his hair, smiling.

"Even you know that. How could I not?"

"Just get up and be quiet."

"Yessa master, yessa."

"Kindle?"

"Yes?"

"Get upstairs, it isn't safe."

She nodded and hurried up the stairs, taking one last uncertain look at her friend's hardened, stoic face.

Eisen placed the fire poker upon the wall hanger to the left of the fireplace, then he started toward the door, seeing that the men were dismounting and heading in his direction. Turning back to the still seething salamander, he bent and grasped the warm iron in his hands once more and lifted it free of the wall and enclosed it in the folds of his long coat. Then he placed his specs upon his face and ambled easily to the door, forcing his expression into obscurity.

The men who stood before him were three in number, and all wore the plain, austere, long-tailed vestments that were the unmistakable ensign of Michael Montferiat's profligate sway, as if his words, his ideals, had been transmuted to cloth, flesh and blood. The man who spoke first wore a broad, snap-brim hat and glasses darker than Eisen's own. He was the shortest of the three and moved with a kind of slithering elegance.

"You Mr. Torquiam?"

"I am."

"We all iz looking fer a man here bouts, you seen any men come through here recent like?"

"Who exactly are you looking for?"

"I think I'll be asking the question, iffn ya don't mind."

"And if I do?"

"Well, that's a problem then, ain't it?"

"I don't think it needs be."

"Oh good, we kin come in then?"

"First, I would like to know whom you are looking for and why."

"Luce Montferiat and Kindle... something, don't know her last name. Nope, not really sure iffn she has one. She's a friend of yours, I hear."

"No. I haven't seen them."

The man with the dark glasses took out a cigarette and then lit it with extraordinary showmanship. He took a long, heavy drag off the smoldering cylinder and then exhaled directly into the coffin maker's face. The two large men behind the smoker began reaching for their guns. Eisen stood still and silent. The man with the dark glasses smiled caustically and then took another drag before speaking, turning to each of his men with great gesticulation.

"He hasn't seen them, you believe that? He hasn't seen them! Oh, what about Johnson, Stockholme Johnson that is, and his boys. Ya'll seen them? Cuz we know they came up here to see you."

Another gust of smoke wafted into the coffin maker's face, but this time he did not let it drift about him. This time he moved and brought the stove iron out from behind the inner folds of his duster, arcing it up and across, catching the smoker across the brow and dropping him instantly. The man to the smoker's immediate left pulled for his pistol, but Eisen was too fast and followed the momentum of his first swing, spinning around and catching the brute in the gut. Next, the coffin maker struck out with an overhead swing that knocked the shooting iron from the last thug's, now mangled, hand. He howled with pain and then went silent as Eisen smashed the poker into his jaw and raised it to strike again. Eisen inhaled deeply, surveying his handiwork, then turned to the door.

Kavaria stood with his pistols drawn, hanging limply at his sides; he looked impressed.

"Well, I spose ye won't be needin any elp after all."

"Put those away."

"They could still be alive."

"Exactly, put them away."

The outlaw did, but only hesitantly and with great disdain. He then bounded to the fallen goons and began checking their vitals as Logan moved from the background and stood near the fireplace in confusion.

"Eisen, what is going on?"

Kavaria ignored the drunkard's words and addressed his host.

"Only our black-lunged buddy still breathes; the rest are dead."

Eisen looked to the ceiling and then let the blood-spattered poker fall from his hand. He ran his nervous fingers through his hair and then again, realizing quite belatedly that he was sweating copiously.

"Well Eisen, what do you want to do with him? I kin get rid of him, if you're all puckered out."

"Bring him in and put a pillow under his head."
"But he's just gonna try and–"
"Bring him in and put a pillow under his head."
"You're disgustingly self-righteous, are ye aware o'that?"
"Just do it."
"Fine. But you'll regret it."
The outlaw carried the unconscious man inside and laid him out near the fire, as Logan thrust a pillow underneath his bleeding skull. Logan rose with his gaze fixed upon the dying man.
"Eisen, what's going on?"
"Do you know this man?"
"Yeah, everyone knows everyone in this town. His name's Malky. Or, Malkenson, Andy Malkenson, everyone just calls him Malky. What the hell were you thinking?"
"See those two men out there?"
"Yeah."
"They were drawing their guns, they were going to shoot me – that is what I was thinking."
"Sorry. Just... it was so sudden. Damn, what was wrong with you, Malky? Why would you come here?"
"Is he a friend of yours?"
"Used to be. Story for another time, a better time."
Kavaria gave a curt little chuckle.
"A better time? Oh, the vanity of sentiment."
"You shut your mouth, Kallista, before I shut it for you."
"How'd a body go about that, exactly?"
"Both of you be quiet. If he comes to, I need to question him, and I can scarce do that when you're both bellowing like two territorial apes."
A thought seemed to suddenly occur to Logan. He rose and dashed to the front door and scanned the tree line.
"What is it, Logan?"
"Those three you took out could just have been a scouting party. There could be more of them out there. I'll go and take a look, you just make sure he doesn't die, all right?"

"I promise, Logan. I'll do everything I can."

Kavaria shook his head, melodramatic and severe. Once Logan had dashed out the door, the outlaw bent over the unconscious thug and plucked out his cigarettes, sticking one in his mouth.

"He's going to die. You know that as well as I do. You killed him, he's dead, he just doesn't know it."

"I'm aware of that, Kavaria, but the last thing I need is Logan at my throat. I told him I'd do everything I can, so that's what I'm going to do. Tell Kindle she can come down. And Kallista?"

"Huh?"

"Behave."

He smiled his jackal smile and ambled up the stairs.

When Kindle laid her eyes upon the carnage her friend had wrought, she gave a shrill gasp of despair.

"If I hadn't of come, if only I hadn't–"

"No, I'll not have you blaming yourself for their actions. I'll not allow it."

"If only I'd never come here..."

☼

Despite the coffin maker's best efforts, Malky died five hours after falling into unconsciousness. They buried him and the other two men in the far-off clearing where, previously, Johnson and his men had been interred. Logan wept silently as he lowered his friend into the cold, mirthless earth, little beads of sorrow speckling the skin, of the living, of the dead. When the bodies had been buried Logan looked out at the mounds of red-gray earth before him and leaned heavily against his shovel. Kindle watched from the tree line, saying nothing, feelings mixed, contorted and pregnant with gloom. Next to Logan, the outlaw and Eisen straightened up from their labor and stuck their shovels into the ground.

Dead leaves stirred and all was silence.

When the silence was broken, it was Logan who broke it.

"Now, we think we're something, sticking this storm out, staying here, think we're making some kind of statement. But it don't mean a damn thing."

Eisen placed his hand on the man's shoulder and looked him in the eye, holding his gaze, steady, affirmative.

"It does to me."

"Eisen, this is one storm you cain't weather. Michael is going to come here and kill you. That's the long and short of it, sooner or later... unless you run away, or... take Kindle back to him."

Kindle stepped boldly from the shadows of the trees, as if ready for a fight.

"I'll go. He won't send anyone after you, if I go back to him."

"Luce Montferiat came to the cabin last night when you two were sleeping, he was raving about his son. He said that Michael had tried to kill him."

"No, I know Michael, that's too far – he wouldn't go that far!"

"You don't know the man, Kindle. You've known him only barely longer than me. Luce is dead, so it doesn't matter what you do. As soon as Michael discovers this, he'll use it as an excuse to see me hang. Or even if it's not that, he'll use the absence of his men. He said he'd see me broken."

Logan whirled on the coffin maker with great concern.

"What happened, you said he was dead?"

"He fell, tumbled down a gully and cracked his skull on a rock, there was nothing I could do for him, nothing."

"Did you bury him?"

"No, it was dark. I can't remember where we were. You must understand, Logan, we don't have time for that. My mind has been muddled, I haven't been thinking straight. A defensive strategy will only be my undoing, because you're right, I can't weather it and I know it. However, I have a plan, but, Kindle, you would have to be willing to work against Michael, to... betray him. Can you do that?"

"No. He's my friend."

"And he has since gone about throwing the town into chaos and costing innocent people their lives! Damn you and your sentiments, this is serious. I need you now, more than ever, don't abandon me. Don't let your weakness consume you as you let it before. Or don't you remember?"

"Don't say this to me."

"You remember how you were ready to throw yourself from the church tower? Don't you remember how I stopped you, how I saved you, me, not Michael. And you repay me by throwing in your lot with him. If that is where you stand, then you may as well leave me, but know that in doing so you're leaving more than just me to die, much more. For your friend is one tyrant with an unmistakable taste for blood. Human and very, very warm."

Logan stepped up beside the coffin maker where he shook with his fury, so stark and consumed by its intensity that his whole body quaked with it.

"Go easy on the poor girl."

"No. Not now or ever will I soften myself to half truths and lies for the sake of feelings, yours or her own, or any others. It is lies and half truths that have slaughtered an entire caravan of performers, it is lies and half truths that frenzied the people of that town to see Kindle and I as cursed and possessed. Now Strade will be returning with a marshal and enough men to quell this business, but whether he'll arrive before Michael hangs us all for some made up crime or ill disposition, is impossible to know, which means we have to act and quickly."

"What are you going to do?"

"Something I should have done a long time ago. It's time I faced up to him alone."

"That's just stupid – they'll hang you, Eisen, they'll hang you stone dead."

"They might, but then they'll have to take the responsibility. They won't blame it on me, they won't be able to, perhaps then they will understand."

Kavaria broke in with something almost like concern.

"Well maybe they might, but right now I don't understand."

Before they could continue, there came a clangorous bang, then another, slamming roughshod against the tree trunks and resounding with aftershocks down their ears and through their blood.

Gunshots.

Coming from the direction of the lodge.

Kavaria patted the coffin maker on the back and gave a childish chortle.

"Best of luck, boyo."

Then, before anyone could stop him, or even try, he took off into the forest as the cadenced sound of hoofbeats drew within the party's earshot.

"You two run for it, get out of here. Go."

Instinctively they hesitated, wavering with their indecision like the seaworthy sail of some great vessel under the mastery of indeterminate winds.

Then came a voice of supreme confidence, surging through the air and swelling the empty spaces between the boughs as if it were the portents of some grand manifestation.

It was Michael's voice.

"We know you are here, Eisen! Do you hide? Do you game? Poor manners, I expected better from a man of your... how shall we say it? Intellectual distinction. I just want a chat. I'm looking for my father and Kindle. Are you out there, Kindle? You've no reason to hide from me. You know that. Come out."

Eisen could see in Kindle's eyes that she could barely restrain herself, that she wanted to go, wanted and yet knew the danger, knew the futility of reconciliation, knew she would be walking toward her own destruction.

The coffin maker shook his head, but she began moving toward the lodge regardless. He grabbed her arm and, gritting his teeth, spoke but a single word. "Run."

He released her and she nodded and then turned and ran off into the trees, Logan following close behind. Eisen tightened his black-gloved grip upon his shovel and flipped his collar up, then inhaled and exhaled like those waiting to die and jogged up behind the nearest, wide-trunked tree.

Waiting.

The sound of hoofbeats was so close that the coffin maker could hear the attendant animals' breath and the low, hazy din of muted conversation. He looked around the trunk of the tree and saw that Michael was accompanied by seven men, all larger and more physically imposing then he. Michael led the party and rode like some newly crowned suzerain, his head tossed petulantly into the wind, ruffling his immaculate, back-swept hair.

To Eisen's left there was a large cluster of boulders surrounded by thick shrubbery and long snaking lengths of vine which hung here and there from the high, twisting trees. He ran quickly to the boulders and discovered a small gap between the two largest rocks, a kind of roofless cave. He vanished inside, cloaked by the hard shell of stone from eight hungry eyes. He brought the shovel up by his face, both hands upon the handle, eyes spinning about from side to side with the sound of the horsemen only a stone's throw from his quaking frame.

The wind was still and the sunlight dimmed under the influx of a massive gray cloud bank.

Somewhere there came the calling of an owl; a warning, perhaps.

Once again Michael's voice came boiling up through the trees, but quieter this time, meant only for the ears of his men. A failed endeavor.

"Split up. Two of you with me, the rest look over there, we'll meet up by the cabin if we don't find them soon. It's getting dark, these woods are not a becoming place to be in the dark. Things stir here in the lightless hours. Things which no voice, however fair, however reasonable, can quell."

He listened as the five remaining horsemen rode off. Only Michael and his two companions remained; one of them stopped just beside the boulders and dismounted.

"I've just gotta take a piss, Michael."

"You bare some refinement in your use of language, Tomes, but fine, just be quick about it. We'll be just beyond that clearing there."

They rode on, leaving the man, Tomes, alone with the coffin maker, who quickly scrambled up to the top of the pile. His back was against the side of the left stone, and his feet pressed himself upon the right. Thus braced, he was able to slowly ascend to the top of the left boulder, his shovel still at his side. Once he had reached the top, his shovel scraped against the rounded stone surface, hissing with the friction. The sound of boot steps stopped, and for a long moment Eisen held his breath and body completely still. He could see the man Tomes, he was standing just below the coffin maker, his hands around his belt buckle and it half loosened; his ear was cocked and his eyes squinted into the darkness of the cave. Eisen drew back from the edge as the man tilted his head up, pressing himself flat against the stone and shutting his eyes tightly. Then came the sound of urine flowing and boots kicking idly at stones; he released his breath, a sigh of relief.

The man's horse stood ten feet behind its master to Eisen's far right, so close he could nearly jump upon the animal. Eisen scanned the surface of the boulder, eleven by ten feet wide, and discovered a large number of little flake-like stones laying all about. He scooped one up in his free hand and aimed for the tree near the horse.

He pulled back his arm, rose and let the stone fly. It struck the tree and shattered into a dozen pieces as its discharge rang out, and threw the horse into a sea of panic. The beast bucked and whinnied and rose and tossed itself about, attracting the attentions of Tomes, who whirled with his pants about his ankles and his genitals in his hand.

"What the hell?"

Tomes scanned the trunks and the shrubs, discerning nothing but green and gold and bark and vine. When he turned back around, the coffin maker stood before him and slammed the flat of the shovel into his skull. The force of it broke the man's nose and sent him spiraling to the ground where he crumpled in a mangled heap. The horse shrieked once more and then bounded away into the clearing, where, already, Michael and his remaining companion had pulled up and turned. They rode back as quickly as they could, but when they got to the boulders, the only thing they found was Tomes laying on the ground in a pool of blood, his horse long gone into a leaf-shrouded distance.

Michael pulled his horse up short of the body and gazed on with a look that was equal parts amusement and profane disgust. His companion, a muscular man of great height, with a bushy beard and long, unkempt hair, swung down from his saddle and bent to the prone figure.

"Dead. Someone damn near turned his face into mush."

"That I can see, Jonesy."

"Think it was Eisen?"

"No. It was very likely that brute Logan, who as yet remains aloof from his position as deputy and from the fold of my congregation. From what I hear, the two of them are friends. Still, he's supposed to be the law."

"Hell, you're the law round here now, Michael."

"Yes, a pity they haven't learned this yet. They will, in time."

"Well, anyhow, I don't like this. Maybe, you think, maybe we all pushed him too far?"

Before Michael could reply, the coffin maker surged out of the darkness of the cave and brought his shovel down into Jonesy's head. Staggering, the man clutched at his skull, howling in pain as if it were filled with insects, chirping and humming and biting. His screams echoed throughout the small, windless vale, dampened by the overgrowth. Eisen kicked the man in the stomach and then brought the shovel to his head once more, a fitful trajectory.

The screaming ceased.

Eisen turned slowly away from Jonesy's corpse and fixed the preacher with his gaze, raising his shovel and pointing it directly at the mounted man's head as he spoke.

"You've no gun – bit of a mistake."

"More than a bit. Though not quite as grave as your own."

"You started this, not me."

"A man must bind himself to principle; his own and the principles of those higher than himself."

"Who, your God's?"

"Yes."

"Your idealism has cost your father his life."

Michael looked on, completely unfazed, unblinking and expressionless.

"Did you kill him?"

"No, he fell and fractured his skull."

"As you have fractured Jonesy's, and many others, I take it. Tell me, what became of Johnson and his men?"

"Kavaria killed them. I tried to stop him, to save them, but he wouldn't stop."

This mote of information was the first which the coffin maker presented that seemed to conjure a change in the immaculate preacher's visage. He furrowed his brow mildly.

"Kavaria Kallista is dead. I should know, it was I who oversaw his hanging."

"Yes, well, ya should't'ave paid better attention, boyo. Off your horse, now."

The preacher and the coffin maker both turned to the boulders whereupon Kavaria Kallista stood, grinning from ear to ear and very much alive.

"I see, perhaps, in place of a rope, a bonfire next time," the preacher replied as he dismounted calmly and stood looking up with clement irritation at the outlaw upon the high, looming altar of stone.

"Auto de fe? Yes, very dramatic. But I don't think ya'll be gitting that second shot anytime soon, Mr. Montferiat. In fact, boyo, I don't think you'll be getting it at t'all. If you've words with your Lord, best say them now."

With that the outlaw drew a pistol with his right hand, cocked back the hammer and aimed at the wide-eyed young preacher's head, all of it occurring with the fluid majesty of a seasoned gunfighter, taking less than a second.

"No, Kavaria, not for him."

"Get your head on straight, lad, he's no different than those pissants you, rather impressively, snuffed out just a few moments ago."

"He's different, he's worse."

Michael turned apprehensively to the coffin maker, fear squirming under the oppression of his taciturnity, like frenzied salmon fighting upstream to breed. Even still, the steel of his conviction sharpened his words, thrusting them portentously about as if nothing much had occurred to his detriment at all.

"You're not a cold-blooded killer, Eisen. It would behoove you to give up this particular ghost."

"Of course I'm not, but here there are no ghosts. Here there is only the wild solitude, the loneliness of the mountain-wood and vale... which you will explore."

"What madness are you talking about? I'm not exploring."

"You don't have much of a choice in the matter."

"Threats will not avail you. I'm not afraid of death. My Lord will provide."

"As he provided for your friends here? They, doubtless, men of faith. Isn't that so?"

"God will punish you for your transgressions. I am merely an avatar. An arbiter of justice. If it is not me that sees your punishment through, another shall, it is only a question of time."

"Running out for everyman."

"Not for me, coffin maker."

Eisen walked out to stand before the preacher and then drove a fist into his gut and raised the shovel above his head, heaving with rage, his voice cracking like overheated glass.

"You run, Michael, you run as fast as you can."

"My Lord will provide."

Eisen slammed the shovel into the preacher's shoulder. He gasped and howled, squirming upon the ground with terror and pain mingling for dominance, neither finding success, both finding outlet.

"Save your servant, oh Lord, save your servant!"

Eisen hit him again, this time far more forcefully.

"You murdered a pregnant woman, her friends, a carnival, all YOU! Your father! Ledru! Statletter! All was your doing! What Lord would provide for that?"

"Shut your filthy mouth, you are unfit to–"

But another shovel blow lapsed his protest into pain. He grasped his bleeding leg and withered uncontrollably with agony.

"What Lord would provide?"

The coffin maker hit him again.

"WHAT LORD WOULD PROVIDE?"

So acute and insurmountable was Michael's pain that only a muted wail escaped the festering prison of his lips, his eyes saucer wide and his nostrils increasing like melting flesh.

The forest, soaking in the tortured man's disinterred moans, knocked the noise strangely about its sturdy wooden bars and lengths of columned green and gold, as if the source of such distress were not human, but something profane and terribly ancient.

"What Lord would provide for the likes of you?"

"Please, don't kill me–"

"I thought you weren't afraid of death? Your Lord will provide. Isn't that so? Or were you lying to me? Were you lying to me, Michael?"

"No, no more."

"Were you lying to me?"

"Yes, yes! Is that what you want to hear, damn you!"

"And what Lord would provide for you?"

"None, I am... I am filthy, I am unworthy, none, none! That's what you want to hear, isn't it!"

"You are less than unworthy – say it. Say that for me."

"I-I...I am less than unworthy."

"Again."

"I was only doing what I thought was right! Can you say any different!"

"Say it again."

"I am less than unworthy."

"I am a murderer, a defiler, a distortion – say that for me."

"It had to be done. It had to be done, don't you understand?"

"Say it."

"I am... a murderer, a defiler, a distortion."

"Yes, good. Now, do you remember your words? That's all right, I'll remind you. 'I will see everything stripped from you and dispossessed, and alone you shall wander the wastes; perhaps God will show you mercy then, in your hour of despair... I doubt it. I, certainly, shall not.' Remember? Yes, I see now you do. Now." Eisen straightened up and slung the shovel up about his shoulder and looked off toward the mountains. "Run. Run and don't look back."

Without another word the trembling preacher scrambled backward upon his arms and legs like some kind of malformed crab and skittered to his feet, then dashed off into the trees. The coffin maker watched him go and disappear over the crest of the hill into the distance.

Kavaria whistled and crossed his arms, walking up behind the coffin maker, still smiling, still jovial.

"That was one helluva show!"

"Yes, and for you it's the last you shall ever see."

"What?"

Eisen spun and swung the shovel into the bandit's left leg, then pulled back the instrument and slashed down upon the man's throat, gashing it deep red. A sickly sanguine spray painted the cold October stone and speckled the coffin maker's shoes.

Gurgling with his own blood and numb with shock, the bandit still managed to cling upright, upon one knee, his head tilted loosely up, meeting his murderer's gaze and uttering his last and final words.

"Good... show."

Kavaria Kallista smiled as Eisen hewed once more into his neck, nearly severing his head entire, killing the brigand outright. The outlaw's body slid slowly to the ground, as if, even in death, some immortal remnant of his passion clung to his gushing flesh, his draining skin.

When it was done, Eisen stood straight and high and breathed deeply of the crisp October air, filling his lungs, his nostrils with the revitalizing aromas. His eyes drank deep the darkening sky, and his feet held firm the leaf-strewn-ground beneath them, and in that space and time it seemed as if those two parts were no longer in separation, but one continuous whole.

Then the coffin maker turned his shovel to the ground and began to dig.

Chapter Thirty-Five

Afterimage of God

When Kindle and Logan returned to the coffin maker's cabin, he was gone, and only a lonely entombment of risen, weathered stones remained. Kavaria's trademark diadem laid out, ceremonial and cold-glistening in the rising light upon that mysterious burial mound, sole indicator of whom the tomb contained.

The duo looked to each other with furrowed brows, wordless and silting in a narrative beyond their collective comprehension.

Kindle walked toward the gray-stone memorial, slowly through a hissing gale and knelt to the dew-soaked ground, touching the stones and the cold, metal crown.

"This belonged to Kavaria," Kindle whispered, more to herself than to her grim companion, who moved to stand beside her, gazing likewise upon that wasted monument.

"That means..."

Though the words distressed her, Kindle nodded to herself and spoke without turning to Logan. "It means Eisen killed him."

Logan bent to the grief-sundered woman and placed a firm and reassuring hand upon her shoulder, lowering his voice and motioning to the trees.

"You know he had to run. Same as we do. It isn't like he left you."

"I know. That isn't why I grieve."

"Why then?"

"Because so many had to die before he did."

"It weren't his fault, weren't your own, either."

Finally she looked to him, and he nearly flinched from her gaze, so dire and strange was its effect, so steeled with renewed resolution; some sudden realization. An epiphany.

"There is no fault. We are as we are."

"That is?"

"The afterimage of God."

And with that she withdrew the diadem from its pedestal and placed it upon her now expressionless brow.

☼

Fairson looked out of the smoke-fogged windows of the quaint, wooden farmhouse to the rolling emerald fields beyond, stretching all the way to the old mountain pass that let out into the forest and Eisen's lodge. He wondered of the man he had come to adore, as brother in arms, adviser and lover, wondered where he might be and if he thought likewise; thought of him.

Jen Arlington stood behind him, a cigarette stuck defiantly between her lips, oddly spaced in the failing light. She moved up to the young man and laid her thin, wind-chaffed arms about his shoulders, letting her head loll gently against his own.

He smiled and plucked the coffin nail from her lips and jut it to his own with a devilish grin.

"Oh, that's the way it's to be, is it?"

"Afraid so, ma'am."

"You're intolerable sometimes."

"At least it's not all the time."

"Oh, please, you know I'm only joking."

He smiled again and puffed on the cigarette, the smoke drifting cat-like to the rippled cherry rafters, coiling in one misty mass like some ethereal serpent.

"I know you're joking because I know how you feel."

"And how do I feel?"

"Helpless. I know I do. I've never felt more helpless in my life, or more cowardly."

"You're no coward, Fairson. If it wasn't for you and Eisen, I... well I don't rightly know what would have become of me, but knowing Kallista, it wouldn't have been good. We grew up together, and even back then you'd put yourself down like this. It eats me up inside, Gerald."

He rubbed her arm and took another drag before he spoke, still gazing out unto the verdant fields, gently rippling like an ocean tide.

"I know. Sorry. You were always the strong one, Jen, it was always you."

"Oh, what good is this kind of talk, anyway? Remember what Kallista said–"

"Kallista?"

"It surprised me like as you to discover the man had so much of interest to say."

"What did he say?"

"Every day above ground is a good day."

"And you're saying we're not acting like it?"

"Well, we ain't."

He nodded and handed the cigarette back to her and untangled himself from her body, moving closer to the window as their hosts shuffled in from their daily toils. They were simple folk, ragged and raw-stiched. The men were bearded and gruff with a rumbling timbre meant for galley song; and the woman, modest and wise, with downcast eyes that would just as quickly be replaced by rackety, half humorous reprimands, cowing all in their path. They were a large family; Winslow, the patriarch; and Marie, his wife; their three daughters, Wendy, Cale and Jane; their sons, Roberts, Peter and Gareth; and finally a stable hand by the name of James Fresco, a poetic lad with a passionate temper.

It was this homely conglomerate that had given harbourage to the two escapists when they had stumbled unwittingly upon the sprawling rural homestead. A thing many generationed and blood built, over 500 acres, half of it farmland, all of prosperous.

And it was at that very hour, at dinner, when all, save Fairson, had gathered about the resplendently set dinner table, that a fierce knocking resounded from the front door. Old man Winslow moved to the door cautiously, as if he feared it were blood-lusting brigands. He opened the door, however, to reveal only a swarthy, slender man with bushy brows and a curious accent.

"A letter, for Gerald Fairson."

"And whom is this letter from, son?"

"I don't know. He paid me to bring it here. You take it, yes?"

"Fairson! Come over here."

Fairson did as he was asked and eyed up the mysterious harbinger. Fairson had seen him before, one of the newer oil workers, brought in from some forsaken field in the Middle East, didn't know his name.

"Who sent you?"

"I told your friend, I don't know. He wore a hood. I must go. Here."

He handed the letter off to Fairson with great care, as if it were some fragile, ashen construct, and then booted off into the rising dark. Then the sound of forest calls, owls and bears and things more dire and unreconciled with the flighty flutters of the young man's imagination.

Jen called from the table.

"What is it?"

He opened the package, and from it fell a small piece of paper, red and very rough, and inside remained a very fine scrap of parchment. Unfolding, he read the only words upon the page, a single line.

See you soon.

He looked to the two red squares of paper; they were tickets for a steam ship.

Fairson looked to Jen and smiled.

☼

When the travelers came upon the man, he had been dead for some time, deep serrations in the bone and something upon his throat, the collar of a cleric.

"A priest, surely," one of that vagrant number spoke up suddenly, his voice wavering uncertainly, fear in every timbre.

"Why do you say that, Issac?"

GRAVE.

"The collar."

"Aye, could be."

"Wonder what kilt him?"

"Well, whatever is was, it was big. A wolf, maybe."

"Those claw marks look more like a bear than a wolf."

"Or one damned big wolf. Ain't no bears round here."

"Either way, I ain't staying to find out."

"Me neither. Come on, sun's going down."

And with that they exited that forsaken veil, that stony assemblage carved by ancient hands, and left the skeletal remains of Michael Montferiat to their eternal slumber.

Part Three

Many Years Later (Epilogue)

E'en from the tomb the voice of nature cries,
E'en in our ashes live their wonted fires.
-Thomas Gray

Epilogue

When the reporter arrived at the town, he found it strangely empty, as if someone had picked the whole vastness of that jumbled aggregate and shook it free of all inhabitants. Not a car in sight, not a man or woman on the short, rain-slick road.

It was a small town much like any other; bars and kids, smoke from a failing factory, the red rim of the dying sun subsumed under the blanket of gray-blue clouds moving northeast and quickly; harbinger of some future calamity, unseen and economic. Fickle lightning sounded the hollow drum of the atmosphere in the great ambit of the floodplains as the rain increased its reasonless assault upon the hovels of that crumbling infrastructure.

A lone man stood at the far end of the road in the town square, white umbrella in hand, looking upon the encroaching vehicle, a rarity. The reporter slowed the car to a crawl and looked again through the rain to the plaza, but the man with the umbrella was gone, only a fuzzy afterimage remained. The driver arched a brow and titled his head up, then inhaled and turned into the inn, wondering if the man in the rain had been a figment of his overtaxed mind.

He parked in the back lot of the local auberge and walked around to the front door, holding the high collar of his raincoat tight about his slick and shivering neck, guarding against the icy rain. He had heard about the tsunami and its trailing effects on the radio and had dressed for the occasion. But even still, he found himself chilled and shivering when he finally managed to pry the door open against all providence of the wind.

Throwing himself inside the small room, he nearly toppled to the floor. Restraining himself, the man paused as the door slammed behind him with a jingling of bells, and the tenants turned. He could, at first, barely make anything out, so dim were the lights and so thick was the place with smoke. Cigars and cigarettes of all makes and flavors. The heady smell of it mingling with the pine and rosewood of the bar and the liquor therein contained. There was only a handful of individuals seated at the small cluster of booths and tables. The reporter ignored them completely. They, however, did not reciprocate likewise. Aggressive stares and mumbled gossip were this outsider's muted greeting.

A stranger in a strange land.

Only one man stood behind the bar, and the reporter quickly realized that the man was a woman when she turned round to face him. Look at the arms on that, he thought to himself, saying nothing, smiling awkwardly and shuffling forward. Dripping water and not noticing. He walked straight to the counter, still shivering, and nodded to the burly woman.

"Name's Giles. Giles Dren. I reserved a room, called ahead and said I'd be coming today."

"I remember. That's fifty."

"One hundred and fifty?"

"Just fifty."

"All right. You need to see identification?"

"Why? You got something to prove?"

Giles looked to her strangely and then smiled awkwardly, realized she was jesting, or at least seemed to be. He wasn't so sure of that, but decided to barrel on regardless, digging out his wallet and gingerly plucking two twenties and a ten-dollar bill and sliding them elegantly across the counter.

"No. Nothing to prove, ma'am."

"Why do you looked so excited? I know it ain't none of my damned business, but.. hell, I cain't remember the last time I saw a face like yours."

"'A face like yours,' and what's wrong with my face?"

"Oh, goodness sakes. Nothing's wrong with your face. I just mean it ain't the most promising place for excitement, that's all."

"It is for me."

"If ya don't mind my asking, why is that?"

"I don't mind in the slightest. What's your name?"

"Candice."

"Candice, I just so happens that, through various what-have-yous and so and forths, I managed to hear that there was a manuscript of a certain series of events that took place in this very town some, oh, 200-odd years ago, give or take. Anyhow, I'm a collector, you see, of stories. I'm writing about the time period and looking for inspiration, and this may be just what I'm looking for."

"You said you was a journalist."

"I am. Of the present, and the past."

"You just take care, not every book is meant to be opened."

"Is that something you heard off of a late-night horror flick?"

"Yeah, sure."

She slid him the key, somewhat disgruntled by his flippancy toward her warning. He furrowed his brow and then snatched up the key with a broad smile.

"Room 3B?"

"That's right, mister."

"Thank you ever so kindly."

"Yeah, sure."

☼

Giles was awakened by the screeching of his telephone, and so clangorous was its knell that he nearly threw himself clean of his bed from fright. Snatching up the receiver, he hissed, "What is it?" running a thin, white hand through his dark, bird's nest hair.

"Fine way to greet a business partner."

"Caldwell? Lenny Caldwell?"

"Who else? Now, I have the manuscript, if you want to see it."

"Well, of course I do, it's why I drove all the way to your cozy little community. And let me tell you, it wasn't exactly a picnic getting here."

"No. It's somewhat hard to find."

"It's in the middle of a desert, course it's hard to find."

"So, you still want to meet then?"

"Yes. Today?"

"That's fine. That's what I was thinking. How about at my shop, at eight?"

"That's in two hours."

"And?"

"Nothing. See you in two hours."

"You know where my shop is?"

"Haven't a clue."

"Want me to tell you?"

"No. It's more fun this way."

He hung up grinning and ran another hand through his hair. He then jumped up, began singing "Rambling Man," then showered, dressed, and hurried downstairs. He paused, thought better of it, and finally decided to slide down the broad, wooden railing, old and very finely polished. As he reached the bottom of the stairs, sliding free of the banister, he met with the unfriendly gaze of nearly a dozen motley patrons, all glaring as if he had just murdered an innocent child right in front of them.

"How do you do? Name's Giles, won't be a tick, but whilst I'm ticking, least you could do is crack a smile – you only live once." He wagged a finger.

He postured invitingly, openly and humorously, like some stately jester of old, his legs straddling the beer-stained floor and his arms out-thrust to the denizens as if in anticipation of an embrace. Their glares only hardened. Dren's face fell slightly, and he looked to Candice, where she stood dutifully behind the bar, polishing a musty, water-stained glass.

"Well then, Candice, a drink for me, drinks for the house – drinks all around. On me."

He whirled on the glaring patrons challengingly. There was a pause, silence like a thunderclap, then a great merry bustling as they waddled, stumbled and swaggered to the counter, some smiling at their generous provider, others nodding gravely, but respectfully. Only one of the men didn't rise, he crossed his great burly arms and then, with a muttered curse, left through the door into the rain.

"What's eating his apples?"

A thin elderly man with four missing teeth clapped an arm on the reporter's shoulder, shaking his head, as if gazing upon some unruly child.

"Dont you worry bout im. He just don't like strangers, is all, an you're bout the strangest stranger this town is ever likely ta see. Here's to you, partner, bottoms up!"

Most of the other men nodded their heads and followed the old patriarch's lead, raising their glasses and toasting their guest convivially. He reciprocated the gesture with a broad smile.

"Here's to me."

☼

It didn't take Giles long to find Lenny Caldwell's print shop. The town was large for its population, but still not very big. The print shop was a house much like any other in that time, white stucco and black shingle roofing, two windows to the front and a low, pale blue door that jingled with the bells hung from its back.

Giles walked in and beheld a most inspiring sight; stacks upon stacks of books, flying about in every conceivable direction, as if they had sprung suddenly from the floor. The owner himself stood at the far end of the room, hunched over a long wooden table that seemed to have been stolen from some ancient pirate's ship. Upon the desk was a single book, a dull green lamp with a dull green shade, a messy pile of magazines and a silver bin-container housing a high mound of business papers.

Crinkling of plastic.

Lenny Caldwell, in a cheap, if fashionable, suit, set his candy bar upon the desk and turned to face his guest with a searching expression. He was a lean, wiry man, hungry looking, predatory, with deeply tan skin and dark green eyes. He was smoking, and his fingers were stained faintly yellow with nicotine.

"Well, having fun yet?"

"Of course. So, where is the manuscript?"
"Right here, I've been waiting over an hour for you with everything prepared. Come, take a look."

☼

After having thoroughly delved through the pages of the masterful holograph, Giles was persuaded to take a ride with Caldwell at the latter's persistent urging, saying only, "I know of something you'll be interested in; something to show you."
Giles readily agreed, and they left into the pouring rain and headed for the printer's spacious minivan. They drove out of town and into the mountains via the forest rode. All the while they spoke of the manuscript and of the coffin maker it described and the mad preacher and the bandit of the wasteland.
"Do you know whatever became of your great grandfather after he wrote that book?"
Lenny shook his head.
"Well, you're not the only one. No one knows. He just vanished. All record of him just stops after several failed publication attempts. My father said he was a strange man, you'd probably have enjoyed his company."
"Well, I certainly enjoy his writing. Why haven't you published it before?"
"I don't know, big work load, I suppose. No, that's a lie, I don't know. It just didn't seem right, doing it without his permission."
"The man's long dead."
"Aren't you a bundle of sympathy."
"Of honesty."
"Sure."
The landscape grew more lush with every passing second, as if the ecological boundaries had been hyper-compressed. One passing by would never have fathomed that a great desert lay just behind them. The trees of the forest grew thick and high, their boughs tangled and skeletal, looming.
An hour and a half later they arrived at a little clearing where stood an old lodge, a lodge which looked strikingly familiar to

the eager, young writer. Lenny parked in front of the ancient house which was connected to the main road via a small dirt way. Giles nearly leapt out of the passenger seat, so intense was his passion, his curiosity.

"Don't tell me this is the lodge from the book? Eisen's lodge?"

"One and the same. Good craftsmanship, I guess. Damned thing, it'll never fall down, folks in town say, it's gotta be over 500 years old by now."

"And the history it must contain! Can I go inside?"

"Sure. Cain't think of a reason why not. I thought you like to see this, but... there's something else. An extra treat fer you." Lenny Caldwell paused and arched a brow, crossing his arms and coughing.

"You're bouncing, do you realize that?"

"I'm excited. It's not my fault you're a sad, sappy sucker."

"A what?"

"Nothing. Thanks for this, my friend."

"Course."

After Giles had satisfied himself as to the curiously untarnished house, leaf strewn and creaking, he returned to the car, where Lenny shifted up and headed even higher into the mountains. A thought occurred to Giles as the trees grew thinner and more sparsely, as the stone rose up like the wall of some monolithic prison, as the air cut and the sky went purple gray with a resurgent horde of thunderheads, roiling in from the wastes like battleships from some ghostly armada. The rain increased.

"How high does this road go?"

"Not very much farther up."

"Don't tell me that means we have to walk to wherever it is we're going?"

"All right, I won't tell ya. We don't have to go, we cain turn around–"

"No, no – I want to see it, whatever it is."

"Only reason I didn't tell ya, is I know how fond of surprises you are."

"Oh, more than you know."

Indeed, just as Lenny had predicted, the road came to an end several miles later. They parked at its extremity and hiked through the deluge up a steep ascent.

At the apex Giles paused and looked down and out at the great bowl of the valley and the town within it and the wasteland beyond. He grinned and continued on and crested the rise, gasping as he did so.

"What is this place?"

"I showed you the section from the book where they found the preacher's body, the cliff dwellings. Don't you remember?"

"Yeah... this is magnificent."

Before them loomed a massive cliff, and from its deepest root to its highest peak the stone had been carved and wrought by native architects, long since departed and forgotten; a monument to their times, wisdom and folly of man interred in the edifice.

Running quickly inside to evade the rain, the two paused in the entrance, catching their breath and looking around. Giles began wandering about and found a staircase cut out of the stone, a kind of stepped natural incline. He climbed it and discovered a vaulted room full of strange animal bones orchestrated in a series of concentric circles, containing something, and it in the center held.

Giles furrowed his brow and walked gingerly into the middle of the room, over the bones, and bent to examine the artifact at its center; a mask, bone-white and smiling. He picked it up and carried the queer token back down to the entrance of the labyrinth and remarked of his find to Lenny, who was utterly enthralled by the discovery.

"In a circle of animal skulls, you say?"

"Yes. But I suppose I've seen weirder things."

"Like what?"

"Actually, I've no idea."

Staring at the storm, fast approaching, and the trees before it, Giles Dren raised the mask to his face and peered through its macabre portals. He recoiled from it in shock and confusion.

GRAVE.

Caldwell, taking notice, laid a hand upon his shoulder with grave concern.

"What is it?"

Giles shook his head.

"I thought I saw a wolf."

www.ingramcontent.com/pod-product-compliance
Lightning Source LLC
Chambersburg PA
CBHW071335020726
47502CB00001B/107

* 9 7 8 0 9 9 6 2 8 1 2 0 1 *